ROADSOULS

ROADSOULS

a novel by
Betsy James

Aqueduct Press

Aqueduct Press, PO Box 95787
Seattle, WA 98145-2787
www.aqueductpress.com

ISBN: 978-1-61976-091-2

Library of Congress Control Number: 2015955946

10 9 8 7 6 5 4 3 2 1

Cover and text illustrations © 2016 by Betsy James

Printed in the USA by Thomson-Shore, Inc.

Acknowledgments

I would like to give special thanks to Craig Werner, who can see in the dark, and to brilliant readers Vonda McIntyre, Shannon Guinn-Collins, Diane Hersh, and the late Dr. George Hersh. Also to Ken Hause, who, though Farki can ground him, now and then can ground Farki.

And, of course, to Ursula K. Le Guin. The ring of her hammer leads us into the heart of the Mountain.

Who We Are

Wind is the prairie tide. We are the wind.
There is no wall the wind cannot unbind.
Rain is the prairie tide. We are the rain.
Rain turns citadel to sand again.

Build proud, build high; wind will unmake it.
Build for eternity; water will take it.
Even the gods in their high town
Are by wind and rain and the Souls brought down.

Waysong. The Roadsouls.

Two Stories

All life too small, all walls
too close for breath, the living heart
crushed to a fist, and the old stone gods
stone.
Pain beyond pain.
Lift up your hands!
Be seized!

Calling the Roadsouls. Welling-in-the-Mountains.

 He was nothing but eyes and fire and bullshit, that boy—that man, not yet eighteen, red-haired, mocking the plaza girls with kisses, burning like a torch in daylight.

On the morning of an autumn day he rose from the sleeping platform in the Men's Hold, the center of the universe. He slapped hands with his brethren, ate bread and meat, baited the girls at the village gate by waggling his cudgel in front of his hips. The girls jeered, but their eyes did not. *We are the men of Creek, we walk like lions.* In the line of young hunters he walked first—his younger brother, Set, envious and worshiping, stepping where he stepped. He always walked first, his bow in his hand.

When they ran along the cliffs it was he who ran first. He saw the hawk in the air and thought, To see what the hawk sees—oh, if I could fly!

At the cliff's edge was a jagged rock. He gathered himself to jump to it. For no reason—just to jump, to shout, to stand at the edge of the abyss, laughing like a god.

His mind and his fate spoke then so instantly, one after the other, that five years' brooding had made no sense of it.

Jump
> Don't jump

Jump
> The rock's bad

Jump
> Don't!

Jump!

He jumped with his whole body, joyful as a stag. His feet kissed the rock, the rock turned, it fell.

And he flew.

When they could find a way to climb down to him, they strapped him in a litter and took him to his mother's house. Not that he knew; it was a month before he opened his eyes, and they opened on unchanging dark.

He never went back to the Hold. As soon as he could walk he made Set take him to the ruined bothy, well outside the village, where they had played Roadsouls as children. He cursed and berated Set until his brother half led, half pushed him out there and left him, with a rotten tarpaulin for a roof, a kettle full of water from the creek, and a haunch of smoked pig.

Set shouted, "You're fucking mad!" There were tears in his voice. "Die out here, then! I'll be back tomorrow."

He lay shivering, rolled in the bald bearskin that was all Set could pilfer at short notice. He made his body rigid against the cold, his jaw against anything like tears. At last he slept. At some still hour he woke to feel the frost his breath had left on the bearskin, and something small and warm creeping at his thigh.

A rat! He cursed, pawed it away. It made a tiny sound that stopped his hand, and by the time he could think *kitten* it was back at his thigh, mewing and burrowing. It butted his fingers with its round head.

"Where have you come from?" He gathered it to his chest. It crawled around his neck screaming, looking for nipples.

He was terrified it would leave him. He picked a shred of meat off the haunch that hung from a nail on the wall, chewed it, offered it at the head end. Smacking noises meant it was eaten. He chewed more; that was eaten, too. At last the creature settled under his chin, kneading his jaw with its claws.

"Stop that, you little shit," he said through his teeth. It let him stroke it, its body lithe as water. "Brook," he named it. "Robber. Nuisance. Tick." With his hands cupped around the cat he fell asleep.

A brown girl in a brown smock, not quite nine, clinging to her mother's hand and staring at a lion.

It was harvest fair. The lion was chained by an iron ring to the axle of a Roadsoul wagon, gilt and green. The Roadsouls stole children; she leaned into her mother's thigh. Then she forgot her mother.

In some lands the male wears a mane of dark fur, but on Mma's mountain, purple above the desert of Alikyaan, both male and female lions are sleek and tawny red. The girl could not tell the sex of this one. To her smallness it was great. It flexed its claws like a house cat and yawned, white teeth, red tongue. Its eyes were gold.

A boy in torn green silks said, "Stroke the lion, Miss?" He held out his hand. "One penny to stroke it."

She had no penny. And who was she to stroke a god? She stared. The lion stared back. Her mother dragged at her hand, whispering, "Drop your eyes!" She did not drop her eyes. The lion stretched, it lowered its head as though it bowed to her.

When the fair was over she sat cross-legged in her mother's cubicle—it was tiny, for her mother was only a fourth wife—and tried to draw the lion on her arm with urda paste. It looked like a mouse. She wiped it off. When her brothers came yelling and waving sticks she ran after them.

Cobalt sky, red earth, and purple mountain—Mma's mountain, the tallest. Close to, the river ran blue-brown between the desert fields. Turtles plopped from the bank, blackbirds whistled in the reeds. The shepherd was bringing sheep across the gravel ford, and Jip, her Jip, was running them. While her brothers pretended to spear fish in the shallows, the shepherd let her call.

"Stay!" Jip poised, quivering. "Now!" she cried, and he ran like joy.

But her brothers were hunters. "You have to be the deer," they shouted, and chased her to the granaries. She hid from them in the dusty dim among the sacks of corn.

In the forecourt a hawk screamed. The boys rushed out after it. She crept from her hiding place, alone for once. Girls were never left alone. She squatted in a shaft of sunlight that struck through the powdery air, and with her finger, in the grain spilled on the floor, she drew the lion. This time it came right: curved claws, long cat-body carried low.

The granary door swung back. She did not hear it. She drew the sweep of the long tail.

The lion disappeared under two sandaled feet.

It was Tumiin.

He took her wrist in his right hand and drew her up. He called her his little flower, eh? And how had such a flower bloomed from a plain, dry branch, eh? And who had got her those night-creep eyes? His own eyes roved over her, he pressed her against the grain sacks. He smelled hot, like a boar. She heard her own voice in a whine of terror, could not move, as his left hand sought, sought in the dusty odor of grain.

The door creaked. He half loosed her; she jerked away and scrabbled up the grain sacks like a rat, up, up. He caught her left foot, dragged her down. For an instant he held her against the sacks. With his lips to her ear he whispered, "You speak one word, chit, I kill your mother."

He let go of her foot. She fled up the sacks again, into the shadows. It would be easy for Tumiin to kill her mother. He was an important religious man.

She heard him say, "The brat was playing in the grain. Take her outside and slap her!"

When his heavy footsteps had faded, the grain warden gestured her to come down. After a moment she obeyed. He did not slap her but knelt, held her shoulders, and made her look at him. "Do not ever go near Elder Tumiin. *Ever.* Do you hear?" His eyes were kind, but they burned as though to say more than his words.

She nodded. Looked down and away.

In time her birthday came. She turned nine, put on white robes of uncut cloth and went to live on the Maidens' Balcony. Tumiin came there sometimes. Never to the inner rooms, and Ganu, the Maidenward, was always there, but when he came his eyes were on her, always. She watched for him. She could not help watching. Sometimes she drew a lion with urda on the sole of her left foot, the one he had grabbed, like a charm against him.

On the Maiden's Balcony girls were kept safe and whole, they said. She had lost the fields, the river, and Jip, but it was a fair trade.

1

The dark has a language. I don't speak it.
I try *Please. Hungry. Sleep.*
The dark thinks I understand
and speaks too quickly.
I repeat the one word I am sure of:
No! No! No!
The dark takes my hand
as if I were deaf and blind,
and holds it to his lips.

      Anonymous. On a slip of paper dropped in the Grip.

He had been weaving at the sash loom all day, but the sun was leaving. He put out his hands into shadow.

The pattern was called Ravens' Flight Over Pines, but Raím had made it trickier by asking, What if the ravens were harrying a hawk? At the border he wove the hawk—tight, hard, wanting to break out and get away.

He unhooked the loom and groped to the bothy's open door, then to the edge of the dooryard. The scrub was loud with bees. Fronds that must be yellow with autumn bloom brushed his palms, his bare waist, his mouth.

8

Five years. Five years, except for one tiny time when he had held a girl in his arms and kissed her, and by his greed and grasping had lost her. Now, they said, she was big with the baby of another man.

Somewhere in the sky a nighthawk twanged, *beent!* Pinprick clicks of bats. From the creek, the deep double *huu!* of an owl.

He went back to the loom. Brook would come home, he would come in the open door, bringing the bigness of the world with him, and though his paws scarcely made a sound Raím would hear him come. Brook would topple against his calves, and his tail, like a silk rope, would whip across the backs of Raím's knees.

"Brook," he said under his breath. "Robber, nuisance, tick. I'll wring your goddamn neck. Brookie."

Brook did not come home. Raím took up the hawk's thread until he wearied. Went to the door again and shouted *"Brook!"* into the big night. Cursing, he crawled into his rat's nest of blankets and slept. Rose. Slept.

He waited six days and nights. The owl called by the river, and Brook did not come home.

❧

He went into the village sometimes. Not often. As a weaver he had memorized scores of patterns—Lizard and Mouse Meet in the Same Burrow, Badger Bites Snake, Clouds Over Straight Cliffs—and it was this map-making that got him down the creek path to the village, counting taps of his stick.

He knew the Men's Hold by its odor of smoke and singed hide. Dogs barked, but no human spoke. The south wall of the village gave off heat and an echo. The main gate smelled of urine; it was custom for men to piss at the foot of the arch as they came and went.

He pissed, then went through the gate. Heard his name spoken softly by startled voices. Scowled. Knocking with his stick, he made his way to his mother's house. He had not returned since the weeks he had spent there, in a dim back room, after the fall that had taken his sight. At that time he had lain in double dark, as the suddenly incomprehensible world went on and on; he had lain utterly still, because, if he did not move, what had happened would not be real.

As an initiated man he ought now to wait at his mother's gate and call, "I stand here. Do you ask me in?" Instead he walked right into the courtyard garden. Spice of tomato leaves, of rosemary in sun. He heard a whimper under the echoing portal and spoke his little sister's name. "Thoyes?"

Scuff of bare feet, door-squeak. He stood on the flagstone, ants running up his legs. The door squeaked again. Garlic and onions and soap: his mother. With a sound like a cry she began the sound of his name. Stopped herself. Said formally, "What discourtesy is this?"

He did not answer. The ants bit his ankles, they ran up the stick to his hand and bit him there, too.

She said, "Come in, then." He bowed his head and entered.

His mother was the headwoman's daughter. She touched his curls, made him touch the lintel and say the house blessing before she laid her cheek against his.

Her cheek was wet. He flinched away. She offered him a glass of the wine she made herself. He refused it and asked for tea, which would not make him soft. Sat at the same scarred kitchen table where he had eaten until he turned eight and went to live in the Hold with the men. The same smoky peppers perfumed the oven's heat. Water fell, *plink!*, from the same clay cooling jar into the wash pan.

His mother said, "You no longer shave?"

"No."

A soft paw touched his knee. He brushed it away. She said, "Do you still have that cat?"

"No."

After another silence in which he heard someone at the doorway, probably Thoyes peeking around the jamb, his mother said, "I shall speak to Zella. She always has kittens."

He shook his head. His mother set a plate of plum cake near his hand. He broke off a piece. She said, "Are you a Roadsoul? We have forks." He ignored her and ate.

She said, "So."

"I'm going away." The words came out of his mouth and startled him.

"Away? Where?"

He could not think of anywhere, so he said, "Ten Orchards."

"Ten Orchards? What is there for you to do?"

He could not think of anything, so he made a scornful face. His father came in, soft-footed as Set, with the older sister who had been sent to fetch him.

"He says he's going to Ten Orchards," said his mother.

His father said, "Eh." Sometimes he came out to Raím's bothy, where he sat silently or perhaps talked about weaving. Now he said, "So. You're here at the house."

Raím shrugged.

"Ten Orchards?" said his mother.

"I've got friends there."

"Who?"

"Friends."

His father's voice came muffled; Raím knew he was pulling his mustache, left side, then right. "You're welcome in the Hold."

Raím shook his head. His hand was sticky with plum cake but it did not seem manly to suck his fingers; he wiped them on his sash kilt. "I'm leaving tomorrow. Don't know when I'll be back."

"How will you get there?" said his mother. "Will your friends come for you?"

"Yes."

That voice in himself that always almost spoke said, *I'm your son, dead already. What's it to you?* But it did not speak. His eyes filled with tears. He said "Going." Rose, blundered out of the kitchen so fast he cracked his head on the doorframe. Blood poured down, he could say "Shit! Shit!" and rub his eyes while he rubbed his forehead.

In her little frog's voice Thoyes said, "He walked into the post."

☙

They sent for his brother. Set led him to the Hold, wrestled him out of his bloody clothes, and sat him naked on the sleeping platform next to the line of Great Looms. One side was called Sunside, the other Starside. From this line of looms, the stories said, everything in the universe grew forth: the mountain full of lions, the town full of girls, and all the world beyond it. Raím sat at the center of the universe.

Set brought him a rag to hold to his forehead. "Shove it up your ass," said Raím, and threw the rag into his darkness. One of the Hold hounds came over and licked his eye.

Set said, "What do you mean, you're going away?"

"Get fucked."

"Who's this friend in Ten Orchards?"

Raím turned his back. Set left. Raím wanted the dog to stay and push its whiskery snout into his ear, but it did not. At the window a wasp buzzed, battering against the glass.

Night fell. He sat on the edge of the platform wrapped in a quilt, sucking down a bowl of soup and trying to shut his ears to the sounds he had not heard in five years.

Whisper, snick, hush of thread at the looms. Hiss of urine into the mordant pot. Male laughter, bets made, rattle of dice. Henno and Ros and Kim spoke among themselves, softly. They were not by nature soft speakers. Once they had been his seconds, reliable as hounds. It dawned on him that they were afraid of him.

At this thought he sat very still. His mind cringed from it, as one might cringe from looking under bandages at a wound.

Set came in, smelling of night and freedom. Lest he show the least pity Raím shouted, "Damn you, what have you done with my clothes?"

Set cursed. Articles of clothing began to wrap themselves around Raím's head. One boot caught him on the ear; he put up his arm in time to ward off the other. He set the soup bowl on the edge of the platform but the platform had disappeared, the bowl fell and smashed.

He began to dress. Only the boots were his own. "Where are my clothes?"

"They were filthy, Mother's washing them."

He cursed and put on the loans: loose breeks, hip cloth, tunic. He was cross-gartering the breeks, fighting a puppy for the garter, when Set said, "Where the hell do you think you're going?"

"Ten Orchards."

"The hell you are. And at goddamn midnight?"

"Better than listening to your crap. Mother's got my stockings, too?"

"Puppies ate them."

Raím pushed his bare feet into his boots.

"By the goddess," said Set, grinding his teeth. "Here's a pair of mine. I'll take you to Ten Orchards and to hell with you. Only wait till morning, you clot, you're not worth a night's sleep."

"Honor?"

"Honor. First light. If I haven't killed you by then."

"I'm dead already," said Raím. Heard Henno and Ros and Kim cease whispering. "First light, then." Fully clothed, he rolled up in the quilt and forced himself into the dark of sleep.

2

The fallen ash leaf,
beaten to and fro,
cries, "Did the tree spurn me,
or did I let go?"

Autumn Song. Creek.

"A lion," said Siibi. "With a fawn in its jaws. Blood."
He held out his fat little forearm, his fist that still had
dimples.

Duuni said, "There is no room for a fawn."

"*Fawn.*"

She took his wrist. His skin was lighter than hers, fair as new
copper. She could see the lion on it, crouching, and the fawn. Siibi
was Tumiin's first wife's son, and what Siibi wanted, Siibi got.
She squeezed a line of *urda* paste onto his arm, where the death
was that only she could see. Under the fine brass tip of the press
the fawn's speckled body grew a slim neck, a wild, terrified eye.

"Where's the lion?" said Siibi.

"Coming."

She drew sharp teeth sunk in the speckled back. Siibi
breathed through his mouth. So did the half dozen little clan-
cousins and side-sibs who leaned on her shoulders to watch the
fawn grow its fate.

"Duuni," said Riinu. Her hands were wrapped in pretty rags; Duuni had drawn doves on them and sealed the designs with lemon sugar. Come morning, the dried paste would be washed away to reveal a picture that would last a week or two, its stain dark in the skin. "Duuni, how do you draw?"

Duuni laid in the snarl around the teeth of Siibi's lion. Two days before, she had drawn a lion on the sole of her own left foot. Urda was delicious to draw with. It was made with rosemary oil, and its harsh, summer odor warmed the inner court of the Maidens' Balcony.

Also on the air was the odor of honey beer and sausages broiled with *frenc*. The roar of the harvest fair in the forecourt floated down from the cobalt sky. Duuni Esremachaan had not been to a harvest fair in eight years.

Riinu leaned harder. "How?"

"The lion is there already. I lay down the line where he is."

"You can see him?"

Her hand paused. Was it seeing? She had not seen a lion since before she turned nine. She had not seen a fawn since then either, except dead.

"Lion!" said Siibi. He kicked her ankle.

She made her hand move. To Riinu she said, "I can feel the lion there. He makes himself with the line."

"Like embroidery. Just, you don't mark the cloth first." In the weaving villages on the river—Alikyaan, Muukra, the half-dozen heaped, stone-built towns—girls thought of everything in terms of cloth. The cloth of Alikyaan was holy, never cut; only heathens and Roadsouls wore cut clothing.

Siibi said, "I'm not some girl's old embroidery!"

Duuni nudged her hair out of the way. It was black, all curls, and at seventeen she should have been wearing it up. She should have been married, with her own room in her husband's compound and her own baby. And at that moment she should have been in the loom room weaving her wedding robe, not drawing on the puppy-tumble of side-sibs and girls too young to have their own battens.

Should is a heavy garment.

She drew the lion's flourished tail. At its feet, the river's ripples.

"Put fish in it," said Siibi.

She drew two fish.

"Now the blood. *Red* blood."

"It is already red." The color of an urda drawing is in the mind, not in the line.

"I want it red!" He jerked his fist away and raised it. "*Real* red!"

"The paste is blue. When you wash it off tomorrow the line underneath will be gold; then it will turn brown."

"*Red!*" he said. "I want it!"

She said nothing. He was Tumiin's first wife's son.

He struck her hard under her left eye.

She caught his fist. "Be careful, the lion will smudge," she said in her mother's voice, patient, neutral as earth.

He pointed at her. "Dirt! Wine puke!" Certainly he had seen wine puke, being his father's son. Duuni said nothing. Looked down and away. He had spent his words; he screamed, when she caught his fist he writhed like a weasel, and bit. Lion and fawn smeared across her robe, her hair.

The damasked curtain of the outer court rang on its rings. Ganu came in, huge in her uncut robes and grim as washday. She seized Siibi by the sash of his tunic, plucked him off, and surged back through the curtain. His screams diminished to silence. The little girls huddled, looking down.

Ganu came back. She said, "Siibi is a good boy, if not provoked."

Duuni should not have provoked Tumiin's son. She should not have been drawing on the children. She should not have been playing the granary, so long ago.

Perhaps she should not have been born a girl.

A heavy garment.

"Fetch your batten," said Ganu. "Go to your loom."

☺

In the loom room the clerestory windows went from cobalt to black. In the forecourt the fair was loud. Earlier Duuni had peered down through the screen of the Maidens' balcony at the vendors of cakes and knives and glass, the traveling medicators hawking cures for gout, the Roadsoul mountebanks on the watch for children to steal. Leaguemen and paidmen offered milled yardage, rum, pale girls for sale as servants or prostitutes. Prayer merchants painted on cheap paper any god one wanted, for blessings or sorcery. Far away lay Mma's mountain in its purple haze. In the loom room, no sound but the scratch of the weavers' combs.

Ganu's glance was hard. No doubt her stories of bad girls and bad women—usually from Muukra, always ending as corpses or sex slaves—were in her thought.

Duuni's thought was, I shall have a black eye.

She slunk to the altar on the west wall where Mma, riding the crescent moon, looked on the seated girls with downcast eyes and sweet, patient face. From the rank of battens at her feet Duuni took her own, two feet long, carved of cherry wood like red honey. Her mother had made it for her: smoothed it with sandstone, brightened it with oil, and put it in her daughter's hands with a blessing and a sad look.

Her mother had always a sad look. That had used to make Duuni angry, but she could never show it. Her mother was like Mma, patient and sweet. Of what use was anger? She had borne eight children, and all her daughters but Duuni were dead. Her sons, too—which was to say, her sons had gone to the mines, or to be paidmen, for they were not of a status to get wives. She was newly widowed; her sorrow now was that she must marry again.

It was the custom: a hunt-brother took his dead comrade's wife as his own, lest she want. But the hunt-brother of Duuni's father was Tumiin.

"Mma," Duuni said under her breath. She touched her left foot. There was nothing she could do. As when her father got drunk, her mother got a black eye, it was how Mma had woven the web of the world. That is why all the saints are women, Ganu said.

Duuni tucked her batten between the threads of the warp. Passed the shuttle across. The thread she laid down would lie against her body in the grave. What she wove—it lacked two fingers' width of being finished—would be her wedding robe and, someday, her shroud.

Of its own accord her hand stopped. She looked at the thread that trailed from her fingers.

A shadow dimmed the doorway. Her mother entered, soft step and bowed head, and knelt on the rug next to Ganu. Something was wrong. Duuni's hand tightened on the batten. Had Tumiin died? But that would be something right.

Ganu's glance was cunning. A foreknown thing, then. Duuni's mother's head drooped like a frost-killed flower.

"It is appropriate," Ganu said to her. "And a baby will make it right. Mma mends all." She turned to Duuni. "Finish your length, lazy girl. At the new moon you shall be married."

"*I?* But it's Mother."

"Both of you."

"Both? Who…"

"Elder Tumiin will take both of you. Then you and she will have each other."

Darkness. Smoke. Through it Duuni saw her mother's head, bent and turned away. She knew her mother had said no, and it had not mattered. It would never matter. The thread Duuni laid down, back and forth, would lie along her rotten flesh, and it would never have mattered, ever.

There was nothing she could do.

She set down the shuttle.

She drew her batten from the warp. Every eye on her, raised by her rising. She smelled the rosemary in her hair.

She carried her batten to the altar. Under Mma's face she set one end of it on the floor, the other against the wall, and her bare foot in the middle.

It snapped like a bone. When she turned to face the rest, whatever had filled her had gone back into the void, and she was only herself, standing in the loom room. But inside she was falling: a shot bird, a cut rose.

Falling, no one to catch her. No one at all.

❦

First Ganu beat her with a heddle rod.

She began by slapping, but that was shock and temper. She slapped Duuni across both cheeks, then caught up the rod and beat her shoulders.

Duuni said nothing. She was a kite with a cut string, no earth to fall to—turning and tumbling down through balconies of cloud as empty as air.

When Ganu had worn out her arm she snatched Duuni's hair and pulled her past the altar and the broken batten, past the crowd of children and women that by then had gathered, to the goods closet, and shut her in the dark.

Duuni lay unmoving on a pile of rugs. Each thought fell apart.

She thought, I broke my batten. Mma cannot mend it. I broke it at her altar—as if I broke it *for* her. But that would be insane. I am insane.

She thought, I shall say I am sorry. Mother will make me a new batten, I shall finish my length and marry Tumiin, a baby will make it all right. She felt his great hot belly pressing her, pressing her mother. O Mma! She would never marry Tumiin.

She thought, I must pray. But she could not call on her whom she had blasphemed. She stayed in the void, not even falling, hung in the air.

So.

Surge and murmur of voices outside the door. When it opened at last, it was to Ganu big in firelight, behind her the women of the clan huddling and whispering like balcony girls. Duuni's eye had swollen shut, she saw only half the world. Ganu pulled her to her feet. She took Duuni to the altar, the broken batten. No one had touched it. "Pick it up."

Duuni gathered the pieces. They were real.

"You are to be beaten," said Ganu. "Be grateful that is all. You are young and stupid; the elders know this. Vicious girl—you have broken Alikyaan."

The broad stone arc of houses and holy rooms, bedrooms and balconies, the great forecourt under the sky—Duuni, a stupid girl, had broken it. She knew she had broken it, for the void had rushed in among the stones.

Ganu pushed her out the door of the Maidens' Balcony. The married women followed; the maidens and children stayed, like lambs watching one of their number led to the knife. She thought, I am to be beaten in my ragged old robe, and felt ashamed. That was all she could feel.

There were no torches in the iron wall brackets but the moon shone, fat and waning. Fear made everything strange, as though seen through tilted glass—fear, and the knowledge that Alikyaan was broken, and she had fallen through the cracks.

A glimpse of the forecourt, loud with music and shouting and smoke. Someone was roasting lamb with *frenc*; a man's voice sang like a cry. Ganu did not lead her there but to a courtyard outside the sub-council room, where a crowd of men was growing. Each held his staff of office in his right hand.

Duuni had seen judgments, she had cringed behind her mother's skirts as elders brought their staffs down across boys' bare backs. Only once had she seen a woman beaten. An elder's staff must not touch a woman's flesh; he beat her through her robes, and even so he broke her rib.

The world went shapeless, wild with shadows and the noise of the fair.

She raised her eyes to the one who was to beat her: Tumiin, big-bellied in his robes, his staff in his right hand, the carnelian set in the end of it winking like an eye. Of course. She belonged to Tumiin, daughter and betrothed.

Ganu pressed her shoulders: kneel.

She knelt before the blue cascade of his robe. She could smell him; he had drunk wine. His feet in new sandals were calloused, the toenails thick as claws. He rested the butt of his staff between the great and second toe of his right foot, on the sandal, so that it should not touch earth.

He spoke. All the councilmen spoke.

It was above her head they spoke, of disobedience and foulness and redemption, while she looked at their feet and thought about the toes of babies, so clean and sweet you could put them in your mouth like new peas.

I could draw babies' toes, she thought. I could draw those man toes too, gnarled like trees, and follow the line upward to the sinewy legs, the strange genitals like those of the Unclothed Gods, the round bellies, the bearded, angry faces. If I followed the line through all that, looking truly, would I know what a man is, and be safe?

Her eyes followed her thought and she looked into Tumiin's face, his mouth an open hole in his beard. His eyes had not expected hers. They widened; his raised staff had already begun its downward stroke.

Her hand pulled the thin robe to one side.

The staff struck her bare shoulder. She cried out. Yet there was room to think, My hand did that.

Shouts. Tumiin dropped his polluted staff. It hit the flagstones with a clatter, he snatched it up and raised it with a roar. Duuni huddled her arms over her head.

The blow did not fall. A scuffle, Ganu shrieking, and another voice—oh, her mother's!—pleading, as Duuni was grabbed by her robe like a puppy by its loose skin, yanked to her feet.

She could not understand how to walk. Lost one sandal. Saw her mother's white face, heard her call her baby name.

Tumiin half carried her out of the sub-council court, down a flight of stairs. She lost her other sandal. Torchlight and dazzle, the forecourt. Uproar. Only men. Tumiin, shouting, held her against his chest, hiked half into the air.

He calmed, or seemed to. The words that had been flying about like dust settled, and she heard them.

"Oh, she will," he said. She saw his face as it had been in the granary when he called her his little flower. "Paidmen," he said.

"You won't get much for her. With her eye like that."

"She'll do in the dark," said Tumiin. "And it's dark. Leave me." The men looked at one another, scowling. "She's mine," he said. "Go!"

He dragged her into the crowd. When she stumbled he jerked her upward, as one would train a leashed dog. Braziers round and red, faces of the crowd alight with fire and wine. Bakers hawking sweets and pies. A man pulled a monkey on a chain. Tumiin bore her across the forecourt toward the watchtower, black against the starry sky. At its foot the paidmen, the slave market, the dark of the granaries.

Weakly she struggled. He laughed.

A fiddle's squeal. Gilded carts. Men and women in cut silks made eerie by firelight, ragged children chattering in a heathen tongue. They looked right at her. So did the animals painted on the wagon canopies in bright colors touched with gold: bears, snakes. A lion.

A painted lion. It fixed her with its painted eyes.

For a penny she could stroke it...

A hiss. A roar. Everything moved, even the paintings on the carts, a ripple in the river of the world.

And the lion was loose, leaping. The crowd shrieked, surged back scrambling, knocking down tents, no room to get away, the lion stink stronger than Tumiin's, coming, a bright darkness.

Tumiin shoved her in front of him, shield or offering. One hot blow; his hand slipped from her shoulder and the lion was past, it knocked her down but someone grabbed her up again into struggling and yelling on all sides. The press began to break free, like moving water.

Tumiin's scream. A horrid, gugging snarl.

Something snagged her robe. She fell against a wall that moved sideways, the whole world moved. Above her a girl's face, Riinu's, not Riinu's, moved sideways with the wall. She raised her hands toward it.

The girl said in the Plain tongue, "You coming with us?"

Duuni said, "*Yes!*"

Women's laughter. Hands took her wrists. A falling tent pole clipped her on the side of the head, she let go but the hands did not, with a rip they hauled her in like a fish from a ditch and flung her into darkness. More laughter, wild. "It's a girl!" For whatever had trapped her robe still held it, and she was naked as the day she was born.

The girl who was not Riinu leaned out the open back of the wagon; a hand snatched her back. She plumped down beside Duuni and said with satisfaction, "Lion got him."

Wheels groaned, the wagon bumped faster. Shouts, screams, a roar that must be Alikyaan, ruined, crumbling to the ground. And over it all—impossible!—the laughter of babies.

Hands shoved her down, rolled her in a shroud. Creatures crawled on her. "He the one beat you?" said the girl. "That fat townie the lion got? Joke's on him." The shattered universe began to dim at the edges, as if Duuni were going blind. "Gya! He blacked your face all right."

Women's laughter. "Seen your own face, Nine?" "What's that on your face?"

"Pie," said the girl. "Nobody wanted it. If they did they wouldn't of let it be took by the Roadsouls."

3

To each being its task.
Beaver builds. Deer leaps. Wild dog
laughs at the moon, makes
the child wake in the dark and wonder
what walks without sun.
Our task is the task of water—
of the world
without us in it.

    Waysong. The Roadsouls.

 The roar of Alikyaan's ruin faded to the hiss of poplar leaves. Blind in her shroud, Duuni fell through the void she had loosed. Fell and fell.

Blackness; motion; whistles and cries. Creak and groan of the wagon, many wagons, traveling on and on.

When she woke at last, truly woke, it was to jolting grayness and cold. Something tugged at her hair. A rat! She could not move.

"Hey, you." More tugs. "You ain't dead, I heard you squeak."

A woman's voice said, "Uncover her, Nine."

"I'm *trying*. Wake up! We've got through the Grip."

The world rolled over and over, spilled her into dim light that jerked and swayed. Laughter. She was naked. She scrabbled for her shroud, a tattered quilt.

"Half frozen," said Auntie.

"No, she ain't. The babies slept on her. *I* slept on her." Prodding. "Sit up, girl. You're took."

"Get her a warmer wrap, she'll thank you."

A creature crept at her, dragging its body like a fat reptile. She shrank away. It broke apart and became the ragged child called Nine, in trousers and a jacket of padded silk, trailing a faded comforter. "Get warm," she said, and flung the comforter at Duuni. "What're you scared of? Curled up like a pillbug. *I* wasn't like that when I was took."

"Squealing like a piglet, you," said Auntie. "Talking fast as a traveling medicator. Farki'll sell you to Doctor Amu."

"Not Amu! He stinks of rum." Nine nudged up. A little warmth began to seep through the comforter. "Pillbug, if you just lay there the babies will tromp you."

Duuni's ears rang, there was a great tender lump on one temple. She pulled the comforter over her head.

"We saw all of you already," said Nine. "Bare as a fish."

"Let her be," said Auntie. "She'll come out when she's hungry."

"*I* ain't hiding, and you ain't giving *me* anything to eat."

"Too busy flapping your lips."

"I'll shut up."

"Pigs might sing," said Auntie.

There were holes in the comforter. Through one of them Duuni saw what happens when a girl disobeys the elders.

She lay in a tilting wooden coffin. Its lid was a glowing arch; shards of light pricked through it to glint on demons sprawled on rugs and cushions. Ragged imps tumbled on torn rugs, creeping or tottering as the world swayed.

"I see you," said Nine. Duuni turned her face away from the hole. "Auntie," said Nine, "is everybody in Alikyaan like that?"

Auntie did not answer. Duuni thought, Is anybody in Alikyaan like me? Women do not break their battens. Therefore I am not a woman, I am not real.

She clutched the comforter to her breasts. The rosemary tang of urda paste still clotted her hair. The demons gibbered, the coffin rocked. Nine jolted against her, singing.

> I'm a pillbug, I'm a pillbug,
> Can't run and can't fly,
> And if you look at me
> I'll curl up and die.

Duuni put her eye again to the hole. Nine stared back. "You're took. Get used to it." Her eyes were shiny as molasses. "Some man been getting at you? Well, he ain't here."

The gleaming demons became women dressed in brilliant silks. They glanced her way, sardonic and mild, as if they stole Alikyaani maidens every day. The imps were babies or toddlers, all except Nine.

Duuni parted the folds of her hood a little.

"Pillbug's coming out!" Nine snatched Duuni's hand in her thin, dirty one. The hood fell back. "Gya, he gave you a shiner all right, that fat townie the lion got."

The lion! "It...was it real?"

"Ask Fatso in the bed sheet, the one was dragging you," said Nine. "Not like he's answering."

That gugging snarl. Duuni whispered, "What have I done?"

"What have *you* done? That old man beat you blue, and you think it's *your* doing?"

Alikyaan broken, Tumiin torn apart, the universe torn apart. And it was she who had done it. She had torn apart God.

"I'll tell you what you did," said Nine. "You lifted up your hands and said yes, and the Roadsouls took you. You'd rather be with Fatso? You like to get beat around?" She prodded Duuni through the comforter. "There's plenty'd be glad to beat you, and not so many hungry lions."

"But...it was a *painted* lion!"

"So?" said Nine.

◌

"What's your name?"

The light had risen. The babies—there were eight of them—toddled and babbled and clung. The women chattered gibberish mixed with rags of Plain like the non-pattern of a crazy quilt, and cast on Duuni soft, mocking glances that she would not meet. Only Nine spoke to her.

"What's your name? Mine's Nine. Anyway till I'm ten." She looked seven, scrawny and brown, her uncombed hair in elflocks. "What's your *name*? You ain't *deaf*."

"If she isn't, you'd deafen her," said Auntie. She was a handsome woman with a lean, seamed face. Like the rest, she sat on the long bolsters that lined the wagon bed, dandling a skinny baby that sucked its fists.

A clang, like pots banged together. The world stopped.

A woman's voice, the driver's, said, "Out and down!" The riders rose, the wooden back of the wagon opened, wind and sunlight poured in. The women's bodies, as they bundled out, were ringed with glory.

Nine, following, turned back to Duuni and said, "Don't you have to pee?"

Duuni said nothing.

"Come *on*, or pee down your leg." She hopped out. After a moment, cowled in the comforter, Duuni shuffled to the door on her knees.

The air was sharp with pine and fallen leaves. Winds cracked in the sky. She crept across a narrow wooden porch, down three steps, and put first one, then the other bare foot into the cold, fine dust of the road.

The red track twisted down through empty table-lands furred with pines, flat-topped buttes like citadels, each immeasurably taller than the walls of Alikyaan. Above them loomed a mountain, enormous, snowy, unclothed as a god; it had devoured Mma's mountain, the one she knew by heart.

On either hand the road stretched away. A dozen canvas-topped, painted wagons stood ahead and behind, their mules fidgeting in harness. Dusty, gaudy men checked wheel-rims, drank from water bags of woven flax. A black-haired youth led a tall black mare.

Duuni cringed against the wagon side. "Come *on*, Pillbug," said Nine from behind a bush. "We ain't going to wait for you to pray."

There was no privy. The toddlers squatted in the road. Holding the comforter high, Duuni stepped into the scrub where no one could see her and made water right onto the ground. Nothing happened except that she felt better. She turned back to the wagon she had traveled in and saw, painted on its canvas cover, the lion.

The same painted lion, but dim now as shadows in a cloud. The lion—the *lion*—was not there. It was loose in the world.

She crept back up the steps. Peeping out, she watched a woman milk a goat into a tin pail, children drink the milk in turns from a tin cup. When everyone had climbed back in, some of the women were different; where there had been eight babies, now there were ten. Stolen children! Every age from newborn to four or so, black-skinned, fair-skinned, coppery, heads shaved or sleek or curly. One had a cleft lip, another a crooked arm.

Duuni thought, They might at least steal nicer ones.

The door shut, the wagon jerked and rolled. Nine slid aside a panel in the door. There behind them, like a painting on a courtyard wall, were the wagons and that alien mountain. Snow streamed from its peak, a ghostly flag.

She cleared her throat. Whispered, "What...what mountain is that?"

"Hey, Pillbug said something!" said Nine. "Same mountain as the other side. Where we took you."

It could not be the same. Mountains do not change. Mma does not change.

"That mountain's got a lot of sides." Nine leaned out into the billowing dust. "Back there we took a pig, and you, and this horse Farki fancied. Plus there was the lion and all, so we cut through the Grip. You were like dead, we laid the babies on you, it was cold." She teetered on the window ledge, pointing. "There's the Grip, that pass. The folks that watch it, you don't want to mess with them. But they owe Farki, and you're Farki's. Though sometimes—" she shrugged "—they'll steal a girl even if she's Farki's, they can't help themselves. So we hid you."

Duuni thought, I am Farki's? Who is Farki?

"We're in the Hills now, going to Ten Orchards. Business, then camp in the woods. Farki'll trade the horse, we'll eat the pig. And you—" she looked Duuni over "—we'll dress you good. Nobody'll know you."

Duuni thought, People do not change into other people. Mountains do not change.

But she had seen another face of the mountain, like a new face on the moon. And who was Farki?

✆

Auntie said, "Get her some clothes, please."

Nine teetered from knee to knee of the seated women and grubbed in a chest. Returned with a bundle of rags, dumped them at Duuni's feet, and held them up one by one. "Shirt. Trousers. No skirts, we ain't got extra. Leggings for under the trousers. Wooly hose. Boots." The stockings were not mates, the pointed boots had been chewed by puppies.

It was all cut cloth. Duuni would not touch it. She crouched like a fawn that, as evil approaches, keeps still and silent as its mother has taught.

She thought, As *my* mother taught. And evil happened anyway.

She slid one hand against the pile of rags. They were silky and cold.

"We're almost to Ten Orchards," said Nine. "You want to go naked?" Duuni looked at her hand as it touched cut cloth. "Auntie, I think Pillbug's slow-witted."

"Wit in one world is witless in another," said Auntie. "When you're took, it's a different world."

"I was fine right off."

"Cockroach at a dinner party."

Nine sorted through the rags, holding them against her scrawny body while the women made comment in Plain: "Can't dress a stick!" "Take nine of you to fill that." "What'll you use for bosoms, a featherbed?" Some who laughed were scarcely older than Duuni, but dressed like mountebanks in silk and linen, trousers and smocks.

Duuni's hand would not pick up the clothes.

"Gya," said Nine.

❧

The sun rose higher. Slowly the view of the mountain changed. The girls in motley dragged up the canvas wagon sides, and Duuni could see the track ahead.

"Ten Orchards," said Nine. "There's the market."

Yellow-nipped poplars lined a river, smoke rose from many hearths. The outlying houses were stone like the many-storied arch of Alikyaan, but instead of being heaped together they sprawled singly, with red tiles like a snake's scales. Walled gardens shed their last roses.

The wagons drew in a little. The road began to fill with more people and carts than Duuni had seen in her life. Most faces were gold-skinned, with reddish hair like Alikyaani slaves and eyes the color of sky; they watched the Roadsoul caravan with curiosity and suspicion. Barrows and handcarts pitched on the ruts. Carters cursed, shouted, cracked their whips. Nine leaned out and returned the carters' curses.

A scrum in the street. Shouts, not in children's voices. Flung stones rattled off the cook pots that hung from the wagon side.

Every head in the wagon turned. Auntie said, "There."

A man screamed.

Duuni shrank into her corner, as the broken craziness of the void streamed back in a rush. But Auntie, smiling, said, "Ah!" The wagon paused. Creaked forward.

Yells, a thump that was not a stone.

"*That* one?" said Nine. She leaned over the open side. "You coming with us?"

A voice—young, despair itself—said, "*Yes!*"

The silken women moved. An angular shadow darkened the air; the wagon jerked, the babies squealed and fell over, and across Duuni's lap fell a naked man.

Long legs, long arms flailing. He grabbed her. Broke into bitter laughter.

She screamed.

But a dozen hands pinned him. His face changed, he dropped her and fought like a boar in a net. She could not get away. Everywhere silks, heaving bodies; one of his wild fists hit her side. He grabbed her foot—her left foot, that Tumiin had grabbed in the granary, that she had painted with urda to keep safe.

This time she yelled, she jerked her foot from his grasp, flung her whole body across his arm and stopped him.

Stopped him. She, with the rest. One had a knee on his wrist, others sat on his chest, his legs. Duuni began to sob and could not stop *that*, lying naked across his arm. His eyes, stone blue, looked through her as if she were not there.

A child said, "He crying."

He had stopped struggling. Still she felt the tension in the arm that wanted to *do* something: hit, smash. She let go of it and scrabbled for the comforter. Outside, a last flung stone hit a cook pot with a clang. Laughter and shouts of "Good riddance!" died away.

He lay still, staring upward with wet eyes. Nine passed her hand over his face; he did not blink.

"Blind as a bat," she said. "How'd he know to lift up his hands?"

"How'd *you* know?" said Auntie.

"I just knew."

"There."

4

The soul's hand
has an eye.

> *Carved on a rain-worn stone.*
> Welling-in-the-Mountains.

It was still early when Raím and Set left for Ten Orchards. The air smelled like ice. Juncos in the bushes made a sound like agates clicked together.

The road ran along the creek, and Raím told himself he could have followed it alone. Set would not touch him but worried and chivvied his every step, saying, "Look out!" and "For hell's sake!" until Raím said, "Damn it, give me your cudgel end!"

On they went through eight miles of dust, one at each end of Set's cudgel. Carts passed. None offered them a lift. Raím imagined the stares, the curt nods, Set's fuming shame; he began to enjoy himself and ambled more slowly, listening to the beat of herons' wings as they rose from the water.

The edge of Ten Orchards was the stink of billy goat. Children chanted in high voices.

> *Blind man, beggar man,*
> *Penny in a tin can!*

They threw rocks. Set dropped his end of the cudgel and chased them. A squeal, then loud spanking and wails. Set came back, took up his cudgel end, and said between his teeth, "Tell me where you're going."

"To the fountain."

"Be damned!" The well with its fountain was where the girls came to fill their water pots and the men came to tease them. Set would not want to be seen there with a cripple. "I'll take you to the market," he said. "If you've got so many friends in Ten Orchards, let them take you to the fountain." He towed Raím through the winy odor of fallen apples, the stinking middens where turkeys chuckled.

Once Raím had been one of the lads at the well, shirtless to show off the bear scars on his back, and even—if he bent casually—a glimpse of his initiation tattoo, a blue serpent that coiled around his hips. The girls had looked him up and down, cast on him water and insults. "'Ware slops!" they cried. "My grannie's chamber pot!" He had leaned on his hard thigh, drenched with blessings, with messages, saying, "That's no grannie's pot. Come here, sweetheart, and let me fill it," until the girls ran out of words and left, laughing, colored up with heat and promise.

Now he could not even find the fountain. The girls he had baited were grown and bedded by other lads, and the insults were real.

> *Blind man, beggar man,*
> *Rubbish on a pie pan!*

Set hurried him on. Raím wished he could get hold of a pretty girl now—Seliki maybe, she had had fine brown hair, a round haunch, and a tongue of honey and vinegar. He would seize her, embrace her, yes, at the very well. He would say, Here's what it comes to, darling. I am the death's head at the wedding.

In the middle of these stone thoughts he tripped over a wandering piglet and fell full length into a puddle. The pig ran off squealing. "Get up," said Set, prodding him with the cudgel.

"Leave me!" He scrambled to his feet. He could hear the market's murmur and clash; he smelled onions. "I know where I am."

"Tell me, then."

"Damn you!" But Set would not leave him otherwise. "Market's there, through the arches."

"Who is it you know here? You've been lying. Who?"

"A girl."

"You wish! You'd beg from a girl—"

Raím swung his stick, felt it connect with a satisfying thwack. Set belted him right back. He bore it. Set would not continue; it looked bad to belabor a blind man. "Get away from me," said Raím.

"With pleasure." Set shoved coins into his hand. "Here. Thoyes gives this to you."

"Thoyes?" Raím stood with the coins in one fist, his staff in the other. Where could his sister get money? She was nine years old. "Set?" he said to the air.

No answer.

He listened. Many footsteps, on dirt and cobbles. He felt the coins. Not many. Thoyes had pet chickens; perhaps she had sold them.

He turned toward the market, rapping with his stick.

☙

Five years ago he had known plenty of people in Ten Orchards, perfume and ribbon sellers, leatherworkers, blacksmiths, the hafters of knives. He had wandered the booths with his lads, drinking beer, stealing peaches, begging angry grannies for their granddaughters until driven off by the watch.

Now no one spoke to him. Surely they recognized him; they had gossiped about him for five years. But no one spoke.

He rapped and groped along the cobbles to the north side of the market square, where a stone cleft down the middle was the Mother's shrine. There was one such at each market entrance. One was to say a blessing there, and set one's hand on the stone.

He would not say the blessing. But he laid his hand on the stone, which was greasy with touching, a gesture so familiar that as he made it he saw the market before him as if his eyes were sound.

Fruit and vegetable sellers to his right. Flower sellers to his left. Beyond, the stink of butchery with its staring cows' heads. Then the spice merchants, the sellers of dried fruit and candy, of incense and whetstones and tea. Bolts of coarse linen from the League's mills in Rett. Autumn apples, squashes bright as coals, yellow corn, and dark green kale. And men and women from all the villages around, each in the clothes that told their origin.

Hunters from Ladderlake in green cloaks, the borders of their hip cloths woven with the hand sign. Filchmeadow men, who as everyone knew had sex with pigs, in bright orange woven with the foot sign—yet another reason to mistrust them. Nagknoll lads in breeks, no hip cloths even; they never ogled the girls, why would they bother? Sometimes even Roadsouls, those people outside custom or clan.

Raím fingered the hem of his own hip cloth. Being of Creek, it would be brown, with the bear's eye woven in red. He thought for the first time, Do the hunters of each town on earth believe the universe was created outward from the center of their Hold?

The idea made him uneasy. He put it aside. Lads from other Holds were stupid; probably all of them had sex with pigs.

He stepped forward into the dark.

All around him were the quick sounds of footsteps and wheeled dollies, the odor of spoiled fruit and frying meat. In a reek of stinkhallow and wild celery, a traveling medicator droned his wares: "Health! Vision! Sanity!" A parrot shrieked. Bodies jostled him. He gripped his stick, stretched out his hand,

walked forward, and bumped into the parrot's cage. The parrot
bit him through the bars.

He groped down the aisle and into a pile of cantaloupes. The
fruit seller rapped his wrist. He cursed her, took one brave stride,
and landed with his hand on a woman's large bosom. She beat
him with a duster while her neighbors screeched, "Sumiyu, are
you so hard up?" and "Brem, the beggar lad's after your wife!"
Someone, presumably Brem, fetched Raím a clout and shoved
him back toward the aisle.

A tug at Raím's tunic. "Hey, mister! For a penny I'll take you
where the beggars sit."

Cursing, Raím aimed a flat-handed smack that missed the
boy and hit Brem. Brem smacked him back, seized his jersey,
marched him down the market aisle, and dumped him on the
cobbles near the sounds of falling water and slow-rolling carts.

"Here you are with the beggars," said Brem. "The fountain's
over there—and you don't owe me a penny."

Raím passed Thoyes' money from his left hand to his right
and hurled it at Brem's voice.

Sound of coins falling, of children shrieking as they scrambled for them. Set's voice. "What have you done? All the money,
Thoyes sold her hens—"

"You spied on me!"

"You can't take care of yourself! Who'll see to you? Who'll
bring you meat? That's my jersey and tunic you've got on, and
my breeks. The hell... What are you doing?"

Raím was yanking off jersey and tunic, loosening the cross-
garters from the breeks. Piece by piece he threw the clothes at
Set's voice: the hip cloth and the boots, too, until he stood naked
by the pattering fountain.

The girls squealed. The grannies cackled, "Oh, what a pretty man!"

He groped at his feet, found his staff, broke it across his knee, and threw that, too. Turned his back on Set and the fountain, lifted his hands, and took two strides into the dark.

It received him. His hands were seized by other hands, one narrow, one wide. They moved sideways; he had to fall. Fell against a rumbling wagon, was dragged. Above his head a child's voice said, "You coming with us?"

Thoyes! Not Thoyes. "*Yes!*" he said.

Hands laid hold of him, hauled him over the side of the cart, and flung him into a heap of silk that moved, there were legs in it. The cart bounced and banged. Gabble of onlookers in the square, Set's shout.

Inside the cart, peals of laughter. Girls! He had fallen in a brave place. He laughed too. Grabbed for a slender waist that slipped away.

His outstretched arms were gripped by many hands. The world jerked; the earth he had been tied to, that had struck and blinded him, dropped away, and he fell.

Fell and fell.

He cried out, writhed, grabbed for anything: a girl's slender foot. She screamed, wrenched it away. His arms were weighted by bodies, someone heavy sat on his chest. A babble of babies...

Babies?

In wet darkness he heard his own sobs. Then a girl's, the one whose foot he had grabbed or maybe that other girl, the one before, who had wrenched herself from his grabbing and was lost to him.

A baby voice said, "He crying."

"Gya!" said the voice he had thought was Thoyes'. "These newies, they don't *act* like they said yes."

A woman's quiet voice said, "Be still."

His sobs, and the girl's, trailed off. Pinned by many hands, he lay in the swaying dark.

Stillness spread through him like frost on a winter pool. He thought of that constellation, the starry Hunter, outstretched and falling, falling in the coldest sky.

They lifted him to lean against knees and thighs. When he began to shiver, they covered him with something, cloak or skirt. Across his lap they laid a tiny child, asleep, perhaps to be warmth for each other. The cart rocked. A scent of rosemary; he was in his mother's garden, hot and quiet and quivering with bees.

He did not sleep. He leaned against the women's thighs, empty. Traveling.

5

I had a dog, my dog was blind,
I stuck a pin in his behind.
Dog went mad, I was glad,
Give me all your money or I'll tell my dad.
Skipping rhyme. Rett.

Weeping, Duuni nursed her foot and looked at the man she had stopped.

She had painted the Unclothed Gods, and at every equinox of her life had watched the Wall Warriors dance, so it was not his nakedness that shocked her but his color. His face and chest, his arms and legs were freckled and bronzy-brown, but his hips, untouched by sun, had the translucent gleam of milk when the cream has been skimmed. Around them was tattooed a blue serpent, so dark it seemed to rise from his flesh. His hair and beard were red, like a torch in daylight.

The women pulled him up to lean against their knees. He sat as though stunned. When the babies crawled over his feet he did not move; he let the jolting of the cart shake him, and began to shake with cold.

"Give him the comforter," said Auntie.

The cut-cloth rags, scattered in the struggle, were fished out of the corners. Duuni clutched the comforter to her breasts. Nine tugged at it. "You got clothes, Pillbug. He doesn't."

The blind man's face said, Everything is gone.

Duuni let go. Nine pulled it away and threw it around his shoulders. He did not seem to notice. Duuni did not know how to dress herself in those clothes. Nine, raking through the heap, said, "I'll help you."

Burning with strangeness and shame, Duuni dressed in cut cloth. The babies crawled and gabbled, the motley girls watched casually, as though this were no strange event. Nine turned the garments right side up in Duuni's hands, saying, "Were you born in an *anthill*? Didn't your mother teach you *anything*?" There was a knit cap; Duuni's hair was so thick it popped right off. "You got nice hair," said Nine. "What's your real name?"

Whispering: "Duuni."

"That's a joke! In Roadsoul talk, *dooni* means brave. You're Pillbug, that's all."

☙

The cut clothing clung to her body, it felt as though she would not be able to get it off. The trousers were loose and full, double-layered against the cold; they made her have two legs. The tunic that went over the shirt was quilted like Nine's, faded green silk with gold flowers. She touched the buttons, flower-shaped and pink, one missing; her fingers tingled with risk. She was so slow figuring out how to button them that Nine did it for her.

Nothing belonged to the world she knew—not even her body, embraced and divided by forbidden cloth. With both hands she held the foot Tumiin and the blind man had grabbed, comforting it before it must disappear into wooly hose and boots as sharp as trowels. The image of the lion she had drawn on the sole was still dark.

"Hey," said Nine. "Look what Pillbug's got!" The women leaned, murmured. The toddlers took wet fingers out of their mouths and pointed. "Dicey, he draws on us kids with urda, but his lions, they look like frogs. Some prayer merchant draw that?"

Duuni whispered, "I did."

"*You* drew it? Gya, you're *good*. Lookee, she drew it herself. Hey—will you draw on us?"

Whispered: "I am sorry."

"Huh? How come?"

Whispered: "I have no urda paste."

"We can *make* some." Nine scrabbled in a box, drew out a stoppered jar of greenish-brown urda powder and shook it.

Whispered: "I have no lemon juice."

Nine got up, fell over the blind man's bare shins, poked in a different box. Fell over his shins again, brought Duuni a tin cup and three withered lemons. Fetched a knife, squeezed the lemons, added the powder. The others looked on with calm interest, nursing babies that were maybe their own, maybe stolen.

"But..." There were prayers to be said when you mixed urda paste. Duuni could not say them. She could not say the name *Mma*.

"What next?" said Nine.

Whispered: "Holy oil."

"Got none. Bacon grease be all right? And speak *up*, I can't hardly hear you."

"It must be rosemary oil." Duuni thought—for an instant only—Who was it who first said how things *must* be?

"We got that. Kills lice." Nine fetched a bottle, stirred the mix with a bent spoon.

"*Holy* oil."

Nine raised the cup. "Thanks, all you gods! There."

At the harsh, warm odor of rosemary the blind man turned his head. Duuni said, "It must sit overnight. And...I have no urda press." Hers had been generations old, worn by years and lives of prayer. "I am sorry—"

42

"You *act* sorry all the time, why d'you want to *tell* people?" Nine wedged the cup behind a trunk. "Dicey has that squirty thing. If I get it, will you draw on us kids?"

Duuni looked down and away. Nodded.

"Deal." Nine held her palm out flat. Duuni looked at it. "Slap my palm," said Nine. "Gya, it's like teaching a *baby*." She picked up Duuni's hand and made a limp slap with it across her own. "You were doing good there for a minute. Don't go deaf and dumb again, we already got a blind one."

The blind one had turned toward the odor of rosemary with a look almost of longing. He was lean as a spring wolf, and his face was so angry—or so frightened, Duuni could not tell which. She shrank into the alien clothing.

Nine looked from one to the other. Shook her head. "Neither of you is going to last long among the Souls."

 The odor of rosemary called him back to himself. Kidnapped by women and babies; he had no idea where he was. Did not want to find out, because if he did the world would start up again. He could not forget the sobbing of that girl, a desolate sound so exactly what he felt himself that he had to hate her.

Beside him, a small child banged on a pan. Then it seemed the pan was filled; he smelled chicken and onions. The child ate noisily.

Raím said, "I'm hungry."

Nobody gave him anything. He slid his hand sideways, thinking to filch some. The child smacked his nose. He cursed and groped, thinking to smack back, but in an instant he was pinned to the dusty rugs by silks—a falling man held by the sky. *Falling!* To keep from crying, he cursed.

"Auntie, we could put him back out. And her, she just sits there."

"They've said yes."

"If they say yes, we've *got* to take them?"

"They're Farki's now."

"She's a pillbug, and he's a pig."

"Room for all creatures in this world," said the voice named Auntie. "Including fleas."

"Jumping about. That would be me?"

Raím said, "Let me up. I won't fight."

Soft laughter.

"Please," he said.

Cautiously, the silks let him go.

He sat up in the swaying dark. Pulled the comforter across his lap but was too proud to put it back over his shoulders. The smell of lunch continued. He said again, "I'm hungry." Thought. Rubbed his beard. "Please, I'm hungry."

As if it had been waiting for him, a fat sandwich was nudged at his hands. He took it, opened his mouth; the sandwich disappeared into blank air.

He was beyond rage, in a kind of mad despair. A child giggled, a woman prompted it softly. "What do we say? Tell the laddie what we say."

Warmth leaned at Raím's ear, and a tiny voice said, "T'ank you."

He thought about this. Said, "Please, I'm hungry." The sandwich bumped his hands. He grasped it. "Thank you," he said.

The whisperer put its stockinged foot in his lap, fell over, and said, "You welcome."

ᔕ

He breathed onions, licked his thumbs. The child who chattered so much in Plain was called Nine; whether boy or girl he could not tell, but because the voice was like Thoyes' he thought of her as a girl. The unknown language around him was eerie, fluid as water. Pillbug's corner was silent.

He said to the air, "Who are you?"

Nine said, "You yap like a townie. You a beggar?"

Screw these people. "I'm a hunter."

44

"Must hunt pretty big things, since you can't see 'em!"

"Bears." Surely they had seen the long scars on his back. "I go into the cave alone. I stun the bear with my cudgel." He gestured with his fist. "It's for the girls," he said. "Until I bring a girl her bear, she isn't a woman."

Shrieks of laughter. The women snatched his hands and held them to their breasts, their bellies: they were already women, he had had nothing to do with it.

He had daydreamed of such a moment, with himself as hero and lover. The babies clambered on him, squeaked, put their fingers up his nose, and crept away.

⑥

He half slept, jolting against warm thighs. Odor of dust, of pine woods, then wood smoke, voices, barking dogs. A rustle of silk; the legs he leaned on left. He was alone in the empty cart.

He did not know where Creek was, or his bothy, or his mother's garden. That scent of rosemary hung in the air. He put his face in his hands, felt his cheeks wet. "Oh, gods," he said aloud. "What have I done?"

A scrabble at the open door. Nine said, "Pillbug! Do I have to tell you *everything*? It's camp, come to the fire and get warm."

Pillbug crept past him, light as a moth, so slight the cart did not shift when her weight came off it. He had not been alone. She had seen him weep.

No one invited him to the fire.

With a curse he threw the comforter aside, groped to the open door of the cart, and stood, naked and disdainful, before whatever was out there.

He was greeted with cheers—or were they jeers? He felt the air with one foot. The off mule backed a step, the cart jerked, and he fell backward onto a pile of tin plates.

Nine's shout: "Beggar's playing the tambourine!"

He clambered down the porch-like steps and stood barefoot on pine needles. Gripped the cart. Chatter and comment in that strange tongue; he could not tell whether it was about himself, could not imagine it would not be. He smelled cedar smoke. The fire must be over there, but if he let go of the wagon he would fall forever into limitless dark.

His hand would not let go. He lunged; his hand stopped him.

"What's the matter with you?" said Nine, somewhere to his left.

"Nothing. Take me to that fire."

No answer.

"Please," he said. "If you'd take me to the fire?"

Her child's hand took his wrist. He thought, It's Thoyes' hand! Near fainting with a strange terror, he let go of the wagon, made his feet step up and down on the needles that pricked without piercing. When her hand let him go he grabbed after it. "What d'you want?" she said.

"What...what place is this? Please."

"Middle of the woods."

"Which woods?"

"Our woods. All woods are our woods. How come you didn't bring that comforter, you trying to show off? You ain't got but a button."

"I'm *cold.* I threw away my clothes."

"Stupid. What's that snake about you for?"

"Because I'm a man."

"You wish!"

Appreciative laughter told him everything had been heard by unseen others, no doubt including the Pillbug girl. "*Who are you?*" he said to the world. "*Where have I come to?*"

"Might be half an answer to that," said a man's voice, gentle. "But we'd have to want to answer."

"I want to know who you are!"

Laughter. "Who are we?" "Not the same as we were a moon ago." "'Cause now we got puppies!" a small voice piped.

"What tribe is this?" said Raím.

"You mean where have we come from? Or what are we called?"

"I don't care!"

"Then why ask?"

And after that no one would answer at all.

He stood. And stood. He thought of striding off into the frosty woods. Of these people struck dead by vengeful gods, himself by a merciful one. Of Set coming after him, cursing, throwing a shirt at his head and shouting, "Get home!"

None of these things happened. He got colder. His nose ran. He smelled roast pig, heard the sizzle of fat.

"Please," he said, too softly to be heard. Then, louder, "Please. If someone would please take me nearer to the fire."

There was a little commotion. Nine's voice: "I won't. He's a pain in the butt. Let *her* take him." Then, nearer: "He ain't going to kill you. *Nobody's* going to kill you. I never saw such a baby."

Smell of rosemary. A soft, flinching hand was pressed into his own. She had seen him cry; he jerked his hand away.

"If you two ain't the worst we ever took! Figure it out yourselves," said Nine, and stumped off.

A still, rosemary-scented space a foot or so away was Pillbug. Except for his old cat, Brook, he had never known a being so still.

The pig continued to smell like paradise.

He turned his face toward the Pillbug-silence. "Yanking at somebody's hand is a rotten way to lead."

No answer.

"I'll put my hand on your elbow. You walk, I'll follow." He hated to follow.

No answer.

Through gritted teeth he said, "Please."

A little, startled movement. He found the elbow, lower than his own, and put his hand on it. It was warm. A sudden safety, as though he were at last attached to earth. Tears pricked his eyelids. He got hold of himself. "Thank you."

No answer. But the elbow moved, it led him to the fire's heat. There was a log to sit on; he forgot to thank Pillbug and sat, feeling proud of himself. He would ask *her* who these people were. But she was gone, as if she had never been. He had never known a girl like that: a girl trying not to exist.

From nowhere a cloak fell over his shoulders, a plate of pork and roast carrots was put in his hands, a tin cup of red wine. "Thank you," he said. It was bad wine, delicious. Surely it was Pillbug who served him, for he smelled rosemary; now she sat on the same log, a little to his right. He shouldered up under the cloak and leaned toward the space where she was. "Food's good, eh?"

No answer. He edged toward her. "You're with these folks?"

No answer.

"They're a bit strange." Perhaps she could tell him who the hell they were. "To me, I mean. As a hunter—" He remembered the response this had brought and said hastily, "That is, when I had my sight I was a hunter. These days I'm a weaver. I thought I'd have an adventure. Leave it all behind, and just go."

No answer.

"Blindness—I don't let it stop me," he said to her attentive silence. He thought of her arm under his hand, so warm. "You're kind," he said, and reached to feel it again.

Nothing there. As if she had chosen not to exist.

He felt stupid. And angry enough to keep edging down the log until he nudged up against a different and very solid girl who laughed and nudged him back. What luck! To hell with Pillbug. He put his hand on the girl's knee. She put her hand over his, laughed, leaned close and said, "Bonnie blind lad, where will you sleep?"

Oh blessed night, of wine and girls and roast pork! A vast grin took over his face. He elbowed aside the cloak to show her the blue serpent, took her hand, and said, "I can sleep anywhere."

"Good." She withdrew her hand and gave him a brisk pat. He rose. She whisked away the cloak. "With the puppies, then."

The puppies lived in an open cart, on a torn quilt and a heap of straw. Raím stole the quilt and rolled up in it. The squirming pups—there were six—licked the pork grease off his face. Away by the fire there was laughter, a violin.

The bitch came back, growled at him, made up her mind and flopped down with a sigh. The puppies scrambled for her teats. Raím edged closer in the dirty straw and drew the quilt over all of them together.

The puppies gave off heat like a stove, the bitch whuffed and galloped in her sleep. Lying in his own dark, Raím felt the larger darkness beyond and thought of an enormous, sighing forest, a night sky brilliant with stars.

He put his hand down at his side. A sticky tongue licked it. He slept.

The blind beggar had prayed into his hands, "Oh gods, what have I done?" Duuni had seen women show despair, but a man, never. Perhaps he was a two-sexed person, a pervert. She had had to bear his big hand on her arm.

But he was easy to escape. She sidled beyond his reach. His strange, light eyes shifted, seeing nothing; her own scurried here and there around the Roadsoul camp.

On summer nights in Alikyaan she had slept in the courtyard, looking up into the sky milky with stars and streaked with meteors, deep; yet always at the edge of vision were the courtyard walls. She had gazed at that bigness from a *place*.

Not here. Carts and wagons stood helter-skelter. Screaming children ran in drifts, wind-tossed pine woods stretched away. Over this chaos the sky glittered unbound. Even the moon was in the wrong corner of the sky.

When they arrived there had been wagons at the camp already, and many fires. The children, all ages, were in constant motion. She could not tell girls from boys; in hodgepodge rags all of them played with babies, scrubbed crockery with sand, hauled water, fetched kindling for the fires. Likewise the adults, in their fairground silks: both men and women carried boxes from the wagons, spread tarpaulins on the ground, shook out vast feather-beds covered in milled linen. A girl unharnessed the mules; a man carried an infant in his arms.

She thought, Perhaps all these people are two-sexed? She waited to be ordered where to go, what to do. No one said anything.

An old woman spread a length of uncut cloth on a cart's tailgate. Alikyaani green cotton, finest weave—it was reserved for the councilmen's robes at Sun's Return, but could be bought at festival for gold. For a moment Duuni's heart came home through her eyes. She thought, Did Mother weave that?

The woman took up a pair of iron shears. *Snick! Snack!* The holy folds fell this way, that way. She snatched a child out of the crowd and tried the cloth against her, pinching up gathers; sewn, it would make a little frock.

A tug at her own cut-cloth hem was Nine, clutching the cup of urda paste. "Pillbug! I got Dicey's squirty thing. Just, don't tell him. After supper you'll draw on us?" She held out her arm, grubby gray at the wrist. Behind her the ever-moving shoals of children had merged to a bunch.

Should Duuni ask permission of Farki, to whom she belonged? Who was Farki? What should she do? But the children dragged her to the fire, sat her on a box, and brought her a plate heaped with pork and fixings. What she could not eat they polished off like dogs. Nine poured the urda paste into the leather bag and screwed on the brass nozzle.

Duuni thought, Nine stole the press from this Dicey. I shall be killed. I don't understand anything, these people are mad, I can't bear it!

Then she thought, Would I rather be married to Tumiin?

She said to the children in Plain, "Your arms are dirty. Wash them, or the design will not take." They ran off, splashed in a tin basin, came back. "With *soap*. Also I shall need sugar water, very thick. And lemon juice."

"You got bossy all of a sudden," said Nine. "Do what she says, you kids."

They returned with clean arms. Duuni took Nine's scrubbed wrist. "What do you wish me to draw?"

"A snake. Like the one on him over there, that rude beggar." Nine leaned like Riinu, warm. "Make it be eating a mouse. With blood."

The fire blazed up and crackled. Duuni said, "I will not draw it eating a mouse."

"How come?"

"Because I will not."

"Can it be a poison snake?"

"No."

"*You're* no fun. Oh well, any kind of snake. Watch this, you kids. She's *good*."

The placeless chaos of the campsite settled. There was the snake, waiting to be drawn; Duuni could see it, winding round Nine's wrist to rest its bright-eyed, slender head on her palm. In pungent rosemary it crept out of the stolen brass nozzle and onto Nine's arm.

As on the loom Duuni had watched the thread travel back and forth, now she watched the line weave what it would. She drew the snake's delicate tail. The little plants it crawled through, clover and thyme. Poised on their leaves, a honeybee.

"Blow on it," she said. "When it has dried I shall paint it with lemon sugar to set the pattern, and wrap a rag around it. You may wash off the paste in the morning." There would be a morning. "Take care it does not smudge."

"See?" Nine held out her arm. "I *told* you she was good!"

Duuni looked up. Around her, careful not to block the fire-light, a crowd stood: children in front, then adults. Auntie was there, the motley girls from the cart, the young man who had led the black mare. A short, strong man with a mustache and gray-ing curls gave Duuni an appraising glance. Nine said, "Farki, look! She can be carnie!"

"Might," said Farki. His voice was very deep.

"Townies would pay." Nine blew on her arm. "Don't bump me, now." The rest of the children came crowding and clamor-ing, "Me! Me!"

Duuni thought, Farki. I belong to him. She dropped her eyes, looked down and away.

Then she thought, *No.*

She looked up. But Farki had gone; so had Auntie and the others. Only the blind man was left, sitting on his log. Someone had brought him a cloak and a plate of dinner.

A clean wrist nudged hers. "Can I have a turtle? With wings?"

The next child wanted a pig. The next, a cat with pants on. Then a spotted horse, a monkey, a dog in love.

"What does a dog in love look like?" she asked the tiny girl who asked for it.

"Like a dog," she said.

Duuni drew a dog. She drew a fish, a fox, three praying man-tises. She was afraid she would have to draw all night, but when the moon touched the pine tops women came and carried away the children, their arms wrapped in rags.

The urda paste was almost gone, her nose was full of the smell of it. She sat on the box rubbing her stained hands, waiting for Farki's deep voice to say, *You. Come.*

Nine, tousled and yawning, said, "Ain't you coming to bed? If we don't go to sleep it won't be morning, and we can't wash the paste off."

The feather beds on the ground were already full of children. Duuni slid in among them, squirmed out of boots and trousers, but left the tunic on, too tired to understand buttons. Nine put her head on Duuni's neck and was asleep in two breaths.

Somewhere, the sound of rushing water. By starlight there was nothing painted on the canvas wagon top at all. Tumbling toward sleep, Duuni thought, Where is the lion? Is it in the forest, following us? And where will the blind beggar sleep?

In her dreams they became one being, man and lion, red and gold.

6

Bowl that's full, you can't fill it.
Meat that's cold, you can't chill it.
Locked and barred? Smash it! Break it!
Sapless, rootless? Let the wind take it!

  Hopscotch rhyme. The Roadsouls.

Smell of damp grass and wood smoke, hard ground beneath her hip. Her bruised eye itched. Still dreaming, Duuni thought, I have not cleaned my teeth.

"*Hssst.*" Something prodded her back. She came awake with a gasp, clutching the quilt.

"You shouldn't jump like that," said Nine. "Your soul's a pack rat, when you sleep it leaves you and goes gathering, if you wake that quick it can't get back and you die."

Morning sun poured through the scrub pines. Clink and crackle of kettle and fire, mild snort of mules. Smoke rising in raveled skeins. Dozens of wagons, in linked meadows where hobbled horses grazed like deer.

Duuni was the only one still under the eiderdown. A crowd of children, frumpy with sleep, held out to her their wrapped arms and said, "You been sleeping and *sleeping.*"

She waited for everything to turn back into Alikyaan. It did not. She said, "All right."

"Meet you by the creek!" They left in a flock. She tugged on trousers and boots, thinking, Cut clothing is warmer than robes.

"Come *on!*" Nine bellowed, far away. "A *slug's* quicker than you." Auntie, stirring pork bits at the fire, looked up and smiled with half her mouth. Older children spread the eiderdowns over bushes to dry. Duuni scuttled to the creek, catching the toes of her boots on stones. Nine said, "My snake, you think it's cooked?"

The creek water was so cold it was hot. Duuni told the children, "You may wash off the paste yourselves." Of course they pulled the knotted rags too tight and she had to undo them with her teeth, but in the end the blue-black paste was scrubbed away. Dogs, turtles, mantids shone on clean arms. Wet children scattered through the camp, shouting in Roadsoul and Plain.

"*Eee!*" said Nine. "My snake, it's the *best*! I'm going to show that blind man!" She turned to run.

Duuni caught her tunic. "None of you said thank you."

"We forgot."

"When the blind beggar does not say thank you, no one helps him."

Nine hung against the slack of her tunic. "He's getting what he needs. Same as you."

"What do you mean?"

"You said yes to the Souls. What you need, that's what you get." She began to giggle. "Let go my shirt!"

"If I let go you will fall down."

"Right."

Duuni let go. Nine fell down. Then she rolled over, sprang up, and rushed off waving her arm. "Going to show him!"

"He is *blind!*"

But she was gone.

He woke shivering and disoriented, smelling puppy shit. Something scrabbled at the side of the cart. "Hey, beggar!" The child named Nine. "You still breathing? Look at this."

Raím sat up, straw in his ears. "I can't see."

"I know *that*." She seized his finger and used it to trace a curving line down her arm. "It's a snake like you got. Pillbug drew it, too bad you're blind as a mole. You cold?"

"No."

"You're all over goose bumps. Farki's got a tunic for you."

Lest the tunic be snatched away, Raím said hastily, "Thank you."

"He took it off a dead man."

"Then I thank the dead man. Where is it?"

"He'll give it when he feels like. Better use that quilt."

He would not walk about wrapped in a puppy-shat quilt. Someone was making porridge that did not smell like home porridge. Who *were* they? Where was he? He could hear a creek; if there was a creek, maybe he could wash. It would run down from the east, the same as the one at home...or would it? It was not the same creek...or was it? What if he had traveled in a circle?

He tried not to hug his arms around himself. To the place where Nine had last been he said, "Where does that creek flow from?"

She answered from his other elbow. "The *mountain*. All creeks do."

"Are we near a village called Creek?"

"Which one? There's two called White Creek. Then there's Stony Creek, and Creek Bend, and Creek Meadow, and Little Creek. Plain old Creek, there's a bunch. Four-five."

"I mean the Creek where the men are hunters. Where... where they walk like lions."

"Townie," said Nine. "They all say that."

Raím turned his face to the sun. "Is that east? For sure?"

"Gya!"

"*Why am I here?*" He did not know whom he asked.

"You got that look a baby has," said Nine. "When they're just born they have this look on their face, like *Huh?* You're here because you lifted up your hands and said yes."

He could not remember saying yes in his life. He threw away his pride and beat his arms around himself, trying to get warm. "That girl, Pillbug. Did she lift up her hands?"

"Sure, else she wouldn't be with us."

"Is she a townie?"

"From Alikyaan. Farki says maybe she's carnie, but you don't look good for much."

No language made sense; the world was liquid, unreal. He had to know *something* for sure. Anything.

"Nine. Are you a girl or a boy?"

A squeal. "Auntie, she says townies got to know which way's east, where the privy is, and whether you got a dimple or a handle, else they get nervous." Nine stood up in the cart and shouted, "*Auntie!* He asked about everything but the privy!"

You said yes to the Souls. What you need, that's what you get.

Duuni, stirring porridge at the smoky fire, thought, What do I need?

She had never asked this. There had never been a choice. She could not answer.

What the beggar needed at the moment was a shirt. Nine had led him down to bathe in the creek, then had brought him, wet and shuddering, to the fire.

Auntie's long hand took the porridge paddle from Duuni's. "Farki has a tunic for him. Will you fetch it, please?" She pointed. Under a broad juniper stood a dark blue wagon dimly painted with a moon, a sun, flowing water. Farki's wagon. Dust rose about it, as if from dogs fighting.

Duuni did not move. Two children came running to show her again the winged turtle, the loving dog. "Take the children with you," said Auntie.

They took Duuni's hands, swinging and squealing. Then she could walk, kicking her own ankles with the boots' sharp toes. But the closer they came to the blue caravan, the more she thought, I am taking children to a man who owns women.

She was afraid to stop walking, but she gathered them close. They thought it was a game, like a three-legged race. At the wagon a group of young men, stripped to their clouts, watched a pair of wrestlers in the dirt; that was the dust cloud.

Duuni stopped. A man ran toward her: the black mare's young master, with eyes like a man of Alikyaan.

She pushed the children in front of her, as Tumiin had pushed her between himself and the lion.

She saw what she did. She gasped, whirled about, faced the children the way they had come and gave them a shove. Cried, "Run!" and turned to face what must be.

But the children ran in wide circles back to the young man, they swarmed his legs and stuck out their arms, crying, "Look what she drew!"

He nodded approval and put out his hand. "I'm Tam Chivi."

She would not touch him or tell him her name. It was the children who said, "We're to ask Farki for the shirt!"

Tam Chivi jerked his chin toward the wrestlers. "Ground, and he'll be up." He turned to watch, standing next to Duuni easy as if she were a man. She thought, I am wearing cut clothing; maybe he thinks I *am* a man?

His bare shoulder was dusty and brown. She wished she had a veil to hide her bruised eye. Then she looked at the wrestlers and forgot him.

They moved like snakes in a dance, like flames or pouring water. Then a hand slapped the dirt. At a yelp, "Ground!" the sinuous motion broke into Farki and a boy who groaned and laughed as he lay on his belly, saying, "You've killed me!"

Farki stood. His eyes were green, small, and deep. Duuni stepped behind Tam Chivi; Tam Chivi stepped away; she made herself drop her hands from her breasts, and said, "Auntie... For the beggar..."

Farki brushed sand off his arms. With a rolling, bent-kneed walk he went to the blue caravan and returned with a packet wrapped in milled cotton and tied with strips of rag. Held it out to her. "Tell him he's welcome to it."

The children pestered at Farki's legs, showing him their arms. From the fire Nine shouted, "*Pillbug!* He's freezing his butt off!"

Duuni waited for Farki to tell her his will. He said nothing. "Thank you," she said. Her feet wanted to run but she made them walk, back across the tussocky field to the fire. The children came with her, skipping and singing.

☙

The beggar hugged himself, clothed only in smoke. Sniffed heartily, scowled. "Pillbug?"

Was he saying she stank? And her name was not Pillbug. "Farki has sent you a tunic."

His *Thank you* sounded like *Curse you.* Yet the poor man was blind; she could be courteous. "I will untie the wrapping for you."

"You think I'm a cripple? Be damned. Give it here."

Naked ugly beggar! He would worry the knots like the children, and she would have to do for him anyway. "I will untie it," she said coldly. He cursed; she untied the knots; the tunic fell open in her hands.

It was linen, heavy and cool, knit onto a wool underlayer. Wait—not knit but crocheted. No...embroidered, perhaps? She held it close to look. Brocade? A dense, doubled cloth with greens and browns in the ground of it, the wide panels across chest and shoulders embroidered with a tree. Around the tree, a hundred animals drawn intricately in indigo ink—no, not ink but thread. And not knit or crocheted or embroidered, but woven.

Woven.

She turned it in her hands. Who had made it? How? It was cut cloth, for it had sleeves and cuffs.

The beggar raved and pawed the air. "Give it to me!"

"Wait. Wait." She searched for the wound where the noble cloth had been cut. It was seamless. A little ragged rent in the breast as if from a dagger, that was all.

She thought, Woven whole!

"I'm a weaver," said the beggar. "I can untie any knot!"

"A *weaver?*" Weavers were women—only and ever women. She held the holy shirt away from that pervert.

"You think a blind man can't weave? I'm the best weaver in the creek." He paused, bit his lip. "In *my* creek."

He wove in a creek! If that madman got the tunic, she would never see it again close to. Had it been woven by gods?

"*Pill*bug!" said Nine. "If he dies of cold he's too tough to eat."

Duuni held the tunic to her mouth. Then, as one would give up a child, she laid it across the beggar's groping hands. He snatched it, spoke his vicious "Thank you." Stopped. Hefted the tunic. Felt it with long fingers. "What is this?"

Perverted, blind, and witless. That such a marvel should go to him! "A tunic."

He felt inside the sleeves, followed the selvage with his hands. "It's woven whole," he said. Her mouth fell open. He touched the cloth to his cheek. "Who wove this?"

"I do not know."

"Where did you get it? Ah—Farki. If I knew who Farki is. If I knew what anything in the goddamn world is. Here." He held it out to her. She could tell he did not care who she was, only wanted someone to look. "Feel this interlock? It's impossible. If you were a weaver you'd realize—"

"I am a weaver," said Duuni. Then, "I *was*."

His hands stilled on the cloth. "But you're a girl. I know by your voice." His brows drew down. "You mean...where you come from, women can be weavers?"

To ask that was to say there were places where women were *not* weavers—places full of perverts and devils. Or else everything the elders and her mother and grandmother and all the ancestors of Alikyaan had taught about the world, forever, was untrue.

Maybe even Mma.

"Yes," Duuni said slowly. "Where I come from, women are weavers."

"In Creek...that is, was, my village...a woman may not even look at a man's loom." He spoke as if they were alone, the two of them. Turned his face aside. "I don't have a loom any more."

"Neither do I."

"I think I've gone mad."

She might have said, *So have I.* The blue snake coiled above his white groin; a strangeness came over her, and she said nothing.

He regained his scowl and fumbled the tunic over his head. "So I'll be a madman instead of a weaver. An honest calling, what the hell."

Nine pointed with the porridge spoon. "Look at the beggar, ain't he fine?"

He was. Bearded, bare-legged, the beggar looked like a lord. His red hair blazed like a torch.

"Looks better on you than it did on that dead man," said Nine.

Duuni put her hand on his elbow. "Step back from the fire, the sparks will peck the cloth."

He followed her easily, like a dancer. "Thank you," he said. It sounded like *Thank you.*

 He had shown his loom to a woman once, the girl he had been in love with. That had been radical enough. But for a woman to weave! He fingered the neck of the tunic, marveling. His hand stilled on the cloth. Suppose a woman had woven this?

The thought made him squeamish. He decided not to think it. Instead he thought about what Pillbug smelled like, rosemary and girl.

Something rapped his ankle. He clutched it and cursed. "I've been standing here with your porridge for an *hour*," said Nine, kicking him again.

"Didn't know you were there." He put his hand down into the bowl.

"There's a *spoon*," said Nine.

He sucked his fingers. The spoon was put into them. He forgot to say thank you, remembered and said it twice, quickly. Felt backwards with his heels for something to sit on, stepped on a dog, was grabbed from behind, steered sideways, and set down on a crate. "Thank you," he said again. He thought, Gratitude is my staff. With *thank you, thank you*, I tap my way.

The porridge was bitter with strange herbs, and he did not like it until halfway through the bowl. The conversations around him made no sense, even in Plain.

"Praying mantises, one, two, three."

"My doggie's in love!"

"If you would like a flying cow you may have one. Later." That voice was Pillbug's. She had lifted up her hands and said yes...her hand was soft...

Nine said, "Want some tea? You. Beggar."

He rounded on her. "You little... My name is Raím."

Around him the bizarre conversations stopped. "Ooh!" said Nine. *"Auntie!"*

Auntie, when she could speak, said, "Fine name."

"Raím," howled a dozen children. "Raím! Raím!"

His grandmother had named him for his great-grandfather, a legendary hunter who had lost his right arm to a bear. He said, "It means Lightning Bolt."

"Flea Butt," said Nine. "It means *Flea Butt!*"

"In your ignorant tongue!" He sprang up, scattering the last of the porridge. "Fucking savages!" Men's hands grabbed him from behind, held him while he struggled. "If I weren't blind you couldn't do this!"

"But you are," said a voice, amused.

He panted. Slowly the hands released him. He felt around for the box. Sat down.

"Give him his tea, please, Nine," said Auntie.

Nine nudged his hand with a mug. He made a fist; the tea spilled. She refilled the mug and brought it back, giggling, "Here's your tea, *Raim.*"

He took long breaths. "Thank you," he said.

"You're welcome, Flea Butt."

The tea was scalding, it tasted like pine pitch and made him straighten his back. Nine nudged a basket full of pine nuts at his hand and sat down next to him, cracking nuts with her teeth and spitting out the shells as if nothing had happened. The bustle and clatter of camp went on.

He ate his handful of nuts. Risked the question, what the hell. "Nine. Please. What tribe is this?"

"Souls." But all tribes are souls. Children came close, their voices so clotted with laughter they kept having to stop their chant and start over.

> *Raim, raim,*
> *Haik haum haim!*

"*Ra* is your butt," said Nine. "*Eem* is a flea. That song's for skipping rope, it means, *Flea Butt, Flea Butt, jump over the moon!*"

He heard Auntie's laugh with the rest. Pillbug must be grinning. He knew, suddenly and absolutely, that he must go home.

Ten Orchards first. Someone at the market would show him the road to Creek. Perhaps Set had saved his clothes, or his mother could find clothes for him, or the men of the Hold could weave them on the double line of looms that was the center of the world. He would know where he was, what men do and women do, and how to behave under the eye of the sun. His name would not mean Flea Butt. All he had to do was get away, hide until the wagons left, and wait for a cart going back toward Ten Orchards. He had been a hunter. He knew how to keep still. And he had a warm tunic.

"Nine," he said toward her laughter, "where's the privy?"

"Auntie! He *said* it!"

"Tell me," said Raím.

"What d'you want a privy for? There's a *forest.*"

"Where is it?"

"Where *is* it? All over! That's how a forest is!"

"Take me there."

"Well, ain't you a god."

"Please."

"Mister Please and Thank You."

"Please."

Nine took his hand. "I'll take you to the edge of the road. You can bang your head on a tree your own self."

"Thank you."

She tugged him away from the subsiding laughter, the half-smothered fires. When they came to the road he said, "I don't understand your people."

"Oh, they ain't mine," said Nine. "Well, now they are. I was took, same as you and Pillbug."

"Kidnapped?"

"Huh? No. I lifted up my hands, I said Yes, oh, yes! and I was took. I was six years old."

"But...what about your family?"

"They'd never care. I was just one more."

Raím tried to imagine Thoyes carried off by this mad lot. "If I were your brother, I'd care."

"You can be my brother if you want."

She said it so easily. He was touched. He squeezed her calloused little hand, felt guilty for what he was about to do.

At the road's edge she said, "There's a ditch, then it's forest."

"Nine. Did you never try to run away?"

"My god, no. I was a mill rat, down there in Rett." Her hand slipped out of his. "Go on, now."

He almost said *Goodbye*. Crossed the ditch and entered the woods, groping tree to tree. The sounds of camp grew distant. He could not move as quietly as he had when he was sighted, but he was not noisy. When he was sure he was out of sight, he got down on all fours like a lizard, careful of the tunic, and crept.

The bushes were thick and cold. Frost had softened the summer undergrowth; when he felt the limp stems heavy above him, he crouched motionless in hunter's trance, barely breathing.

Nine would come seeking him, calling. And Pillbug. He waited for the dismay, the shouting, the fruitless search. His feet got cold. There were halloos, squealing axles, clopping hooves. Then silence.

No one came looking for him. No one called his terrible name.

7

Ayah, ayah! Babe without a cradle,
Laid in the greenwood on the bare ground.
Ayah, ayah! Nothing to cover you,
Until the leaves cover you without a sound.
Ayah, ayah! Babe without a cradle,
Nothing to hold you, nothing to hold,
Nothing between you and the wide wilderness
But the wild wind—and the wind grows cold.

      "The Abandoned Child," *Song.* Greencliff.

"He's gone," said Nine.

Duuni waited to hear who was gone.

"I said he's gone. You deaf?"

"No."

"Then how come you don't say, 'Who's gone?'"

Because in Alikyaan one did not ask questions. One waited. Sooner or later something was said, and one went back to the loom.

The caravans of the camp had mingled, re-divided, gone on. Duuni saw Tam Chivi on his black mare, but in her wagon half the women who ignored her and the babies who sprawled and gabbled were different from yesterday's. Or so she thought; it was hard to tell, for yesterday they had all just looked like Roadsouls.

They had begun to climb the mountain. Behind them through the open window the wrinkled hills and plains were ever-changing, like a mirror held at different angles, reflecting a few things Duuni could name: pine trees, a sandbank, a creek set about with willows.

Other things were strange at first and then, from long ago in the fields along the riverbank, a memory would rise. Flick and glitter on creek water: a trout's jump. Round, bright eye: a rabbit in the grass. For eight years she had seen those beings only dead and ready for the kitchen, or painted on a wall; now she looked and looked.

There were many more things—glints, motions, cries—that she could not name. When Nine said, "He's gone," she had been kneeling at the window, gazing back as world upon world dreamed away into dust and distance. Far away, somewhere to the west, lay the sea.

Nine poked her. "I don't know how you *breathed* till we took you. Say this: 'Who's gone?'"

Duuni shifted her eyes from the trillion worlds. "Who is gone?"

"Flea Butt."

Of course she knew the beggar was not in the wagon. But when everything is new, how do you know what is usual and what is not? She said obediently, "Where has he gone?"

"Ran off. Sometimes they do. They change their mind, they think they can run away from yes. The Souls, we don't wait. You don't want your life, you don't get it. He ran off into the woods."

With the tunic, the wonderful tunic. "He is blind. Perhaps he is lost?"

"He'd of hollered."

"Some wild animal…" She caught her breath. The lion! Following the caravan!

"Getting killed ain't quiet. Nah, he ran. Too bad. That was a master tunic. Farki says a master tunic knows where it needs to go, but too bad it had to go with old Flea Butt. He can't even see it."

"He—" said Duuni. Stopped.

"Go *on*. That place you came from, they give you the stink eye every time you opened your mouth?"

"Yes."

"Well, get over it."

"He saw it with his hands." Long fingers, the nails pared short.

"Like I showed him my snake." Nine stuck out her arm, grubby now. "When it fades, you do me another?"

"Yes."

"Or a toad," said Nine. "Only probably you won't do a poison toad. Let's get down alongside the cart and walk."

☙

Nine trotted like a dog in the choking dust, but Duuni had no strength in her legs. For eight years she had sat at her loom; she had danced, but where had there been to walk? As wagons came jangling from behind, she stumbled on, feet blistered, heart thumping.

A voice above her head said, "Lift?" Tam Chivi, on his big black mare. He leaned down, held out his brown fist. "Give me your hand."

A man. She did what he said without question.

He pulled her straight up into the air. She gasped and grabbed; he set her in front of him, astride in her cut trousers, his arm about her waist. His body was hot. His knees moved, the mare moved, his arm held her close.

She fell into terror like fire. The horse broke into a rattling run that flung her this way, that way, pinned by his arm. He laughed; from the side of her eye she saw him, his teeth white in his dusty face.

They drew up to the buckboard of her wagon. "Hey up, Auntie," he said. "Losing things?"

"Getting them back, seems," said Auntie.

To Duuni he said, "Hop!" When she did not move he picked her up and dumped her next to Auntie. Somewhere in the dust cloud Nine squealed, "Me too!" The horse wheeled, and in a moment she appeared, clinging to his hand and chittering like a monkey. He swung her up alongside Duuni, grinned, and rode off.

Nine rubbed her face on her sleeve. "What're you blubbering about now, you silly Pillbug?" For Duuni was sobbing, touched and untouched, alive.

"Let her be," said Auntie. "Dust wants rain."

⑤

She stayed on the buckboard as the autumn day grew warm. Sometimes the road ran across a hillside, sometimes along a lively water lined with poplars or sandy cliffs that still held the cool of night. Always to the left was the flank of the mountain, high as thought, dusted with new snow.

Now and then they passed a little settlement. At first the houses were like those of Ten Orchards, stuccoed mud with roofs of red tile, and Duuni thought, So that is what houses in the big world look like. Then they passed through a village where the houses were built of round stones from the creek, with roofs of gray slate. Farther on they were black mud brick with thatch. She could not imagine there would be so many kinds of houses in the world.

I am seventeen in years, she thought. Yet I am still the age I was when I entered the Maiden's Balcony: nine.

At every place a clutch of children scampered out to watch from a distance; women followed and snatched them away. Nine waved. Sometimes a child waved back. They passed through a poor village in a clearing in the scrub pine, where the houses were ramshackle, and the worst ones, on the far edge of town, were little more than shacks. Scarcely had they entered the forest on the other side when a tattered figure darted out of the trees, laid a heap of rags on the road's verge, and ran back into the shadows.

Auntie said, "Ah!"

From the purse at her waist she took a silver coin. She gave it to Nine, who leapt from the buckboard and ran ahead like a hare, dropped the coin in the rags, and lifted something in her arms. The wagon drew even with her; slowed; Auntie reached down her big hand, Nine grabbed it and was hoisted up, clutching to her shoulder a naked baby.

"*Peeuw*," said Nine. "And he ain't nothing but bones."

The wagon had hardly passed before the ragged creature darted out, snatched up the coin, and vanished again into the wood. Man or woman? Duuni could not even see a face. The baby thrust out his arms and legs as though he were falling, and weakly wailed.

Auntie, driving one-handed, inspected him. Said, "Give him to River."

Nine disappeared into the wagon, and in a few minutes came back without the child. "He took goat's milk. Bet he pukes it up."

"Did the same yourself," said Auntie.

Nine flopped down on the buckboard. "That baby's a skellington, he ain't worth coin."

"And you were?"

"You got me for *nothing*."

"Worth every bit of it." The caravan rolled on. Auntie began to sing.

> *Here we come a rolling,*
> *Hillery, hollery, hi-ti-o!*

Other voices took up the song. Duuni whispered to Nine, "A baby cannot say yes!"

"Sure he did. You saw him lift up his hands. That little, they say yes real easy. If he was too sick Auntie'd have said to put him back."

"But the...mother, whatever it was. She ran away. If you had put him back, wild beasts—"

Nine shrugged. "They'd eat him." From the wagon came that thin wail, then silence. "Sleeping," said Nine. "Or puking. Skinny little bones."

The sun sank west. The line of wagons rolled into a bigger town. Greencliff, said Nine, but the Souls' name for it was *Wheem.* "Means 'Looks Worried,' because everybody there does." The houses were white stucco among yellow laurels. There was a village wall, with a gate.

The men at the gate looked worried, all right. They did not let the caravan through, but waved it along to a big field busy with people who were building booths, waving hammers, arguing, and carrying sacks about. So many people! Duuni whispered to Nine, "Am I permitted to go back among the babies?"

"Huh? If you like those little barfers better than all this fun. But tomorrow you're on."

"On?"

"On show."

The slave market. The draggled, beaten girls.

"Carnie," said Nine. "Farki says. You're to draw on kids with urda, penny a go."

"*I?*"

"Who else? I can't draw a cat, even. Just a circle with a tail."

"But—"

"I'll help you mix the paste," said Nine. "You need a carnie name. Fancy, so the townies think they're getting their money's worth. I'll make you one." She gazed at the sky, chewed on her thumbnail. "Lady Lovely the Ducky Drawer."

"Ducky—"

"Townies, they think kids want little fuzzy smiley things. Kids, they want spiders. Or slugs. You can name yourself anything you want. What did you always want to be?"

The only thing Duuni had always wanted to be was invisible to Tumiin. "I—"

"Give me some *ideas.* How come you draw so good?"

Duuni, how do you draw? Slowly, as if to Riinu, Duuni said, "I...the being is there already. I lay down the line where it is. As I draw, it changes itself."

"Magic talk," said Nine. "That's good carnie."

"It is not magic."

"Townies think it is, that's what they pay for. Here's your name: Nightweaver, She Paints Your Dreams. *Night* on account of we black your face with soot so folks can't see that shiner."

"Nightweaver... You said people want rabbits."

"They want thrills," said Nine. "That's why they go to fairs, their lives are so boring they have to get drunk and poke bears with sticks. We give them what they want."

"But I cannot—"

"Wish you'd stop talking like that. You sound like a League-man preacher. Say *can't*."

"I *can't*," said Duuni. "I cannot be a show in a carnival!"

"*Can't, can't, can't*," said Nine. "You've got to earn your keep. You lifted up your hands and said yes."

Duuni's mind darted about like mouse in a bucket. "The blind beggar—how could he have earned his keep?"

Nine shrugged. "Some folks ain't good for anything at all."

 It became ordinary day. Squirrels in the trees, jays scrocking in the bushes, a light, cold wind. A cart came squeak-and-clop along the road, going the wrong direction. Raím let it pass, then sat up and shook the twigs out of his hair.

He crept toward the road, found it by falling into the ditch. Where the caravan had camped, only the creek was loud.

He sat down on the verge. Another cart came, going toward Ten Orchards this time. He stood up, holding out his hand.

The cart passed, clopped away.

Carts were few on this road, and fewer in the direction he wanted to go. It was a long time before another came. As it drew abreast of him he took a step toward it, his hand held out, and got the sting of a whip across his palm. He drew back, cursing. Heard a woman's query, a man's answer: "Dirty beggar."

He sat down again, his hands on his knees. The next cart that passed he did not hail, nor the next. He sat without thought; none he could bear presented itself. After an hour or so, a screeching of ungreased axles came down the road in the wrong direction, away from Ten Orchards.

It stopped in front of him. A rusty voice said, "How are you, my man?"

Raím swam up from his iron trance. "I am in good health." For safety's sake he added, "Thank you."

"You are well-spoken," said the voice, a man's. "And wearing a fine tunic. Are you sitting in the ditch to some purpose?"

"I was hoping for a lift to Ten Orchards."

"Why then, you are in luck! I am going straight to Ten Orchards, to the market fair."

"You are?" said Raím. "But…Ten Orchards is that way."

"Er, no. It is *this* way. I realize you are—" the man coughed delicately "—somewhat deficient in vision?"

The map inside Raím's head turned head-to-tail. He put his hand to his eyes. "I am blind, yes."

"Terrible, terrible," said the man. "Shouldn't happen. Climb up here with me, son. Come on to Ten Orchards, maybe we can do something about it."

"Thank you," said Raím, hearing only the name of the town. He groped along the side of the mule until something nudged his ear: an old hard hand with big knuckles. He grasped it, scrambled upward until he sat on a high buckboard next to tobacco and rum and sweat.

"About your blindness." The cart lurched forward. "That's a right handsome tunic you've got."

"Thank you. What about my blindness?"

"No need to suffer it, boy," said the man. "Ignorance. Folk should know better."

"*What?*" He swayed on the high seat. "Please?"

"Blindness. So curable. You'd think folk kept you in the dark on purpose."

"*Curable?*" said Raím. "No. I fell from a cliff and struck my head."

"The cause is unimportant. Once the darkness has been established, it sets up a...a roadblock, you might say." The voice became firm, imposing. "I shall explain. As you and I travel this road to Ten Orchards, so the light that falls upon your eye travels to your soul to be read. Were all well, you could see. But darkness has diverted the flow of light to its own use—tucked it away and saved it up, as you might save gold. How long have you been blind?"

"Five years. Who are you? What are you saying?"

"I am Amu the All-Doctor." His voice deepened. "Purveyor of health, vision, and sanity. We are discussing your slight problem, a diversion of light."

"Tell me."

"Five years," said Doctor Amu. "That is a wealth of light you have stored up."

Without realizing it Raím had gripped Doctor Amu's arm above the elbow. "I know nothing of this."

"May fools be cursed! Have you a family?"

"Yes."

"Do they care for you?"

Raím thought of the person he had been since his blinding: arrogant, hateful to Set, his mother, the world. "Perhaps they don't care any more."

Amu slapped the reins on the mule's rump. "Plenty of families go bad. But there's a law in this universe, lad, that draws good to those who deserve it. Who'd have thought you would step, by chance, right into the path of Amu the All-Doctor?"

They jingled on through the dust. Raím, sweating, said, "What is the...what do you mean, the light is stored?"

"It is difficult to explain to someone untrained in medicine."

"Give me the explanation!"

"Darkness. In your case, darkness brought on by the shock of the fall. Why, you knocked yourself so hard you let darkness into your head, right behind your eyes. A fever can do it too, as no doubt you've seen."

"I have. Go on."

"Don't you feel, sometimes, that you can *almost* see? If you looked hard enough?"

"Yes." He felt that all the time. Unbidden, tears welled and spilled. He wiped his eyes with his sleeve.

"Careful of that tunic, my lad. Five years. Five years of images stored up like salt fish, like pressed flowers—"

"You can free them?" Once more Raím seized him by the arm. "Will you heal me? I can't pay you. But if I could see again I'd weave for you, I'd bring you riches from the village of Creek. You would never want—"

"Hush," said Doctor Amu. "First things first. Someone blessed as I am with the skill of healing cannot set his mind on payment. You are in need; I am generous. Where did you get that tunic?"

"Tunic? This? It was given to me. Doctor Amu—"

"That weaving. It's from Welling-in-the-Mountains, by the look—a most famous Gatehouse. Why anyone would give away such a—"

"It's off a corpse."

Doctor Amu stopped fingering the sleeve, but said as though to himself, "Who's to know?"

"Doctor."

"Yes. Your eyes. Young man, we must certainly restore your sight. This very night. What is your name?"

"Raím."

"Strange name! In my mother tongue it means 'left-handed.' Such a name would be considered unlucky."

"It has not been lucky." He was grateful not to be Flea Butt, at least. "Will we be in Ten Orchards tonight?"

"Ten Orchards? We are not— Ah. Yes. We are going *toward* Ten Orchards, but we shall not be *in* Ten Orchards tonight. Never arrive dirty at a market town. Camp outside, wash, and march in looking your finest. I know of a little hut, with a stream nearby to wash in. Humble, but sufficient."

"How long does it take? To pull away, to cast away the darkness?"

The cart lurched and rattled. "Hmh. A lad of your age, strong... I should say that by tomorrow morning your eyes will be opened."

"Tomorrow morning."

"Aye. But for now let's get along and find our little shelter."

They jangled on down the road. Raím asked how Doctor Amu would cast out the darkness. The doctor explained, in detail so complex that Raím, though impressed, could not follow it. He sat on the lurching seat, more aware of his blindness than he had ever been before.

He had never allowed himself to do anything but fight it, trying to wrench from it anything he could get. And it had given him nothing. Until now.

Now, because he was so soon to lose it, he could know it; could almost be grateful for it, as for a dark night that will have a morning. Sounds: creak of harness, swish of the mule's tail, *cronk!* of a faraway raven. And odors: pines, wet earth, grassy tea offered in a bottle stoppered with a corncob. The mule's farts were fragrant. Raím's eyes brimmed. That girl, Pillbug—how could he have wanted to banish the scent of her? If she were here—

"Don't wipe your nose on that sleeve," said Doctor Amu.

He hardly dared let his mind touch on his return to the Men's Hold: the astonishment, the triumph. His place again by the fire.

"What is your profession?" said the doctor.

"Hunter," said Raím. "And I can weave."

"The men of the Hills are remarkable for that skill. They nearly challenge the Gatekeepers of Welling."

"Who are these Gatekeepers? They'll never weave better than the men of Creek."

"Don't say that, boy! The world will take you for a bumpkin. The Gatekeepers of Welling weave better than anyone in the world. As for who they are, ask me another riddle! Or ask them yourself; when your eyes have been opened, go to Welling-in-the-Mountains, just south of the great mountain, beyond High Moles of the Mines." The doctor rummaged under the seat. "But that's for another day. Here is bread and cheese."

It was hard bread and moldy cheese but Raím was glad of it. As he gnawed he thought how he might indeed visit Welling-in-the-Mountains. He could go anywhere, travel the world. But as the sunlight's heat slanted toward evening a strange thing happened: he began to be afraid of having the darkness taken away.

He pushed the thought aside. It came back. Would he be able to find his way in the world of light? He had grown used to living by the maps in his head, tracing his way by the warm angle of the sun... But so poorly, he thought. Now, for example, the sun was setting in the wrong part of the sky.

They came into the tang of wood smoke. "Ten Orchards," said Raím. "I smell the fires."

"Eh? Ah! What a wise nose you have. You must hunt like the wolf. Yes, we are nearly there." The sun had quite withdrawn its heat, and Raím, barelegged, shivered in the fine tunic. "Let me help you down," said the doctor. "This way... Sorry, I should have told you to duck. But here we are. Even a heap of straw for sleeping, and a bit of firewood. I'll have us warm in no time."

He built a fire that warmed the little space where they were: a shepherd's hut, perhaps, for it smelled of sheep dung, with drafts at every corner. The fireplace did not draw, but Raím squatted by it, alternately hot with elation and cold with a terror that enraged him. "When do we start?" he said.

"Get back from the fire, lad, the sparks will mark that tunic. I must run a little errand, I lack a few things for my doctoring.

I'll take the mule and leave you the cart as collateral, eh! I'll be back before you know it."

He was gone an hour, perhaps. When he returned he brought, among other items, a sausage. Raím could smell it, and licked his lips.

"None of this for you, I'm afraid," said Doctor Amu. "Your belly must be empty. Cruel of me to bring it, I suppose, but I need my strength." Munching. Odor of garlic. The doctor hocked, spat, rubbed his hands together, and said, "Now."

Raím had been sitting motionless in the straw, his feet tucked under for warmth. He could not tell whether his trembling was cold, or fear, or joy.

"All right," said the doctor. "Let me have a look." His big, calloused hands found the scar hidden in Raím's curls. Gently they lifted his eyelids, peered within. "*Full* of light," he murmured. "Full of images. I swear, I can nearly see them."

"What...what if all of them at once—"

"Harmless. A dream. Like water pouring from you, pouring out. It will be a few days before you are in balance again, light and dark; expect it to be strange. But worth it, lad. Worth it, to have your eyes opened."

Raím nodded, furious at his own shivering. Listened to the doctor make his preparations. "My mortar, where have I... Ah! Here. A little hawksfoot... Fire stone... Grind it finer..."

A plume of pungent, changing odor wrinkled Raím's nose. Spearmint he knew, and wild celery. There were smells he did not. The doctor grunted as he worked pestle in mortar. "I'll administer this in three portions. And you'll enjoy it, boy! I've denied you food, but the vehicle for the medicine is none other than Ten Orchards' finest homebrew. Spirits for the spirit, eh! The herbs spoil it rather, but in a good cause. Here, take a sip. Can you bear the taste? A sip only, and tell me."

He put a tin mug into Raím's hand. One sip: coarse, weedy, sharp. "I can bear it."

"Give it back, then, and I'll put in the real miracle." A crackle, a pungent, male smell, like leather.

"What is it?"

"You think I would tell you? And lose my living—? There now. You've a right to know. But not a word, lad. Eh? Eh?"

"Never."

"Gullsleaf. That's what it's called. And there's only one place it grows: out of the eyes of sailors, drowned and washed up on the shore. Makes you shiver, does it? But think of those lads, happy their dead eyes will loose the grip of darkness. Be glad."

Raím tried to be glad. The gullsleaf was odorously ground and added to the spirits.

"Now then," said the doctor. "Drink this—and I'll have a spot of undoctored spirits myself. Drink the first draught, then two draughts more. I shall lay my hands on your eyes, and you'll tell me what happens as they begin to open. You'll sweat; that's the kidneys casting out the blockage. I'll stoke up the fire, we'll burn the dark away. And then, my lad—" The hard old hand gripped Raím's shoulder "—you'll have a morning such as you've not had these five years."

"Give me the drink," said Raím.

He drank. It was not so bad. He hurled aside his fear and grinned, as he had used to when he drank with his comrades in the tavern in Ten Orchards. "A fine jug."

"Is it! Is it!" The doctor sipped his own. "How do you feel?"

"I can feel the liquor." For it was strong; it was not long before the warmth of the fire was ample. He felt a terrible happiness. He lived his darkness wholly, like a child shut in the woodshed who knows his father is there to open the door. "Give me the next cup."

"You are ready?" Again the doctor put the mug into his hands. This time the calloused hands went over Raím's eyes. "Tell me what you see."

"Lights," said Raím, who was beginning to be drunk. "But there are always lights. Lights in wheels, and lights in patterns like a quilt, like water bugs moving in schools—"

"Watch them," said the doctor. "Here is the third cup. Drink. My hands are on your eyes. The light is moving, I can feel it. The dark is shifting. Watch the light and tell me what you see."

Raím drained the cup. The light moved in a great wheel, he had seen a dance like that, a circle with torches, he could not tell whether what he saw was real or memory. Light in slow procession, formal; light like a flower opening, the center bright. "I see faces," he whispered. "Almost. Faces...white arms in a circle...girls..."

"Ah!" The hands that covered his eyes were sweating. Or perhaps it was he who sweated, for the doctor said, "Get that tunic off, I'll lay you to the fire."

The tunic vanished, the air was hot and freezing, the girls poured their dance before his opened eyes, white arms crossing and uncrossing. His body gave a great heave as though he were hurling up his very kidneys, and the whole world turned to light.

৯

He knew nothing else until the shivering morning. He was still blind. The fine tunic was gone, and so was Amu the All-Doctor. But he had been pulled out of his own vomit, and kindly covered with straw.

8

Wear the mountains down, fill the valleys up.
King, put a penny in the beggar's tin cup.
Bring the mighty low, help the lowly stand.
Beggar, give your penny to the hurdy-gurdy man.
Tune for the Hurdy-gurdy. The Roadsouls.

"I cannot do this."

"Say *can't.* I'll make you look like a night of stars." Nine waved a brush full of thick white paint.

"Do not touch me."

"Say *don't.*"

"Don't touch me!" Duuni snatched at the brush as Nine tried to lay it on her cheek. "I shall paint myself!"

"Gya, you're getting bossy. Say *I'll.* Oh well," said Nine, surrendering the brush. "My stars are wobbly." She held up a bit of broken mirror. In it Duuni saw her own face, blacked with soot from mouth to hairline. The swelling around her eye had gone down. Nine said, "Will you paint me, then? I'm barking."

"Barking—"

"For you. I'm your barker." Nine stuck out her chest in its shabby finery. "Step up, lords and ladies of Greencliff! See Nightweaver, She Paints Your Dreams! Draws on your kiddies their heart's desire, lasts two weeks guaranteed one penny step up! So," in her ordinary voice, "I want a star on my forehead."

"Then hold the mirror still." Duuni began to paint her own face. Her hand shook. Outside the cart the world roared with hammering and shouts, the crashing muddle of festival that for so many years she had looked down upon from the Maidens' Balcony. Now she was to be in the middle of it, on show.

That morning Nine had dragged her to see where she was to sit: on the midway, in a red tent painted with tarnished silver stars. Next to it the lads were rigging a wrestling ring. Tam Chivi was there; he saw Duuni and grinned.

Now, as she painted, Nine said, "You look good. Like a Roadsoul." She had scrounged for Duuni a flounced skirt, an enormous flowered blouse, and a hooded cape. There was an unlikely apron of purple velvet to wear against urda stains.

"Auntie put rugs in your tent for the kids to sit on, and one over your chair to make it a throne. You're the night goddess."

"I am…*I'm* not a goddess."

"Quit saying that, it's bad business. You're Nightweaver, She Paints Your Dreams. You can be boring old Pillbug later. Paint me." She knelt at Duuni's feet with closed eyes. On her blackened forehead, Duuni painted a big star with little stars around it. When she held up the mirror, Nine capered in her green silks. "Eee! I'm *beautiful!*"

Duuni said, "I painted your dreams."

"Then you know how to paint me to be a tight rope walker?"

"I do not, I *don't*, know what I know any more."

"You're cuckoo," said Nine.

⑤

"Nightweaver, She Paints Your ow, you little bugger, don't shove," said Nine. "You jiggle the goddess, I'll smack you."

"You may watch," said Duuni to the children who crowded round her throne. "But you must not bump my hand."

They stepped back but leaned forward: a shuffling pack of village children, fair-skinned, with curly red hair like the blind beggar's. Boys in short breeks, girls in skirts or loose trousers, eight and nine and ten years old, leaning to watch as Duuni washed and dried the first downy arm. Outside the red tent, the carnival smells of candy and broiled meat lay on the air. From the wrestling ring next door came grunts and thumps, a voice shouting, "Ground!"

A girl with thick braids knelt against Duuni's thigh. In a trembling voice Duuni said, "What do you wish me to draw?"

The answer was so low she could not hear it. The girl's face was full of fear.

Duuni said, "It does not...doesn't hurt." The girl bowed her head. Duuni thought, She is afraid. To her I am a dream painter, a goddess.

Me.

She made her voice gentle. "What shall it be?"

A whisper: "Two fish."

"Are they swimming along? Or in a circle, nose to tail?"

The girl looked up. Her fear was less, for she had to think. "A circle."

The instant she spoke it was as though Duuni had seen the fish already, waiting to appear on the child's plump arm. She began to draw. The paste was cool, a little stiff; later her hand would warm the press, and it would flow more easily. She forgot the festival smells, the wrestlers' groans and yells. Brisking their fins, the little fish called the line out of the urda press. The other children breathed, leaned, nudged their heads together.

"There," said Duuni.

"Ah!" They craned to see. The girl smiled. Not at Duuni; she had forgotten Duuni. She smiled at her two fish.

"Sit here," Duuni said. "Blow on it. When the paste is dry, Star Tamer will wrap it for you, to set until tomorrow."

"Don't you bump it either," said Star Tamer, craning with the rest, "or it won't look so good as my snake."

The girl sat on the worn rugs and blew. The rest jostled patiently, Star Tamer quibbled over pennies, Duuni washed the next arm.

A larger shadow dimmed the tent: someone's mother. Looking worried, of course. The fish girl held up her arm. "Mama!" The woman's sharp glance went from the child to Duuni, asking, Who are you? Is my daughter safe with you?

Duuni thought of her own mother, who had not been able to protect her. "The design will last two weeks."

The woman frowned. She looked at her daughter's arm, and her glance softened. "Very pretty, Leili." She smiled at Duuni and said, "We call her our little fish."

The woman withdrew to busy herself at the booth across the way, glancing in now and then. Duuni thought, She trusts me with her daughter. Then she was terrified, as if that trust meant she must protect all these children, in the world full of elders and paidmen.

The hopelessness of that made her small corner of it real. She grew calm, she watched the girl's bent head as she blew on her arm and wondered why, for her, there must be two fish instead of one, swimming in a circle instead of a line. As she washed the next arm, a boy's, she thought, *I like this. I like this.* She could not remember thinking that in her life…yes, she could. When she had run on the riverbank with the dog Jip, blackbirds calling in the reeds.

"Do two rats fighting," said the boy.

"I do not…don't…draw biting things or blood."

"Two rats *wrestling*. Like them out there."

From next door came thumps, grunts, laughter. When she looked at the boy's arm she could see them, two rats like fat wrestlers in a knot. The paint around her eyes felt crinkly and tight: she was smiling.

"Hold still, then," she said, and began to draw.

ᕚ

By late afternoon she was sure she had drawn on every child in Greencliff. Pigs, dogs, moons, cows, mice, lightning, snails; eagles, cats, lilies and suns—as if each soul, with grave face and outstretched arm, came to ask for its emblem. Sometimes she said no—to a killing scorpion, a snarling wolf. Then she wondered whether it was right to say no. For if a person's soul harbored a snarling wolf, would it not be best to show it?

No child asked for a lion.

Nine collected coppers from hot fists. Duuni's hands were stained and weary. In the late afternoon they closed the tent, stirred up a batch of paste for the morrow, reopened and went back to work. A gaggle of ten-year-old girls set up camp on the rugs, whispering, watching as each of their group was painted. "Come back tomorrow, after you wash off the paste," said Duuni as Nine wrapped each arm. "Show me how it looks."

"Nor don't you peek, or your arm will wither and fall off," said Nine.

Early dusk. The braziers were lit; the noisy fair became a moil of shadows. The line of waiting children thinned and vanished. Duuni was washing her hands, hoping that was all, when a big body stepped into the tent.

It was a tall farmer in cut breeks and tunic, smelling of dust and sweat. He grinned, rolled up the sleeve of his shirt and said, "Nightweaver, will you paint on me?"

Duuni shrank. But Nine in her streaked face paint bounced at his knees like a little dog. "Three pennies!"

"Three? My dreams for a penny, that's what I heard."

Nine pointed to his burly arm. "That ain't no pennyworth."

"Two pennies, then."

"For that? That's *acres*."

He laughed; he liked to think his muscles were acres. Fished in his pocket and handed her three pennies. He knelt where the children had knelt, rolled his sleeve above the elbow, washed his arm in the bucket, and laid it in Duuni's lap.

Sparks of fire flashed at the edges of her eyes. At the tent door a shadow moved.

Then she saw who the shadow was. All day one or another of the wrestlers, in sweated clout, had stopped to look into the tent, glimpse and glimpse; this time it was Tam Chivi. He glanced at the farmer. Said to Duuni, "You need a hand here, shout."

She nodded. Nothing would happen. The Souls would not allow it.

She touched the farmer's big arm. He said, "If you'd draw a raven, ma'am. I'm of the Raven clan." He was not leering, only cheerful; he had had a cup of wine and did not look worried at all. On his arm she saw the raven, black in a black circle, with a bright eye. It steadied her hand as it called itself out of the urda press, out of his arm. He bent his head to watch his raven grow. She smelled man and wine, yet her hand did not shake.

"Blow on it until it dries," she said, and her voice did not shake. "Then Star Tamer will wrap it."

"That's a fine thing," he said, eyes only for his raven. "Brothers, have a look."

There were men at the door; but some were the Roadsoul wrestlers. As the farmer showed the raven to the crowd her hands did shake, not from fear but from some other thing—as if she had leapt from a cliff and, instead of falling, had flown. She wanted to weep. Even more she wanted to wash the paint off her face.

She wrapped the farmer's arm and sent him off. At the clink of coin she looked up in dread that it might be another customer, but it was Nine, closing the tent flaps. "Farki says that's enough," she said. "Here's our pay."

"Pay?"

"Well, sure. Our cut." Nine dumped a fat handful of copper into the lap of Duuni's skirt. "Farki's raising your price. He didn't know you were so stinking good."

Duuni had never owned a penny in her life. Here was a fortune in pennies. They had a metal smell. She said, "I don't want them."

"Don't *want* them? Are you *crazy?*"

"It is...it's too much. What would I do with them? I am not a person with money!"

"You are now. Gya, put them in your pocket, *I'll* show you what to do with money."

Duuni washed her face, pulled off the ragged silks, and put the pennies, heavy, in the pocket of her cut-cloth trousers. Nine stuck her head out of the tent. "Tam Chivi! Can we come fairing?" A murmured reply. Nine pulled her head back in. "We'll go with them. Don't go alone, got that? We're rich women, and there's paidmen." She took Duuni's hand in her own, still wet from washing, and tugged her out of the tent into the carnival.

☙

With Tam Chivi were two more wrestler lads, bare-chested, wearing hip cloths over their breechclouts. Their names were Ducktail and Shank. There were two Roadsoul girls as well. Shine was slow and easy; Duuni had seen her dandling the skinny new baby. Sleepy was brisk as a dog, she walked next to Tam Chivi and joked like a boy. Nine pirouetted and skipped.

Duuni had not spoken to boys since she was eight years old, yet as they breasted the rowdy festival crowd she walked so close to the others that Shank laughed and said, "Don't crawl up my leg, girl!"

"Pillbug ain't no braver than a bunny," said Nine, trotting to keep up.

"And you're no wiser than a gnat."

"Bite you, then."

"Swat you."

Aisles of booths, all jammed with fairgoers who strolled, ate, laughed, shouted to neighbors and rivals. What Duuni had looked down on from the Maidens' Balcony she now saw as one who walks on earth.

Roadsouls in their silks were everywhere, juggling, fiddling, singing, yelling in front of a closed tent, "Day-Night the Beard-ed Princess, Half Man, Half Woman, two pennies a look!"

"I made up that name too," said Nine. "Put *night* in, makes it mysterious."

Duuni thought, Two pennies a look! Why, an urda drawing is worth at least as much as a *look*.

She wanted to see someone who was half man, half woman. In Alikyaan it had been very clear what a woman was, what she could do, what could be done to her. Right down to her day-robe: brown for a girl, white for a maiden, red for a married woman. Yet Shine wore a blue silk skirt and a man's white tunic; Sleepy wore high red boots with cut-cloth quarter-breeks that bared her knees, and her hair was cut short as a boy's. And they were beau-tiful. Lads' faces changed when they looked at them.

There were booths with silk blouses and overskirts. Duuni wondered how much they cost, now that she was rich. A woman sold caramel apples on sticks; the others each took one, and when Duuni did not, Sleepy laid money on the counter and put one in her hand. Duuni dug for her pennies, but Sleepy said, "My treat. That means you don't have to pay."

Duuni thought of the blind beggar, how for him the world must have seemed to arrive at his hand out of nowhere. Like him she said, "Thank you."

Sleepy gave her a shrug and a smile. When they turned to the clothing booth next door she said, "What would look best on Pillbug, d'you think?" The wrestlers stood wide-legged and jok-ing as Sleepy and Shine held shawls and blouses against Duuni's rags, saying, "She should wear salmon, it suits her. Oh—she's gorgeous in turmeric, nobody can wear that color but Pillbug!"

The merchant, a sour little man, wrung his hands for fear they might drop the candy on his goods.

Duuni put her shoulders back. She held out her pennies and pointed to the blouse in Sleepy's hand. "Please, I would like to buy that."

The merchant snatched the blouse away. "Come back when you have money, you dirty Roadsouls!"

Without argument Sleepy, Tam Chivi and the rest ambled on, gnawing their candy apples. Duuni scuttled after them, though not before she saw Shine, out of the merchant's sight, mark a silk blouse neatly with a sticky thumbprint.

Sleepy told Duuni how many pennies a new silk blouse cost, and her riches dwindled. But there was plenty to spend a penny on: the sword swallower, the snake charmer, the penny toss where you could win a genuine crystal plate—they said it was a genuine crystal plate. Painted gingerbread, candies wrapped in bay leaves, hot spiced tea. Shine flirted as she bargained. When she bought a rattle for the babies, the man wanted four pennies but Shine said, "That's high," blew him a kiss, and got it for three.

Here and there among the crowd was a child Duuni had drawn on, guarding a rag-wrapped arm or carried half asleep on her father's back. There were Leaguemen, whom Duuni had never seen up close: tall, pale, grim in dark tweeds and broad-brimmed hats. Paidmen, in twos and threes; the little Roadsoul group closed up and hurried past the scarred men in stained leathers, patched woolens, nicked iron.

Though Duuni could not buy a silk blouse there were silk ribbons, and rings that shone so brightly they must be gold. There were bracelets of glass beads in every color, with chevrons and flowers formed in the glass itself. While the traveling medicator next door droned his wares like a religious chant, the bead merchant jangled necklaces in hanks and sang to the same rhythm, "Beautiful, hard, cold—but laid to your skin, I warm!"

He had set up torches to show the colors, made strange by night and fire. There was a bracelet of green glass beads overlaid with blue ripples. Duuni turned it in her hand. Sleepy said, "Buy it, Pillbug."

"Health, vision, sanity!" droned the traveling medicator.

"Beautiful, hard, cold!" sang the bead salesman.

Duuni did not know how to choose anything. She put the bracelet back.

It grew late. They turned toward the Roadsoul camp. Nine rode piggyback, clutching Tam Chivi's hair. They passed again the tent where the hawker, hoarse now, chanted, "Half Man, Half Woman, two pennies!"

Duuni stopped. Said, "I want—"

"Hey, Pillbug said she *wants* something! World's coming to an end!"

"I want to see the Bearded Princess."

The others burst out laughing.

"Yes." Her own voice, clear. "That's what I want. My treat," she said.

"Eee, *Pillbug!*"

Had she not earned that money? Was it not hers to spend as she liked? She said, "I have enough to pay for everyone. I want to see her. Him. Her."

"*Aaa!*"

Tam Chivi swung the squealing Nine from his shoulders and nodded at the tent's entryway. Angry, blushing, Duuni dug in her pockets for the coins, but he touched her arm and said, "Don't pay."

"It is two pennies each—"

He shook his head. Indeed, when the man keeping the door of the tent saw Tam Chivi he smiled and waved them in.

She was distressed that it could not be her treat, awed that Tam Chivi could go anywhere for free. Shine and Sleepy and the rest crowded in behind them. Late as it was, there were no other spectators; they stood on the dusty trampled grass in torchlight from the door. Before them, on a platform that was the back of a cart, stood the Bearded Princess. She had one hairy leg, one smooth. A grass skirt covered her privates, but one of her breasts was a woman's in a spangled red halter and the other a naked man's, hairy as an ape's. The ape side of her mouth had a beard; the other side was hairless, with painted red lips.

Duuni stared with revulsion and relief. So that was what a person looked like who was half man, half woman! *She* did not look like that. Perhaps wearing cut-cloth trousers had not made her half man?

The Bearded Princess scratched her armpit, said "What are you doing here, you little warts?" and turned into Dicey, who drove the oxcart and owned the urda press.

"Pillbug, she wanted to see you!" said Nine.

Dicey grinned, beard and red lips. He turned this way and that. "Front view. Back view."

Duuni was so shocked she spoke aloud. "You are not a beard-ed princess!"

"Eh? And you are not Nightweaver, She Paints Your Dreams?"

"No!"

"I have seen your work, and I think you are." Dicey curt-seyed in his grass skirt, then crossed his arms and laughed his booming, ox-driver's laugh. "So perhaps I *am* a princess. For the moment." Then, "Hist!" he said, as a group of drunken farmers haggled at the door. He made his voice false and high. "Leave royalty to its travails."

Duuni wanted to stay and understand what was real and not real. Tam Chivi had to tug her by the shoulder, and even then she went staring backward.

"Dicey's ugly both halves," said Nine, yawning.

Shine said, "Pillbug, you never spent your money," and Sleepy said, "You should have bought that bracelet. It might not be there tomorrow."

And Duuni wanted it. Now that she had seen the Bearded Princess, she wanted the bracelet desperately. Tam Chivi jerked his chin back toward the thinning midway. "Come get it?" He shoved Nine toward Shine and Sleepy and waved Duuni to come along with the lads. She went with them, walking alone with men. The moon, quiet in the sky, rode on unchanged.

They had forgotten which booth it was, and found it only by the singsong of the traveling medicator: "Health, vision, sanity!" *That* booth they might have found by the smell of his medicines; and he stank of rum. The bead seller's torches had burnt out, and he was beginning to pack up. Duuni was afraid the bracelet had been sold, but he remembered which one she had held and found it for her. She asked the price. When he told her she stood straight and said, like Shine, "That's high."

He laughed. "Tell you what, sweetheart. One kiss and you can have it for free."

Shank and Ducktail laughed. Hot with shame, Duuni shook her head and paid full price. Tam Chivi clasped the bracelet on her wrist. The beads chinked together. Next door the traveling medicator's voice had dropped from singsong to a secretive whisper. To someone unseen he said, "Also for sale, a genuine master tunic from Welling-in-the-Mountains. None like it for the price."

A master tunic! Were there so many in the world? She craned to see. Behind his counter the fat little man held up a tunic.

She drew breath to say, *That's the beggar's!*

But there was not light enough to see it properly, and she had made a fool of herself twice already. She said nothing, even when Shank pointed to a prayer merchant who shuffled her papers together on a makeshift table and said, "Pillbug, you could do that." As if Duuni might wish to be a blasphemous old painter woman, conjuring sorcery and foreign gods.

She stumbled back to the eiderdown and the sleeping children. She lay for a long time fingering the bracelet, looking up at the stars that were not painted but real. *Were* they real? Or had someone painted them? How could you know?

Next morning the bracelet still shone on her wrist, green and river-blue, but the cheap cord held only half a day before it broke and the beads were lost forever in the grass.

9

Heavy to carry, this head.
Heavy to carry, this heart.
Buckets too full
On a road too long.
Set them down in shade, oh my soul!
Share the water.

     Song. Red Creek.

He stank. The straw stank. Whatever the drink had been, it had given him diarrhea. His head hurt so badly he could barely breathe, and the soft ticking of ashes in the fireplace told him that soon he would be without any fire at all.

At first he thought he would not move. He would lie still until he was as still as the ashes, and as cold, and at peace. But his hand betrayed him and pushed a little straw onto the coals.

The heat was sweet. He sat up, groaning. Groped about. Found wood and pushed it into the flame. Hunkered, his head in his hands.

The weather had turned wintry, or perhaps they had come higher on the mountain. But what mountain? He picked up a thread of thought. Dropped it. Rubbed his hands together and remembered the tunic, its warmth, the feel of its weft. He thought how Amu the All-Doctor would feel between his hands, and, now that his eyes had been opened, how he might thank him.

That it was morning he knew by the cries of animals—crows, cattle, cocks—neither close nor far. Early morning, for no one had come yet to inquire about the smoke from the shed. Because Doctor Amu had said the place was Ten Orchards, Raím assumed it was not.

There were three small logs left. He squatted with his stinking backside to the fire.

Voices.

He did not move. His head hurt.

Outside, men's voices, low and brief, in his own Hill tongue but some barking dialect. Sound of the door being knocked back on its hinges, and the yell, "Who's in there?"

Raím said nothing.

The door clapped to again with a bang. "Naked!" said the voice. "A madman!"

The murmur of voices went on. Raím might have shouted, explained. He could think of nothing to say; could not think.

A creak: the door opening a little. "What a stench!" The door shut.

Raím tried to stand. Squatted again, holding his head.

"He's sick." The voices alarmed now. "A poxy madman. Plague!"

He tried to speak. From his mouth came a moaning grunt.

"Keep the door shut. The plague! Damo—what think?"

"Set the thatch," said the voice that must be Damo's.

"It's Monsa's shed."

"Are *you* mad? Monsa's poxy shed! Will you kill us for old thatch? Set it! At the corner there."

"If he—"

"Damn you! Give me the fire!"

Raím rose to a crouch. Running in a dream: one, two, his legs stepped him the miles to the door. He fell against it.

"He's coming out! Hold the door!"

In the tang of scorched straw Raím laid his forearms on either side of the door jamb. Found words. Spoke them through the crack.

"Not plague," he said. "Hangover."

Silence. Busy crackle of fire. He thought, I'll die warm.

This thought sharpened to reality, then fear. A commotion outside; the door was opened against him. He sat down with a grunt.

"Dirty swine! Come out!"

"Here comes Monsa!"

"Screw Monsa, I nearly saved him from the plague. Get out, you! Take his ankle, Sig."

"Nay, he's shat himself."

"Take his ankle! What are you, a murderer? Lads—look at the snake on him!"

Dragged out on his back, Raím stayed like that, clutching his head. The burning shed made a grand heat. So did Monsa, until distracted by Damo's promise of new thatch and by inspection of the serpent tattooed around Raím's hips.

There is nothing like a fire. A crowd began to gather. Women's voices, neutral and concerned; girls' voices, laughing. Raím sat up, tried to brush the straw off himself.

"Take the poor creature indoors."

"Who'd wash him? Arlie, look at that snake."

"And not a hand on him anywhere."

"Maybe he's sitting on it?"

"Becca! Imagine a man sitting on his hand!"

The girls' bold laughter. "Maybe *you'd* like to sit on his hand. A bonnie man like that—"

"*What's this?*" said a terrible voice.

Raím had been holding out his hands, dumbly, because these people seemed to think he sat on them or had none. At the voice, he set them on his thighs and sat up straight.

"What are you up to? Baiting a bear cub?" The voice was sharp, vigorous, that of a woman not young. "Who set this fire?"

A pause. Damo said, "That dirty beggar did."

"Nonsense. You set it yourself. Am I right, Monsa?"

"Right," said Monsa with a sigh. In a village one cannot lie for long.

"Damo, your lying tongue is dirty already. Lick this man clean."

From Damo, an angry hiss. The woman said, "If I were a goddess I would force you to do that. But I am your aunt, so you will wash him. In hot water. In my barn."

"He's a drunk," said Damo. "He's puked on himself."

"And you never have? Do I not recall, behind Horsetail Tavern—?"

"Get up!" said Damo to Raím, and shoved him with his foot.

"Help him up," said the aunt. "Sig, take his other arm. And you girls go home. If you need to gape at a naked male, I've got a goat."

Raím was helped unkindly to his feet. A girl said, "He's got no hands on him anywhere."

Raím said, "I have hands."

The crowd murmured, as if an animal had spoken. "He can talk," said Damo. "But he's got that snake on him."

"Serpent," said Raím. "We wear the serpent. We are men of Creek."

"See, Ta Ba?" said Damo. "A madman!"

"I am from Creek!" said Raím. "What place is this?"

"Creek. And you're a madman."

Half walked, half dragged, Raím murmured, "Nine says there are many Creeks."

"Then ten say it," said Ta Ba, the aunt. "The proper name of this village is Red Creek." A roar of rusty hinges. "Put him in the straw there. Damo, fetch water and heat it. Use the pot I scald the pigs in."

Damo jerked Raím's elbow. "Walk, souse. Open your eyes, you're not blind."

It doesn't show, thought Raím. For this moment, they don't know. He felt so grateful he turned closed eyes toward Damo and smiled. "Thank you."

"Crap on yourself," said Damo.

"Did."

ᕼ

Damo brought water but did not heat it. Muttering, he left. Muttering, Ta Ba ordered him fetched back. This was done by a group of men, unhappy, efficient, brief. From this Raím guessed that Ta Ba was important, perhaps the headwoman.

He had burrowed down in clean straw in a cold, medium-sized space that, from the way it muted sound, was full of fodder. Smell of horse and cow. Outside, where hens crooned, the snap of fire and splash of water.

"Get your ass out here," said Damo. Ta Ba must have left. Raím rose and shuffled toward the voice, cracked the bridge of his nose on something, and put his hand over his eyes. Damo took his elbow and steered him. "Pig! You got me in trouble with her. I hope you're as sick as you look."

"Sicker," said Raím.

Overseen by low-voiced men, Damo scrubbed him with soapy water and a rough brush until he felt indeed like a scalded pig. He bore it with his eyes closed. Damo toweled him with a burlap sack, cracked him across the butt with it, and said, "Tie a ribbon on him! I'll show him at the fair!"

Laughter. Damo smacked him again. "Piggy, piggy!"

"Enough," said Raím.

"To the fair, lads! A talking pig—I'm a rich man! A talking *sow*!"

The wet burlap came through the air once more. In the map of his mind Raím watched it come, neat as a shuttle between parted warps. All he need do, and he did it, was grab the burlap and pull.

Damo came to him like a dance partner. In that perfect embrace Raím hooked his legs from under him. Damo went down with a grunt. He was big, no taller than Raím but heavy and limber. He whipped his back like a pike tossed on the bank, and grabbed.

Raím, eyes closed, met each grip as water meets water. In crystal darkness he saw without vision, as though his skin had eyes. He set to work.

"Stop him!"

"Keep them out of the fire!"

"Get hold of him—"

Other hands, other knees entered the pattern he was making. He removed them. Got the thing right, lying flat the way he wanted it. Hands intruded again; he took them off; they stayed off. He finished his weaving. Stood, wobbling a little. Suddenly his nose was bleeding, his head throbbed so fiercely that he knelt again and held it in his hands.

Silence, except for the hens making small talk. He opened his eyes. Raised his head and turned it this way, that way. "I'm dirty again," he said. "Take me where the water is. Please."

"By the holy," said Monsa. "The lad's blind."

No one would touch him, but a warm bucket was set down by his knee. He splashed away the dirt and blood. He knew exactly what he had done to Damo, and expected the groans he heard. "I pulled his shoulder out of the socket," he said. "Bring him here, I'll put it back."

"No, no!" said Damo.

"Then have the bonesetter treat it. If he can't, come to me and I will."

"No," Damo said again, but faintly, for they were carrying him away.

"Wrestler!" said a new voice.

Because it had not been wrestling, but a fight, it took a moment for Raím to understand the title meant him.

"She's sent you clothing. The headwoman. If you want it."

"Thank you." The shirt was patches on patches, but the hip cloth and sash were fair enough cloth. There was a knit jersey with the elbows out. Raím put the clothes on, raked his fingers through his beard.

"She has soup for you in her kitchen. For beggars, she does that. But listen: Come to the Loom Hold, wrestler. We'll kill a sheep for you."

The ragged clothes were freshly laundered and smelled like autumn smoke. Raím rolled the tattered sleeves above his elbows. "I will eat her soup," he said. Not out of gratitude toward Ta Ba nor superiority toward the men, but because, sick as he felt, the thought of fresh mutton made his throat work.

A little frightened boy was elected to lead him to the kitchen. This he did by keeping well out of reach and scuffling with his feet.

⑨

The kitchen was stone flagged. He stood before the fire, so sick and worn he swayed on his bare feet.

"Sit down," said Ta Ba. "I saw that fight. A good thing to happen to Damo, I might add. The village should thank you. There's soup on the table."

He groped for a bench. A bowl had been set for him, a spoon floated to his hand.

"So. How did you, a blind man, get into Monsa's shed? I will know."

He could not eat. He put the spoon down and said, "My grandmother is the headwoman of Creek."

"I am the headwoman of Creek. On this creek you are not the headwoman's grandson. Why were you in Monsa's shed, and why don't you eat my soup?"

To both questions he said, "I was drunk."

"Very drunk. Why were you drunk and naked in Monsa's shed?"

"Because I drank. My tunic was stolen."

"Ah! A master tunic, green and indigo and red?"

"I don't know what color it was. There was a dagger's rent just here." He touched his heart.

"That's the one. A traveling quack was hawking it in the tavern last night, I'm told. Nobody bought, so he was off with it. He'll peddle it at the next fair, I don't doubt."

"It was given me. As you gave me these." He lifted his ragged arm. Remembered to say, "Thank you."

"You're welcome. That was bad luck or bad judgment on your part, for it was fine weaving."

"I'm a fool," said Raím.

When the words were out he realized two things: that all his life, even when he had been the best hunter in Creek, he had privately felt a fool; and that he had never admitted it, even to himself. He could have crushed himself like a beetle with contempt.

"Good," said Ta Ba. "I don't want any pious mendicants in my kitchen. If I know Doctor Amu, and I do, he put more than liquor in your cup."

"You know him!"

"I know ticks and toothache, too. The soup can wait. You want tea."

Hot tea was set before him. It tasted like blessing. "You are kind."

"I have these things to give, it is no hardship. The potion he gave you—was it to be a cure?" Raím bent his head. "For your eyes? That old cur, someone should knife him. Indeed, someday someone will. Plenty have taken the cure from that quack, and waked with a hangover." A little silence. "Even me."

"You? *You* bought a cure from Doctor Amu?"

"Oh yes."

"And got a hangover?"

"The worst. Though more from bad herbs than alcohol, I think."

"What were you...what was it to cure?"

"An ill as desperate as yours," she said. "Or so it seemed. A long time ago. It felt like life or death, then."

From her voice he knew she would not tell him what ill. "Were you cured?"

"No."

He sighed. He drank tea, listened to the rustle of the fire, rubbed his feet on the cold stone floor. After a while he said, "Why are you so kind? I'm a beggar." For so he was.

"I do not think you have been a beggar for long."

"I'm a weaver." He drank more tea. "I have no loom any more."

"I have a loom," said Ta Ba. "But it is broken."

A loom! "I could fix it. Maybe. I'd fix it for you. May I fix it? Please."

"No need. It was my husband's, and he is dead."

"But I could mend it. It should be mended. A loom shouldn't sit idle—"

"You may look...that is, you may tinker with it. But you must eat something. After that wicked doctor's cure—"

"I need the loom." Raím rose. "Show me the loom."

She took his hand. Her own was almost as big as his. "Come along, then," she said. "I'll bring your tea."

⚬

Later she brought him soup. Much later, near evening, she brought a worn old pair of leggings with the bands to cross-garter them, and leather shoes mended with rawhide on both toes. "Day is done," she said. "Come away from that."

"No," said Raím.

He lay on his back on the stone floor, working at the treadles, whose hinges were stiff with rust. He had never known a loom like this. He did not understand it.

The looms he knew were attached to the roof beams, or were simple straps that hitched to your sash. This loom had a swinging beam that pulled the heddles all at once. He had walked his hands over it, mapping it, feeling the mouse-gnawed warp break under his fingers. "I'm busy," he said to Ta Ba.

She stood in the doorway, silent. He felt her there. He did not mind. At last she said, "It is strange to watch you work in the dark."

He realized he had been smelling lamp smirch and roast lamb. It was night. He was famished. He sat up, whacked his forehead on a crossbeam, crawled out spitting dust, and let her lead him to the kitchen.

"Tell me your name, weaver, and I shall call you by it."

"Flea Butt."

"Your name."

"Raím. What does that mean, in this place?"

"Nothing in particular. Although a *raímanlek* is a laundry bucket."

"Not what my godfather had in mind." It felt strange to be happy—almost like pain, an animal moving in his chest. He wanted to weep, so he said sternly, "It's a crime that loom's not used." She gave him a hot washcloth, and he buried his face in it until the tears were gone. "It's not like the looms I know."

"It is built like the looms in the linen mills in Rett. But those looms are bigger than this room."

That was a tall tale. "You've seen the mills in Rett?"

"Long ago. In my novice years I traveled with a friend. Then I married, and brought my husband home to my village."

"Novice?"

"To a master. A Gatekeeper."

Reluctantly: "Amu said a Gatekeeper wove that tunic."

"Yes. In a Gatehouse. Do not feel ignorant. The small villages think the Gatehouses are full of sorcerers. Certainly my neighbors think that."

Raím was not surprised that he did not understand this talk. He was getting used to not understanding anything.

"I had skill in painting," said Ta Ba. "I ran away to a Gate-house and was novice to a master there. For a while I traveled and plied my trade at the fairs, but in the end I found my fate lay in village politics. Art, weaving, politics—the skills are the same," she said. "Only the means are different."

"I knew a girl who could draw in urda. That is, they said she could."

"Then I wish for her that she may find a Gatehouse. If you are a skilled weaver, I wish that for you also."

Her words were a mystery, but her tone was clear. Raím said, "Why should you do this? For a stranger, a madman!"

She sighed. "Come eat. Why do we think ourselves mad, when all we are is young?"

"I am not young!" Had she not seen the serpent at his waist?

"Yes, you are. I am kind because it pleases me. Because you are young and blind, Damo is an irritating fool, and scraps from my rag bag happen to fit you. Eat. Here are knife and fork."

He ate. Again that desperation filled him, joy, like a biting animal. He ate, ate more, did not want to stop eating because he might have to talk or feel something. He did not know what might leap out in his words—perhaps that biting creature, bright and strange.

"It makes old women happy to see lads eat," said Ta Ba.

He wiped his mouth on his wrist. He had not thought how odd it was to find a loom in a woman's house; a loom was male as a breechclout, and more private.

But Pillbug, girl weaver. He said cautiously, "You don't weave?"
"No."

It occurred to him, dimly, that a traveler might ask what the custom was for men and women. Stammering, he said, "In this village, do men show their hidden things to women?"

Ta Ba laughed. "Now and then."

He heard what he had said, and blushed. Said stiffly, "In my village, weaving is men's work. Secret."

"Secret? Not here it isn't! Weaving's the gossip of the town—how long, how much, how often. The men pay more attention to their looms than to their girls."

"Women can look at the looms? Then what... Forgive me. Those things are not to be told."

"Are you asking what men here keep secret in the Hold?" said Ta Ba. "Wrestling. It is never to be seen, except at the ceremonies—and you wrestled a champion to the ground in my hen yard."

"I don't remember what I did."

"Damo will have some hand-shaped bruises to match his tattoos. That is what they tattoo here, on the thigh: the wrestler's hand, with an eye in the palm. That was why they said you had no hands, but a snake. Serpents disturb them."

Too strange. "You say *them.* Yet you are of this place?"

"I was born here. But in my painting years I was a prayer merchant. My fellow novice is a master now; she still travels fair to fair, though winters she teaches at the Gatehouse." A laugh. "Now and then, I wish I were still a prayer merchant, not aunt to a whole village. *Ta* means aunt, and my name is Bayami. Ta Ba." He did not want to know her name, it was too intimate. She said, "Those who range the world learn to see their home village with different eyes."

"To see takes eyes."

"You are quite aware of what I mean."

He said nothing.

"Life at a Gatehouse, among novices from so many villages—that is a journey in itself. My Gatehouse was in Welling-in-the-Mountains." In her voice there was a little longing. "At the source of the river that is called only the River, where the water is still narrow—steep and rushy. By the time it has rolled the leagues down to Rett, it is wide; its waterfalls drive the looms." She chuckled. "Those looms would make the lads here stare. They are big as houses."

Still he did not believe her. On Ta Ba's loom there were nocks for the warp; he had counted a finger length and multiplied: nine hundred nocks, like the ribbed edge of a shell. It was not possible for the looms of Rett to be bigger than that.

"Do you have yarn?" he said. "If you have yarn I'll warp this loom. If I can warp it I can fix it. Maybe."

"I have linen thread. No one has touched it since my husband died." She moved away from him. "The hired boy sleeps by the kitchen fire. He'll lay a second pallet for you, and tomorrow you shall mend the loom."

By touch and echo he felt his way outside to the midden and stood listening to the frosty night. Dogs barked; far off, a wild dog answered. From somewhere, maybe the Loom Hold, came the tang of cedar smoke and the sound of a drum.

Shivering, he returned to the kitchen and rolled up in the ample blankets. A huge cat, as unlike Brook as a cow is unlike a roe deer, trundled onto his chest and sat down.

He did not think about being blind. Or about Damo, or Pillbug, or what a Gatehouse might be. He thought about how, on Ta Ba's loom, the rows of little wire heddle eyes moved the warp up and down, slipping between each other like weeds crisscrossing in a current.

⑤

By afternoon of the next day he had two handspans warped. Ta Ba brought him a hank of thicker yarn; he took it, forgetting to thank her, and shot the first weft across.

The loom wove a plain linen, chilly, as though cold resided in it. Always before, weaving had been silent work. Only the soft whip of weft through warp, the scratch as it was combed into place. But this loom spoke, *creakity-rackety-thump*; it swung, it rocked like a cradle. He thought in shapes, in textures. His mind sat on the delicate surface of itself, like a water strider on a pond.

Ta Ba said, "The warp is blue and the weft is green. This village weaves cloaks, only; we buy shirt linen from the big looms I spoke of, in the League's mills."

Nine's hand in his own. "Children work there," he said.

"Yes, poor mice. I've seen the retting ponds, bigger than our millpond, and the children hauling out the rotted flax stalks. Water to their armpits, and their lips blue cold. Sometimes they drown."

"Whose children are they?"

"There are plenty of children in this world," said Ta Ba. "We are fond of starting them. There are more children than suppers for them."

"Then…their parents give them to the mill?"

"Or sell them."

He wove in silence. The strip of cloth grew a little. "My mother bore ten children. Six lived."

"Were you hungry?"

"In spring."

"If you were hungry only in spring, you were lucky."

He thought of the patio full of rose trees, the careless long table with plates of corn bread, the brothers hitting each other. "Still—to sell your children!"

"This world is big and strange and sad. What brought you out to wander the roads, when there was food on the table at home?"

He shrugged.

"Did they cast you out?"

"I'm too strong to cast out!"

"I would not want the task. Are you going somewhere in particular?"

Nosy old woman! Another shrug. The weft broke. He made himself so busy, smoothing the ends and laying them in double, that when she said, with amusement in her voice, "Why don't you go to my Gatehouse at Welling? Most of the novices there are blind, or beggars, or mad—that is, according to their neighbors," he scarcely heard her.

Then he heard her. He fell into a rage so brilliant it stood out from him in invisible rays.

She said, "It would suit you."

He wanted to scream, *I am not mad!* Yet he had leaped to the cliff's edge, knowing it was bad. Through gritted teeth he said, "I'll go to Welling in the morning."

"That is too soon! The loom is just mended. Will you deny me the pleasure of feeding you?" Her voice was laughing and sad at the same time. He could not understand women! They were never where you left them.

He stood. "I'll leave right now."

"Ah—I have offended you. What is it?"

"I've got a mother. I don't need two. Feed your own children!"

"I have none," said Ba. "Hence Doctor Amu."

He had begun to grope toward the door. He stopped. "That's what the cure was for?"

"Barrenness. Yes."

"It...did it make you vomit?"

"Oh, yes. I vomited up Leaguemen and paidmen, a horse and cart, two circuses, a sailing ship. When I had done, I had never been cleaner. Nor had my house: my jewelry, pots and pans, my husband's axe and toolbox, all were gone."

Because tears pricked at his eyes Raím said, "I'll find Amu! I'll kill him!"

"Ah, no. I had a good lesson. I live the life that is mine, now, not someone else's."

He blundered his hand toward her. "I'm sorry."

She took it. "There are plenty of children. Only not my own."

"Is it as bad as being blind?"

"Oh, lad!" She took his other hand, kissed both and laid them palm to palm. "What a gift you are! I do not doubt for a moment that some girl, some morning, will lie in your arms as happy as the rising sun."

He did cry, then. Yanked his hands away, banged his head on a hanging lamp that dribbled hot oil, yelled, and scrabbled out of the jersey.

She put a compress on his shoulder. "It'll blister," he said crossly.

"Yes, it will. Stay here awhile, and wake that loom. I will tell you about the Gatehouse at Welling."

He shrugged. Put his hand on top of hers.

"Bright weaver?"

"I'm hungry."

She cuffed him gently. "Thank you."

✿

But next morning, when after three bacon sandwiches he went out behind the kitchen to piss, a voice in midair said, "Beggar."

He turned his back on it.

"You, then," said the voice, young as his own. "I don't know your name. Wrestler."

He turned around again. There was a stone wall behind the yard; the voice came from above it, the same voice that yesterday had called him Wrestler.

"My name is Raím." Mister Laundry Bucket.

"Raím, then. That lad you grounded, Damo? He asks you to come to the Hold."

"To be meat for dogs? I'm not stupid."

"No treachery! He wants you to spit on him."

This was too strange for comment.

"On his shoulder," said the voice. "You pulled his arm out of the socket. If the enemy spits on it, then."

"Then what?"

"The hurt heals." The voice was astonished, impatient. "Damo asks you to come spit."

Still strange. In Creek, one caught a toad and bound it alive to the hurt. When the toad died, the pain went away. "He wants me to reset the joint?"

"That's done. He wants spit."

"And why should you not kill me, if I step out of this yard?"

· "Kill you! Then how would you spit? And the Lord of the Ground would kill *us*, for harming one of his own."

"Who is the Lord of the Ground?"

The owner of the voice whistled. "Where do you come from?"

"Creek. A different Creek. Near Ten Orchards."

"I've heard of Ten Orchards. The girls are ugly, they say, and the men gabble like turkeys."

"The girls are pretty," said Raím. "Like apricots."

"Hmph. Who do you worship in the Hold there, if you don't know the Lord of the Ground?"

"The One who wove the world."

"Ah! We know that god. He's little. He's servant to the Lord of the Ground."

Raím, who had traveled, said, "The world is big. There are many gods."

"Hmph!" said the lad on the wall. There was a chill, theological silence. "Then you won't spit?"

"Why? I'd spit, then you'd beat me."

"I swear we will not. By the Lord of the Ground I swear it."

Raím thought of all the ways one could swear and break an oath. If one's fingers were crossed. If one carried a hare's ear unseen. If the deity in itself were crooked. "The Lord of the Ground—what's his province?"

"The ground! He is god of us, the wrestlers. You walk upon him. You dance here for a little—and you're a nimble one—but in the end he'll have you. When you're grounded in the fight we say, 'He took you.' And in the end he'll take you for good. They may not know him in your place, wrestler, but he is there. His name is Lord of What Falls."

"We know him," said Raím with a creeping vertigo. "*I* know him."

"Then by his name I swear, and I swear for my brothers in the Hold: No harm shall come to you. Come spit."

"Show me where the gate is," said Raím. He did not so much as think of Ta Ba, but stepped forward as lightly as he had leapt to the rock, for now he had a name for God.

⑤

The lad called himself Tass. He was friendly and easy, he told Raím where the gate was and waited for him to blunder through it. "Don't want to step on her property," he said. "She's got a tongue like an adder."

When Tass fumbled at his arm Raím took hold of his elbow and said, "Just walk." They ambled jerkily, like two goats tied together.

The sharp breeze was full of the odors of the Hold: cedar smoke, half-cured hides, mongrel, and man. Dogs came barking, then put their wet noses behind his knees. There was a deep murmur of talk, and a new sound: a repetitive knock, many knocks, like heartbeats in big chests.

He stopped in his tracks and lost Tass's elbow. "Looms. The looms, I hear them. In my village they're silent."

"Silent? Wrestler, your village must be lonely."

Tass slapped aside a leather curtain, and they entered the smoky fug of the Hold. The dancing thumps slowed, stopped. Like a dog surrounded by a strange pack, Raím stood stiffly while around him unseen men gathered, murmuring. His back was as alive as his front; he knew how close each body was, almost its height and shape. A perfection of danger, like the moment one entered the bear's den.

Someone said in Plain, "They say you've got a snake on you."

He pulled off the ragged tunic, pushed down the sash to reveal the serpent, and crossed his arms.

They barked about the bear scars on his back. "You'll heal Damo?"

"In my land," Raím said gravely, "the enemy must piss on the hurt."

A consultation of barks. "However," they said, "here one spits. You are agreed?"

"I will do what you wish."

They led him to Damo, who lay on a pallet in the silence of hate. His unbound shoulder, when Raím felt it, was swollen and hot. Raím spat on his palms and rubbed the spittle in, gently, while Damo hissed with pain. Raím had seen a shoulder reset before, and had felt it in the healing; his hands remembered.

"In my place we put drawflower on it to pull out the pain," he said. "Or a toad; a toad is good."

There was no enthusiasm for the toad. He rose, wiping his hands on his thighs. Damo did not thank him, but Tass said, "Come, eat with us."

᥆

The three bacon sandwiches had been nothing. He ate mutton stew and smoked trout with corn mush cooked stiff and served in slabs. They wanted to know about the bear scars. When he told them, they were puzzled. Girls here were not initiated to womanhood by going to the bear. Girls were archers, dedicated to the mountain, the Lady of the Sky; until they married they carried their bows with them always. They were bold hunters, and chose their own lovers. These men did not know by what rites girls were made women; the question embarrassed them.

They asked why he was blind. "The Lord of the Ground," he said. When they asked why he wore a serpent he said, "For that same god!" He had not thought before that he, so tall and bright-haired, wore an image of the most low. The rightness made him shiver. He threw the trout's bones toward the fire and said, "In my land, we say the serpent is the weft of the cloth."

This led to talk of looms. Ta Ba was right: the men of this place were mad for looms. Guiltily he thought of her, of the Gatehouse she had said would suit him, the unfinished weaving on her loom. He must find someone to lead him back; but Tass was guiding his hands to worn crossbeams, the tight plane of a warp.

The loom's voice and motion—push, swing, pull—how could this not be holy? But here it was only a prized possession, said Tass, like a spear or a girl. Better than a girl, because one could play with it among one's fellows in the Hold.

It made Raím uneasy, this speaking of girls as if they were dice or fishhooks. He thought briefly of Pillbug, put the thought away and lay on his back in the lint under Tass's loom, exploring. Sometimes he spoke a tender sound, as if to his lost cat, Brook. Tass drew him up to sit at the polished bench. He wanted to drive the weft down the long path between the warp planes, but Tass took the shuttle out of his hand. Raím understood. It was Tass's loom.

From his pallet Damo said, "Use my loom, Snake."

Raím sat still, wary as if he had been offered the loan of Damo's girl.

"Use it," said Damo. "Spit on it, maybe it'll weave better."

Laughter. Like a pet bear, Raím was led to Damo's loom, the shuttle put in his hand. The men liked his new name, Snake; they repeated it to one another but not to him, so he knew he was not one of them.

"I won't be using the damn thing," said Damo. "Go ahead. This Hold has no boys' loom, and mine's too sturdy to be harmed by clumsiness."

Tass pushed Raím down on the bench and put the shuttle in his hand. "Show us your skill."

"Weaving is not shown," said Raím. "It *is*. And in my place we use a different loom."

"Handy excuse," said Damo.

Raím rose and blundered in Damo's direction. By the time he got there Damo had scrambled off the pallet, saying, "Truce, Snake. I don't know foreign ways."

"I'll go back to your aunt."

"Was she that good?" said Damo, behind him now.

Raím knew it was hopeless. Turned to begin his lunge anyway; was stopped by the word *good*, which dropped like a rock. "Yes, she is good."

A laugh went round at Ta Ba's—Bayami's—expense. And he knew she was good, impeccable; she had taken in a blind beggar covered in vomit and turned out a man who knew he could weave. He must go to her.

Later.

"I can't reach you to kill you," he said without heat. "Take me to the loom and show me the skills of this place."

They tugged him to the bench. The loom was poorly warped, when he shot the shuttle across it stopped halfway. He said, "How did that lad shoot with a limp bowstring?"

Everyone laughed except Damo. They slapped his back, taught him dirty names for the loom parts, offered him yarn. They were young like him, they did not talk of mysteries and old sorrows. By afternoon Tass had gone to Ta Ba's house to shout, from the safety of the stone wall, that the beggar would return to her in a day or two. For now, he would sleep at the Hold.

10

Steady,
slowish,
alert,
alive
line
   staying
   in this
   its
   instant

     Graffito on a drawing board.
     Welling-in-the-Mountains.

Duuni dreamed she was a sorceress. She raised her batten; there was a crack like lightning; a great rent opened in the world, earth to sky. She started back with a cry. Too late: the whole world poured outward toward the rent, bearing her with it in formless chaos.

She woke, crept out of the eiderdown, put on her boots, and went to the fire, where sleepy children warmed their hands and men spoke in low voices over strong tea. Women called from fire to fire. A party of ravens flung about in the air, shouting *graak!* as if the sky itself were stirred to motion. It was cold.

She ate breakfast, washed dishes, washed babies. She knew the names now of the stolen ones, those who did not come and go with their Roadsoul mothers but stayed in the wagon, which Nine called the newie cart.

The dream was still with her. She wanted to pray. Instead she made the babies' names into a chant and whispered it as she scrubbed.

> Maidy and Midget,
> Toady and Bones,
> Rags, Tig, and Larkin.

Bones was the skinny baby bought for one silver coin, who, when he was not yelling, slept and slept, his belly rounder now. She had not seen any Roadsoul make sorceries over him or use any magic but goat's milk. Nor had she seen a Roadsoul pray.

The new sun struck through the camp smoke. As she had done yesterday, she stirred the urda paste, put on her finery, painted her face. She painted Nine's face, gathered paste and press and Nine, went to her booth, shook out the rugs and laid them straight, set her low chair in the same place as yesterday. She was about to sit down, pull up the hood of her cloak, hunch her shoulders, and settle to work the same as yesterday—as if she were at her old loom, her batten in her hand.

In the middle of sitting, she stopped.

Nine said, "What're you waving your bottom in the air for?" and pinched it.

Instead of answering Duuni went to the doorway of the tent and stood there, shadow cold and sun hot, looking up and down the busy midway.

The world torn open. She thought, The cicada cracks its hard jacket, it splits its whole body and draws even its delicate legs out of their casings, and creeps out new, and does not die.

Nine pinched her again. "Hey, you deaf?"

Duuni whirled and grabbed her. "*I am not deaf!*" She wanted to hit; instead she tickled hard. Nine shrieked and fought. In an instant they were running out the door, Nine squealing, "Truce! *Truce!*" until they fell over the ropes into the wrestling ground and jumped up filthy, laughing so hard that Duuni sat down again.

Tam Chivi plucked Nine off and held her dangling. "This yours?"

Duuni shook her head. Could not speak for laughing. She got up, beat the dust off Nightweaver, She Paints Your Dreams, ducked back under the ropes and into her tent. Nine came to the door, still giggling. "Eee, I'm not coming in, you're a maniac!"

"I'm done being a maniac."

"Says you!" But she came in.

"Says me."

᳚

The day rose. Yesterday's children came to show Duuni the designs on their arms, now amber-gold. "Put your arms in the sun, it will darken the drawing," she told them. They stood in the door of the tent holding their arms to the light. "Be patient," she said.

Word was out. A wave of new children found her. Then the adults.

The first was a farm wife, Duuni's age but big with child. She stood in the doorway, watching Duuni draw a cricket on the arm of a boy not much bigger than a cricket himself. Yesterday's girls had taken over the arm-wrapping and the instruction of new children; Duuni had only to wipe her hands before the pregnant woman sat down, smiling to herself, and held out her arm. "A line of quail, please," she said. "The mother, then the little ones."

Nine said, "Three pennies for big people."

"I know. Nightweaver drew a raven on my husband's arm. But I want quail. For luck."

Duuni washed her arm. Surely it was her first child; under her smiles was a stillness, as if she knew that childbirth goes hand in hand with death. On her fair arm the line of quail waited to be made visible, as Duuni had seen them long ago in the willows along the river. She drew the busy mama, the babies like fuzzy thimbles dashing to keep up. .

The woman smiled more. The girls, proud to instruct a grownup, wrapped her arm and told her she must be patient. She left, holding her arm carefully, but soon came back with a woman who wanted a butterfly.

So it went: women and girls, sometimes a gawky hunter asking for a wolf's head on his wrist, grinning while his fellows stood in the doorway cracking jokes, craning to watch the wrestling that went on next door to shouts of "Ground!"

Nine jingled the penny sack. "We're richer than those miners up in High Moles, that burrow in the mountain all their lives."

Duuni's brothers, men of low status, had gone to work in the mines. Or perhaps they were paidmen now, like the ones who slouched and leered along the midway. "It's only pennies," she said.

"*Plenty* pennies." Nine turned to hide the sack under the rug.

A big shadow blocked the light. Three big shadows. A big arm reached out and a big voice, a roar, said, "Rich, eh?"

The whites of Nine's eyes flashed in her blacked face. In the doorway stood three paidmen, big and made bigger by their patched and rusty shoulder harnesses, helmets pushed back from greasy hair. In uncombed beards their grins showed missing teeth.

"Sure, you're rich. Give's a little, now." His seeking hand, Nine backing away.

They were inside the booth now. More laughter. "She don't want to give's her pennies. Draw's a pitchur, then, and we won't take them. A little pitchur." They were drunk, Duuni had seen Tumiin drunk, had seen her own father drunk and hitting her mother's face. "Pitchur or pennies, eh!" The biggest of them knelt where the children had sat. Thrust his filthy arm into Duuni's lap. "I want a lion."

She could not breathe. Not think. Barely see, as though the world had gone dark except for one patch of light, that bare arm. He prodded her with his elbow. "Lion."

"No."

Who said that?

She thought, *I* said it. The mad part of me, the part that broke my batten.

Again it said, "No."

He pressed his elbow into her belly. "Said I want a lion, carnie bitch."

A whistling in her head. The patch of light shrank to a pinpoint. "No."

His big arm struck her off the stool. She sprawled across the rugs, the whistling went sharp as a shout and suddenly there were real shouts, light, the yowl of men fighting, bare-bodied men and men in armor rolling on the trodden grass of the midway. As Nine shrieked and jumped in the doorway Duuni scrambled to her feet, saw the paidmen in their hauberks pinned to the trampled ground by a half dozen wrestlers. Too late, the festival constables came running with staves and got in a few whacks.

"Eee!" said Nine. "You get 'em!"

Tam Chivi stood up out of the pile, dusty and grazed, then Farki. The constables tied the paidmen's hands. A crowd gathered; the constables yelled questions.

Everyone turned to look at Duuni.

Nine danced like a monkey. "Tried to steal the money, he! Tried to make her paint him, she says *No!* and he hits her, she says *No!* again and *No!* and they came, the wrestlers, you saw! Eee!"

There was a lot after that. Duuni said Yes, Sir and No, Sir to the constables who were not much interested now that the fight was over, just paidmen, what do you expect? People stared, Tam

Chivi grinned his white grin. But what Duuni remembered was Farki dusting his forearms, watching her. His quiet face.

The crowd moved on. The children, who had scattered like mice, crept back chattering. The designs on their arms had darkened properly now. The girl with the two fish came to Duuni where she sat with her heart still quick, patted her knee and said, "Miss Nightweaver. Were you scared?"

Then Duuni cried so hard the night sky and all the constellations turned to water, and the paint washed away from her black eye.

She let Nine redo her face with crooked stars. Nine made the middle one extra big. "Gya," she said. "Some Pillbug."

⌒

That night Duuni worked late, for after the children had gone their parents kept coming, asking for clan emblems and any pretty thing they could think of. A girl her own age brought a potsherd painted with steps and spirals and asked Duuni to draw that design round her forearm in a band; it looked so well there was a rush for painted armbands that went on almost until the beer booth closed. Afterward she went out with Tam Chivi and the rest, down the crowded midway. This time she was able to treat them all to cakes and sweet tea. They praised her and teased her and made jokes she did not understand.

All but Nine were Roadsoul born. She did not know what a Roadsoul was, if not a sorcerer and thief; she watched them as she had once watched the creatures of the riverbank, cautious, entranced. Tam Chivi especially she watched. He never said much, as if the world were so easy there was nothing to say about it. She could have looked at him forever, as one might watch a stallion in a field.

When they heard her new bracelet had broken they bore her back to the bead seller's, to harangue him in fun and see whether he would give her another. He would not, but while the others were laughing and cajoling she edged over and looked at the medicator's booth.

It was empty. Just stained boards. Sleepy saw her looking and said, "Need a cure, Pillbug? A love philtre?"

Laughter. Duuni shook her head. She was troubled about that tunic. What if it had belonged to the beggar, killed by a lion— *her* lion, that she had loosed unknowing and that now walked free in the world? The cloth had not looked torn...

The bead seller was trying his bargain with Shine, beads for kisses, and gaining only laughter. He tried it on Duuni, who only blushed. "*I* need that philtre," he said with soulful eyes, for he was young and good-natured. "But not from that medicator skunk. He'd sell his mother to a tanner and steal the finished hide."

When the others moved on, Duuni hung back a little. The bead seller leaned over his counter. "Changed your mind about that kiss?"

"No. But...did you see a tall, blind beggar at the medicator's booth? A little older than me. With a red beard." She had never spoken so many words to a man.

"And how old might you be, sweetheart?"

She backed away. He saw her fear, and raised his hands to reassure her. "Toughen up, little one. It's a rough world. No, no tall, blind beggars. Just short, fat crooks. If you're wise you'll keep away from Doctor Amu."

He blew her a kiss. He was so nice; a sudden lightness made her pretend to catch the kiss in her hand. She kissed her fingers and laughed.

He came right out from behind the counter, saying, "Oh, you darling!" and she bolted like a rabbit back to the others, who strolled joking down the midway.

She took Nine's sticky hand. Nine yawned and bumped against her as they walked. "What'd you ask him?" she said.

"If he'd seen the beggar. Flea Butt. Last night that medicator was selling a master tunic."

"If Amu said it was a master tunic, it wasn't. Some rag painted to look like."

"He only sells in the dark," said Shine. "The darker the better."

"Old Flea Butt was in the dark, all right," said Nine.

They laughed. So unkind! Yet their faces were not cruel. Duuni thought of the wind that blows, and of the trees that must stand in the wind and bend, for if they do not bend, they break. She thought of the beggar's arrogant, stiff back.

She said softly, "Maybe everybody's in the dark. *I* am."

"Nightweaver," said Tam Chivi.

☙

She began to see how to set the selvages of her loom. That was how she thought of it: in the new, cracked-wide-open world, how not to fall, boundless, through boundless air, yet not to go stiff and break.

In the evening before she slept she must mix urda paste for the next day, gather and tear enough rags for wrapping, and mix paint for her own face and Nine's. She must keep clean.

Those were her selvages. Once those things were done, she could do whatever else was asked of her: cook, wash dishes, help with the children, or be still and watch as the strange world revealed itself. She could sit calmly, painted and cowled, and ask each soul who came to her booth, "What would you like?"

The day after the paidmen's fight the bead seller came to her booth. He did not recognize her. She said, "What would you like?" He smiled and said, "A turtledove." She drew that, and he went away pleased. She watched him go, thinking, Shine would have flirted. *And how old might you be, sweetheart?* I should be seventeen, she thought, but when I left the Balcony I was still nine years old.

Dicey the Bearded Princess came in his day silks. He had fallen off his platform and sprained his ankle, the un-hairy one, and could not work. "Draw on it, please," he said gloomily. "It'll make me feel better."

She was still uneasy with his half-and-halfness, but she said, "What would you like?"

"A duck. I'm fond of ducks."

She unwrapped his swollen ankle, drew a duck on it, and would not take his money.

"I won't have to shave for a while, anyway. You're a sweetheart," he said, like the bead seller, and hobbled off. A sweet heart; that did not seem a bad thing to be.

And then it was the last day of the fair. Everyone was weary. The constables were irritable and most often to be found at the beer sellers' booths. Two wrestlers had wrenched knee or elbow, leaving Tam Chivi and Farki to do most of the work. When Duuni had a moment, she stood at the door of the booth and watched them ground the townies for bets. She knew nothing about wrestling, yet when she watched Farki her mind went alert and still, the way it did when she drew.

He had said nothing to her yet, done nothing.

She was standing thus, watching him, when to the booth came an old woman, round and robed and gray, walking slowly with a cane. She scowled at the low stool and said, "If I could get down there, I would never get up again."

Duuni gave her the chair she used herself. The woman sat down like snow sliding off a roof. She was short of breath. "So you paint dreams," she said.

Nine, who had been lying on her back playing cat's cradle, bobbed up and said, "Three pennies!"

"What are three pennies to four score years, kitten?" With the slow fingers of the old, the woman untied a worn purse, counted out the pennies, tied it up again. "It is not a dream I want but the goddess. Will you paint her?"

Duuni said, "Mother, I don't know the gods of this place. Is there no prayer merchant in the fair?"

"A bumbling wretch, he could not draw the sun at midday."

"Nightweaver, she can draw *anything*," said Nine. "You just say."

The woman smiled, but only a little. "I am dying," she said. "I want you to paint the goddess on my hand. When I go to that other land I shall hold up my hand—" she held it up "—and greet her. She has given me a good life."

Duuni put her own hand to her heart. "I? You want *me* to do such a thing?"

"Why not? I have seen the raven on my grandson's arm, and the quail on his wife's, and the fish on my great-grandniece's. Now I have come to ask for what *I* want." A wicked look. "I am napping, they think."

"*Four* pennies," said Nine. "What you want is mighty serious. Or five—"

"Stop that!" Duuni took her shoulders and hustled her out the door. "Go watch the wrestlers. I'm working."

"Gya!" Nine stuck out her tongue, but she went.

Duuni returned to the old woman. Twisting her hands together, she said, "Mother, I can't paint what I don't know!"

"Ah, but you must know her: Imoy, the consort of the sun."

"I know only the goddesses of my own home. When it was my home."

The woman gave her a sharp glance, as if she would ask where home was, and why Duuni was not there being a decent girl instead of daubing strangers in a carnival. But she held out her hand and said, "I shall tell you what Imoy looks like. She is goddess of that mountain there. She rides the sky on the crescent moon, as if it were a boat on a river."

Duuni caught her hand. "But that's..." Mma, goddess of the mountain, consort of the sun. She could not speak her name, let alone paint her. "I knew her in my own land," she said. "But I can't draw her."

"Why not, child?"

She looked at the woman's crooked old feet in their slippers. "I blasphemed against her. She would curse you because of me."

Silence. Duuni waited for her to lean on her stick, and rise, and go.

Instead she put her hand, cold as a frog's, under Duuni's chin and made her look up. "You are too young for curses. There is only one true blasphemy, and that is unkindness." When still Duuni said nothing, she said, "What is her name, in your land?"

Duuni could not speak it.

"Draw her for me." The woman held out her palm. In the town called Looks Worried, she did not look worried at all.

"But…perhaps here she is different. The world…the world is very big, and different in every place."

"I have never been farther than ten miles from Greencliff. But the goddess is the goddess. However you paint her will be right."

"It will last two weeks."

"That will be long enough."

Duuni knelt and took the old hand into her lap. It was thin-skinned, soft. She stroked the palm as one might smooth cloth before embroidering it. Gazed into it, afraid of what might show itself.

There she was.

Duuni drew a dark crescent for the goddess's feet, her cloaked body, her smiling face calm as Auntie's. It was Mma, yet not Mma. She began to draw her eyes as they were always drawn, two downcast crescents.

She stopped. She looked again into the old woman's hand and drew the eyes as she saw them: wide open, looking straight into her own. When she had finished she could not stop looking at them, open for the first time.

"Aye," said the old woman. "Imoy, there she is. Here we paint her looking down to see us, but this is better. Her eyes are open, she will know me."

Duuni blew on her hand. When the lines had set, she wrapped it stiffly to keep the paste in place until morning. Scarcely had she finished when the woman with the quail on her arm came

125

running with her husband, crying, "Grandmother! What are you doing here?" and there was a quarrel such that Duuni thought the old woman would drop dead right there, before the color even took. But she was pleased with herself and rapped the grandson with her cane. They bore her off.

Nine came back from the wrestling ground, angling like a scolded cat. "You could have got paid extra. Tomorrow we pull up and go, so no more pennies till we get to High Moles fair."

Duuni said, "Some things are not about money."

"Gya!" said Nine. "Don't ever go into business."

❧

The caravan left Greencliff. Stakes were pulled, tents hauled down. Limping, the wrestlers fetched the pastured mules and harnessed them to the carts. A few children came to show Duuni her work, the lines still golden; their mothers called them, and they were gone like autumn birds.

Duuni climbed into the newie wagon, where the babies tumbled on the rugs and a few women—she had begun to learn names, Lacey and Barley and Snail—sat joking with Auntie. The wagon pulled into the crawling line of carts, and the now-familiar jolting began once more. The field where they had camped was only trampled squares where tents and wrestling-ground had been. In a week, less, it would be just a field again.

Nine hung out the rear window, trading insults with the townie children who ran alongside. Duuni held on to her sash, sure she would fall; saw she would not, and let go.

Barley sang softly.

> Goodbye, farewell, you rolling old river,
> Goodbye, farewell, you rolling old sea.

In an undertone Duuni said to Nine, "Where are we going?"

"Townie! Right here." Nine plumped back into the cart and grabbed Maidy across her lap. "Hey. Do you know where babies come from?"

Of course Duuni knew. Her mother had been frank and bleak. She felt embarrassed; then she thought, What if Nine is asking because she doesn't know? She has to know! What if some Tumiin...

Stammering, she said, "Yes. I do. Now, *listen*, Nine. The man... The woman..."

"Not *that*. Everybody knows that. I mean *our* babies. He's from Lilypond—" Nine pointed to the curly little boy called Toady "—and Maidy's from Dale, that we call Stick-in-the-Mud, and Rags is from Esker. And old Boney there, you saw where he came from. He's fatting up all right."

Under the soft singing of the women Duuni said, "In Alikyaan—" was Alikyaan in the same world? "—they say the Roadsouls steal children."

"Well, we do, kind of. Midget here, she was by the road yelling, nobody about. We just took her, otherwise the wild dogs'd get her. Didn't leave a penny. She was so skinny you could see her butt bones. Hey, Midgie?" At her name the child lifted her arms, now round and fat. Nine said, "*Peeiuw*, you stink," gave her to Duuni, and fetched a clean rag for a diaper. The older babies went bare-bottomed; the women knew by their cries when to hold them out over the road—mostly. "We buy some, and take some, and give some away. Guess the dogs get the rest. Or the mills." Nine dropped the dirty diaper into the bucket that swung behind the wagon, tickled Midget hard and loosed her into the throng. "I was took from the mills. I was big, though."

For the first time, Duuni thought, Maybe that is why Nine will talk to me? The Roadsoul-born just smile, or joke, or sing; they never explain. "What was it like?"

"Like now. Fall of the year. I was crazy." Nine bared her teeth. "I said yes, all right, but then I bit people. Auntie, she'd hold me so tight I couldn't move. I thought Farki'd do what that overseer did to us mill rats, and I'd try to bite him. When we got to the Gatehouse I'd throw food and smack the mice and all."

There had been a gatehouse in Alikyaan, a little stone cubby where the chief Wall Warrior slept. But "Mice?" said Duuni.

Nine waved her hand. "Kids. Babies. In a Gatehouse there's lots of Mice. We bring them. Like we're bringing you, like we would've brought old Flea Butt if he hadn't got stupid and run. We take people where they're supposed to go. That's what we do, the Souls." She took up Bones from his nest of rags and blew on his belly to make him squeal. "In the Gatehouse, that's where we winter."

On they went, tilting and jarring. Tiggy clung to Duuni's leg. Duuni let her questions fall and rode on toward wherever it was she was supposed to go, watching the mountain change slowly, like a jewel turned in the light.

ᕦ

All day the wagons traced a dusty line on a red mountain road that ran along a creek rough with great stones. River poplars, yellowing with cold, rustled *hush, hush,* over the rush of the water.

Duuni thought, Perhaps the old woman is dead now, and raising her hand to Imoy.

They camped in a glade by the sprawling water. When Duuni went with the rest to gather firewood, she smelled hearth smoke: they must be near a village. Farki and his lads, limping and slow, went that way on some errand. They returned empty-handed, laughing among themselves.

Dusk crept out from the poplars and made the campfires into little worlds. Duuni left the heat and chatter to creep under the comforter with the babies. The poplars hissed, the stars burned far and chill. Even the voice of the creek was cold.

A rustle and nudge made her jump. Nine burrowed under the comforter, wriggled out of her rags, and snugged up to Duuni tight as a dog. "I know a surprise," she said.

"What is it?"

"Ain't telling. It's tomorrow. You'll see."

She would say no more, only giggle. Soon she was snoring. She gave off heat like a stove. The stars were a thousand thousand campfires.

11

I don't need to understand
men or children:
I don't need to be God.
I don't need men
to understand themselves:
I don't need them to be God.
I need men to understand
that they do not understand
themselves, or women,
or children, or God.

    Shrine poem. Welling-in-the-Mountains.

The next morning Tass led Raím to the millpond to bathe and swim. Raím marked the way in his mind, thinking, Afterward I'll ask him to take me back to Ta Ba's house.

But instead he went back under Damo's loom. The hides that made the walls of the Hold had been thrown back to let in the low sun. Everyone was outdoors; he heard scuffles and grunts, smelled the sweat of great strain. The men of the Hold were wrestling.

No one had said anything to him. Wrestling was holy; he had not been made part of that holiness by a tattoo on his thigh and rites he could only guess at. He understood this. He himself had crouched under a Great Cloak, beaten through it until he was blue from shoulder to waist; the cudgel that beat him had been put into his hand, he was a man then, and could be tattooed with the snake.

Thinking of that time and that boy, he ignored the wrestling as he would the sounds of lovemaking in the next room. When Tass came to him and said, "You. Snake. Will you try a fall?" he did not understand what was meant.

"A fall." He did not like falls.

"A wrestling fall."

He sat up, stretched his arms to crack his back. "I'm not tattooed like you."

"But you know some things," said Tass.

"About wrestling? It's not holy, in my place."

"They say a flood will come and drown the unbelievers. Damo was the best; how could you pull his arm out, if you don't belong to the Lord of the Ground?"

Raím said nothing.

"He took you," said Tass. "The Lord. He rescued you out of that false Creek and sent you to teach us your sorceries. We know this by the bear scars on your back: the bear in his cave belongs to the Lord."

It was a welcome of sorts.

Tass pulled Raím to his feet. "Come. We'll mark you."

This meant that handprints in some odorous paint were pressed onto his thighs in lieu of a tattoo. By then he was naked like the others, prayers were barked, he was doused from behind with a dipperful of scented water. They made him scratch his belly with his fingernails, like a bear. He obeyed, feeling silly.

He had always been a fair wrestler, strong and hard, and could pin his opponent by sheer muscle. But the encounter with Damo had felt different. What he remembered of it was quietness. A simplicity; there had been instants when hardness had nothing to do with it. He had flowed around Damo's body like water, run through him and re-formed like a wave. As though

Damo had pinned himself, and Raím had done nothing but wait, and turn, and wait.

He did not know what that magic was.

At home the lads grappled anyhow in the dirt. Red Creek had a formal style. Wrestlers met first in a round of ritual holds. Raím was clumsy. He groped, flailed, put his elbow in Eineg's eye. Lying where he had been pinned, he thought with detachment that he had failed again, nothing special. He got up, back into the starting stance, his hands on Eineg's thighs.

That stillness rose in him.

Eineg's shoulder against his. Eineg whole, himself whole: an unpredictable pattern. When Eineg drove in and gripped, Raím gave way like water, gathered himself, levered Eineg into a fall, flowed out from under him, and wedged his knee on Eineg's back.

Eineg made the croaking bark that meant he was grounded. "Ah," said the rest. From the sidelines Damo, sneering, said "He looked like a woman diapering a baby."

Raím swung toward him to do damage. Paused. Because that was what it had felt like: as though he and Eineg had fulfilled some gentle act, the baby's flailing absorbed and guided by the mother, and in the end both as they should be.

"How did you do that?" said Eineg, slapping the dust off. "Damned if I could get hold of you."

Raím did not know how he had done that, so he said nothing. The rounds began again. Attentive now, Raím felt for how he fought.

His impulse was to be sinew, to force his opponent down. But these lads were vicious wrestlers, they met strength with strength. Tass pushed Raím's face into the dirt and said, "*Thus we wrestle!*"

Raím spat dust, rose. Next time, when Tass drove in with his levering thighs, Raím gave up.

He gave up as snow melts on a windowsill, as a woman surrenders to a lover. Tass entered him and passed right through.

Raím re-formed, rolled over, turned to sinew again, and pinned him face down.

"By the Lord," said Tass between gasps. "You're there, and then you're not. Yet you're bigger than I am. What is it you do?"

Raím said nothing. Thought, That softness, like fainting into water. Is that what it's like for a woman? *Surrender, be entered.*

Am I half woman?

"The Lord of the Ground turns your bones to water," said Tass when the bouts were over. "You're no snake. A snake has bones."

"I've got a bone," said Raím, swaggering, to drown the thought *I'm half woman.* He wiped his face on his shoulder. "I'll go to the millpond and wash."

"Not yet," said Tass. "There is a rite to unlock you from the Lord."

"I am unlocked. That's why I could pin you." He left them and followed the smell of water back to the pond. In a little the rest of them came too, barking among themselves.

The pond was big, a small lake. Raím swam out and back, shallow to deep to shallow, with long strokes. As he made a shore turn, Tass caught him by the wrist. "By what magic do you know where you're going?"

"Feel of the sun. Smell of two goat pens."

Tass laughed uneasily and gave him a friendly shove. Raím swam underwater as long as he could, the weeds stroking him. When he came up it was still with him: *I'm half woman.*

He swam away from the sound of the others, fast, splashing, with anger and gristle and force. Felt his arms lengthen, stiffen, pull; soften and fold; rise, lengthen, stiffen again. When the voices were distant and small he turned on his back and floated on the skin of the water. He had come to some shore, for whispering cattails and water grass surrounded and surely hid him. He did not care whether he could find his way back. The water was warm, the air cold.

Something fell across his face. He brushed it off. It fell again; he brushed it off, flailed, then stood on the mucky bottom, water to his thighs. Heard, close and muffled, the laughter of girls. Then singing.

> There comes a bonnie beggar
> Unto a lassie's door,
> Says, "Would you marry a traveler lad
> That's new come from the fair?"

He understood: They had been tickling him, as he floated, with a plume of water grass.

He forgot he was blind. He forgot five years, he laughed, he splashed toward them and fell over. By the time he had sloshed to the shore—a steep rock ledge that jutted into the pond—they were gone, laughing louder as they ran.

This being half woman, he thought as he swam, following the men's voices back to the far shore, it must be like blindness. Sometimes people can't tell.

ᕤ

His cock kept falling off. True, it reattached itself, but he woke rattled from the dream and groped out into the frosty dawn to piss heartily. He must get away to the silence of Ta Ba's back room, where the rhythm of weaving would settle his heart.

But when the sun was up, the lads wanted to wrestle. Reluctant, clumsy, he was pinned and pinned again. The others laughed, relieved: the foreigner's magic had worn off. He got angry and fought them. Was grounded, Eineg's knee on his neck and one cheek grinding the dirt.

I am half woman.

No!

Half woman.

What his pride would not admit, his body knew. It surrendered, turned to water under Eineg's knee, flowed up and embraced him. Eineg bore down like a log on a flood; Raím went

134

loose as a wave and kept him rolling. Eineg grunted and thrust; Raím welcomed him, parted and flowed, then turned to iron and twisted one arm across the other's back.

"Ground!" said Eineg, gasping. "Let me up! That was sorcery. Get him off me!" He slapped himself to get the enchantment off. "His body melted," he said.

"No it didn't," said Tass. "You pinned him, he squirmed up and pinned you. That was all."

"He changed your eyes, then."

Damo said, "A blind man—you think he hasn't magic to change eyes?"

"He won fair, get over it," said Tass.

"*You* fight him, then!"

Tass came forward and set his hands on Raím's thighs. "They want your blood," he said in a comradely whisper. "If it is not witchery, tell me what you do."

Grateful, reckless, Raím whispered back, "Be a girl to me. Give way, for if I begin my thrust I must finish it, and then you have me."

Tass pushed Raím away with a laugh. "Oh, so that's it!"

"What? What did he say?" said the rest.

"His words were for *me*." Tass's hand came out of the invisible world and pinched Raím's cheek.

Raím took the hand, which was attached to an arm, and began to remove the arm from its body. This work was mysteriously stopped. When he came to he was lying face down in mud, bleeding, and somewhere an old man was shouting about profanation of the wrestling ground. He was picked up by the arms and walked, staggering, to lean against a wall. Slid down it to lie on the ground. Sat up, holding his head; the lump on the back of it had stopped bleeding.

He thought, I want to weave. Just weave, and nobody talk to me.

135

But the person who spoke was Tass himself, still frightened and angry. "Would you die, Snake? Why did you do that? Where a grip won't stop you a cudgel will."

Raím did not answer.

"My arm is half out," said Tass. "What's the matter with you? You invite me, then try to kill me." Grim amusement came into his voice. "Is that how they do it in your country? I shall not travel."

"I didn't—" Raím began. Stopped. For it would follow that the woman half of him would invite a man.

He would not let himself not think it. The girls at the pond... had that been because he was also half man? Or was he all man, but only half the time...?

His head hurt.

"Did not what?" said Tass. "Invite me? Try to kill me? Just wanted a haunch to roast for dinner?" He was laughing now, still grim, but pulling Raím's head forward to look at the knot. "Lek hit you. Be glad it wasn't Damo. Stay there, I'll wash it."

"Do the rest of them know—"

"Why you tried to rip my arm off? No more do I. By the holy! I've a bruise under my shoulder blade the size of my fist. You'll have to spit on it," said Tass.

Raím said nothing. He let Tass bathe him. He had to notice Tass's hands, deft and efficient, because he would not let himself not notice. Tass rubbed him dry with sacking and brought him his clothes. The others were still wrestling, still whispering; he heard his name, *Snake*. Head sore, neck stiff, he groped back to Damo's loom and crawled under it, comforting himself with yarn.

For the rest of the afternoon Tass came and went. His hand, with his warmth behind it, came floating to rest on Raím's ankle or thigh; he paused to sit on the loom seat and talk of heddles, battens, weft, in the detail peculiar to the men of this Hold. It was not the complexity of weaving that intrigued Tass, but that of looms: how the parts fit together exactly, and made sense.

Raím lay under the loom, working and listening. He told Tass a little about the looms of his own hold. The others came in, bantering warily. "Tass, don't pick up that snake."

"Snake!" said Tass. "She-bear, more like." When it was time for sleep he moved his bedroll next to Raím's, laid his arm over him like a hunt brother at cold camp, and fell asleep.

He snored. Raím lay awake in his always-dark—embraced, comforted, terrified.

So be it, he thought. The solace of that friendly body, that warm arm; but it was a hard arm, not soft and rosemary-scented. Yet surely his woman half must like that hardness? It was all only strange. Unbelievable that he, Raím, should lie here, fallen from some cold height; yet the place he had fallen to was warm.

Tass's sleepy thumb moved on his chest. "Snake."

Raím moved, to show he had heard.

"Don't kill me," Tass whispered. Raím heard his smile. The hand moved to his face, stroked it. Tass's hand wanted him to turn his head.

Because his old life was gone, Raím let Tass turn his head. Tass kissed him. He was prickly; Raím put up his hand to push him away. As he did so he thought how many girls had made that gesture to push away his kisses—that gesture exactly. He had considered it a challenge to see how far he could get, and disregarded it.

Tass disregarded it. Grunted, settled himself close. "She-bear. You said, 'Be a girl to me.'"

Around them, the quiet sounds of the others' sleep. Raím's mind gabbled in an undertone, saying, When women said stop I never believed them, I kept pressing, why shouldn't he? A man, oh gods, what's it like to fuck a man...

An image rose in his mind: two men sparring with cudgels.

He tried to shake it. It grew stronger. It curled his mouth under Tass's kiss, it shoved Tass backward and made room for Raím to laugh, to roar with laughter until the whole Hold sat up and barked, "*Shut up!*"

He rolled onto his belly and howled into the blanket. "What's the matter?" said Tass. "Madman! What is it?"

"I can't." A gasp, and off again into laughter. "You stink same as I do."

Somebody threw a boot.

In the end he got hiccups. They lay facing each other, wrapped in their bedrolls, Tass's fist in Raím's. Whispering into the dark, Raím said, "I'm half woman. I think I am. But not in my body, exactly."

"I'll teach you that part," said Tass. "You teach me to wrestle."

"It's when I wrestle that I'm half woman."

Tass stroked his curls. "You're crazy."

"Quit fussing at my hair." He pulled Tass's big fist close. "Be my brother," he said, and thought of Nine.

"Don't want to be your damned brother." Tass rolled away. Rolled back. "Just a little. Snake—"

"Shut up or I'll kill you."

"Get fucked."

They chuckled, turned away, and slept, butt to butt.

◎

In the morning Tass was still joking and eager. To please him Raím asked his help to get to the millpond, though he could have found the way himself. Tass scrambled his map by leading him to a different bathing place, from which he could not get back without help, and would not leave until Raím had promised to wrestle later.

He should go to Ta Ba. But she would scry out his womanness and speak truth. He shook like a dog, stripped, and waded from the grassy bank. His splashes echoed from a rocky ledge—was it the one from which the girls had baited him? This time the water was ice, as if it had come from peaks already snowy, and when he climbed out again the air felt warm.

He dressed, scratching his beard. Groped among the little straight trees of the shore until he found one he liked, an aspen sapling bare of leaves. He broke it, dragged it to the sunny side of the ledge and took out the knife he had borrowed from Tass. Whittling, whistling, he made himself a stick.

The wood under the bark was silky as damp skin. He trimmed the branches, pushing the knife with his thumb and whistling "The Bonnie Beggar," so absorbed that when he stopped whistling to try the height of the staff he barely noticed that the melody went on for three notes before it stopped.

The woods were still. In the distance, cattle lowed. He took up the tune; the other whistler joined him. They went on raggedly together to the end of the measure.

The whistler was above him. Raím set his shoulders against the stone and sang.

> There comes a bonnie beggar
> Unto a lassie's door,
> Says, "Would you kiss a traveler lad,
> New come from the fair?"

A light voice nipped in.

> "Why should I kiss a beggar lad
> With neither kith nor kin?"
> But at one blink of his bonnie blue eye
> She's opened the door to him.

A girl's voice.

> "If you marry a farmer lad,
> A farmer lass you'll be,
> But a beggar lass can wander the world—
> Ah, come along with me!"

Raím sang. The girl sang with him. The smothered laughter of two or three others hung behind her singing. A bold one, then, with her cohorts.

> She's kilted up her silken gown
> Above her lily-white knee,
> And he's raised up his ruddy staff,
> Straight as an aspen tree—

Here the voice on the rock squealed, as if the singer had forgotten what the verse said until she sang it. Her companions laughed. Scuffling, low argument—S*top! Come away!*—with laughter breaking through it like little fires through a smother of brush.

He flushed all over with delight, anger, desire. He was safe to taunt, for he could not catch anybody. The laughter and whispers went crackling away into the wood. When they were gone he sang the next verse anyway. He began it angrily, but by the end he was sad.

> As bird into the mossy nest,
> As hare into the ground,
> As weeping child to mother's breast,
> As sword into the wound...

—and from above, on the rock, the light voice sang with his.

> As sun at bright midsummer
> Into the dark does win,
> As man into a woman,
> That beggar lad went in.

The voice sang too fast, and got to the end of the verse before he did. He bent his head and trimmed the stick. A pine cone hit his ear. Another.

"There's more," said the voice. "Sing it."

He did not answer.

"Sing."

"Not to you."

"Why not?"

"It's too pretty."

"*La!* It's coarse," she said, and giggled.

"The words aren't."

"If it was only coarse, would you sing it with me?"

He whittled.

"*Tcha!*" Another pine cone. "The lads of your land are cowards."

He whittled. A branch poked him. He said, "The other girls are watching from the bank to see how brave you are to make the beggar sing."

This time it was a bigger stick. It hurt. He whittled. "The lads of your place are rude," she said.

"True."

Wheedling: "Sing it."

"What did you wager the others that you could make me sing?"

"The loan of Mari's green overskirt."

"No prize for me?"

"A kiss," she said, bold as could be.

"What if then I don't let you go?"

"You die," she said. "The arrows are already nocked."

He had forgotten the girls here were archers. His skin glowed with the arrows pointed at it. "Who's the best shot?"

"Steffy. She is aiming at your eye."

"My eye!" He laughed. "Why should I mind dying?"

A pause, as if she had not considered this. "Well…you're very pretty."

"I can't see myself."

"Do you want to die?"

"Sometimes."

She was silent for a while. If her friends held their bows drawn, their arms were tired. At last she said, "Your voice is

141

sweet. But the words—you say them all foreign, like a duck quacking. I'll sing, and you follow."

She sang. Raím joined her.

> The rushing creek did crest the bank,
> The hawk did crest the hill,
> The wave did crest the bonnie strand
> And on the sand did spill.
>
> She's risen up alive with child
> And brought him to her mother:
> "Here is the lad I love the best,
> A beggarman no longer."

From the woods, ragged laughter.

"Now I'll kiss you," she said, breaking her way downward among the brush beside the stone.

"No. You've had your song. Go, be happy in Mari's overskirt."

"I keep my promises."

Warm hands pulled his head down, warm lips kissed his mouth. From the bank a shriek went up. She was tall, she smelled like girl. He held her; thought of arrows; let her go. She hung on his neck and bit his lip, so that he gasped and grasped after her in spite of himself.

But she was gone. He heard her laughing.

"Wait," he said. "What—"

"My name? I won't tell you!"

"No. What...what color is your hair?"

"Can't you...oh! It's black. And curly." She fled. He heard her scolding the others on the bank.

"Black and curly." He leaned on the rock, set his forehead on his fist. "Oh god!"

ᕙ

He did not wait for Tass to fetch him but groped along the shore with his new stick until he found the smell of the goat pens, and so back to the Hold. Tass was surprised. He was mending a weasel trap and let Raím feel it, how it broke the weasel's back but left the pelt unharmed. While Raím counted with his thumbnail the turns of fine cord that padded the jaws, Tass leaned on his shoulder and said, "So—in your place, men do not love men?"

"Sometimes. It was never my way."

"I have a girl," said Tass, "and I'm telling you, it's simpler with a brother. What were you doing yesterday, if you weren't asking me to your bed?"

"Wrestling."

"Doesn't it start there, often as not?"

"That's wasn't what I meant." Words were clumsy. He could have woven it: soft threads and stiff threads mingling, resisting, giving way to one other. "When we wrestle again, just we two, I'll show you."

"Now," said Tass. But the shouts of a hunting party announced a fat doe to quarter and roast. Then the lads must show the hunters their new pet and his snake tattoo; then it was night. Tass edged and leaned, but Raím turned away and slept, or pretended to, thinking of the lips that had kissed his.

The next day was one of rites in which Raím, an infidel, could not take part. A wrestling match went on for hours. Raím worked at Damo's loom, wishing he could weave a girl's mouth, soft and open. It would have been courteous to find his way back to Ta Ba's; but she was old.

Late in the day, Tass came to him, sweaty from the ground. He brought Raím his aspen stick and took his hand. "Come away, Snake! There's a clearing in the woods by the pond. No one will see us."

"I've told you, no."

"Not that. You promised to show your holds to me—just me. The lads are at the ground, and outside the ground one must be careful. Wrestling is not for women to look upon."

Raím rose, stretched, and took Tass's elbow. If they were seen, it was without comment; they were lovers now. Tass led him to a sandy clearing in the oak brush not far from the lapping water of the pond. There, again and again, he tried to pin Raím with blunt, robust grips; again and again Raím tipped and rolled and vanished out of his arms, flowed up behind him, brought him down. Tass was like Tass's weaving, straightforward and plain. He would not have understood Hawk Harried by Ravens.

"Show me step by step," he said, spitting out sand. "Tell me where to put my head."

Raím, panting, said, "Up your ass."

From the oak brush, a squeak of laughter.

"By the Lord!" Tass leapt up, barked at the bushes, waded into them. The girls laughed as they fled.

"Hussies!" He sounded truly shocked, but with swagger in it. "They ought to be pilloried. But then—girls like to look at men."

Raím rolled his head to loosen his neck. "Who's the black-haired one?"

"Which? Yanna? Or Ellie, hers is curly—" said Tass. Stopped. His arm came out of nowhere and locked around Raím's throat.

Raím twisted once and laid him down. From the ground Tass said, "You are the devil himself!" His voice was furious, cold. "How does a blind man know the color of her hair? Have you spoken...have you touched her? You think because you can wrestle you can have her? Since you won't have me? Fucking beggar—"

"*Stop.*" Raím rubbed Tass's face in the sand. To make everything stop, everything: the word *beggar*, the lips that had nipped his and vanished, the black hair he would never see. When he got aware of himself he had his knee on Tass's neck and Tass, too, was saying, "Stop," in a hoarse whisper. He took his knee off. Tass scrabbled away.

"Sorry," said Raím.

Tass breathed like a dog snoring. "I could put a knife through your heart!"

Raím lifted his hands, dropped them. "Then it would stop, all right," he said, not to Tass. "That would do it."

"*What are you?*"

"I don't know."

There was a silence. The girls rustled in the oak brush, not giggling now. Tass cursed, rose, and went after them.

But it was not girls this time. Men's voices. Tass answering, low. Raím crouched, ready to be jumped. Heard Tass say, "...or he'll kill you." Decided to hurt as many of them as efficiently as he could.

But Tass came back alone. "To the Hold," he said. "Follow me."

"Who was that?"

"Nobody. Men. I told them don't touch that beggar, he's a witch."

"If I'm a witch, why are you leading me to the Hold?"

A silence. "You are our guest." Instead of taking Raím's hand he gave him one end of the aspen stick and led him that way, as Set had done.

၅

No one would wrestle with him. But nobody jumped him. He comforted himself with the rhythmic back-and-forth of Damo's loom, weaving quietness. Thoughts rose and sank like animals that rose from the underbrush to stare, but not to pursue him. Pillbug. Ellie. Ellie's mouth.

A warp thread broke. He cursed.

Night came. Tass did not lie next to him. Raím slept as if on hunter's watch, waking each time a sleeper turned, a dog went in or out.

Nothing happened. Morning came. No one spoke to him. The air around him was empty, as though no one dared enter that space. When the day was well begun he said to the emptiness, loudly, "Tass. Will you lead me to Ta Ba's house? Please."

A silence. Then Tass said, "After you swim."

"I've been discourteous. I should have gone to her—"

"After you swim. You like to swim. I'll lead you." A silence. "We can go now."

Raím was so grateful to be spoken to that he said, "Yes, please. Thank you." Everyone had stopped talking to listen; he felt like an idiot. Tass brought him his staff, let Raím touch his elbow as they walked.

Raím said, "Yesterday. Sorry I was rough."

"No matter."

"I was—" He was on the brink of telling Tass what it felt like to be called beggar, blind, incapable. But Tass would think him stupider still; he said nothing.

The pond smelled damp and fresh. Again Tass took him round to the shore near the ledgy stone, and said, "I'll fetch you later."

Raím gripped his arm a moment. "Thank you." For the risk of comradeship, however slight, the touch of a hand. Perhaps he could learn to make love to Tass after all? He did not think so. "Wrestle with me. I promise I'll keep my temper."

"Hmh," said Tass. But he did not say no. His footsteps faded on the path.

It was enough. The sun burned through the mist in patches. Raím swam out and back, out and back, then followed the goat smell to shore and struck out along it to find the ledgy stone. There he sat naked on the verge, his back against the rock, and felt the sun.

He was almost happy. A bird he did not know whistled in the forest, a little wind blew, and every now and then a shower of pine needles trickled into his hair.

He brushed them out. More fell. He brushed them out again, stretched his arms. More needles; a pine cone.

"Damn," he said. Heard her chuckle, there above his head.

From sheer habit he looked up. A pine cone fell into his open mouth. As casually as he could manage while spitting, he bent his head so she would not see his enormous grin.

She tickled the back of his neck with a twig. He ignored it, panicked with delight. She dropped pine cones, one after the other. He shook his head, pulled his shoulders away from the stone and said, "The children here are a nuisance. I'll go."

"You'll miss something good." It was Ellie, all right.

"What might that be?"

"I haven't thought of it yet. Stay, while I think."

"I've no patience."

"Wait! I've thought of it. I'll ask you three riddles, and if you answer right you can kiss me."

"And if I answer wrong?"

"Then *I'll* kiss *you.*"

"That sounds fair."

"All right. Here's the first one."

> Sweet girl in a green gown,
> No prettier lady in our town.
> What am I?

Raím thought. "A daisy."

"No! Me, in Mari's overskirt. You've lost already, and I've won."

"No fair. I can't see colors."

"That's so. Another riddle, then." She thought.

> Soft as a rose cheek,
> Round as the moon,
> Warm as a puppy—
> Taste me soon!
> What am I?

"A peach," said Raím.

"A *peach!*" She pelted him with cones. "It's a mouth. *My* mouth."

"I like peaches."

"And not me?"

"Compared to a peach?"

She hit him with the twig. "One more, to be fair. This one is easy. Listen."

> Press at my secret gate,
> Knock early, knock late,
> Press harder, leap through!
> What am I? I dare you!

Raím turned his face up to her. To hide his blind eyes he covered them with his hands, as though this were hide-and-seek. "Ah, now. I could never guess that one."

"No?" She crept down the rock a little, closer.

"Never."

"If you don't guess, no kiss at all."

"Give me a hint."

"No hints."

"Is it warm?"

She laughed.

"Is it open now?"

"Yes."

"Lean down, then, and I'll whisper."

Rustle and scratch, odor of girl and crushed mint. Curls brushed his mouth. "Tell."

He whispered.

She leaped away, laughing, slapping him with the twig. "What minds men have! No! It's the weir gate of the mill pond!"

This was where he should have leapt after her, caught her, kissed her over her false protests. And then.

Instead that stillness came upon him, that strangeness, as if everything drew into the center. He stood. She came back, flapped at his chin with the twig. "You're odd," she said. "And you're stark naked."

He woke to ordinariness, full of confusion. Forced his hands not to cover his groin. "What do you want me for? If you're just teasing me, Miss, then damn you."

"'*Miss.*'" She dusted his face. "They say you're the son of the Lord of the Ground. Where did your mother get you?"

Raím was pretty sure his mother had gotten him from his father, who looked just like him. But the Lord of the Ground was a better father to have.

"She lay with the Lord," said Ellie, "and got you. And you go about as a beggar, like the one in the song. Anni and I guessed."

So it was real. The girls here chose their lovers, Tass had said. He need do nothing; she would make of him whatever she wanted. Casually he crossed his hands in front of himself; it was necessary.

"What happened to your eyes?"

"I gave them to the Lord of the Ground."

"That's a cruel father. Would you...would you strike that bargain with a son? If it were your son?"

"Never that!"

"I want my son to be a wrestler."

His body prickled with desire. "How do you know you'd get a son?"

"I can pray for that part. It's the wrestling I can't give him." She crept close. "I promised to kiss you if you lost."

"I've lost." Laughing, he dropped his hands, opened his arms. "I've lost, lost."

She came down the bank and kissed him.

A rushing force had him. He was falling, as when he tossed away his eyes. She whispered, "Not here, not yet!"

Here. Now.

"Stop!" she cried against his mouth. Like a fool he paused, and from that least slackness of his hands she slipped like a lizard, like water between fingers. "Not on this muddy bank," she said.

"Where? Wherever you want. Ellie—"

"There, in the meadow."

"Give me your hand—"

"No! Follow me."

He followed her laughter, stumbling, crackling among the cattails. His heart and parts preceded him. The clutter of reeds changed to hummocky grass, he smelled the tang of wood smoke, horse. Where she was taking him? "*Ellie*—"

He was seized from all sides.

For a crystalline instant he thought it was she who had seized him, miraculously many-armed. He did not fight.

Then he fought like a bear taken in a net, forgetting everything, lunging in his old brute style. There were many, they had his arms and ankles, they twisted coarse sacking over his head. In a moment he lay face down in the dirt, somebody's foot on his neck.

A barking voice, Tass's. Ellie barked softly back.

"Easy as that," said Damo. He tied Raím's wrists and ankles, rolled him over.

A half-familiar voice said, "He had better be whole."

"He's whole. Only probably bent himself, falling on it."

Laughter. Through the burlap that swathed his head Raím sobbed, "*Bitch! Bitch!*"

"She's my girl," said Tass.

"My sister," said Damo, and kicked Raím in the ribs.

"Whole," said the cheerful voice.

"Mucking about, you," said Damo. "Fucking foreigner, pissing on our rites, got the devil helping you, lusting after our women. Now you're a slave. Hope you like it."

"Tass—" said Raím.

"Go," said Tass. "Maybe you'll belong there, wherever they take you."

That was all. Raím was rolled to and fro, inspected, muttered over in an unintelligible tongue. Hoisted, tossed onto something scratchy. Quiet voices, the clink of coin.

"Done," said Damo. "Ellie, here's your share."

"I don't want it."

"Take it! Offer it to the Mother."

Tass said, "Come away."

What Raím lay on began to jolt and creak. "His stick!" said a child's voice. "Gya! Go get his stick!"

The aspen staff clattered into the cart. Raím said, "*Nine!*"

Scrabbles, clambering, a soft thump. "You're ours, you old Flea Butt," she said, bouncing on him. "We bought you."

12

The steam at the kettle's spout,
The flame at the candle's wick,
Rest on an emptiness
Invisible, quick.
The word at the poet's lip,
The line at the painter's brush,
Rest on an emptiness.

Hush.

Shrine poem. Welling-in-the-Mountains.

"Surprise!" said Nine. "Told you there'd be one!"

It was not to him she spoke. Bound hand and foot, Raím lay face down on rugs—the same rugs as before, for they smelled of wet babies. A voice he could not place said, in accented Plain, "But he never said yes!"

"In Ten Orchards. You heard him. Say yes to the Roadsouls, you can't unsay it."

Roadsouls. That at last he could name his tormentors changed nothing. He panted through the burlap that wrapped his head, as if to draw in light and reason. His cheek, his knees, his knuckles bled.

Nine bounced. "We paid *money* for you," she said, to him this time. "Not a pig, even. Real gold, that Farki keeps in his belt."

The burlap was pulled away. He turned his face to one side and could breathe, but not think, not feel. The cart lurched. Low murmur of voices, odor of babies and rosemary and dust.

As before, a tribe of toddlers had been set to play on the floor. They made a mountain of him, creeping, tumbling, poking their fingers in his ear.

He gave a grunt of rage. Thrashed and heaved as much as he could, which was not much. A child bumped its head and wept; the rest fled.

For a minute or two he was left alone, king of babies. Then the caravan stopped. He was lifted, still in his bonds, placed sitting on the back platform of the cart, and tied there, wrapped in the comforter with only his head free. The cart jerked, rolled on.

Above his head Nine said, "Old Flea Butt, he sure knows how to make it hard."

He thought how hard he would make it for anybody who touched him, if his hands were free. Dust smoked up from the track. At first he pushed his face into the quilt. Then he gave up and hung in his bonds, swaying with the motion of the cart, and ceased to think at all.

A low voice, the foreign one. A girl's. "Beggar," it said.

He ignored it.

Soft, as if it were a secret: "Beggar. Are you thirsty?"

Then Nine's voice, penny-bright: "He knows how to ask for water."

"*I* am asking." Low but firm—angry, even. He thought of a bobcat kit he had taken from the den of its dead mother, darling as a kitten; it had bitten his thumb to the bone. "Beggar. I can reach you with the ladle. Do you want water?"

What did he want?

To be free. To see. What good was water? He turned his face away.

153

Above his head Nine said, "Show you what works better."

From nowhere, from the heavens, a bucketful of cold water burst over him. He straightened, sputtered, cursed, struggled in his bonds. The babies laughed, the world smelled of wet dust, of rain.

The soft, resolute voice attached a name to itself: Pillbug. It said, "You Souls have never been so cruel to me."

Nine set down the bucket with a clatter. "You ain't him."

At last the afternoon went chill. The wagons stopped. Sounds of making camp. When the men came to untie him, he fought them, one to six. They pinned him, tied him again, and bound him to a tree without even the comforter. Snugly, so that he could not hurt himself.

Smoky fire, dinner smells. Nine came to stand in front of him and said through her full mouth, "You want something to eat? Notice I'm asking, even."

He would not answer.

"You sure are a stinker." She went off, returned with the comforter, and tucked it around him. Gave him a wet kiss on one eye. "G'night, brother."

He sat like stone. Roast goat, songs and foreign laughter; then only the wind in the trees. The place where Nine had kissed him felt sticky and stiff.

He wept. At last he fell asleep.

ⓢ

He woke so cold he thought he was dead. When the men came to loose him, he could barely move his mouth. They must have been concerned for their investment, for they carried him to sit between two fires, still tied, but with his hands free. From beyond grabbing range they passed him a mug of soup. He took it, and burned his mouth.

When he had finished it Nine brought more, standing well away. "I ain't coming near you when your hands are out," she said.

"I won't hurt you. But I'll kill the rest of those dogs. I'll break their backs."

"They'll keep you tied, then, and you'll wet yourself."

In the end it was this near humiliation that brought him to say to the invisible world, "Loose me. Please. I won't fight."

Someone said, "Swear on your manhood," and a laugh went round. But they half loosed him and led him into the woods on a leash, then gave him a hunk of bread and cheese. They tethered him with four lassoes around his waist, slip-woven so there were no knots he could untie. It was how one staked a mad bull; his vanity made the bread taste better. The sun came up, a blessing.

A man's quiet voice: "Are you fighting?"

"No."

"What if I loose you?"

"I won't fight."

The voice was not far off the ground: a small man. One after another the ropes slacked, fell at his feet. Raím stroked his hands down his body, once, to be sure they were gone. "Who are you?" he said.

"Farki."

"Farki, then." He rolled into Farki like a mudslide.

There was a brief, liquid confusion. Something came back at him—not a man's body, for Farki barely touched him, yet he was lifted, spun like a ring on a stick, hung in midair, and abandoned. He fell like a rock, onto his back.

No breath. No thought. Pain, air returning in sips. Roar of laughter and comment. Of admiration, probably not for himself.

"Ah." Farki's voice had a smile in it. As if he dressed a baby he tugged the ropes over Raím's head to his waist, then tied his wrists. Raím did not try to stop him. Farki said, "The daylight's in you somewhere, and the night, and all the stars."

Sound of carts being packed. Men pulled Raím's stakes and led him to the wagon. "Untie my hands?" he said.

Laughter.

"I swear I won't fight. I swear on—" He laughed bitterly. "There's nothing to swear on."

"That's so." They sounded cheerful. They tied his legs and arms and sat him outside again, on the wagon's stepped back porch. He could just rub his face on his shoulder. The wagon jerked, rolled.

Nine leaned out the window above his head. "You were pretty," she said.

He said nothing.

"Flea Butt. You were *sweet,* the way you came at Farki. Like a wave on the ocean."

"Shut up."

"Sha'n't. How'd you learn to fight so pretty?"

"I'm not pretty. Leave me, you little blowfly."

Nine began to sing, flapping him with something, perhaps a jump rope. The song was about a bad pig. Each verse ended with a flap and the shout, "*Sow!*"

He could be a martyr about pain, but not this. "Get away! If I could lay hands on you—"

"You can't, though. What's happened to you? Old Pillbug here's got brave, but you've got nastier. I said you were a pretty wrestler. Farki's took to you."

So the rosemary girl must be there, watching this. "He took me down," said Raím.

"'Course he did. He's the best in the world, and knows the best. We were passing Mosquito Palace—that's what we call that village—and Farki sees two men wrestling by the pond. 'There's a good one,' he says. 'By life! It's that beggar took such a long shit in the woods. Maybe he's for sale.'"

"For sale!"

"Everybody is. Find out the price, is all."

"What's Farki want with me?"

"A couple of our lads got hurt, and he doesn't want to fight all the townies himself. Wish I was big, I'd do it."

"What townies? What for?"

"I think it's your *mind* that's blind. For money. At the fair. Comes a big bumpkin like them that sold you, he's cock of the hen yard, got to show off for his girl so he says, 'Bet you three coppers I can ground that sorry Roadsoul!' Then Farki lays him out. But Farki doesn't want to do it all, so it's to be you."

Raím rubbed his chin on his shoulder.

"I'll make you a name, like I did for Pillbug." Nine flapped him with the rope while she thought. "Here's you: Bad Blood the Blind Maniac, Eats Human Flesh."

"Go get Farki. Tell him I'll fight."

"Like you get to choose!"

"Go tell him."

"There's a word I ain't hearing."

"Please."

"You're welcome. Can't tell him," said Nine. "Not till we stop for the night. *Sow!*" She flapped him with the rope.

Pillbug's voice, clear and low. "Stop that."

"How come?"

"It's cruel. Leave him alone."

"Well, ain't you the queen." Nine leaned down to Raím's ear. "Pillbug says I ought to stop being cruel to you."

"Pillbug can go to hell, and take you with her."

"*Sow!*"

So the day went on.

⦿

That night's camp was among pines resiny with the heat of the afternoon. When the fires were lit, Raím was brought to Farki, surrounded, and untied.

Farki was indeed small. When Raím held his arm out straight Farki could walk under it, singing under his breath.

> It's kiss and be kind to me, maidens of morning,
> Kiss and be kind to me, maidens of day.

Raím was starving, sullen, his skin prickling under the stares of the spectators he could hear all around him. Most comments were in the tongue he supposed was Roadsoul, but some were in Plain.

"He's too long in the leg, Farki."

"Bred mean, like Ari's hound."

Farki continued to sing. To Raím he said, "Do you know how to fall?"

A harsh laugh. "Oh yes!"

Farki said, "Lift me, then."

"What?"

"Seize me and lift me."

Raím hesitated. But hadn't he walked into the cave when the bear was in it? He found Farki with his ears, then his hands. Farki simply stood. Raím took him round the middle—the barrel chest and thick, soft waist of an older man—and wrenched him into the air.

Farki did not leave the ground.

Raím wrestled, panting. Farki was stuck to the earth. Raím thought he must be tied there, and felt his ankles for the rope. The watchers laughed.

Farki put out a short, thick arm and nudged Raím with it. "Pull me over your shoulder."

Raím pondered. An idea opened like a flower: how he had wrestled with Tass as both man and woman. He seized Farki's wrist and swung softly round. Farki came unstuck. Raím dragged him over his back, Farki came as though weightless, sailing through the air.

"Ground!" said Raím. Then, "Ah—" as he in turn was weightless, then stone. He landed hard, rolled into somebody's legs.

"Those bumpkins will break you," said Farki as Raím rubbed his butt. "You were not falling. You were standing sideways in the air, praising yourself. Get up now, and fall."

Raím got up and, at Farki's hand, fell. Fell again. And again. As often as he fell, Farki said he was not falling. And Farki did not tire.

Nor did the onlookers—young men, by their voices, and some women. Nine yelled, "Go, Flea Butt!"

He lost his temper. Farki threw him harder. He despaired. Farki threw him harder still.

Before each throw, Farki had begun to speak. Brief words: "Drop it." "Open." "Die." Raím thought they were curses, but spoken so quietly they sounded like instructions.

He could understand if Farki wanted him to die. It was a fight, wasn't it? But why would Farki buy him, then kill him? Well, he would not be killed. Next round, as they groveled in the sand, he rolled over and drove his fist at Farki's mouth.

The fist did not arrive. It was taken like a baby's hand, and Raím pulled after it until he was face down with Farki's knee on his neck and his arm twisted half off his body. He cried out.

Farki said, "What do you lust with?"

Raím panted.

"You in particular," the quiet voice answered itself, "lust with a cudgel. And cudgels break." He released Raím's arm and walked away.

The lads came forward and replaced Raím's tethers. They sat him on a box and put bread into his hands. He ate. Heard a small baby's coo and cry. Somewhere across the fire Nine chattered, not to him. He wished Brook were there to fall against his ankles.

There was a step soft as Brook's, and a mug of wine nudged his hand. Odor of rosemary: Pillbug, come back from the hell he had wished her in.

He wanted to say, *Forgive me for cursing you.* Too worn to get the words out. Said, "Thanks."

"You're welcome."

ᕙ

That night they tied him in the puppy cart. The puppies were bigger already and made better cover. He did not want the dreaming night to end, did not want to wake to himself, filthy and sore and the same person he had been when he fell asleep.

In the morning the caravan did not pack and move. Farki untied him, saying, "Up, and to the ground."

Raím crept out of the cart and to the wrestling ground, where he was thrown and told to die until breakfast. After breakfast he was thrown some more, tethered to doze until the afternoon, roused, and thrown.

As an experiment he said to Farki, "Thank you."

"You're welcome," said Farki, and threw him again.

Farki was little and dark, with bow legs and short-fingered hands. The beggar was long and big-shouldered, and rage smoked off him like a torch flame, yet each time he tried to close on Farki something happened that Duuni did not understand.

They had camped for some days in that spot, a black-earth meadow with no view but up at the mountain. The wrestlers and Dicey nursed their hurts. Duuni was not afraid of Dicey any more; he had a pet raccoon and a bad back, and had given her the urda press to keep. Auntie had given her flint and steel in a sash pouch, and a little knife so many times sharpened there was hardly any blade left. Sleepy and Shine had brought her a red silk skirt, laughing because it went twice round her slender waist. There were dry branches to gather for the fire, clothes to be mended, bread to be baked in the cast iron kettles. Skinny little Bones had learned to laugh.

The older lads went hunting, without much success. It was the children who set snares for birds, deadfalls for squirrels, and little nets for rabbits, and came back with their bags full. Nine could catch trout with her bare hands; she caught a bag full of

160

grasshoppers, pinched each one behind the head, and roasted them in the ashes. Duuni went with her on her hunts, learning the mountain world. She gathered seeds and wild roots; those she would eat, and squirrels and fish and even little birds, though she felt sorry for them, but she would not eat grasshoppers.

Nine offered some to Flea Butt, still tethered like a bull. He cursed. "Townies," she said to Duuni, munching. "Both of you. They taste like pork cracklings."

All this; and yet. Asked anything directly, the Roadsoul-born rarely answered. When they did it might be with a joke, a song, a look; or they might answer in Roadsoul. Their names were music: Noonday and Faraway, Sila, Willow, Lea. But sometimes their names changed; Shine and Sleepy traded theirs back and forth the way they swapped their flamboyant shirts and stockings.

Of the Roadsoul world Duuni learned little, and that mostly from Nine. You stayed with your parents until you were twelve, perhaps; then you were given to a relative to travel and learn, while your parents took in a side-sib. Shine and Sleepy lived with aunts or second cousins, worked with the rest, then lolled and strolled and flirted with the boys.

Duuni did not join them. She did not know how to flirt.

As for Tam Chivi, with him she grew shyer and shyer. She could not look at him if he might see her looking; when he did catch her glance she blushed till she thought she would faint. He said little. He was not for speaking with but looking at, beautiful as the mountain. On his tall black mare he began to ride into her dreams.

Of the beggar she did not dream. Around his waist, above the snake tattoo, Farki had clasped an iron band with a chain to it. His hair grew matted, his beard thick. For him there was no featherbed, only a heap of straw and the filthy quilt; but the puppies liked him. She heard him whisper, to no one, *You think my life is worth living?*

Her own life had begun to be real, though so different from her life in Alikyaan that sometimes she woke in the night thinking she had died and was living some other person's life.

Still, her greatest trouble was the lion.

At the Greencliff fair she had been so busy and frightened that she could ignore the painted lion, now barely visible on the canvas of the newie wagon. The dusty cloth had taken on the color of the earth the caravan rolled over, red or yellow or black. Anyway, she tried not to look; but here in the meadow the dew darkened it, wind blew the dust away. She had time to remember Tumiin, to grow frightened all over again.

One night, the fourth or fifth in that camp, a shadow blinked between her eyes and the lion's. For a moment she thought the blind man had stood up beside the wagon, but there had been no clank of chains, he was a quilt-shrouded lump. It was Nine, weaseling under the comforter between her and Toady. When she had plastered herself to Duuni she said, "Farki says you're going to paint that lion for him."

"*What?*"

"You're going to paint a new one."

"I never said that!"

"He never asked you. You just do what he says, because Farki's in it."

"In *what?*"

"In what there is," said Nine. "The river. That's why old Flea Butt can't lay a hand on him." She played with one of Duuni's curls, pulled it straight, let it go. "If you don't know the river, how come you can draw so good?"

"I just draw."

"You're in the river, that's how." Nine chewed the end of the curl and painted Duuni's cheek with it. "Farki says when somebody's in the river they say, 'The god came into me.' But the god was there all the time, they just got out of their own way for once."

"But that lion was *magic*," said Duuni. "The way it...in Alikyaan—"

"*Townie.*" In a whisper: "Townie, townie, townie!" Poking her with each word.

"I am not a townie any more!"

"You are. *Magic* is townie. Like that Doctor Amu, he says he'll cure them with magic and they give him their coin," said Nine. "Old Flea Butt, he could pay Amu a lord's gold ducats and he'd still be blind as a shoe. And he ain't never going to ground Farki. He's too proud to give over to the river." She yawned. Sighed.

Stars bright overhead. The lion's eyes. Nine's face open in sleep.

☙

Next morning Farki unchained the beggar, led him to the wrestling ground, and threw him. Duuni watched Farki move. It was indeed like watching the water of the river. Sometimes the beggar moved like the river, too; more often he looked like a man trying to ford it and falling in.

She went to the newie wagon and stared at the lion. She saw that behind it a painted river ran, empty and blue. There were a few reeds and cattails, a river poplar. Cautiously she laid her hand on a faded blue pool; her fingers came away silvered, as if with fish scales.

"So," said Farki.

She whirled where she stood, her arms across her breasts. He stood close. She was blind with fright; then, as if she leapt from a cliff and had one word before she struck earth, she said, "*No.*"

"No?" He inclined his head. Turned, and left.

She sank against the cart. She would be beaten, driven away. Then, with a jink of metal, he was back—but only to lock the slave ring round the beggar's waist and chain him to the axle.

With his bowlegged stride Farki returned to the campfire. Duuni panted. The beggar turned toward the soft sound of her breath. His face was filthy, determined, without hope.

She touched the lion's paw, brought her hand away sparkling with the fish-scale paint. Said to the beggar, "I do not...I don't remember your name."

He jumped, as though the wind had spoken. "Flea Butt."

"Your real name."

"Flea Butt."

"My name is Duuni."

Two breaths. "Farki bought you?"

"No."

"You're his bitch, then. Don't talk to me."

She said, "You don't know who I am."

He straightened as if she had slapped him. Asked coarsely if Farki used her for sex.

"No."

He put his hand over his eyes. She thought it strange a blind man would do that. He said, "I don't know what I have become. My name is Raím. Get away from me. Whatever I touch is destroyed."

She had not been going to touch him. She had not been going to touch the lion, either, yet her hand gleamed with the paint of its faded pelt, and nothing had happened. *I stroked the lion.* It was the same red color as the beggar. As Raím.

She said, "I'm going to paint the wagon. Whether you are here or not makes no difference."

For it was not Farki who wanted her to paint the lion. It was the lion.

⟁

Raím said nothing more, nor did he raise his face from his hand. Duuni went looking for Farki.

Most of the camp were gone, hunting or wood-gathering or bathing in the creek. Farki was splitting wood. His axe rose, then fell. Between the rise and the fall there was a pause, slight, the pause a flying bird makes as it turns here, turns there.

She moved where he would see her from the tail of his eye. The axe finished its swing, the wood flew apart into billets. He picked them up and stacked them. Turned to Duuni, inclined his head.

There was an instant like the flying bird's, when she knew it was her body that was afraid—of being hit, groped, raped. She caught up the hem of her tunic and wrung it in her hands. "I'll paint it."

He nodded. "Nine will bring you the paint."

"But I only know how to draw. Not colors."

He looked at her.

"All right," she said. "Thank you."

A nod, a quirk of his mouth. He turned back to the round he was to split. Raised the axe; brought it down. Two billets. Stacked.

She watched him swing twice more. Then she went back to the lion and looked at what she had said yes to. The beggar still sat with his hand over his eyes. She did not speak to him. In Alikyaani *raiim* meant primrose, a lovely name for a girl.

 Morning, the bustling camp. Still in his mind was how he had behaved toward that girl. He cringed from himself, foul and listless in the puppy straw.

"Up, and fall," said Farki.

Raím did not move. Farki went away.

Nine came. She tugged at his chain, poked him with her toe. "Are you dead? How come you won't play with Farki?"

"He wants me dead."

"No, he doesn't. You cost more than a cow."

"He keeps telling me to die."

"Better die, then. Since he says to." She went away.

Raím sat up stiffly. Said to the air, "I'm not dying for that bugger."

Immediately Farki was there. "Drop your cudgel," he said.

"I have no cudgel."

"No?"

"Go to hell."

Farki stood at the wagon wheel. "Cudgels break. Die, and drop it. Then maybe"—Raím heard his grin—"maybe, someday, you will ground me. For a moment." He began to walk away. Stopped. Said, "What were you before you were a beggar?"

"Hunter," said Raím. "Weaver."

"Now totally blind?"

"Yes."

"I spent my money well," said Farki. He slapped the wagon's flank and left.

The puppies stuck their noses in Raím's armpits. Nine came back and dumped a clinking heap of something onto the ground. "You stink," she said.

"Let me wash in the creek."

"You'd run off. Maybe Pillbug'd bring you a bucket of water, if you're nice."

He half rose. "*I am not nice!*"

"Maybe she'd bring it anyway, before you smell so bad we got to burn the wagon. There she is. Pillbug! Old Flea Butt wants something. I made you a sandwich, even, it's in the box with the other stuff." She scampered off.

Raím sank back. Felt his own blush—of rage, he told himself. Except that he must stink indeed, for he had not smelled rosemary at all. But there was another smell. He said, "Gods, what's that stench?"

"Paint." Another cluttery sound of things being set down: metal, glass.

"Something's dead. What...what did you say your name was?"

"Duuni."

"I'm ashamed of what I said to you. Yesterday."

Silence.

"But it's true whatever I touch is ruined."

Silence.

"And I don't like women."

She said, "I was watching. When they caught you by the pond." He put his face in his hands. She said, "Nine said you wanted something?"

"Water to wash in."

She went away, came back with a bucket of lukewarm water. He remembered to thank her. He had to wash with her right there; his embarrassment made him angrier still. But soft scuffs, rattles and clinks told him she was going on with whatever she was doing, as if she paid him no attention at all. He felt insulted.

The usual clot of children formed around her. They had been warned away from him, for they did not clamber and use him as a vantage point. He leaned against the wheel, damp and lonely, while to his left some process went on that smelled like rotting fish.

The children gabbled in their tongue. Sometimes they said, "What's that?" or "Aaa!" The girl Duuni did not answer, and in a while they went off to be noisy somewhere else. Adults paused, murmured, left. He might have thought Duuni, too, had gone, if it were not for a light, almost soundless rasp. He thought of the scutch and thump of Ta Ba's loom. Once Duuni laughed to herself. Sometimes she spoke softly in a tongue he did not know.

He cleared his throat twice. "Duuni."

No answer. He subsided into gloom.

She murmured foreign words. Then, aloud, "Don't bother me."

He ought to have felt as lonely as before. Lonelier. But he knew what it was like to be so intent on his weaving that he could not talk. He crossed his arms on his knees, felt the sun, and smelled her invisible work.

She did not begin by painting the lion. True, it had summoned her; but she held the brush.

She frowned at the faint tracing for a long time. She knew nothing about color. Except embroidery, and threshold charms drawn in colored sand, and icing on cakes, and the Unclothed Gods on patio walls...well, maybe she knew a little. She would draw over the ghostly line with black paint, then fill in the colors.

One line framed the painting like a cage. She would paint that first. But the lion's paw broke it in one place, its tail in another; it did not keep the lion in. Well, she thought, I'll paint the grass on the riverbank.

Nine had brought a bundle of brushes wrapped in an old shawl, paint in tins and crusty bottles. Duuni put on Nightweaver's apron and filched a battered pie pan to mix the colors in. When she uncorked the first bottle, it smelled so horrible she thought there must be devils in it. The paint was oily, with that fish-scale sheen, and when she tried a stroke it lay on the canvas as if it had always been there.

She began to paint the grass. It looked like brittle black sticks. She panicked, uncorked a bottle of silvery green and painted over and in between the lines. That was better: not so stiff. The paint dried quickly. By shifting back and forth between the black and the green she could make the line look soft.

It was like spring coming. She painted green leaves on the gray-trunked poplars. Behind her the children squealed at the paint smell, nudged and talked. She did not answer them or let them put their fingers in the paint, and after a while they left. Sometimes an older person stopped to watch in silence, then moved on. Perhaps Farki had ordered that she not be disturbed.

If she looked at the canvas sideways she could make out the old painting. At first she thought she would follow what was there, just brighten it. But she began to think about blackbirds.

Under the poplars of her own river, there had been male blackbirds that clung sideways to the reeds, full of themselves, flashing their red wing blazes, singing so loud they were yelling. Now, because he ought to be there, she painted a blackbird clutching a reed with his wiry feet, his braggart head cocked sideways.

That little change could do no harm. Anyway it was half hidden. From the edge of her eye she saw Raím, his braggart head cocked at the same angle. She laughed softly, the way you do when something comes just right.

She painted the sky; the silvery blue paint was perfect. But the sky was too empty. On her riverbank beetles had blundered in the grass, snakes glided like the river current, ducks upended their foolish bottoms. The lion that sprang from the grass should be part of that world, woven into it.

"I am to paint the wagon," she said aloud in Alikyaani. "Therefore I shall paint it." In the sky she painted two cranes, legs trailing. Peeping from the grass, a rabbit. She began on the blue water.

A voice said, "Duuni."

She thought it was her own voice, somehow speaking from outside herself, and answered in Alikyaani: "River, o river." Then she knew someone else had spoken. Without turning her head she said in Plain, "Don't bother me." She was painting a fish, and its eye would not come right. There would be other fish in the river, dark muddlers at the bottom, but one could not see those. She painted a patch of riverbank earth with a turtle on it. Then a dragonfly. Sunlight crept along the canvas.

Her back hurt. She blinked, stretched, looked around. The camp was all but deserted. Away off, a man sat on a stump, mending a boot; he caught her eye, then deliberately turned away.

She stood back to look at what she had done. There was the bright world, squirming, splashing, shining. In the middle of it all, empty canvas, was the space where she must paint the lion.

She mixed red-gold paint. Raised the brush.

Suddenly she was hungry. She could not possibly paint the lion until she ate lunch. Especially since nothing else was left to paint.

She rinsed the brushes in pine-smelling turpentine and fetched Nine's sandwich from the shade under the cart. Someone was still in the world with her: Raím, sitting against the cart-wheel in a cat trance. His ribs barely moved.

No one had brought *him* anything to eat. Duuni unwrapped her sandwich from its cloth. It had been cut in half. She was starving.

"Raím."

He stirred. Arched his back.

"Would you like half a sandwich?"

That arrogant head. "It's yours."

She would not waste time arguing with a blackbird chained to his reed. In a different voice she said, "Therefore it is mine to offer."

He turned his face to her. She wondered whether blind people saw anything at all; if they dreamed. In a surly voice he said, "Thank you, then." He put out his hand.

She gave him half. She would have liked to move away from the paint stink, but that would be rude, since he could not. They ate in silence. She had never taken a meal alone with a man, certainly never with a man clothed only in shackles and a blue snake.

He ate his half in snaps, like a dog. She ate slowly; at least he could not stare at her like a dog while she finished her half. She did not want to look at the lion, but she had to, more worried with each glance. The lion was the reason for the painting. Nine said it did not have magic—yet it had something, some god thing. Else how could it have killed Tumiin? And here she was, with stinking paint in crusty bottles, thinking to paint a god.

"You're painting."

It was Raím's voice. She said, "Yes."

She waited for him to ask what she was painting and why, all the things people ask. He did not. She said, "The paint on the wagon is faded. I am brightening it."

He nodded. Her bites of sandwich got smaller and smaller. She could not make it last forever. She had to look at that blank place in the shining world.

She had painted all around the lion; she could not paint the lion. What would happen when Farki came back and found the ruin she had made of his god work? And he would see what she had put in without leave, blackbird and turtle and fish. She had disobeyed.

She would leave the lion until tomorrow.

Tomorrow it would be worse. She would never paint the lion. She would leave the cart half painted, spoiled. Farki...

She must run away. She jumped up, all body, no thought.

"I have ears," said Raím. He too stood, at the limit of his chain. "What's the matter?"

"I can't paint a lion."

She had not meant to speak. She covered her mouth.

"You're talking like one of *them*," he said. "What lion?"

Through her hand she said, "The...you can't see it."

He hooked his thumbs over the iron around his naked hips as though it were a sash. "By ashes, you little chit—I can't see bloody anything!"

She looked from him to the lion-shaped hole on the canvas and back again. With her hand still over her mouth, she laughed.

It came out as a chirp. He looked bewildered. That made it funnier. It was not fair to laugh when he had no idea, nor did she know why she was laughing in the first place.

"What's so funny? Tell me."

"That you can't see it!"

"That's funny?" But he was grinning, his teeth white in his awful beard. "By the gods, I should be laughing all the time."

"It's...I could ruin it, and to you it would look—"

"—just fine. Yes. Lions, turds, sunsets—all the same. It simplifies life." The bitterness was back, yet still he grinned. "I thought you were painting the wagon." He made an up-and-down gesture, painting a wall. "You're painting *things*?"

"Things." Oh, that lion! Even faded, it shone its truth. "A lion. If I paint it I'll spoil it. And I must paint it—"

"I'll watch. If you start to spoil it I'll say, *Duuni, stop.*"

For an instant that was funnier still. Then it changed to something mad, perfect. "All right." She mixed the paint again, red gold. Raím sat facing her, his eyes open. They were blue. Maybe it *was* the lion they saw, that part of the lion not made of stinking paint.

He heard the first brush stroke, for he said, "Beautiful so far."

It was not beautiful. Her hand shook. The power of the lion would run up the brush and strike her, as it had Tumiin. A fat black dribble ran down and blotted out the turtle's head. The painting was ruined.

Raím said nothing.

Duuni kept painting.

Little by little her hand grew steady. She forgot anyone might be watching, forgot anyone would ever see it. She served the lion; there was nothing of her in it at all.

She did not follow the faded lines. On one soft paw she painted claws curving the way a cat's do when she stretches. She painted the swelling muscles hidden by the fur; she did not know how they ought to be, so she let the lion decide. The mouth with its teeth and red tongue, snarling or yawning. Delicate whiskers, black blazes on the bright face. Last of all, she painted the eyes, looking at her, black and gold.

She wiped the brush. Inside of one breath she was so weary she could not bear herself.

The sun had dropped. Raím sat in shadow now, his chin on his fist. Now and then, a blink of his strange eyes. She cleared her throat.

"Done?" he said.

"Yes."

"It's perfect."

"Thank you."

She should wash the brushes. Soon the camp would return, and Farki. She went close to Raím. She was afraid he would grab her wrist, and then, and then; but she touched the edge of her hand to his fisted one.

He opened his hand and held it upright as if in greeting. She set her hand against his. He pushed lightly; she pushed back.

He dropped his hands to the slave ring. "Gods, you stink of paint. That rosemary was reek enough."

❧

To draw, to paint—that makes something visible. One would think, then, she would want to look at what she had done. Would want others to look at it.

She could not get away from that painting fast enough. With her back to the wagon she cleaned the brushes and laid them with the paint jars, did not take leave of Raím or even pull off her apron, but walked uphill into the pine woods, fast, wiping her hands on her thighs.

She had thought to go just a little way. But each tree called her on to another tree, beyond each rise was a higher rise. She climbed among pine and scrub oak, among sandstone boulders fallen from the cliffs, treading the sand that had weathered off them. Drifted oak leaves crackled underfoot. A stillness flowed down from the hills.

She looked back. Far below in the lengthening shadows the camp sprawled, threads of smoke rose from banked fires. There was the wagon. She was too far away to see the painting, only that it was bright, a poppy in a dry field. Beside it, the same fire color, shone the tiny dot that was Raím's hair.

She climbed on. She could no longer see the camp.

Beneath a high gold cliff she was stopped by the stillness. Of the forest, the mountain, like someone deep in sleep. At the cliff's foot lay a little field of sand. A deer trail led across it, side to side, but the wind had smoothed it; the sand was as unmarked as the moment the world was born.

She wanted to go on. Just go, as a bird flies over water, finding no branch to rest on. She thought, This is how Raím ran away. He walked until he was out of sight, and then kept still.

She closed her eyes and laid her cheek against the stone of the cliff, still warm from the setting sun. Shadows crept up. A ghost of damp rose, and from the valley a breath so slight she felt it only on the hairs of her face. A grain of sand fell from the cliff like a dry raindrop, to join the trackless sand below.

On the deer trail a twig snapped. Into that quiet, the lion came.

She did not look. She did not need to. With her eyes closed she heard the cat step, heavy and light. No other creature walks like that. It came six steps onto the clearing. Stopped.

She did not move, waiting for her death. No fear. No thought. Without seeing she saw the lion's eyes as she had painted them, gold under the frowning brows, each iris a crescent like the moon. The lion bared its teeth. She had a jumbled thought of Siibi, blood. Then she knew it was doing what a cat does, drawing back its lips at the smell of something it does not know.

She did not move. Heard it turn and pad back the way it had come, along the deer trail into the woods.

The stillness flowed back. Her heart, suddenly frantic as prey, was the only moving thing. She opened her eyes, turned her head, and saw the paw prints, round as saucers, pressed into the sand.

She slid down the rock, crouched against it. Every voice in her cried *Run!* But her legs would not move. She waited. The lion did not come back. Her mind came alive again and said, *Don't run.*

She walked back the way she had come. It took one thousand years. The world was almost dark; each breath was her last before the lion should leap on her back. When she came into the circle of firelight her legs went strange, she had to sit on a log and hug her elbows.

She had forgotten the painting. She thought the glances, nods, and slight smiles from the Souls were because she was acting oddly, until the shrieking flock of children found her.

"*Eee!*" Nine tugged her to her feet. "That lion, it's so good it's *bad!* Our Toady screamed, he says it's looking at him and I said get over it, it's Pillbug's, but he wet his britches. Where were you? We thought you ran off like old Flea Butt."

"I took a walk."

"In the *dark*? Get eaten by beasts and deserve it. Farki likes that lion. He likes the fish and things, the turtle." She snuffed heartily. "You smell like that paint. Can I have some on me?"

⑥

Farki only nodded, with the little grimace that was neither smile nor scowl. "That's right work," he said.

She had not gone to him for praise. The lion on the mountain had made human praise something different, and less. She went because she had disobeyed him by changing the painting, and would not hide. Her voice shook, her eyes would not stay on his; but there is fear and fear.

He said only, "Plenty of wagons to paint in this world," and turned again to the iron rim he was knocking onto a wheel.

She put the babies to bed in the eiderdowns and thought about the other side of the canvas canopy. As far as she could tell, it had never been painted. She thought, I could paint a meadow with all the small creatures that live there, mice and rabbits and fawns, and nothing big to hurt them. It would not be the truth about how a meadow is, but a wish has its own truth.

She had said nothing about the lion on the mountain. Nine was asleep already, hugging Toady like a doll. The moon was up, and bright. By its light the painted lion looked black. So did Raím's hair. He sat against the wheel, wrapped in the torn quilt, as still as she had been on the hillside.

She went near him. Not close. He said, low, "You think I don't know who you are? Rosemary and that vile paint." She sat down just out of reach of his long arms.

Raím—I walked into the woods the way you did. The lion came. I am alive.

She did not say this. She just sat, smelling like herself.

He drew his fingers through the sand. Then, as in the afternoon, he held up his hand, flat. She came a little closer and set hers on his—sandy, cool, warming. Their palms moved together as if to invisible signals, like a flock of winter blackbirds.

He let his hand drop. "Farki likes your lion."

She said nothing. He pulled the quilt around himself. It rucked at the chain, and must surely let in the frosty air.

She went back to the eiderdown and slid in between Midge and Maidy, warm as new bread.

13

How shall I cross the river and not be changed?
You cannot cross the river and not be changed.
Nor can you stay on the bank and not be changed.
Which will you have, muscles or roots?
What will you be, doe or tree?
　　　　Skipping rhyme. The Roadsouls.

Farki pushed down on Raím's shoulders. Raím said, "I won't kneel to you."

"I too shall kneel."

Farki unlocked the slave ring, knelt, and laid his hands on Raím's, palm to palm. Raím remembered the feel, last night, of Duuni's hand on his, and pulled his hands away. Farki took them again and said, "Stay with me."

His hands moved. Raím's followed. Raím's instinct was to shove, but when he did his hands slipped off Farki's.

"Attention in your hands," said Farki.

That worked. Farki's hands made circles and zigzags. Raím's followed them, sullen. Something shifted; Raím understood that Farki's hands were asking *his* to lead. A half smile broke across his face. He scowled again, quickly. Farki chuckled.

Raím led. After that they passed the leadership back and forth, sometimes by instants. In Raím's mind images rose and passed: a river; a fish; a girl's mouth. A cudgel, hard and whole.

His hand slipped off Farki's.

"Drop it," said Farki. Half in trance, Raím dropped the image of the cudgel. Their joined hands moved on.

"Open," said Farki. His hand, bearing Raím's with it, rode gently toward Raím's chest. Raím blocked it. "Open," said Farki.

Tense, scowling, Raím let Farki's hand enter the space in front of his chest. Ashamed, as though he had surrendered. Farki's hand slowed, and Raím's was pushing it slowly out, back across Farki's guard to Farki's chest, which let it come.

"Ah—" said Raím, as the tide turned again and Farki's hand moved toward him.

"If you could understand that instant you could be king. Rise now, and fall."

Raím rose to his feet and laid his hands on Farki in the starting pose. Everything had changed. His body paid attention, as his hands had. He was so startled that Farki simply threw him down.

He got up. He tried paying attention with his feet and tripped himself up; found he had shoulders, and they stuck out all over. Then his head got in the way.

"You move like a sack of cats," said Farki.

Angry, Raím came at Farki hard—but now he could feel how brittle he was and how easily Farki broke him. That made him angrier, because unless he was hard he was not a man, and if he wasn't a man he must be a woman. So he was lumpish, and Farki thumped him; confused, and Farki took him apart. But once, by accident, he felt the moment he had felt with his hands, when Farki had passed that living leadership on to him. Even in midair, falling, he felt himself whole: a swallow scything out from its nest and home.

That evening, shivering from a scrub in the bucket, he sat chained while around him dinner was prepared. Odor of night, of wood smoke and frosty dew; somewhere a guitar rang, yearning. He thought of Ta Ba, of everything in his life unfinished, unspoken. Duuni brought him wine in a cup. Her sleeve brushed his face. Tears stung his eyes. He had to curse and bend his head to hide them.

She put a short cudgel in his hand. He dropped it. She picked it up and gave it back to him, along with a pot of potatoes to mash.

❧

Next morning Farki unlocked the chain from the slave ring. Like a sullen ox, Raím waited to be led to the wrestling ground, but Farki was gone. After a little Raím raised his arm toward the clatter of camp—uncertainly, as if his hand were an eye.

Something soft nudged his belly. Nine said, "Get dressed, you old Flea Butt. Farki wants you."

"Dressed."

The bundle she shoved at him was a tunic and sash, trousers and leggings, clout, stockings, and a pair of boots, or what was left of one. Everything was patched and mended, soft with wear. He rubbed his face on it. "Please thank Farki. Tell him I say thank you."

"*You* tell him. And don't you go losing it like last time."

He put the clothes on over the iron ring. Took two steps into the world and fell over the wagon tongue.

"Gya," said Nine. "Chain you or you kill yourself."

He got up. "Where's Farki? What am I to do?"

"Help push a wagon out of the sand. Breakfast, then we move camp." She grabbed his hand.

"Don't yank at me! Here, I'll show you how to—"

"I'll take you." Paint stink laced with bacon and smoke: Duuni. Her elbow, lively as her hand had been, nudged his palm.

Nine sang, "*Pillbug's got a sweetheart! Kiss him 'hind the newie cart...*"

Her singing trailed off. Duuni had said nothing, but Raím, a judge of sounds, read her silence as if it were words.

Nine said sulkily, "Well, *so.*"

"I have business with Farki," said Duuni.

"*Business* with *Farki.* Like you were some headwoman." Nine swung on Raím's new sash, spanked him and ran off. From a safe distance she hollered, "Look out, he falls over *everything!*"

Raím, who had dropped Duuni's elbow, said stiffly, "That's true." She guided his hand back to her arm and began to walk. He followed. He said, "That kid is terrible."

"I wish I were like her."

"*Like* her?"

"She's not afraid of anything."

"She's too young to know better."

After a long silence she said, "One can be young and afraid." He had been stupid again. He shrugged. "How old are you?"

"Seventeen."

"I'm twenty," he said, because *twenty-three* was an old man. He could not think of anything else to say. Her elbow moved away into the world. Someone grabbed him and said, "Put your shoulder here." Other bodies leaned in beside him.

One, two—hup! With a hiss and a groan the cart hove clear of the sand and rolled onto firm earth.

⟡

Squeal of axles, clang of dangling pots. He walked in the dust beside the newie cart, holding on with one hand. When it lurched, so must he, a fierce dance, for if he stumbled he would fall under the turning wheels.

Above his head Nine said, "If you get run over, Farki's out plenty cash."

He did not answer. It pleased him to be worth plenty cash. If the road smoothed out a little, Duuni might see him striding like any man.

The carts were climbing. They splashed across hasty waters that ran down from the left, escaped to the right. At these crossings he swung up and clung to the wagon side, for he could not risk his footing on the wet stones. When the sun said noon, they forded another stream and stopped.

Nine slapped his back. "Dust bag!" He beat at his new clothes, wished for lunch, and would have died before he asked. Duuni touched his hand and put half a huge sandwich in it.

"Thank you." He felt a fool, standing in the middle of the road with a sandwich. Horses trotted past.

"Better come aside." She took his elbow, steered him onto soft pine needles and—o gods!—sat down beside him. She had the other half of the sandwich. They ate in silence. He wondered how he had ever felt she did not exist; her body was as warmly present as a dog's.

He said, "Do you know where we are?"

"No."

"Could you look around and tell me what you see?"

A long silence. "We're in a meadow, by a stream. There are pine trees like pillars, very tall. To the left is the mountain, big as...as night. As day. To the right there's a break in the trees, you can see down and down, to the edge of the world. The earth there is wrinkled. It is red."

He liked the slight formality of her speech. "Are we going south?"

"South and up."

Lower, he said, "Do you know where they're taking us?"

A long pause. "No."

"These people are insane."

"No. They're not *good*." He scowled in agreement. "And they're not bad. They *are*. Like air. Or water. I don't think they have gods."

"Have to be crazy gods. That mad baiting—and Farki! You have eyes, why don't you run away?"

"I'm a girl."

She did not need to say more. If a girl were to run away alone into the big world, there was only one fate for her. As well meet it one place as another. He felt ashamed, as though he were responsible. Shifted the iron ring that galled his waist. "The place they took you from—was it bad?"

"Yes."

"Mine was not. Just—it was bad for me."

"The world is big."

"It's very small. Only what I can touch."

They sat without speaking. Clink of harness, laughter. Slap of a jump rope, children chanting.

Duuni said, "When you dream, can you see?"

"Yes."

"Then you aren't truly blind."

He groped for some bitter remark. In her careful voice she said, "In my land I would have been beaten for asking you that. Maybe killed. I have never talked to a man before. When they pulled you into the cart, when you caught my foot and I said, 'No!,' I had not spoken to a man since I was eight years old."

He sat back. "Not lads your own age?"

"No."

"Why not?"

"It was not done."

"That's insane!"

"Yes. *That* is insane."

Nine's voice came sing-shouting above the slap of the jump rope.

> Prince grabs the princess by her long black hair,
> Princess kicks the prince in his you-know-where.
> Prince can't walk, prince can't talk,
> Princess shouts, "O-U-T, out!"
> *Manners, boys!*

Duuni said, "I've been wondering—"

He waited to hear what she wondered. Seventeen, and never spoke to a man! It made him nervous, as if he had been handed something exquisitely breakable, like a hummingbird's egg.

She said, "If I can bear not to force everything to fit the looms I know…if I let the world begin to weave itself, what might it weave?"

He thought, Who is this girl?

"I hope that does not sound crazy."

"No."

"You said you were a weaver. Do you understand what I speak of?"

"Maybe." What was hatching here was not a hummingbird. "It's just…I can't stand what the world has woven. For me. So far."

She was silent.

He said gruffly, "Thank you for talking to me."

"I like it."

He blushed. Rubbed his face in his hand. "I never talked to anybody like you."

"I don't suppose so. I hope there are not many people like me."

"Gods! Why not?"

She did not answer. He sat scowling. At last she said, "I have asked Farki if I might paint the other side of the wagon. He said yes."

Nine came howling over and tied them together with the jump rope.

⌒

"So," said Nine, skipping beside him in the racket of axles, "did you kiss her yet?"

"Get away from me!"

"She likes you. She doesn't like beards, though."

"Get *away*. Go bedevil somebody else."

She had hold of his hand; he was afraid to let go lest she fall under the wheels. She said, "Pillbug's pretty."

"Shut up, she'll hear you," said Raím. "What does she look like?"

"Brown, like dirt."

"Dirt!"

183

"Like to plant things in. You, you're the color of smoked cheese."

"I'd wring your neck, but I can't let go here."

"Right, ain't I lucky? Her hair's black, like a silk rope unraveled. She won't paint blood on anybody, and she doesn't smile hardly ever."

"Then you leave her alone. Maybe something bad happened to her."

"So?"

"I mean really bad."

She tried to kick him, and fell down. He yanked her back up. "You'll fall under the wheels!" She landed a thump behind his knee. He let go, let his hand trail along the passing cart, caught the back steps and clung there in the blooming dust with Nine clamped squealing under his arm like a piglet.

"You're choking me!"

"Good."

She stopped squirming and hung over his arm slack as a cat. "You ought to kiss her. Maybe she'd smile."

"If she smiled I couldn't see it."

"So? Neither could she, 'cause it's on her own face."

"Oh, god!"

"Which one?" said Nine.

"So," said Nine, "did you kiss him yet?"

Duuni held Toady in her lap; each time the cart pitched, his head bumped her collarbone. She bent and kissed the place where his hair made a spiral.

"Gya, not Toady. *Him*." Nine jerked her head toward the window in the back, closed now against the dust. "Flea Butt."

Blankness. Duuni said, "Raím?"

"Right. Did you kiss him yet?"

She had never kissed anybody except children and her mother. "Why...why would I kiss him?"

"Why not?" Nine was dandling Maidy, letting her nearly roll off her lap before she snatched her back giggling. "You're both took. He likes you. And you're both kind of old."

"I am not old. He what?"

"Likes you. Sure, you're old. You're pretty, though. Too bad Flea Butt's so ugly. If he shaved off his beard, would you kiss him?"

"What are you saying!"

"Huh? Ain't you listening? I said, how come you don't kiss old Flea Butt? You both said yes."

"You terrible child!"

"I'm just *saying*. He ain't had luck with girls, I guess, on account of being such a pig. Is that why you won't kiss him?"

"I—"

"Don't know that I'd kiss him either, come to think. On the lips, I mean. I want a prince." Nine swung Maidy this way and that. "Or a sword swallower."

Duuni said nothing. Nine got up and brought everybody apples. When Duuni had eaten hers she went to the back window and opened it.

Right below her he trudged, one hand on the side of the porch. His hand, his hair, his big shoulders were all creased with dust.

Nine nudged in beside her. Looked down, shrugged. "Oh, well," she said. "Dibs on the prince."

⊚

There was no way he could have known how uneasy Nine's words had made her. Yet now whenever Duuni spoke to him—which was as seldom as she could—Raím turned his head away, angry and gruff.

In the end she got angry, too. Nothing else she felt had a name, or she did not know how to feel it. A great restlessness took her. She crept up to sit with Auntie on the buckboard. Not that Auntie said much. Tam Chivi rode ahead on his black mare. Duuni watched him without thought.

She wanted to paint the other side of the wagon, but day by day the caravan did not make long camp. Duuni fidgeted until she thought her whole skin had wrinkles. Whenever she could, she got down and walked; her legs were stronger, the boots no longer tripped her, she walked or ran as she wished. Sometimes, in that freedom, she dropped back to watch Raím trudge in the dust. She wondered what he looked like under that beard.

The road climbed higher. They were no longer next to the mountain, but on it; beyond the dark comb of trees, the red land rolled away like ocean to the edge of the sky.

Night. They camped among pines whose needles were as long as her hand, and soft. The sun set earlier now, the air was cold.

She went to the wagon, the unpainted side. With her face close to the shadowy canvas she said softly, "I do not know."

With a rustle like a fox, Farki stepped over the wagon tongue.

She sprang back. A dim place in her mind said, *I am always frightened.*

"Soon we will make long camp," he said. He fetched a hacksaw from the toolbox.

"Sir. Who painted the lion the first time?"

"A Gatekeeper."

"I don't know what that is."

Glint of a grin. "A master. One who keeps the Gate."

He left. She had not been shamed for asking. Neither had she understood the answer.

❧

For a long time she looked at the empty canvas. When she walked back round the wagon everyone had gone to a fire down the way where Dicey played a guitar. Everyone but Raím and Nine, who sat together on a crate.

Nine was waving a stick. Duuni looked again. It was a straight razor. Open.

186

She ran, she caught Nine's wrist and yanked her arm into the air. She did not say *Stop!* or *Give me that razor!* but snatched it out of her hand.

"Hey!" said Nine. "That's his!"

Duuni closed the razor. "Whose?"

"Flea Butt's. He's gonna shave."

Shave? He was blind! Yet there sat Raím, with a pot of hot water and the rageful look he wore when he had had to ask for something. Duuni said, "Did you ask Nine to bring you a razor?"

He scowled and blushed. Nine hopped and grabbed, saying, "Give it! Farki sharpened it and everything!"

"Be damned," Raím said through his teeth. "Farki thinks I can't strop a razor?"

"Raím! Nine was waving it around open."

A look of angry shame. "I'm sorry." He held out his hand. She hesitated. Gave him the razor. He turned his back, and, with his face in shadow, began to splash water on his beard.

Nine said, "That old Pillbug! I wasn't doing anything!"

"Good," said Raím. "Keep it up."

Duuni forgot about Farki and the painting. Raím would cut himself horribly. She should take his wrist and say, *Stop!* She should have rags ready to staunch the blood.

But to be thought helpless; to have to do each little, common task in front of everyone, because you could not get away.

She left him and joined the others at Dicey's fire. She could not help glancing over her shoulder at the twin shadows, Raím and Nine. But there were no screams, neither collapsed on the ground, and at last the small shadow led the tall one away. Later, when she had put the babies to bed and slipped into the eiderdown herself, the same shadows came stumbling: Nine leading Raím to his bed under the cart. Farki followed, locked Raím's chain to the waist ring. Raím rolled himself in the quilt and lay down against the wheel.

Nine crept in with Duuni, yawning.

"Did he cut himself?"

"No."

She hardly believed that. "Did you take the razor back to Farki?"

"*No.* That old Flea Butt wouldn't give it to me."

"He…he still has it?" She remembered his whisper: *You think my life is worth living?*

"You wouldn't let me have it, so now he won't either. You're a piggo. He made me take him to Farki, he gave it back himself."

Nine slept. The wind blew in the pines. Their long needles fell, pattering, on the eiderdown. Duuni half sat up and looked at Raím.

Farki had given him a robe made of wolf hides, worn nearly bald; the puppies had gnawed it already. In the moonlight his smooth face was beautiful, like a hand fallen open in sleep.

☙

She could not get used to him. She would glimpse him from the tail of her eye, or shake her hair forward and study him through it. The skin around his mouth was very fair, already shadowed again with beard. At one corner of his lips was a small white scar: nothing compared to the long scars on his back, yet she could not stop looking at it, for it had been hidden.

She wondered what had made it. She turned her mind from him a hundred times a day. The more she banished him the more she thought of him, until she felt so uneasy she avoided him entirely—him and his little white scar.

☙

The number of wagons in the train kept changing. Another caravan might join theirs for a day or two, then part. Men and women came to look at the lion, pointing, speaking in their tongue. Duuni hid, or busied herself with the children. Twice there was another newie wagon; at those times she clung to Rags and Lar-

188

kin and the rest, fearful lest they be swapped for other babies, like counters in a game.

Perhaps among these new faces there were some who, like Raím and herself, had been taken? She never found out. A flock of new children in colored rags would come running with their arms washed, begging for squirrels and fish. Next day they were gone, scattered to other roads before the urda lines had darkened.

The caravan made long camp. Duuni looked for Nine to fetch the paint from Farki's cart, but Nine blatted like a goat, "*Meh! Meh!*," and ran off, so Duuni went to fetch it herself.

Farki was at his improvised wrestling ground. Still her eyes would not look into his. She turned her face away—and there was Raím, new-shaven and stripped to his clout, seeming more naked than when he had been unclothed.

With the paint she scuttled back to the wagon, stood on a chair, and glared at the canvas, furious at her fear. She would paint lion cubs in a meadow. She would make herself paint them badly, so the world would see how stupid she was to be afraid.

She raised the wet brush. Slowly the angry thoughts fell aside. When the children came crowding and gabbling, she did not hear them. She must have seen them, though, for as the tumbling cubs began to show themselves they were like the children: rolling, pestering, clambering on one another. She laid the outlines of them on the cart side and did not think about who might be watching, as long as nobody spoke to her.

She worked as though the air around her were different from other air. Groping for shape, changing what did not work until it did. When she was done she stood back to look. A sound came out of her mouth: *Ha.*

A voice said, "You've finished."

She gaped around, came out of the world of other air to find Raím sitting next to the rear wheel, unchained and dusty, still in his breechclout.

"How did you know I'd finished?"

"You said *Ha.* That's what I used to say, when I knew a weaving was done. Nine says you've painted lion cubs."

"Yes."

"She says they're funny, they're in a heap like the kids."

"Yes."

"She says you don't smile."

"What?" His question came too fast, a pounce.

"Why don't you smile?"

She felt nothing—confusion, a slow blush. She had not known she did not smile.

"You aren't blind. You don't wear a slave ring. Nobody is slamming you to the ground half the day. Why don't you smile?"

"I—I don't know."

He had bent his head. "Do you like what you have painted?"

"I—maybe."

"If you like it, you should smile. Like this." He raised his face, and a slow grin broke across it, amazing, a door opening on daylight.

She said, "*Ha.*" Then she covered her mouth.

"I heard you. Did you smile?"

She thought of lifting his long hand against her mouth so he could feel her smile. Her own hand began to reach for his; she caught it back.

"They say you've painted fine lions."

"They're just—"

"Don't bleat those modest lies. When someone tells you your work is fine, don't mumble. Say thank you." There was his grin, bitter and sweet. "I'm telling you. I, the King of Thanks."

She said, "Thank you."

Then *he* mumbled. "Sorry I can't see what you've painted."

"The paint is wet. On the cubs. But—" she cleared her throat "—if you'd come round to the other side, I could guide your hand over the lion."

She had to bring the chair along to stand on; to reach the high parts they had to crowd onto it together. She took the middle three fingers of his hand as if they were a brush, and painted the lion again.

His hand moved easily with hers. His face was serious; she could see him making the lion in his mind. As she painted each thing she named it. "A fish. Reeds. A dragonfly." Together, like a dance, they built the whole picture. His hand was silvery with the new paint. "And that's all of it," she said.

"*Ha.*"

She turned his silvery hand, laid it across her mouth, and smiled. Then she jumped down off the chair and ran away.

14

I am lopsided.
Even my depths are unequal.
I was made by running water.
    Song. The Roadsouls.

 "What's the matter with you?" said Nine.

"Nothing. Have you seen Duuni?"

"Huh? Oh. Pillbug. She went with Auntie to fetch fire-wood. What are you cross about?"

They had made a new camp, higher and colder. The world smelled like stone. For two days they had been climbing the mountain, up and up. More than once, at fords and gullies, Raím had joined with the other men to heave a wagon out of a rut or up some steep pitch. Overhead, hawks said *kee!* Vultures said *kraa!* He felt the bigness of the sky.

Somewhere in that bigness was the smallness, the warmth of the mouth that had smiled under his hand. He heard her name called by children's voices. Sometimes he smelled rosemary, or that wretched paint. But she did not come near him. He thought of a rabbit, a deer, which will allow the hunter only a glimpse before she flees; for him, not even that glimpse.

He thought of standing by the cart wheel and bellowing like a tied bull, *"Duuni, where are you?"* This thought embarrassed him so much that when Nine sidled back with a ragged jersey she had stolen and asked him to mend it—he had gotten a reputation for mending things—he shouted at her.

She flapped his face with it. "I stole yarn for it, even, and a darning needle. You're the best twiner there is except for Pillbug, she knows more cats-cradle than Auntie."

"Then ask Pillbug to mend it!"

"She's busy. Dicey wants her to draw an octopus on him. That's like a fish thing with legs."

Raím ground his teeth. "Mend it yourself, you little wart."

"Nobody taught me how."

"Curse you! Come here, I'll teach you."

She plumped down by his shoulder, but in five minutes had thrown down the yarn and run off screeching to a game of hide-and-seek; he heard her shout *Allee allee outs in free!* He mended the jersey himself. She brought a second one, for him this time, more holes than sleeves and full of burrs. He mended that, too, and wore it, for the wind had gone cold.

They climbed for yet another day. Duuni did not speak to him. He walked beside the mules. They did not mind his hand, and the dust was less than it was behind the wagon.

Sometimes Nine came to skip beside him. He said, "Where are we going now?"

"To the fair, to get money."

"What fair is so high?" For there was less breath in the air, and the wind was constant. "Only goats live this high."

"Auntie! Flea Butt says High Moles is goats!"

"Goats, and gold from the mines," said Auntie from the buckboard.

"Stuff to buy and sell," said Nine.

"Might sell you."

"I'm too skinny."

"Wouldn't make a broth," said Auntie. "Not to mention the natter of you, like a laying hen."

"Sell old Flea Butt, all he does is eat and get thrown on his head."

"Belongs to Farki. And who mended your jersey?"

"I could've done it myself."

"Cows might dance," said Auntie.

As the carts crept upward, they passed and were passed by League caravans, jangling and slow; by messengers on quick-stepping horses; by porters grunting under loads that Raím could only guess at until, as he walked behind the wagon on a stony stretch, he heard Duuni say, "Tiggy, look. Lanterns and chairs, pots and pumpkins."

He said, "Duuni?" Stumbled, and was dragged a yard or two before he found his feet.

No answer.

The iron ring around his waist burned with cold. Auntie gave him a piece of torn canvas for a cloak. Donkeys laden with sweet split cedar pattered past, urged on by woodcutters' curses; he smelled cedar smoke long before they passed through the thick stone gate into the mining town of High Moles.

A gabble of children and raucous talk. Raím, who all day had been walking next to the mules, heard the tramp of many feet crowding and following. Sometimes a hand touched his sleeve. Odor of spices, incense, midden, and over everything the sharp smell of shattered rock.

Nine had been to High Moles before. As the cart crept through the crowds she scrambled from one side to the other of the rear window, yelling, "Doy Dumbhead, I'll get you! Suki's a muddy-front! Yah!" When the wagon jerked to a halt, she squawked, as if she had tumbled backward into it.

Someone spoke in an unknown, hooting tongue—officially, it seemed, for the crowd fell silent. Raím, in the dust beside the cart, heard Farki answer. That seemed the only formality. But women's voices rose around him; their bodies crowded his, their hands began to pat his wrists, his chest.

He could not brush them off. It was like being walked on by cats. Frowning, he felt his way to the back of the cart and climbed onto the porch; the hands patted his ankles. The caravan lurched and went on.

From the rear window Nine said, "Flea Butt, those ladies like you. Guess they don't know you're a pitiful old blind man."

The wagons stopped. Odor of hay thrown out for the mules. Raím climbed down—but there were the hands again, as if they had followed the wagon. Low laughter; women's voices in that dialect hollow as an owl's call.

Farki came. He brushed the hands from Raím's body and hooted. They left.

Raím had schooled himself not to ask Farki questions, but now he said, "What the hell do they want?"

No answer. Raím cursed. He hung about the wagon, then groped toward the sounds of camp. Sometimes his shoulders were seized, and he was propelled elsewhere or given a rope and told to hold it taut. Fumbling, he found that walls of felt and canvas had been attached to the wagons and laced into a warm warren, snug against the wind. Inside, rugs made a floor, the featherbeds rolled up along the sides. Here and there a gap let in a blade of cold. No Duuni anywhere. He had offended her somehow. She would never speak to him again. That was what she had meant when she laid his hand over her mouth.

He felt his way along the walls. Strong hands stopped him. "Be aware," said Auntie. He stood still, and felt the heat of the iron stove he had nearly laid his hand on. She made him sit on a rolled mattress and gave him a mug of tea. "You will sleep in here with us."

"Have I grown less dangerous?"

"It is winter in High Moles. You are no good to anybody dead."

"Am I any good living?"

"There are those who think so."

"I wouldn't make a broth."

A soft cluck of laughter. The backs of her fingers nipped his cheek. "Nor can you lay eggs," she said, and refilled his mug.

That night he slept in a row with a dozen others. He did not know half the people, but their fleas bit him anyway. Duuni was there; she must be, for across the tent-room he heard the sleepy babble of the babies, like geese settling. But she said no word. It was Nine who slept next to him and all over him, flipping like a minnow until he laid his arm over her to keep her in one place. She held onto his hand with both hers, and was still.

There were three people Duuni avoided. Farki, because he owned her; Tam Chivi, because he charmed her; Raím, because he confused her and made her act so strangely she hardly knew herself.

Farki was easy to stay away from. Tam Chivi was harder. He rode his black mare up and down the caravan line, joking, racing the other lads, dashing the dust off his breeches with his hat. Sometimes he rode close to the open window of the cart, and grinned; once, when Duuni was walking in the dust, he trotted up and held his hand down as if to say, Want a lift? She shook her head and looked away, and he cantered off.

Raím. When she remembered his hand on her mouth, a darkness came over her, and she could not think. He was a matted skein, too many threads: his hand that followed hers so easily, his blind eyes that yet seemed to see the lion, his pride that would never bow, Nine said, until he had broken God's back.

Duuni had tried to comb Nine's hair, so matted and dagged that the comb would not go through it. Nine shrugged and said, "Cut it off, why not?" Duuni sheared her, and she ran off light as a lamb. Duuni wished she could do that with Raím: clip away the tangle of him and drop it in the fire.

He was easy to avoid. She knew how to be silent, unremarkable, small. She wanted him to ask for her, did not want him to ask. He did not ask. She was already uneasy with the eyes, the nods, the approving looks of those who came to look at the painted cubs. She craved praise, yet praise felt awful; she wanted Raím to speak, and feared he would, and when he did not she hated him.

The caravan toiled up the mountain toward High Moles. She felt the lion following.

The road grew stony, then steep. The pines were no longer tall and straight as roof beams but dwarfed, bent away from the wind. The view was southwest, into the gales; there the world grew vast. Travelers and merchants passed on the road, more and more, in strange garments, staring as if the Roadsouls were strange.

Duuni thought, Down in the wrinkled canyons are many, many towns like Alikyaan, and each one thinks itself the center of all being, the most important, specially beloved of the gods.

Above her head the mountain rose as tall as ever, its high peaks white with snow. She watched Raím walk, his hand on the mule's flank. She caught a glimpse of his mouth, and that darkness came over her, dense as smoke.

They came to the town of High Moles.

It lay in a bowl-shaped valley between two lesser peaks of the great mountain. The stony slopes were freckled with rock heaps, with clutters of gray timbers like woodpiles, and hundreds of black dots that she did not understand until Nine, leaning out the window, said, "Mountain's full of mines. Those black holes, they're adits, where the miners go in. They don't come out, either, plenty of them. The mountain gets them."

Duuni thought of her brothers, long gone from Alikyaan, and wondered if they worked there, or had died there. If they were alive she would not recognize them. As the caravan drew closer she saw that some of the holes were black and open, some closed by heavy wooden doors or iron bars.

"Like an anthill," said Nine, "the mines. You go in and down and in and down and you never come out till you're a skellington. There's ghosts in there, and things that suck on you."

"How do you know?"

"Doy Dumbhead said. The miners are taking gold out of the mountain, they have to give her presents and things so she won't swallow them. Then she swallows them anyway. Townies."

In the lands the caravan had been traveling through, the farmers had been mostly fair- or red- or gold-skinned. But in High Moles the people were all colors. At first she thought they had taken their color from the different stones. Then she thought perhaps they were like her brothers, outcast to the mines, but from many different lands. The women wore long cloaks of every hue and pattern: cheap, League-milled stuff, but from a distance lovely as flowers. They seemed bold, and laughed among themselves.

There were many of them. The closer the wagons drew to the town gate, the more women there were, laughing and following. Raím was trudging by the mule; the women touched him as he walked, as if they had never seen such a being before. He clambered up on the porch. Still they followed—their language like owls' calls, *Oo! Oo!*—until Farki shooed them away.

At the foot of a cliff, at the edge of a wide field, the caravan made camp next to a gray boulder worn with caresses: a blessing stone. The felt cushions in the newie cart, unrolled and rigged with ropes and stakes, made rug-floored tents against the wind.

They penned the babies in a corner like a litter of puppies. Tiggy wept; Duuni lifted her out and let her roam, to find for herself what this new place was. As she patted and tasted her way along the wall, the curtain that was the door moved, and Raím stepped in.

Duuni watched that tall man do what Tiggy did: touch the new-made space, bring his face close as though to taste it, listen. He turned his head a little. Very low, he said, "Duuni? Are you here?"

She stood still as a tree. After a moment he turned back to the wall and groped on, found the door to the next room of the warren, and was gone. She picked Tiggy up and put her back, squalling, in her pen.

⑤

The wind never stopped. They cooked outdoors by the blessing stone but came indoors to eat, and slept next to the iron stove. Dicey, Shank, Shine, strangers half-known and unknown, all crowded under the eiderdowns the way the girls on the Maidens' Balcony had curled together for warmth when winter came. Wind cracked at the felt walls. In fitful dark lit by the iron grate, Duuni crept in between Auntie and a stranger girl who wore her hair braided in fours. She whispered, "Auntie, does Flea Butt still sleep under the wagon?"

Auntie pointed with her chin. There he was, a long, quilted range that Duuni had not recognized. His sleeping face was blank.

Nine slept next to him. His arm lay across her body.

A rush of heat. Duuni looked at Auntie. Auntie's face told her nothing. Duuni thought, *But—? Should he—?*

Speak one word, chit, and I kill your mother.

She lay down again, rigid. Nothing happened. Perhaps it was all right? How could she know?

The night wind blew. She slept, dreaming of mines.

 In the morning sleepers known and unknown got up and went out, leaving Raím to find his own way. He fumbled aside the thick felt door and stepped into the cold. The sun had not risen; he did not know where he stood in the map of the world. He tucked his hands in his armpits and listened to the racket of hammers, trundling wheelbarrows. To his left, the voices of Farki and the wrestler lads laying out the ground for a morning bout. To his right, the ting and chuckle of a little stream.

He felt his way to it and put his hand in. It was burning cold. Somewhere at the other end of this water, of all moving water, lay the sea; this thought comforted him, as though now he knew where he was.

Half-running footsteps, a few, then many. Bodies in soft robes closed round him where he knelt, and the hands began to pat him. He stood up and made himself big. Women laughed softly. He pushed his hands outward as though parting a crowd of children, found foreheads and smiling cheeks at the level of his chest.

They settled on him like moths. "Get off," he said. "Get away."

They laughed. Farki came, spoke a sentence in that hooting tongue. They laughed again, gave Raím final pats, moved off. Raím brushed his arms, forgot it was Farki and said, "What the hell do they want?"

"You."

"Me?"

"You are a god. And that is lucky for me."

"A *god?*"

"According to them. Do not grow big on that. They are goddesses."

"According to them!"

"Is there anything you believe that is not according to somebody?" said Farki. Raím said nothing. "You are big, and red, and blind, like the son of the Lord of the Ground."

Raím felt a creeping between his shoulders. "The son of the Lord of the Ground is blind?"

"In High Moles he is."

In his mind Raím saw gods, sub-gods, and versions of gods, red, brown, sighted, blind, short, tall, many-armed—all quarreling over who was to rule which element, be worshiped in what rites by which village, shoving like hordes at a market.

"In High Moles," said Farki, "the son of that god is a god himself: Hosh, Lord of the Mines. Each ten years there is a festival to honor him. The women make offering, that they may have many children and their husbands be safe underground." It was more explanation than Farki had ever given. "For that they need Hosh—and I shall charge them for him."

"For *what?*"

"You anticipate your life. That is why I can throw you," said Farki, and did so.

Raím scrambled up. "You mean...you'll sell me?"

"Rent you. Isn't it a fine thing those women think you are a god? Especially," said Farki, "since you think that yourself?"

Raím stood confused, and Farki threw him.

ᔕ

"Farki says you're to be god of the women of High Moles," said Nine, her mouth full of buttered biscuit. When the rest of the Souls had left to set up the midway she had circled back, stolen Raím's biscuit and made him bargain for the return of half of it. Now he sat next to her on a crate by the fire, sharing breakfast the way he had used to with his sister Thoyes. "He says you're going to give them lots of babies. You going to fuck all of them?"

Raím spit out his tea. "Don't talk like that!"

"Why not?"

"It's bad."

"How come?"

"You're not old enough to know about those things."

Nine grabbed a pan of cold water and flung it on him. He sputtered. "Why do they let you do this? Run around like a mad creature, and throw water, and talk about things that aren't for children—"

"Huh, like they ain't for children! They're how children get *made*, you just ask those ladies in High Moles!"

"But they're not *for* children."

"Gya!" said Nine. "You must of never lived anywhere!"

"I lived in Creek. In Creek no one ever—"

But with these words came the image of old man Esseril, the way mothers kept their girls away from him. And Chesh, in the Loom Hold, who had to be watched with the new boys.

"That's a big old lie," said Nine. "If things happen to kids, how come kids can't know about them?"

He wiped water from his face. "Maybe to *know*. But not to *talk* about."

"How you going to know something without talking?" She gave him a shove in the middle of his chest.

"All gods! Why is it I can't be rude, but you can?"

"'Cause I'm a Soul."

"You are not. Not born."

She slugged him so hard he grunted. Slugged him again. He grabbed both her wrists. "I'm a Soul *now*!" she said, struggling.

"All right. You're a Soul." He pulled her between his knees so she could not kick him. He still had her wrists; he leaned close and said, low-voiced, "Look. Does Duuni know about that Lord of the Mines nonsense? That I'm to... I don't know what I'm to do. Has anybody told her?"

She would not speak. When she did, she said, "I hope they told. You're sweet on her."

"Probably she knows about that god stupidity already. If she doesn't know, don't tell her."

"What'll you give me?"

"What'll I *give* you? You little rat—I mended your jersey, last night I gave you half the quilt and you grabbed all of it, you twitched like a flea, you kicked my shins until morning—"

"You old witch man, I'll tell her if I want! *Meh, meh*!... There she is!"

He gripped her arms. "Don't tell!"

She wrested herself away. "I ain't sleeping next to you no more! I'm telling!" she shouted, and ran off.

Duuni heard what Raím said.

She heard Nine's answer. Through the half-raised door of the tent she saw Nine wrench herself from his hands and come running, crying, "*Pillbug!* Flea Butt, he—"

Duuni ran to meet her. Grabbed her arm. "*Get* into the tent."

"Hey—"

"*Go!*"

Nine looked at her with wide eyes. Ran into the tent. Duuni pulled her knife. Went to Raím where he sat.

"Duuni?"

She said nothing. Raised the knife.

"Is it you?" A dull blush flooded his face. He put out his hand. "Are you here? I haven't been sure—"

"What have you done?"

His hand paused. "What?"

"*Do not touch her!*"

His face blank, ludicrous. "Who? What?"

"You—" She held the knife close to his face, his mouth. She could tell he knew something was there. His face creased into a puzzled frown and something else: longing.

He did not move his body, but his hand moved. Something in her thought, *He will cut himself.* She turned the blade so that he would not. Then she thought, *Why?*

His fingers found the flat of the knife. His face went still.

She gasped herself full of breath. "I take care of the babies. *Always*. And Nine. I watch over her."

His mouth made the word *What?*

"I make sure—" With Nine nothing could be sure, no more than with the wind. She said, "*If you touch her again.*"

His brows twitched down, he blushed to the roots of his red hair. "What? You think—"

"I said, do not touch her!"

"What makes you—"

"I know what you are! Chasing that girl by the pond! I saw you with Nine last night. If you—"

"Listen—"

"Get up. Get away." To speak so to a man. Her weight on the batten, hearing the wood snap. "Go, or I'll kill you. I'll kill you

203

the way you kill children." She pressed the knife past his fingers. They resisted only a little. Laid the blade against his cheek, under the bone.

He did not move.

"Go!"

As if he looked, not at her, but at something that stood where she stood. He turned his face against the flat of the blade, gently, as one would turn one's face against a child's. "Kill me, then," he said. "If that will mend anything in the world. Do it."

She stared at him, at the knife in her hand. Pulled the blade away. It left a little triangular indentation above the scar by his mouth.

She turned. Went back into the tent where Nine was peering through the doorway, hopping up and down. "What'd old Flea Butt do? Why're you trying to stick him?"

What did he do to you last night? She could not ask it. Could not think how to ask it. Raím out there, motionless, sitting on the box.

"What did—" How could she ask? With a gasp she said, "What...what was your name before it was Nine?"

"Huh? Eight."

"I mean, before the Souls took you?"

"*I* don't know. Kitty, it might of been. Or maybe it was the cat they called that. How come you're trying to kill old Flea Butt?"

"Were they...in the place where you were before, were they good to you?"

"In the *mills?* Are you *crazy?*"

"Were there many children?"

"Many as they could get. Paidmen bring them, or that Doctor Amu. Or their folks sell them. My ma sold me. There was nothing to eat. How come you—"

"Were they...bad to the children?"

"Nastier than snakes. They beat us with spooling rods, they'd speed up the looms so no way could you keep your spools full, your hair get caught and pull you into the gears, even." She shrugged. "Those foremen, they'd do anything to you."

"Raím...did he ever...has Raím ever, to you I mean, like the foremen..."

That unbroken gaze. "Somebody done it to you."

Duuni looked down. Looked away.

Toady crept to Nine's legs, stood up and banged his nose on her knees in the wobbly way babies do, as if their heads were too big. Nine picked him up. "Flea Butt ain't done nothing," she said. "I don't know why those High Moles ladies want a god with no manners that falls over things, but Farki says if it's religion, don't ask." She swung Toady back and forth; her cropped hair stood out like a dandelion clock. "There, see, I told. What Flea Butt said not to tell you. That he's got to go be Lord God of Ladies. Oh, and you got to draw on him tonight, so the color sets by tomorrow."

"God?" said Duuni. "Ladies? Draw?"

"Those High Moles ladies think Flea Butt's a god, and he's going to give them all babies. But he's got to wrestle townies first, so Farki says you got to paint him to be scarier than devils."

Duuni put her hands to her head. In Alikyaani she said, "I want to be home on the Maidens' Balcony. I want to be at my loom, with my batten in my hand."

"Huh?"

"Mind the children." She went back outside. She walked right past the man to whom she ought to apologize, who sat on the box with his hands on his knees, stone-faced, looking at nothing. The man she had made into Tumiin.

She would walk out of High Moles, into the wilderness, until the lion found her and devoured her. Much easier than explaining to Raím what she had thought.

ᕫ

She was not in the wilderness. She was in a crowd on the half-finished midway, bodies and voices at every hand, yet as surely alone as when she had climbed the mountain.

No one knew her. She walked on. There were stalls for pottery, leather, spices, cheese. A trodden ring for showing horses and long-haired sheep. A League trader setting up his display, wholesale only, cheap skillets, milled yard goods, rum. A prayer merchant with paint-stained hands, two dusty great hounds at her feet.

At all of this Duuni looked without seeing, as if at a meadow blurred with flowers. There was a traveling medicator, odor of whiskey and wild hemlock.

It was he: the slovenly, red-nosed man who had offered the master tunic. Whistling, he laid out bundles of herbs on the stained boards of a booth. When he saw Duuni he cocked his head and said, "Good morning, young lady. Do you need a cure?"

She needed to be cured of something, she did not know what.

"Ah, but what does a pretty lass want with a cure?" He held out a nosegay of herbs tied with green ribbon. "For you, a love charm. Compliments of Amu the All-Doctor."

A gift; it would be rude not to accept. But then she had to stand there, blushing and unhappy, holding the nosegay while the doctor said, "Lay it under your true love's pillow. He'll dream of you, and in the dawn he will see no other. Now, I'm sure you also need lavender to lay among your linens. Or a little oil of rosemary to gloss that lovely hair—"

She collected herself. "I...I saw you at the fair in Greencliff."

"Did you now?"

"You were selling a tunic. Very fine—"

"Ah, the tunic! From the looms of Welling-in-the-Mountains, marvelous, matchless. Alas, the tunic is sold! Hardly an hour ago." His eyes ran over her ragged silks. "Was it to be for your lover, that lucky lad?"

"No...I just...I wanted—" She wanted to give something to Raím, to make up for what she had thought him to be. She could not give him the tunic, but perhaps she could bring him news of it. "I wondered where you got it."

"Ah, now. A tunic like that has a life of its own. Shall we say *it* chose *me*? I was given the use of it, briefly. It will buy me some dinners—" he slapped his greasy paunch "—and now it is off again on its adventures."

That he was a liar even she could see, yet what he said about the tunic—that in its brilliance it had its own life—rang true. She said, "How do they weave like that, in Welling-in-the-Mountains? It had no seams, I looked."

"You did not inspect it in Greencliff. You know it from some other place?"

"No. Yes. I mean, I saw one very like it. Once."

His sly eyes lay on her. "Almost magic, the master tunics of Welling. Anything made in a Gatehouse is delight and danger together. True art is a fierce fire...and may I suggest, young lady, that you take care how you put your fingers into it?"

"Yes, sir."

"Good. You will live long and healthily. The tunic came to me, it is gone, and life flows on. Commerce, too, hence I return to my question: You need lavender? Or rose lotion for those little hands? Ah, good sir—buy your lass a sachet for her bosom? Only a penny."

Turning, she saw to whom he spoke: Tam Chivi, smiling. He shook his head at the medicator, slipped his arm through hers, and led her away. They passed a baker's booth; he bought her a penny cake, and one for himself. At the Roadsoul compound next to the blessing stone he said, "Don't go out alone. And beware Doctor Amu."

Arm-in-arm with Tam Chivi. She could scarcely think. Raím was gone, the empty box stood by the burnt-out fire. Tam Chivi dropped her arm. "Take care," he said. He never spoke three words when two would do. Nothing about him was confusing. His eyes were black as cherries.

She had a crazy thought to give him the nosegay. Her hand would not do it. When he had left her she stood twirling the posy in her fingers, then laid it on the blessing stone. Aloud she said, "That was Doctor Amu." Who bought children and sold them to the mills. Who spoke truth about mastery.

⟲

In the afternoon she was sitting with Auntie by the stove when Nine came, leading Raím and a flock of children, even some townies.

Auntie said, "Away with you lot."

"We're going to watch Pillbug draw on him."

"You'll let her be while she's working."

"Flea Butt ain't a wagon!" But they whined and left, Nine returning the trades and small change she had charged for the spectacle. Auntie nodded at a sheltered corner where the canvas had been pulled back and the sun warmed the dark felt; then she too left. There was nothing to keep Duuni company but the muffled bangs of midway-building, the wind, and Raím.

New-shaven, in nothing but a wrestler's clout. He had come from bathing in the stream and stood where Nine had left him, shuddering, scowling to prove he was not cold.

She wrung her hands. "I was wrong," she said.

His eyes, which sometimes roved about looking at nothing, seemed to stare straight ahead. "Not if you thought I had done...what you thought."

"I didn't know. I heard you say...something you said. But I was wrong. I am so sorry."

"Tell me what I said."

You speak one word, chit... "Nothing. I misunderstood. I am ashamed. Please forgive me."

"Of course." His voice was dreary.

"The urda is ready." Scent of rosemary, summery and hot.

He let himself be led to the sunny place. Knelt, hands on thighs. With his face turned away he said, "Why haven't you spoken to me, all these days?"

"I don't know." If he would shut up and be simple like Tam Chivi! "Farki says I am to draw on you? Did he say what I should draw?"

"A lion."

She had already knelt beside him, the urda press in her hand. No use to say no. Not to Farki. Her shame became defeat. "Fierce, I suppose. Plenty of blood."

"Blood? If there's blood it'll be mine. I've never grounded Farki."

"But...isn't it the townies you're to ground?"

"So maybe I'll live? Not that it matters. Though since I've been rented out, I'd better live long enough to fulfill the lease."

"As a god, Nine said." By the way he settled his shoulders she could see he was not entirely displeased to be a god. She said, "I don't understand that. Renting a god." Who gave women babies; she would not think about that part.

"Nor do I. But I don't understand much. If I could find a damned thread end in this life, I would follow it. And I a weaver!" he said, as if that were a bad word. "You, too, you say. So, what would you, Duuni? A thread that leads always back and forth, or no thread at all? Choose!"

It was like hearing her own soul speak. She said, "I have a thread. It is the line I draw."

He sat up straight.

She said, "Be still."

"What you just said—"

"*Be still.*" For her eyes were changing. She no longer saw him so much, for she had begun to see a lion on him, a shifting ghost. He was no longer a man, or Raím, or a person whom she had insulted; he had become the place where a lion would show itself. She touched him lightly. Saw where the line would begin.

He was still.

☙

The Maiden's Balcony had had a cat once, a grey tom named Smoke, who fought up and down the roofs and courtyards and came home bloody, his ears in tatters; yet he would sit motionless to be groomed, only leaning a little to accept the brush. Raím was like that cat. His eyes closed. Nothing moved but his breath.

The lion called the line from the tip of the urda press. She was servant to the line, as a dog is servant to the scent of game. Slowly, as though it stepped from the underbrush, the lion made itself seen on Raím's breast: water-pool eyes, triangular nose, dark lips wide to show its teeth and curling tongue—not a snarl, but the open mouth of the lion on the mountain as it had tested a new odor, herself.

The man sat still as a hawk on a branch.

She shook out her hands. "Could you feel what I drew?"

"Lion's face."

"Where did you learn to sit so still?"

"Hunting."

The long body stretched over his shoulder to his scarred back. There was a place that still wanted the line. Wise as a sleepwalker, she set her hand there, drew its outline and filled it with spirals.

Paintings know when they are done. She sat back.

Raím, stirring, said, "You drew your hand. Why?"

"I don't know." She blinked up from her trance. "Don't move. The paste must set, then I'll seal it with lemon sugar. And wrap it some way." She had not thought about how.

"Nine said she'd bring rags when she comes to fetch me."

"Will she remember?"

"By next week, maybe." He sat motionless, hands on knees. The sun shone, falling west. Outside the alcove the sounds of the world went on, but where they sat was still as a riverbank at dawn. A bit of wind got in and stirred Raím's hair.

He said, "What was it like in Alikyaan?"

She did not answer for a time. "Maybe I don't want to remember."

"So bad?"

"Some of it." She tried the paste on his arm. Still sticky. "Most could bear it."

"But not you."

"There were women whose lives were worse than mine. Much. Yet they bore it, and did not break their battens."

"Perhaps what they broke didn't show."

She was frightened, as if he had seen her without eyes. "You said your place was not bad. Yet you left it."

He started to raise his hand to rub his face; remembered, sat still. "Perhaps I leapt out of that world. When I blinded myself."

"Tell me that story."

He told it. "How many times had I jumped to some cliff's edge? I had the best life gives, yet I chose to jump. I felt myself choose."

In her eagerness she leaned forward and laid her hands on his. "Did a devil make you choose? A god?"

"No."

"How do you know?"

"I know."

She said, "*Ha!*," as she had when the painting on the wagon was right.

"Yes. That."

He began to raise his arm, but her hand was on his and stopped him. "What made you choose, then?"

In the slow voice of one who has brewed a thought for a long time he said, "Maybe...the world beyond my loom. It said 'Jump; learn how vast I am, how ignorant you are!' And I jumped."

Her hands on his. "Before I broke my batten something rose in me, from somewhere I did not know."

The wind blew. A leaf of sunlight crept in and lay on his cheekbone under one eye, where she had pressed the knife.

She said, "How did you get that little scar by your mouth?"

"My mouth?"

She touched the scar.

"My cousin hit me with a hoe."

"Oh."

She tested the paste on his arm. It was dry. She took up the brush and began to lay on the sugar seal, thick, beginning at his neck and passing down slowly over the lines on his back. He said, "I have to sleep in this glue?"

"Yes."

He muttered a curse. With broad strokes she sealed the lion's face on his breast. She said, "Sometimes I want my old loom."

"I, too."

She sealed his arms and hands. Far away, Nine was teasing someone. "Don't move until the sugar dries," she said. Groping for a rag, she put the drippy brush crosswise in her mouth and spoke through it. "Oh, be blessed, Raím—you're so sticky!"

"Kiss me."

In the little alcove, no sound.

She said, "What?"

"Kiss me, damn it. Duuni. Nine will be here in a moment, and I'm not to move." A silence. "Please?"

The sun shone. She took the wet brush from her lips, leaned across his knees, and kissed him.

Sweet. The sugar, the living man. He flushed dark under the dark lion. And there *was* a world beyond the loom, for it could not be Duuni Esremachaan who said, "Say thank you," and, softly, laughed.

"Thank you."

As he spoke, Nine ducked into the alcove waving a huge, ragged, milled-cloth shirt printed with purple comets. "Old Flea Butt got polite?" she said. "Must be the end of the world!"

His hands were still on his knees. He said, "I can't move, or I'd smack your butt."

"You can't move?" She dropped the shirt and ticked his feet.

◎

She wanted to be by herself. Not to think. She wanted to stand absolutely still, invisible as a mallard chick in its weed-colored down.

But the carnival had begun: tents up, ropes strung, booths and counters hammered down; shouts, arguments, the mixed aromas of mule droppings and garlic and dust. For the moment her task was the babies—those from the newie wagon as well as stranger babies who were brought, left without comment, then taken away. She was frantic that Bones or Midge or Tiggy would be taken. The babies fought. Nine came begging for a new snake to show the townies, so as Toady screamed and Midge yanked the hair of a stranger child, Duuni must be half in that drawing place and half in the pen of mad infants, smelling wet diapers and burnt sausage and urda and so crazy with what had happened she thought she must wither like a moth in fire.

And Raím was right there. Not close; he had said nothing more, he had eased the old shirt over his sugar armor and let Nine lead him to sit at the smoky fire before the tents, mending harness for Auntie, careful to keep his gestures small. She watched his bent head.

She could have asked Nine to mind the babies for a moment. She could have gone to him and said *Are you warm enough?* or *Can you bear the sugar seal?* or *Who are you?* She could have said, *I have never met anyone like you,* or even *I love you so much I shall die of it.*

She did not go to him. As if she, too, were sealed in armor—brittle, sweet, invisible.

His long hands turned the harness, pulled on the waxed thread.

15

My body is made of glass.
My body is made of greening wheat,
of slate and lavender and light and nails.
Don't come to me with some rote word!
Go weep. Go walk.
Go lie in the dirt until the spears
of bear grass grow up through your belly bowl.
Come to me then, and we'll braid
like the silt of two rivers.

        Shrine poem. Welling-in-the-Mountains.

"Gya, look what Pillbug drew!"

"Where is she?"

"Those townies see you, they'll piss their britches!"

"Where's Duuni?"

"That lion'd scare the hair off a bald man. She's getting dressed to be Nightweaver. Don't put your shirt on! You got to show her how the color set."

Raím opened his mouth to say, *Take me to her!* Shut it. Put his shirt on. With the flour sack Nine had brought him he rubbed the freezing creek water from his hair and dried his feet. Said, "The lines haven't darkened yet."

"How do you know, you old blind man?"

"She told me they wouldn't. Take me to the wrestling ground. Please."

So he had asked for a kiss and got it. What was a kiss? Once he could get as many as he wanted. Oh gods, he wanted his arms around her. To pull her close, close against the lion she had—

He fell headlong over a tent rope. "You old Flea Butt," said Nine. He got up. It was not good to go to the wrestling ground longing for a girl. Rage worked better. He thought about Doctor Amu.

☙

The mountain ridge was high; the sun rose late. By the time it had warmed the frost off post and stone, he stood on the wrestling ground in his clout, trying not to shiver. The borrowed cloak barely reached his knees. The murmuring crowd that pressed the ropes was already dense; from the food booths came a whiff of gingerbread and hoppy beer.

Farki's deep voice: "Bright Blood the Blind Magician, best wrestler on earth! Strong as the mountain, come try a fall!" Nine had wanted Bad Blood the Blind Maniac, Eats Human Flesh, but Farki had said Raím was a ladies' god and that name would be bad for sales.

Raím settled his feet and let the tangle that was Duuni drift to his mind's edge. This morning, as every morning, Farki had thrown him.

"Bright Blood the Blind Magician!"

Voices hooted in dialect, but some spoke Plain. "Blind?" "Look at his eyes." "He's to be the Hosh, God of the Mines!" Farki took away the cloak. From the crowd, a subdued roar, almost a groan. "Lion! The Hosh!"

Raím felt silly. He folded his arms across the lion he could not see. Duuni's lion; he put his fists on his hips instead, and scowled with embarrassment. Shouts. Coins chimed on a spread bull hide. A cheer went up: "Naxali! Naxali!" and someone scrabbled through the ropes. Farki led Raím to the center of the ring to shake Naxali's hand.

Only once had Raím wrestled a total stranger—Damo—and that had been in rage. Detached now, anxious, he tried to sense the being in front of him, but the memory of Duuni was all over him like the lion, almost in his arms.

Then she was gone. This was not she.

For the first time he understood humans to be similar in some ways, with head and trunk and limbs, yet each, like a map of being, different. The man before him was broad and big—but he was hollow. As Farki and a village referee set his hands and Naxali's in the starting pose, he thought, Strange—this man's life is all in the surface inch of his body, and none inside.

This so startled him that the man nearly grounded him in the first fall. Gasping, he rolled to his feet.

"Naxali!" the crowd shouted. "Naxali will ground the Hosh!" The big man laughed.

This time Raím was ready. He had forgotten Duuni. He wanted to explore this thing, a body that was all on the outside. He did not ground Naxali right away. He could have, now that he knew he was wrestling something structured like a pumpkin. Instead he turned the man this way and that, finding out about him.

Naxali got angry, and twice nearly pinned him. It made a great show. But always Raím could find that hollow center and roll him round it. When he grounded Naxali at last, almost gently, he felt like thanking him.

Naxali put a joke on it and limped off. Coppers clinked as Farki gathered them. Raím heard Nine's voice, distant as a fly's, shouting "Bright Blood!" The crowd said, "Hosh! The Hosh!" They urged another man into the ring. "Petoysa!"

Petoysa was not hollow. He was solid and lively—but only the top half of him. His legs felt as though their owner occupied them only fearfully: they were watery, cold. When Raím discovered this he knew how to ground Petoysa, but it would have been unfair to spend his money so fast. And he wanted to learn about leglessness. It was like the moment when, newly blinded, he had found he could recognize different yarns with his hands.

He folded Petoysa's translucent legs backward. The man slapped the ground, and Raím rose away from him. This time he whispered "Thank you," in the Plain tongue. Petoysa laughed; he was fair-minded. Raím said, "It's your legs."

"You are the Hosh," said Petoysa, and vanished into the world Raím could not see. Farki rattled coins in his fist.

There were three more challengers. One was a man so puffed with pride there was almost nobody there to wrestle; another a man so careful of his face that Raím could make him do anything he wanted. The last man was whole, balanced, and quick, but so sodden with something, sorrow perhaps, that in the end he simply gave up.

Raím grounded them all. As he rose away from his last opponent, whispering "Thank you," he wondered how many of these men had girls in the crowd whom they had wanted to impress by grounding Hosh, son of the Lord of the Ground.

Nine's hand slipped into his. "Bow," she whispered. "Look *mean.*"

He bowed and followed her from sand to stony dirt to the worn rugs inside the Roadsouls' warren. There she jumped on him, yelling "Flea Butt! Flea Butt!"

Farki said, "Well, well." Auntie put a mug of tea into his hands. He would not sit down. His face kept smiling for him. Nine recounted the matches in detail. "So old Flea Butt grabs his leg, and the fat man—"

He was desperate to know whether Duuni had watched him fight. He drank his tea. Farki said, "Why can't you ground me, eh? What changed?"

Raím had no words. He had felt detached, meticulous, as when he improvised finger weaving; as though a path had opened, so that what he did as a weaver could walk over and visit

what he did as a wrestler. "It was…push. Then fall open. Like…
I don't know."

"Like making love," said Farki.

"What?"

"Making love. You were a man one moment, a woman the
next."

It was one thing to suspect it of himself, another to hear it
spoken—and by Farki. "I am not!"

"No? Then you must be a dull lover."

Mug and all, Raím's hands made fists. "Are you calling me
a woman?"

Farki said, "Try a fall with me."

Raím set down the mug and stalked after him, straight into
the wall of the tent.

They did not wrestle in the ring but in an open courtyard
in the middle of the warren. Raím tried to read the body facing him, as he had read the wrestlers of High Moles. Farki was
unreadable. There, but not there. Like water. Raím might say,
"This is the creek," but were he to grab the stream in his fists he
would have no creek. Farki's legs were solid, then fluid; his body
was hollow as Naxali's, then a crazy rolling center that tipped
Raím into the dirt. He was hard as a club, then soft as a doeskin
that wrapped Raím and gathered his arm behind his back. Raím
slapped the earth before that soft force should draw his arm out
of the socket.

Farki said, "Like lovemaking, no?"

"That's lovemaking?" Raím got to his feet, rubbing his
shoulder.

"The goal is different."

"I make love the way *I* want!"

"And how does she feel about that? The woman who made
you a lion?"

Without warning even to himself Raím shot his fist toward the warm patch in the world that was Farki. Nothing there. His body followed his fist, and he sprawled on the sand.

He turned over and lay on his back. Could feel Farki, a shifting being or beings, somewhere off to his left.

"What's he doing?" said Nine.

"Lying about in the dirt," said Farki.

"Get up, Flea Butt. They're shouting for you. They've brought a big man, he's ugly as a privy seat."

Raím got up. Nine took his hand; he jerked it away, but she grabbed the waist of his clout and tugged him by that, saying, "You got to show off and be god."

He followed her back to the ring.

She had a glimpse of him washing off the urda in the icy stream, naked, the lion golden on him. He did not come to her.
Nightweaver's tent was dusty and chill. She was cold even in the depth of her hood; the children who came to be drawn on had blue fingers. But work is work. Ganu had said that. Duuni drew turtles, crows, toads.

Nine kept running out to watch the wrestling and add her shrieks to the grunts and yells, then scampering back to stand in the doorway. "Paints your dreams, two pennies!" she bellowed. Farki had raised the price. And at Duuni, "Go watch him!"

"Who."

"What d'you mean, who? Old Fl…I mean Bright Blood. He's wiping them up. You could go watch him for a *minute*."

"I'm working." Ganu's voice.

Nine put her fists on her hips. "Bright Blood, he's out there doing the real with your lion on and you sit here like some old lady never moved from her chair in her *life*, you could get hit by lightning and *die* and you'd never have seen him."

Duuni stood. Dropped the urda press, half ran out the door.

219

It was crazy crowded. She had to shove and elbow and then stand on an upturned bucket to see over the crowd, kept having to grab people's shoulders, nearly toppled onto the prayer merchant and her two dusty dogs. Her hood fell back. First she saw a smoke of dust, then the shape of two bodies, locked.

Grip. Breath. Grip.

In the locked bodies, a little shift, as when you lean your weight from one foot to the other. A howl from the crowd. The shape broke in two. One half stayed on the ground. The other rose away from it: Raím, staggering, wiping his face in the crook of his arm, the lion on him all mirked with dust.

"Hosh!" the crowd roared. "Hosh!" Duuni came down off her toes.

"A pretty fighter," said a rusty voice at her elbow. "Incurably blind, I understand."

Doctor Amu. She teetered; he put out his hand to catch her but she gathered her robes, jumped, and dodged back through the crowd, scrabbling for her hood. In the tent she found Nine and a little girl who held up her blouse to bare her belly, on which Nine was drawing a large, strange chicken. "I gave her a discount," said Nine, surrendering the urda press. "She got a lot of chicken for her money."

Duuni wondered what the girl's mother would think for the next two weeks. She wondered what she had seen, and what Raím was, and what, oh what, she should do.

🌀

As in Greencliff, it was the children who came to Duuni first, then the adults. But in High Moles it happened sooner. It was still morning when the first miner came into the tent, his burly forearm scrubbed.

"Nightweaver, paint for me the face of the sun."

"Four pennies," said Nine, and left to watch the next bout. Duuni spoke with the man a little, to understand what the sun might be to one who spent day in the mine's night. On the breadth of his arm she drew a sun with eyes, fierce rays to shine by lantern light.

From the wrestling ground another shout went up.

Next came a woman as dark as herself, floury and smelling of gingerbread. She rolled her sleeve to show her inner wrist, where the skin was lightest, and asked Duuni to draw the kitchen goddess Li.

"I don't know her," said Duuni.

From between her big breasts the woman drew a necklace with an ivory amulet on which was scratched, vaguely, a woman at a cauldron. Then Duuni could see the goddess on her wrist and draw her, plump and smiling in the rising steam.

"Lovely. *Lovely*," said the woman. "What a hand you have! Fine as the prayer merchant's, and that's fine. Have you used a pastry press?"

"Yes."

"A pretty girl like you…oh, I can see beneath that paint! Why are you with the Roadsouls?" In a lowered voice she said, "Were you stolen?"

Duuni blushed and shook her head. But when she had dried and bound the design the woman said, "You ought not to be traveling with such folk. Do you have a mother?"

"Yes."

"What would she think to see you in this company? Nay, I'm a mother, I can read your face. Was it a lad? Did you run away? Your mother would forgive you." She patted Duuni's hand. "It's a wicked world, and worse for girls. Just think, if you were one of my own."

By then Duuni could say nothing, or even look at her, for her heart had shrunk to the size of a cherry pit. She thought of her mother's bruised, vanquished face, the punishments that Duuni's acts must have heaped on what she bore already. When her client had left she could hardly sit with herself.

Then the woman was back, smiling, with a ginger cake broad as her outspread hand. A cat was drawn on it in piped sugar. "For you, dear."

Duuni stammered thanks. "Such a pretty cat!"

"It's a horse. Oh well, I have not your skill." She cocked her head. Looking about to see they were not overheard, she said, "I come from Windy Heel, that's our booth over there. Marda the baker is my name. Come prentice to me, you and your hand. I'll hide you. I have many friends." She touched Duuni's arm. "Leave these folk. Send word to your mother that you have an honest trade."

Shelter, safety, a trade. No more wandering, never knowing.

The baker looked at her with warm eyes.

Nine skidded in. "You got to see the man they brought! He's gigastic! He's *ugly!*"

Duuni stood up. "Thank you," she said to Marda the baker. "You're so kind. But I couldn't."

As they ran back to the wrestlers Nine snapped the gingerbread from her hand.

 If the man was ugly as a privy seat Raím could not tell, but he was big, all right. His body loomed like a cliff. Raím thought of Duuni's hand, traced on his back, then was desperate not to think of it, as a swordsman tries to ignore the wing-flick of a bird.

The crowd hooted. The shadow of his opponent lay across him, and all thought fell away.

The man seemed to have no shape, only weight and heat. His breath was rank. He patted the lion on Raím's chest, laid his hands on the tattooed serpent. In halting Plain he said, "I break snake," and laughed.

Raím felt slight and brittle. The arms that crossed his in the starting pose were thick as a bull's thighs, bunched with muscle.

A beam of bright fear swung through him, as if a lantern's door had opened and shut.

The big man led him into a formal move. Raím's body wanted to dart and retreat, dart and retreat, like a squirrel; he would not allow it. Stolidly he let himself be swung, remembering how he had swung girls in the dance, his hands at their waists, their petticoats flying out.

He stumbled. Big picked him up like a child and set him right. The crowd laughed.

Raím found the tipping point he wanted and fell, pulling Big after himself. Instead of unbalancing him he found himself hooked and spun so fast his feet left the ground. He rolled; was gathered up, dangled, groomed, set on his feet.

They laughed again.

He found a little crack, a gap under Big's left arm. Quick as a lizard he slipped through it, pulling Big after himself. Big, who should have been on his back and inside out, merely snickered, one arm crossed under the other.

"Sweetie dance," he said.

Once hot, Raím grew cold as iron. He came at Big hard, was broken and flung away. The great arm slammed past his head like a dropped log; he cartwheeled and came unsteadily to his feet.

"You so sweet," said Big.

Raím broke into panic like sweat. In broken thoughts of alarm and interruption, Big was a woman huge as the mountain, himself a tiny miner entering, valiant, between her thighs.

His body squeezed out a bark of laughter. The crowd murmured. A woman said, "He is bold!"

Big's great hands laid hold of his waist. He knew of no way to bring a mountain down; instead he thought of water and melted out of that grasp again, again. It was retreat, it got him nowhere. It got Big nowhere either, and annoyed him. Raím flapped like a salmon in the paws of a bear. This image came to him clearly. Desperate, he went to it and became salmon.

He had felt the structure of his opponent; now he felt his own. With no outer sight to distract him, he looked inward.

Duuni had said he was not blind in dreams.

The idea stopped him cold. This saved his neck, for Big hooked the air where he ought to have been and not where, astonished, he was. Raím recovered, wiped his nose on the back of his hand. *A salmon. What else? What else am I?*

He looked with that inner eye.

A pale flame. Water. A shut fist. Tears.

As he saw, so he moved: up over Big like fire, down him like water. Hard as a fist, then loose as tears.

And? he thought, rolling away.

A woman.

No!

He stiffened. Big flipped him, nearly broke his arm. He rose, staggering. Had time for two breaths and a vision: *A woman. Yes.* Big took him. Raím opened to him, died, was gone from his embrace. *Both man and woman. And still a man.* He saw the long, stroked line of a girl's thigh. Thin air. Rawhide drawn bitter tight. A stone.

He let Big slide in, vanished under him, wrenched one thick leg up and over—heard something twang—drew everything he was into his belly, and sank. Then Big was bawling, slapping the sawdust, the crowd screaming, "Ground!"

Raím let go of the leg. Stood up shaking. Thought, Who am I?

"Hosh!" they shouted. "Hosh!"

"Flea Butt!" Nine's piping cry. Was Duuni there? Had she seen? He tried to look casual. He had seen without seeing, known without thinking, been man and woman at once. And he did not understand a damn thing.

☙

After that no one would wrestle until they had drunk enough to be reckless, and then they were not trying. Yet Raím was nearly grounded by a lad younger than himself, so shaken was he by the knowledge that he was not as he had thought.

He won every match. Nine swarmed his back and hung from his neck, yelling; he plucked her off and hugged her to make her stop. He was sore in every bone, and it was better than anything had been in years. To be nonchalant among men's praise and women's laughter, all the while listening for the voice of someone who rarely laughed.

He knew she was there the way the hunter knows the doe is in the wood. She would never come to him in the crowd. It pleased him to think how well he knew her.

He waited. He washed in the freezing stream. He put on breeks, but in spite of the cold he left his chest bare to show the lion. Farki locked the iron ring around his waist. Auntie gave him supper. As the night noise of the fair rose and roared he waited, ignoring the strangers who wanted to touch him. Even when Nine promised him a lavender cake from the midway he did not ask where Duuni was. He asked to be taken somewhere away from the crowd, somewhere quiet.

"*Quiet?* It's the fair!" But she led him through the maze of the tent, down two cloth alleys to an alcove where all sound was hushed and distant.

He stubbed his foot on something firm and soft. "Where is this?"

"The store place. You said quiet."

"Thank you." He sat down on a sack of wheat.

"You're *old*," she said, and left. He waited in hunter's trance, without thought, but full of slow movement like weather. He knew she would come.

She came. Rasp of a lifted curtain. "Raím."

He stood. Put his shoulders back so she could see her lion. So she could see his shoulders, his breast, himself.

She stayed where she was. "I saw you. What were you doing?"

Not the question he had expected. "Wrestling."

"But *when* you were wrestling, what were you doing?"

"Trying to ground—"

"No. Something was happening. You were…I don't know if you were *doing* it."

A silence. He said, "It was already there. When it changed I just followed it."

"When I draw," she said in her clear voice, "the image is already there. Yet it changes, right where the urda flows out of the press—changes and changes. I just follow."

A gulf, immense; and he had already leapt.

She said, "What are we?"

"I don't know."

But so happy: blind as a worm, sore in every limb, standing in the storeroom of traveling thieves talking madness with a girl he had barely touched. He heard his own unbelieving laugh.

She laid her fingers on his wrists. In half a breath he could get his arms around her.

Something stopped him. He was puzzled. He thought, as with the men he had wrestled, If I could touch her I would know what she is.

He caught the tips of her fingers. Could not get a picture—just panicky motion like a bird trapped in cupped hands, and something else that was steady as a stem. He tried to take her hands. She drew back, until again he held only her fingers.

He said, "Please."

No answer.

Well, damn her—Pillbug going nonexistent? He'd show her she was real! His arms tensed to seize her. And his cheekbone remembered the knife, shaking like her voice as she said, *Don't you touch her!*

"Oh, shit," he said. "So *that's* why you tried to kill me."

Her fingers twisted in his. He jerked his hands away, held them up as if to show some goddess he had not touched her shrine.

Rustle of silk. "*Don't,*" he said.

Silence.

"Duuni. Don't go."

Broken music, the muffled murmur of the fair. She said, "There's nowhere to go."

Nowhere one did not bring one's self along. He thought of himself sick and stupid in Monsa's shed, splashing after Ellie in the mill pond. "Was it your father?"

"No."

"Brother?"

"No." Almost inaudibly, "My hunt uncle."

"What did he do?" He could not believe he had asked.

Silence.

He wanted to shake her. Stubborn, stubborn! A crocus pushing up through frozen ground. He did not know what to do, it made him brutal. "Did he lay you down and rape you?"

"No."

"What did he do?"

Silence. Then, "With his left hand."

Raím said, "That's rape."

"It was my fault."

"*What?* God of gods. How old were you?"

"Eight."

"Be damned," he said, not to her. "How could it be your fault? Eight years old—"

"I was not supposed to be there. I was barely dressed, a red smock—"

"You weren't wearing some winding-sheet? By the Mother! In my land children play naked, boys and girls, and nobody—" But how did he know what their uncles were up to? He himself stripped girls in his mind.

"You think I'm sweet!" she shouted. "You think I was innocent. *I should not have been in the granary!*"

"I don't care if you were naked in the goddamned *temple*," he shouted back. "It didn't give your fucking uncle the right to shove his—"

Her hand cracked across his mouth. He tasted blood, refused to put his arm across his face. She stood weeping like a storm. He said, "Your uncle was a bag of shit."

"He wouldn't have just done it! He was a religious man."

"He was *horny*," said Raím. "All men are horny. Your uncle was a horny *bad* man, he raped little girls. Religious!" He turned and spat.

"He's dead." Heaviness in her voice. So many to take the uncle's place, and so many children.

"Listen. Nothing is ever all right." He laid his hands on her shoulders. She let him. "Kids aren't innocent. Old people wish they were, that's all. Kids are just here, learning everything there is." He licked his bleeding lip. "Too bad that had to be part of what you learned."

A whisper: "I wish—"

"—that you could unlearn it? Good luck."

"I wish I hadn't hit you. Raím. Did you ever rape a child?"

"*I?* All gods—you think that?"

She said nothing.

He turned his face aside. "I won't say every girl I made love to wanted it. At first. But I never—"

"It was love?"

"It was hornyness. But those girls weren't *children.*"

Silence.

"They could say no."

Silence.

No had meant *She's playing coy. Try harder.* "Damn it, Duuni!" Earnestly: "If it was you I'd take it seriously."

Silence.

He let his hands drop. "I'd *try* to."

She made the ghost of a sound, laugh or sob. And then he was laughing too, softly, at the hopelessness of it, and in the dusty closeness of the storeroom she pulled his head down and kissed him.

The hunter stands still, patient as forever, and lets the doe come to him. She had come; and she was not a doe. Not prey. She was Duuni, a person. He thought, I'm not a hunter any more.

And then he was just himself, glad as a king, drawing a girl close and closer, kissing her and dodging the uneasy thought that, depending on the ground, she might be a better wrestler than he.

$\backsim$

"You been sitting here in the dark all this time?"

"It's always dark."

"Seen Pillbug?"

"No," Raím said truthfully. "Where is she?"

"Don't know. I got a cake for her. And one for you, here it is. And Farki wants you."

"Does he," Raím said with his mouth full. He had earned Farki a lot of money. Farki could wait.

"About those miners, the ones going to buy you. They dress you up like Hosh, and the ladies clap, and the men cheer, and there's music and incense and blessings. You're extra lucky, on account of you're blind and you beat them all."

"What truck," said Raím, pleased. "But—*buy* me?"

"Oh, Farki wouldn't sell you. You're worth too much. He's renting you out, with a deposit in case of damage."

"You've seen this ceremony?"

"Nuh-uh, it's every ten years, and I can't talk that High Moles hoo-hoo. They'll come for you tomorrow if Farki settles the price."

"Fee," said Raím. "*Rental* fee." A few days ago he had not given a damn what might become of him. "It's for the one day?"

"Sunup to sunup. You ain't going to eat that?" She snatched the last of the cake from his suspended hand. "They'll dress you fine, and all the food you want."

"Foreign slush," said Raím. He was uneasy about the babies he was to bestow, but to be decked and feasted and made much of—he could bear that for a day.

"Fairtime you got to eat good. We ate doughnuts and potatoes and sweet cream and pork on a stick. Shank got sick, but Tam Chivi said get better or I'll buy you a dose from that Amu, so he got cured."

The world paused in its turning. "A dose from who?"

"Doctor Amu. That traveling medicator."

"He's here? Doctor Amu is here?"

"Nobody's killed him yet, so yes. You know him?"

Raím nodded. He forgot he had yearned to see Duuni's face and yearned for eyes to find Doctor Amu's throat.

"He'd sell you piss for whiskey," said Nine, "and those townies lay down their coin. Even Pillbug."

"Duuni? *Duuni* bought something from Doctor Amu?"

"She talked to him, is all. He gave her a love charm."

Enraged, rising to his feet. "Amu? If I—"

"He gives them to all the girls. Advertisement. A posy, you put it under your true love's pillow and he can't help himself."

"Oh." Raím had no pillow. Perhaps Duuni had laid it where he slept?

"She gave it to that greasy old blessing stone," said Nine. "If you'd kissed her like I said to maybe she'd of given it to you. Anyway Amu's charms don't work. Probably turn you into a weasel."

"Where's Amu's booth?"

"Down there," Nine said invisibly.

"The fair goes on for three days?"

"Right."

"When I'm done with that god nonsense, will you take me to Doctor Amu's booth?"

"You want a love charm?"

"I want him to turn you into a weasel."

"Gya!"

He would not tell Nine his thoughts because of her busy tongue. But when the time came, she would lead him to Doctor Amu by a back way, disguised if need be, and get him pointed right. Not because she loved him, but because she liked a nasty fight.

It would be wonderful.

He stood and stretched himself in the goodness of this day. He had a girl to kiss, a man to hate, glory, and a job. Life was as it should be. "Nine. Tell Duuni to stay away from Amu. Aren't you going to her now?"

"Nuh-uh."

"I thought you had a cake for her."

"Ate it," said Nine, and wiped her hands on him.

16

O wind that rambles the world's roads and rivers,
Carrying seeds and souls, bearing takers and givers,
Masters and slaves alike to their gambles, their graves:
Where do you come from? Where do you go?
I am god of all gods, said the wind,
And I do not know.

      Song. The Roadsouls.

She had told.

And nothing happened. And everything happened, his mouth, his big hands not tender but careful, holding back, trembling as the dog Jip had when he waited, gazing at her eyes, for her to say "Go!"

She would not say it. But she climbed onto a sack of wheat to bring her mouth where she could reach his. She found out why she had drawn her hand on him, right there.

The dusty odor of grain. She said "Stop!"

Panting, he let her go. Pulled her to him again. "Please..."

"Stop."

He held her. Loosed her, still held her waist. "Are you going to run away from me?"

She thought, Someone ran away from him.

Slowly he dropped his hands. She set her own in the middle of his chest. She did not know who she was, if she was glad or terrified.

"Duuni. Look—"

That he should say *look* struck them both as so funny they put their hands over each other's mouths. Darkness. Kisses. "Stop. Raím. *Stop.*"

"Go, then. Get away from me." Opening his arms. "Now!"

She slipped just out of reach. "I'm not running away."

"Thank you."

"I love you."

Silence. Half to himself: "What the hell shall I do?"

"What do you mean?"

"I can't…it's not like you're some…gods, a girl like you. An artist. I'm blind—"

"*I'm* not." How stupid could he be? She did not know what to do either. She thought she might not have to draw lions on her left foot any more, that was as much as she knew. "All I said was I love you."

With his head bent he said, "All right."

"Even if you have to give those ladies babies."

"Duuni—"

She left him. It is easy to get away from a blind man.

๑

In the morning she did not see him.

She blacked her face and went to her tent. Marda the baker brought her a cake in the shape of a man with a sugar smile. Nine left to watch the wrestlers, not Raím this time but Tam Chivi, lithe in his clout. Marda asked again, low-voiced, if Duuni would hire out to her. Duuni said no. Marda said, would Duuni come see her booth, at least? That it was not a real decision if she had not seen what might be.

Duuni had half an idea, then, that she might work for Marda and…oh, something, maybe buy Raím from Farki? Though

233

surely a slave cost more than a silk blouse. She told Marda she would come if she could. When they closed the booth for the noon meal she told Nine she would bring her gingerbread, scrubbed her face, and slipped away.

The baker's booth was within hail of the wrestlers, so she was not afraid. Halfway down the midway Doctor Amu was wagging a bottle in the air. There was the prayer merchant with her dogs, painting some god, perhaps Hosh; a miner looked over her shoulder. His face as he watched the brush move was like Riinu's when she had watched Duuni draw.

The prayer merchant looked up. Duuni looked away, hurried on.

At the bakery Marda waved her to come behind the counter, then back behind a long canvas with dreadful, wobbly paintings of breads and sweets, to an oven cobbled of bricks and tin. She introduced her husband, a broad, smirchy man who grinned and wiped his brow on his sleeve; a shy, smiling daughter; several nieces. She hinted that Duuni might hire on. Gave her tea, too much to eat, and a paper full of good hard ginger nuts "for the imp who works with you, she needs fattening." Duuni thanked her and prepared to go back to her tent, determined to keep Nine from gobbling the lot and guard some for Raím.

Marda kissed her. "Remember, dear, we want you. If you change your mind... Ah! Look, there he is!"

A commotion on the midway, horns, hooting shouts. The crowd drew back. Marda said, "The Hosh!" Men with trumpets, men with picks and mattocks, shovels and pikes. Then oxen, beribboned like girls, pulling a jouncing wooden cart rubbed with gold leaf.

In the cart, Raím.

His head and arms were bound with ribbons like the oxen. He held on with both hands so as not to be pitched out, on his face such arrogant shame it was clear he half wished he would be. But she hardly noticed.

For he wore the master tunic. Her weaver's eye found the little rent over his heart.

"The Hosh." Marda's voice said she was half in love with him, never mind her husband. Her daughter clasped her hands and said, "There never was such a handsome Hosh. And blind! Oh Mother!"

"We shall have good years and good dreams," said Marda. "Duuni, how could you travel with such a man and not fall in love with him? I would hardly sleep!"

Duuni said nothing. She watched Raím out of sight with her hand over her mouth, for his look of embarrassed pride struck her painfully, at once funny and sweet.

"There," said Marda. "Tomorrow you'll watch him consecrate the mine? Come along with us, surely your people will allow it. The ceremony is only once in ten years, and it brings such blessing!"

Duuni thought, Why shouldn't I go? She would ask Auntie if she might. And if Auntie said no, well...*she* did not wear a slave ring. "I'd love to," she said.

Marda clapped her hands. "Tomorrow at dawn. We'll leave the men to bake and just us women go. And should you change your mind about working for me..."

Duuni escaped.

She went straight to Auntie. She felt shy; there was a veil between herself and the Roadsoul-born, not even habit had raised it. She told Auntie the baker had invited her to the blessing of the mines.

Auntie gave her a long look. "Choose for yourself."

Emboldened, Duuni said, "Please, why is it that Raím...Flea Butt...the Hosh...must be chained, but I go free?"

"Tear the mountains down," said Auntie. "Build the valleys up." She turned her back.

Puzzled, Duuni went back to Nightweaver's tent. She came near to telling Nine about the expedition, but thought better of it; Nine would whine to come too. As secret compensation Duuni gave her half the cakes. The rest she stuffed into the leather sash-wallet that held her flint and steel.

"What're you doing that for?" said Nine.

"I don't trust you."

"I can be good."

"Snakes might walk," said Duuni.

 Morning, after an uneasy and exultant night. He had hoped to catch Duuni again before the god silliness, but Auntie roused him before dawn and took him to the stream. He splashed cautiously, though Duuni had said the lion would last two weeks. He put on his patched clothes.

Nine came to fetch him. She tugged him along by his stick and sang, minor and sad.

Raím shivered. "Has Farki rented a man to them before?"

"Think so. Guess those miners can't give their ladies enough babies," said Nine. "Hey. Where was I before I was born?"

" Ah...inside your mother."

"I know *that*. I mean before *anything*. Those High Moles ladies, they get their babies off you and their husbands, but who made me?"

"Your mother and father."

"Nuh-uh. They wouldn't have made me on purpose, then just sell me to the mills. Some Hosh or other, he made me. He should've made me Roadsoul-born."

Raím wondered who her father was. If he knew, he might some day find him and beat him with his fists.

"You take care when you're giving those ladies their kids," said Nine. "The good ladies, you give them nice kids. And the bad ones, don't give them any at all." When Raím did not answer she jerked at the stick. "Hey. You listening?"

"I am not Hosh. I'm not giving anybody any kids. Why can't you learn some manners?"

"'Cause I'm a bad kid," Nine said softly. "Else whoever made me wouldn't have given me to that mum and dad."

"Who you're born to has nothing to do with being good or bad. It's chance."

"No, it's not," said Nine. "Chance is Farki."

☙

Farki touched his shoulder. "They have come for you."

"Tell them to wait until I've finished breakfast."

"They have come. You are not a god yet."

"It's a rental, right?"

"You have my word."

Raím wondered what Farki's word might mean. Farki led him along a low alleyway. Burring murmur of a small crowd. Farki's voice, apt in their hollow language. Raím was taken by the elbows and inspected. Jink of money in a sack—plenty of money, by the sound. He felt smug.

Farki's hand left his elbow. He had meant to ask when Farki would fetch him back, but someone dragged at his sleeve; he pulled away and said in Plain, "Let someone offer me his shoulder, or the butt of a pike."

The haft of some implement nudged his palm. Then it was a long, fast-paced walk. Now and then a hand came out of nowhere to pat him, and was warned off with hoots.

They brought him to a stone wall, cold as a midwinter quarry. The unknown tongue echoed around him like rockfall, pleading, declaiming. He shifted from foot to foot to keep warm. He was having a pleasant daydream about Duuni, hoping it did not show, when without warning there was a trumpet's brass blare, he was seized from all sides and flung into the air.

He came down, thrashing, into a forest of rough hands. Roars of laughter. He was carried some distance, and with another roar flung into a tank of ice water.

He came up clawing, scrambled out and hurled himself in the direction of the crowd. They were hundreds, and smelled of rum; with good humor they piled on him until he stopped squirming. Someone, priest or official, bent to his ear and said in creaking Plain, "Next very good, you like."

He remembered he was a god, that people do strange things to gods and their representatives. They carried him, singing. Screech of big doors opening. A rush of steam; once more he was in the air, but this time he plunged, with a tidal wallow, into a tank of water deliciously hot.

It came to his waist. He stood up in time to hear the doors close. The laughter around him now was all female. He found the rim of the tank and prepared to climb out; a forest of women's hands pushed him back in. "Wash, wash!" said their owners, squealing with laughter.

"I washed this morning," he said. They laughed harder. Obligingly he splashed his head. After shrieks and instruction he understood: he was to take off his clothes and wash, right there in front of—he supposed—all the women in High Moles.

It was strange. Not long ago he would have been thinking to himself, Give these chits an eyeful! Let them want me! But now he thought of Duuni, fighting him, fighting herself.

He wondered what it must be like for the woman.

At least they let him wash himself. He had never been in so much bathwater at once. By the time they let him climb out of the tub, his pride had returned, even a little vanity. He took his time with the warm towel.

They gave him a clout of softened linen. Trousers, heavy and full. A wide sash, stockings, boots with the fleece turned in. He could guess how good he looked, bare to the waist and painted with the lion. He wished Duuni could see him. A woman's hand took his and led him out of the steamy room, down a dismally cold corridor. A heavy curtain met his face. He stepped through it.

A roar: the sounds of a great hall full of people. Chants, incense, smoke. He was led again, then left standing—on a podium, perhaps, to be admired from all sides.

The chants went on. At each pause the crowd, in one voice, cried, "*Woop!*"

Woop? he thought. What the hell?

It went on for hours. He stood. And stood. Weight on one foot, then the other. Each time he moved, the crowd, in an awed howl, cried "*Woop!*" He began to test whether he could make them do it by turning his head, crossing his arms. They wooped like anything.

He was absorbed in this experiment when they uncrossed his arms and dropped something over his head: a tunic. He clambered into it, thinking how badly he needed to piss. When it was halfway on he knew what it was.

He settled it on his shoulders and felt the front panel with his hands. There was the little rent, like a mouth, where a blade had entered. Perhaps only a master was allowed to mend it. The tunic had been washed, and smelled like wind.

He stroked it. "*Woop!*" said the crowd. An official at his elbow whispered, "Hosh likes?"

Raím nodded. Amu, get screwed! Whispered back, "When can I piss?"

"Later."

Fortunately it was not much later, and fortunately there was a privy, so he could be alone for a moment and think. Doctor Amu had sold the master tunic to the people of High Moles. It had come back to Raím, as if it belonged to him.

When he came out of the privy the official chuckled and said, "Hosh feels better, eh?"

"Much." For as the tunic had found Raím, so Raím would find Doctor Amu, and make sure he got what belonged to *him*.

⑨

He had not known it was so tedious being a god. Or so hungry. There were more chants, and anointings of parts of him in water and very sticky wine that he would rather have been drinking. He was required to hold staffs with things on the ends of them he could not see, walked back and forth in spaces he could not tell the shape of. He thought about how hungry he was, and how tomorrow he would tell Duuni and Nine about the woopers. Ribbons were tied on him. He was led onto a cart. He clutched its railing as, in a procession of chanters, it jarred over cobblestones toward the familiar roar of the fair.

Oh, gods.

Beribboned, paraded, the prize pig. He tried to make himself smaller. No use, of course, so he stood straight with flaming face as the cart bounced and tilted down the midway. He heard Tam Chivi's laugh. Heard Nine squeal, "Eee, *look* at him!" Where was Duuni? Hands touched him, were dragged away as the cart rolled on.

The sun set. The cart stopped. He was led out of it and seated in some great hall—the same one as before, or another. By then he was in a vile temper. What use to be a god if he could not smite those who annoyed him with boils or thunderbolts? But it turned out all right. Huge platters of food were set before him: roast beef, fish braised in wine, songbirds, suckling pig. There was fiery spirit, but the experience in Monsa's shed had stayed with him, and he rose from the table nearly steady.

They led him to what seemed a throne and brought a mask that fit over his whole head. He explored it with his hands.

It had no eyes.

A mask is a disguise through which the eyes of the living look out. But an eyeless mask—the idea had an edge. It kept him alert for a while, listening to the endless chant, but he was full of food and drink; he drooped against the side of the throne, now and then elbowed to wake with a snort.

So the day passed, and the night. He woke from a doze and knew it was almost dawn, he could smell it. He was grateful. His head ached; he was tired of being a god, he wanted to be Bright Blood the Blind Magician and kiss Duuni and find out whether, if he took it ever so slowly, she might let him slide his hands under her shirt.

He wondered whether they would let him keep the master tunic.

⑨

The unseen officials took away the mask, led him back into the cart and walked beside it. The air was cold. *Whut-whut* of windblown torches, clink of harness and hobnails. The procession wound upward, up and up. Religion continued in the background: chanting, and mournful instruments of brass or tin. Then they were standing against a cliff—he heard the metallic echo of the horns' squawk. He thought of the stories he would tell, and felt like a rich man.

The cart stopped. They led him out. An annoying picture formed in his mind: what if they took him to a cliff and pushed him off? Religious people did strange things.

A stony path wound upward a long way. It felt high and open. His uneasiness increased. But hands drew him closer to the mountain itself, and he remembered he was a rental. Broken stone underfoot. He guessed he had been brought to the mouth of a mine and was to bless it as Hosh.

He hoped it would not take too long, and afterward there would be breakfast.

It was indeed a mine adit, framed by timbers and closed by a thick wooden door. The men made him lay his hands on it while prayers were said. They pulled him back. The door, with a horrid rusty screech, was dragged open.

From the crowd, murmur and moan. Two men took his arms. He was escorted forward; did not like the smell of it; was pushed another step onto something soft and hard and stiff, and fell forward over it.

Behind him the huge door shut. Through its heavy wood he heard the horns bray, the voices roar. Then horns and voices faded, and there was no sound at all.

17

Over the paidman, over the king,
Over the lady with the diamond ring,
Over the pickpocket, over the queen,
Over the chimney sweep, the grass grows green.
Skipping rhyme. The Roadsouls.

He cracked his forehead on the stony floor and made his darkness starry for a moment, remembering the colors green and red.

Nothing struck him, or moved. No sound but a tiny hiss of wind under the door. He raised his head and craned about. He was sure he was alone. In a beast cave there was always a living odor, bast and scat; here there was another smell, like old leather. Bats? But bats had their own acrid stink, their rustle and pinprick squeak.

He passed his hands along the stony floor until they met the cloth he had fallen over. It was finely woven, wrapped around a barrel. At the top of the barrel was leather. He felt it cautiously. Put his finger up a dry nostril, laid his palm on teeth.

He scrambled backward, wiping his hand on his thigh. But there was another mummy behind him, and, when he scuttled away from that one, a third, a fourth. All wore tunics of fine cloth, and boots with the fleece turned inward.

The bland darkness that had pressed him for years went heavy, the mountain pressing down. His body jerked; his feet did not move. They had died as close to freedom as they could get, some with faces pressed to that tiny sibilance under the door.

He gasped. Sweated. Nothing changed. All was as it had been for a long, long time, altered only by the addition of one Hosh every ten years.

How many?

It was not much, a fingerhold in terror, as a tiny crack in the granite of a cliff face is to a climber. How many Hosh? Five? Five hundred? He did not know where the walls were, or anything beyond his darkness. All these men, he supposed, had been big and handsome and red-haired. Where had they gotten them all?

Farki. And Farkis before Farki.

He was no longer cold. Rage opened in him like a night-blooming flower, so exquisite there was no room for fear. Of course Farki had known. *Rent?* Hardly. There had been too many coins chiming in that sack.

He got to his feet, found the low ceiling with his arm still bent. To hate someone so completely made the world simple. "I'll get out of here," he said, "and find Farki."

But there was no out.

There was only in.

He found the door and felt about with his feet. Huge timbers held up the roof. At the foot of every timber lay a body, sometimes two. At first he could not bring himself to touch them; then he could. Each man had died with his cheek pressed to the wood as if to the tree it had once been, growing toward the light. He wondered which of these cold piles had known his own Farki.

"Brothers," he said. Perhaps even now the Roadsouls' carts were creaking down the roadway, back to the winter lowlands. Duuni would be looking for him.

Duuni.

He cut off the thought, slammed it away. *Never.* Made himself focused, cold.

Because of the bodies he could not pace the measure of the room. He could feel it was not vast. Could not judge the number of Hosh, but there were many; the mountain had been hungry a long time. Some were heaped one on another, but most huddled apart, as though to die against another death had been too frightening, and each had hoarded his little warmth alone.

He returned to the door and traced the right-hand wall. It led to a tunnel, its low arch framed by a timber carved with a sun. He listened. Nothing. Groped back to the door, tried the left-hand wall. It brought him to the same tunnel, the same carving. Only one way to go.

Trailing one hand on the left wall, holding the other across his forehead, he shuffled forward. It was not the way out, but he was not going to die in there with the rest of them.

It was no darker for him than it always was.

The tunnel bent to the left. He trailed his hand across its low roof until he understood that it branched: left, right, straight ahead.

It was a little warmer than it had been at the windy door. Not warm, just the even chill of underground, unchanged by seasons. He kept his left hand on the wall and followed it into an abortive tunnel, a cul-de-sac. Against the back was another Hosh. He stepped over it and followed the wall back to the dividing ways.

He entered the center tunnel. It had a spacious feel. He stopped. Felt forward with his foot.

The floor curved to nothing: thin air.

He felt about for a hunk of rock. Tossed it. One, two, three; then not a stony crack but a thump, as though its fall had been damped on cloth.

Hosh.

There was no room to pass the shaft on the left side. He trailed his hand across the ceiling to the right: no passage there, either. He returned to the junction and tried the right hand tunnel, the last.

This one went deeper in. Shuffling, he came up against a huge slab that had slid from the wall and crumbled. It blocked the passage; no; there was a crack he could get his arm and shoulder in. He turned sideways and tried it. Took off the master tunic and gripped it in one hand while he forced himself through, tried not to think about getting stuck, the rock tight to his chest. Squirmed like a lizard, tumbled forward onto rubble. The air changed, no longer the dry cold of the heights but heavy, dank. Far off, the clink of falling water: *drop, drop-drop.*

He got up, put the tunic on and laid his hand on the left wall. Shuffled through a pile of sticks: a Hosh, just bones, rotted by the damp.

Down the tunnel. His feet stubbed timber. A telltale draft rose, belling the tunic hem.

He tossed a fist-sized rock. One, two, three...and four and five, still falling, until at last, far and away down, he heard a click, then another, as if the rock had glanced off the side of the shaft and never struck bottom at all.

He stood listening to the drip of water far below.

The shaft had a timber headframe, with room to pass on the left. This he did, but beyond the frame the tunnel became a wall of stone. He worked around to the right. The same: no further tunnel.

So.

He could go back to the doorway where the mummies lay. Or he could go down.

Down—that would be easy! The easiest thing in the world.

What bothered him was that he would be a long time falling, probably striking the sides of the shaft, before he hit bottom—if there was a bottom. There would have to be a bottom...would there not? If the shaft was a manmade thing. But what if it was not? What if the miners had found it already there, had made use of it by driving tunnels off the sides, and the shaft itself had no bottom?

He sat down, held tight to the timbers as if the shaft sucked him downward.

The feeling passed. He forced himself to stand. Hiked up the tunic, and pissed into the pit.

He had used to piss off cliffs. It was like cheating at a distance contest, the sunlit jewels drifting away on the wind. Too bad Nine was a girl, he thought. She would have liked cliff-pissing.

Strange that though he could not think of Duuni, he could think of Nine. He leaned over the pit and shouted into it one of her skipping rhymes.

> Mama has a fishpond, Papa has a pole,
> Papa has a fence post, Mama has a whole
> New pantry, tea chest, cedar chest, lock;
> Papa found the keyhole and poked it with his cock-
> A-doodle di-do, cock-a-doodle dee,
> *In* goes the handyman, and *out* goes she!

A slight echo. Warm air rose past his face; the shaft went down forever.

He climbed the frame. The timbers were thick as his body. At the top was a huge iron wheel with a thick rope looped over it. Directly below was a wicker basket, such as two men might stand in to be lowered into the pit.

He shoved at the pulley. It turned a little, with a horrific screech. The arrangement was simpleminded as a bucket in a well, he did not trust it. One's weight would have to be borne by men below who dragged on the rope. In any case, to go down that shaft would be insane.

But the miners of High Moles had gone down. They had built this rig to go down. He could have figured out how to use it, if he had companions other than all those dead Hosh. The rope was too thick and heavy for a rider to pull himself up hand over hand; for the basket to have ended up at the top, the rope must have been pulled on by someone down below.

Or some *thing,* said his fear. He ignored it. What if, down there, there was another way out?

"Where shall I die?" he said. "Up here, or down there?"

It would be as dark in either place. For that matter it would be as dark on a sandy creek bank at noon, though there would be more to listen to. The only sound here was that drip, drip, far below.

I couldn't pull myself up in the basket, he thought, but maybe I could let myself down, if I clung to the rope and used my body as a brake. I'm a madman.

He was almost happy. He got a grip on the headframe and stepped down into the basket.

His feet went through the bottom with a crackle of dissolving wicker. He caught himself, swung from his hands with one foot tangled in the wreckage, hauled himself back up by terror and the strength of his arms. Heard the broken basketry rasp and clatter down out of hearing in the pit.

"That basket should be iron," he said aloud, hugging the frame with arms and legs. "Wicker was stupid." How that kept happening, the world giving way beneath his feet!

He crawled off to think. He could shinny down the rope. It could not go down forever; it had been hauled on from somewhere not impossibly far down, or its own weight would have made it immovable. The far end must be tied off somewhere, at a place people wanted to get to.

What if it wasn't? What if it had been released to hang straight down? What if he got to the end and hung there, dangling over the pit?

He could not be the only man who had wanted more reassurance than the rope. He hitched along the timbers that framed the shaft, feeling about until he found a foot-long iron pin driven into the timber, and another a little below it driven into the stone. They were scaly with rust, but when he kicked them they felt sound. He lowered himself. Sure enough, there was another pin below at a comfortable reach, like a ladder.

He climbed back to the headframe and took stock of how hungry he was, how strong he felt, what might be below. Found himself asking if he should risk it.

Risk it?

He laughed, an ugly sound that echoed from the jagged rock. "*In goes the handyman,*" he sang. Hand over hand, feeling for each step, he climbed down into the pit.

18

The world tears like rotten cloth.
Falling, never striking earth,
falling through earth.
Come, Death!
Death at least real.

      Young shaman's chant. All tribes.

She knew what she had seen.

"We'll have luck these next years," said Marda the baker. "Such a bonnie man as that. A perfect Hosh… ah, but look at you, pale as ash! It's hard to see those souls given to the mountain—and you knew the lad, no doubt. Be glad! The gods love him. Come now, it's done."

But Duuni could not walk, could only stare at the ancient doors, the rusty bar dropped across, the lock rammed home. She was ice, falling through empty air.

Marda prattled and clucked. She hailed a cart full of friends; a tall woman lifted Duuni into it as if she were two years old. Marda and her daughter and nieces climbed in as well, they gathered Duuni against them and petted her, exclaiming how gentle she was, too kind for such sights.

The falling stopped. Still she had no ground, could only pant, could not bear to be touched. She would wrench herself away from those kind women and run—where? To the Roadsouls? To Farki who had sold him?

She raised her head from Marda's bosom. Marda said, "There, duckling! Feel better?"

"Let me come with you," she said. "I want to work for you."

"My dear, my daughter! You know that will delight me! It will delight us all."

She pressed Duuni's head down again, the others clapped their hands and said the whole family would love her. The cart brought them again to the bakers' booth. Marda trundled about, sharing in a low voice the news that she was to be one of them. "Stay at the back," said Marda. "If those wicked Souls come after you, my husband will see to them." The baker nodded and scowled and rolled his shoulders. He was one of those whom Raím had grounded the first day; Farki could stop him with one hand.

Clang, the oven door opened, the air was sweet with nutmeg. The daughter took Duuni by her stiff arms and drew her behind the canvas curtain. "Stay here, no one can see you. I'll fetch a smock, you won't look so like a Soul."

Duuni stood where she was put, seeing him, a hot gold spark dropped into a pit, dwindling, then dark. Suddenly the bakers were lying down, or so she thought; the world cried around her like starlings, "Poor chick, poor kit!" and she understood that it was she who lay on the ground. Marda had her arm around her shoulders. A tin cup banged her teeth. She drank bitter tea, gasped and shuddered.

"You're green as a duck's egg. Have those wicked folk got you with child?" said Marda. "They shan't have you. I sent the lads to scout, they say the Souls are packing their carts, they'll be off southwest down the mountain road. Thieves! We'll hide you, and when the fair's done, it's southeast we're bound, to Windy Heel at the foot of the pass. There we'll winter, my bird, and you shall teach us to draw cats in icing." She tapped Duuni's cheeks with thumb and forefinger, as one does to make a baby smile.

Duuni did not smile. Marda gave her the mug to hold and jumped up to help her husband with the cakes. Duuni did not drink. She had remembered a story of Ganu's, about a princess imprisoned in a cave. A brave and clever prince steals the key, he kills the ogre...

Beyond a gap in the canvas was a gray slice of mountain strewn with mine adits; nearer to, the fair went on livelier than ever. Across its brightness a shadow sauntered. Paused. Odor of sweat and oregano, a rheumy eye.

"Ah," said Doctor Amu. He stepped back, visible to her but not to the bakers' oven dance. "My little friend."

He held a flask of whiskey. Duuni had a cup of tea. He raised the flask to her; unthinking, she raised her cup and bowed her head as Ganu had taught. He chuckled and rocked on his heels. Not from drunkenness; she could see he was one whom drink made careful.

She was careful, too. She looked his way only in glances as she said, "He was wearing that tunic."

"Indeed he was. You've a fine eye."

"You sold it to those people."

"Awesome, how the gods work. High Moles needed a master tunic for the sacrifice; I had one. I am but an instrument," he said, and drank from the flask.

"Will you get it back?"

He paused, the bottle in midair. "Those gates open but once in a decade."

"There were heaps of men in there. Dozens. Men in fine clothes."

He said softly, "Well, aren't you the little Roadsoul."

She shrugged.

"Naturally that very thought had occurred to me. But to desecrate a holy place—" he laid his hand on his heart "—would be a solemn undertaking. More to the point, my lark, were it possible, it would already have been done." He corked the bottle, tucked it in the top of his boot. "What might be your interest in that tunic?"

She tried to look impudent, but blushed till she burned. "I...I wanted to see it close. The man who wore it, the Hosh—"

"Ah," said Doctor Amu, scrying her face.

"It's the tunic! I'm a weaver. I mean I *was*—"

"Not long with the Souls? And now you've found yourself a better place. Resourceful! Adventurous! *And* a fine eye. You'll go far, my lass, indeed you will." He turned away. Stopped as if struck. Turned back, and said, "Hmh."

Duuni said nothing, sick and stupid.

"A thought," he said. "Merely a thought. As I said, were it possible to open those doors, it would have been done long ago. However. It occurs to me that if even the great Doctor Amu, purveyor of health and vitality, believes that impossible, then certainly your common man believes it. Hence your common man would never try it. Hence..." He rocked on his heels. "It seems likely it has never been tried."

She raised her head. He patted his boot, found the bottle and drank, but not deeply. "I am a fool. The great Doctor Amu, and it takes a pretty Roadsoul lass to bring him to his senses."

"You mean you would try—"

"Eh? What? Shh!" He scowled. His wet eyes dodged with thought. "Would you kill the plan before it is born? What kind of Soul are you?"

She put her hand to her mouth; one of the baker's nieces sent her a quick, sympathetic look. Careful not to glance through the gap in the canvas, Duuni whispered, "I can't pay you."

"It is I who should pay you, for nudging sense into an ignorant old man. What an idiot I've been! Telling myself it can't be done. Comes a slip of a girl, not half my age, says, 'Why not?' A mirror held up to a dunce." He glowered. "Of course, they don't die right off. The Hoshes. That's the point, they say. The mountain sucks the life from them slowly; the gods like that. So the lad *in* the tunic—" he blinked his pink eyes "—will be quite alive. And angry. Such a wrestler, he could kill me with one blow."

"He knows me. I'd talk to him. He wouldn't care about the tunic if he could escape from the mountain—"

Doctor Amu dabbed at his eyes with his sleeve. "If I had a daughter, I would want a daughter like you. Why have I no daughters?" He cocked his head. "There now—who knows, perhaps I have. But none like you. Listen. Have you courage enough? Dead men in heaps—can you bear it? Ah. Your face says you can. You *will*." His look was tender. "If there is a living man among the dead, you can bear it."

"I bear what I must," she said. That was true.

"Not like town girls, who must have their cakes." He jerked his chin at the oven. "But nay, lass. It won't work."

"Why not?"

"Scandal. Think of the good wife here letting you go off with me—even the great Doctor Amu. There would be a story!"

"I'm seventeen, I can do what I like."

"Even so, your reputation. If you were my daughter," he said, "I would forbid you to go."

"A man's life is at stake," she said. The bakers were putting up the trays. What was she to do? "And...and a master tunic. Would you throw away—"

"Wait. Wait. And quick with it, or these good folk will think things amiss. I shall send you an escort. Will that serve? A woman. A dignified older woman. Who shall we say she is?"

"My aunt. I've told the baker I might have brothers at the mines."

"Just the thing. Everyone has an aunt, and the whole world comes to the fair. When, when? Stay here, lass; stay where you are, I shall send your aunt right round, asking for...what is your name, dear?"

"Duuni."

"Duuni the bold. My daughter, had I the choice; were I a god, like the Hosh. Ah well, we all grow old. Wait here for your auntie." He turned away. Turned back and said, low and passionate, "How fortunate I was to meet you! But not so fortunate as the Hosh."

He turned, and was gone.

☙

Duuni wished the old woman were her auntie, when she came. Tiny and bent and quick as a wren, patting her arm, patting her face, and embracing her, scolding in soft chirps. Why had Duuni not told her she was in High Moles? Had she come to her senses and left those horrid Roadsouls? And had she been wise at last and taken a position with this good woman?

She clung to Duuni's sleeve. She told Marda, who was at first suspicious, that Duuni was a good child but willful; did she really want to take her as apprentice? Marda answered with spirit that Duuni was good. Duuni stood with her eyes cast down. All this behind the curtain; the family kept stopping their work to listen. Then the auntie must have a long look round the bakeshop to be sure Marda was a decent woman; this ended with them chatting about a peddler they both liked, and hugging each other like sisters. The auntie must take Duuni to buy a garland to lay at the blessing stone, to begin her new life.

"Wise and sweet," said Marda, pulling out her purse. "Nor shall you spend for the garland. But take her by the alley behind the booths, look sharp, and bring her back directly."

"That I shall, dear," said the auntie, tucking the coin in her sleeve. "Child, be quick, for they will want you here."

Swathed in a smock, Duuni pulled Marda's shawl across her face and left the baker's booth without one glance backward. She knew who sold the garlands.

Amu was tossing his wares haphazard into the cart. "Dear Duuni," he said, "was that not well done?" She was shaking, fearful of being stopped, and there was a paidman near, she did not like how he looked at her. "Come here, back of the cart. One moment, while I pay your auntie." He scratched in a wallet, found a coin and gave it to the woman, who had dropped Duuni's arm.

"Eh?" she said. "You thief, knowing what you'll have from it?"

"Ah now, old hen, you're jealous." He gave her a corked bottle. She scowled, received the bottle like gold, stowed it in her shawl and disappeared into the bustle of the fair like a finch into a hedge. He turned to Duuni. "Now. Around back of the cart."

There was a young man there. A paidman. On an inbreath she started back; but Doctor Amu was with her, rum and herbs and sweat, he gripped her upper arm. "Here's our lass," he said, and the paidman's hand was over her mouth, his hard arm round her. "Remember whose she is," said the doctor, and turned to his packing as if there were no time to be lost, though he paused long enough to give her a fatherly look. "Pity about the Hosh," he said. "You and he were made for each other, gullible as kittens."

☙

There were three paidmen. The young one had skin the color of Duuni's, black hair, and a scar down his temple. He was even a little kind; when they were on the road, jangling in the hasty cart, he loosed the gag that cut her mouth, saying, "You scream, it goes on again, tighter." In the half-light of the canvas canopy he showed her his fist. The second paidman laughed; the third looked back from his seat next to Amu, who was driving, and said, "I'd make her scream with pleasure."

Amu tapped him with the butt of the whip. "Users to pay, Greb, and you haven't a penny."

"Trade?"

"For what? Your dirty sark?" They nudged each other's shoulders. She could see past them through the open front of the canopy to the road and the wild land beyond. They had left the bowl that held High Moles, crossed a low pass, and now traveled on the east side of the mountain, heading south and up. She thought of the brothers who had gone out of her life as boys, and wondered if the dark paidman was her brother. If it mattered to anybody; it did not matter to her.

She did not struggle or scream. She could have; there were other carts on the road. Amu had not even bothered to take her ragged wallet. Chained by one ankle, she sat in the cluttered, swaying cart. Not because struggle was useless, though that was so. But because she could not bear any more to be human, in the human world.

They drove on. When the passing carts were fewer they slowed. The men's jokes grew warmer. It was afternoon. The track was rough; they turned off the road, itself no highway, onto a rutted forest lane that climbed the mountain flank.

It seemed early to stop for the night. The drivers climbed down from their high seat. Amu said, "Let's get this little matter over with, shall we?"

Laughter. The second paidman opened the tailgate. She had no wish but to be quit of this world. She saw the faces of Maidy and Toady and skinny little Bones, and wished they had a world to live in that was not this one. Amu unlocked the chain and pulled her out of the cart.

"Lads, I'm a sensitive man," he said. "A bit of privacy, please."

"Gods. Silk sheets?" Greb threw him a dirty blanket.

"Nature's sheets. Sweet tracery of autumnal bush and fern, now get the hell out," said Amu. "You can have her when I'm done. But she's to be sold; you damage her, you pay."

He pulled her to him amid laughter and lewd talk. She did not see them, saw no one but Nine in the grip of the overseers, dirty and jeering, lifting up her hands.

"Now, now." Amu dragged her into the brush. Threw down the blanket. His voice was soft, his right hand like iron; with his left he fumbled under his tunic, below the big belly stained with grease and rum and the grime of the road. "You understand that I must. Just to be sure, dear—to be *certain* you're clear about what you are now. What you are to be." He groped at her, rucking and pawing. "Pants on women, never liked them." His hand found her bare waist. "Perhaps you'll give me a daughter," he said.

She drew one breath. His face was slack, intent. The girl in the granary; Nine with her jump rope, chanting. *Prince grabs the princess by her long black hair...*

She made a strange sound, almost a laugh. Doctor Amu in his rummaging was for an instant distracted. She jerked half out of his grip; he caught her wrist and wrenched it upward as though to hit her with her own fist. "Be glad it is I who am your first," he said, panting, "and not some paidman."

She swung away from him, felt something click in her wrist, swung back and kicked him as hard as she could with her pointed boot, right where the princess kicked the prince.

He shrieked, crumpled to the dirt. She clawed out of the tangled bush. Light, air; the paidmen, waiting their turn beyond the cart, rose as they saw her—angry for an instant, then beginning to run, laughing, as they guessed what she had done, what Amu had not done, what they now could do.

There was nowhere to go. She ran only to run, up the steep, stony slope toward gray pinnacles, above them only sky. Granite scree, low silver plants frost-stopped in bloom. Her feet sent loose rocks spinning down among the bodies that dodged and laughed below her. "Oho! The doe flees! She stands!" Nowhere to go, only the sun glittering at the world's edge.

Climbing, scrambling. Raím climbed with her. She saw him. He sprang like a roebuck, his bow in his hand, laughing and calling, *Come! Come!* That was how she knew he was dead already, for all Amu had said it would be slow: for Raím could see. His eyes met hers, merry as a wood god's. The last pitch was bare scoured rock; as she gained it he ran ahead of her to that shining edge.

Fly! he cried, and jumped.

She ran as he had, the sky enlarging, her heart gone big as the sky. Here was the edge, the white gulf. *Fly*—

Nine's voice said, *Huh? Are you stupid?*

Her foot was on the cliff's brink. Nothing below: blue cloud, wind. Everything in her body cried *Stop!*

She tried to stop. But her heart had already jumped, it pulled her body after it, and she fell.

19

As though there were two ways to go
and I had long ago, unknowing,
chosen one of them.
Too late to go back.
Going forward,
right or wrong.

Shrine poem. Welling-in-the-Mountains.

She looked at the sky. Thought it was water, did not know why she should be underwater looking up. Saw it was sky.

No motion but wind.

Blood in her mouth. She tried to move; screek and chink of stone, sensation of sliding. She lay still. The wind blew. On her left side wet blood was cold in the wind.

Web of twigs at her face: a stunted bush. She put out her hand. Grasped the bush. Began to pull herself up—not upright, just head-up, still sprawled on the scree.

The bush came away in her hand. She slid farther. Lay awhile in the scratty brush, looking at the angle where slope met sky. Saw another bush, growing from a crack like the first. Shiny brown scraps of leaf clung to it, like fairy hats.

She put out her hand. Gripped, pulled, slow as a snake. Rocks slid, spun into silence. Distant crashes.

Her cheek lay against the hand that held the stem of the bush. Her left wrist hurt. Before her eyes were gray stone, orange lichen, gray-green plants tiny as moss clutched tight to the rock. A lizard's-eye view.

She made herself lizard. Did not look down. On bleeding knees and elbows she felt for each crack and ledge as she crept and slithered upward. No thought. She knew which holds were good before her hands touched them. Her left hand was not working right but it did not matter, only her body with the body of the mountain.

She crawled back to the rim and over it. Turned her head to see the foreslope where her instant's hesitation had landed her, and, just beyond the scrub that had hidden her, the straight drop into the gulf. Far below, a hawk circled.

No one. No sound.

She could not put weight on her left hand. She crawled down from the ridge, into the oak brush and the wind-flagged pines. The sun had set, dusk was cold as winter. Soon she would be as dead as if she had slid that last yard; but cold is a kind death.

Only silence. She wept, cradling her hurt wrist.

So.

So the world had changed for her again; *she* had chosen it.

She sat up. The world kept changing; maybe the problem was not the world, but that her teachers had told her it was changeless? Through chattering teeth she said, "They don't know."

And, she thought, I don't either. So I'll just go on, paying attention, for as long as I can. But I can't stay here because I'll die.

She did not know anywhere to go that she would not die. But *down* seemed best. She stood. Limping, clinging to the slope of the mountain, she started down.

ᕼ

The corrie up which she had fled was a chute of gray stone, bare as if giants had slid down it. She kept to the side, among the boulders. At the bottom the road was a pale line in the bluey dusk, winding away on either hand. Of Amu and his troupe only cart tracks in the dust remained.

She could walk along the road. If a beast did not seize her, if she did not die of cold, she would come in time to the main road, and a village. There she might beg help, and take her chances with how the people of that place were accustomed to treat a girl alone.

She stood in the lee of a great stone, shuddering, looking at the road. Turned back toward the east face of the mountain, climbed to a low ridge thick with pines, and entered the forest.

There were gaps between the trees. Animals lived there, bear and deer and fox; she let her eyes be an animal's and found the little paths they had made, walking about in their world. These led her across the ridge and down again, away from the road.

They dropped into a canyon, narrow and deep. High in the darkening sky the wind rushed over the tops of the pines. There was the night's first star. Fallen needles made the walking soft, and the wind had brought blown sand from somewhere far away. Hush and tinkle of a stream that pooled and fell between boulders big as houses, a neighborhood of stone. Trees, living and dead, stood or lay among them in a ruck of downed branches. Against one stone, so big that it had walls and niches like a courtyard, the stream had built a sandy beach.

On three smooth rocks she crossed the stream to that stone. There was dead wood everywhere, and before dusk turned to dark, she had a heap of it gathered, with more to hand. She built a fire against the foot of the biggest stone and lit it with flint and steel from her wallet.

Red flame blazed. Shadowy smoke rose dwindling. She looked at her hurts: gashes and deep scrapes that oozed and crusted, wrist swollen and ugly but perhaps not broken. She took out the shattered bits of ginger cookies and stared at them as if they had fallen from some other world. She ate, drank from the icy stream, set her back against the stone.

For the first time in her life, she was alone.

The fire laid a half circle of flickering color over a curve of water and dark forest. Beyond that the night went on and on. She could feel Raím's ghost in the mountain. He was the darkness around her, with only her little fire to light it.

Perhaps she had gone crazy. But that darkness—his—did not bother her. She spoke to him. "Maybe we could have found a way to."

To what, she was not sure. To make love—whatever love was—without him bullying, her terrified. Or to be two stubborn people, given visions and driven to serve them. Or to live somewhere and eat and squabble and hold each other and have friends, without being trapped forever between the selvages of Creek or Alikyaan.

"We could have been Roadsouls," she said. But that was not right either, traveling and traveling. Her heart wrestled in its harness, panted and struggled until it wearied and lay down, still bound. Aloud she said to the darkness, "What shall I do?"

Bang!

She leapt away, fell on her hurt side in the sand. Looked about. Nothing. Then saw: a slab of rock the length of her arm had burst away from the stone and fallen in the fire.

She thought a door had opened in the mountain, and something would leap out. Crackle of the scattered flames; lap of water, hush of wind. She had built the fire too close, and heat had burst the stone. No door, only a sparkling fresh surface of rock seeing fire for the first time.

She raked the coals away from the stone and found she had made herself a place to sleep, on warm sand between the hot stone and the fire that would keep beasts away. She built up the new blaze, lay down on her good side, and hugged herself. Soon she slept. When the fire burned low the cold roused her, she got up and threw on more wood. Once she woke to see a pair of great gold eyes watching her across the flames, but when she stirred they blinked and were gone.

ᕲ

Stillness.

Not silence; the little stream lipped and purred, burned wood fell softly upon ash. A bird cried, high in the lightening sky.

It hurt to sit up. She was white with ash, and her breath was white. She tried not to have thoughts, for every one was fear.

She should go back to the road and wait for a cart to pass. *No;* her body shrank from that thought. She might ask after the baker woman and her clan; but to do that she would have to go back to the road. *No.* Should she try to win back to High Moles? *No, no!*

And she was so hungry, and there was nothing to eat.

The sun rose above the canyon wall, glittering through pine needles, and lit the tall stone face where she had slept. Under the gray and orange lichen were drawings in the stone. One was a spiral, like water. One was a man and woman holding hands. One was a fish.

She went to the stream. There were three pools there, and fish shadows, and in half an hour she had caught with her hands four little trout that since the time of the stone carver had not learned to be wary of people. She gutted them with her stub of knife and roasted them, grateful for their lives. When she had thrown their bones in the fire she washed her hands in the stream.

That was when she saw the tracks in the sand on the far verge, and knew whose eyes she had seen in the night. But she had known already.

As the lives of the trout became her life, she felt real again and began to sort thread from thread, not thinking, exactly, but setting things out without words. *What now?* She saw that this is the question every being asks all the time, mostly not with words, and that the answer might not be in words.

She knew what her body would not do, which was to go back to the road. She was afraid of cold, hunger, and the lion, but those were clean fears, not Amu's smut or the clotted hardness of the paidmen. If she was to die, she would die like those little trout.

She scratched the coals into a heap and raked sand over them. Amu had gone southeast, the Roadsouls southwest; as near as she could, she struck out due south.

On a mountain you do not walk where you choose. Between stones and brush and unclimbable cliffs she could go only where an animal her size could go: by faint trails along stone ridges, between thickets, through open glades. Where the undergrowth was too dense, the hill too steep or covered with fallen trees, she found her way by clambering, but as soon as she could she returned to the paths. At each divide she took the one that led most nearly south, but because of the mountain steeps she was driven here and there.

She did not wonder where she was. She was on the mountain, walking. To her right, inside the mountain, Raím's ghost kept her company; to her left, somewhere in the forest, the lion walked.

In the hungry middle of the day she climbed a stony hillside to a sloping, sun-brown meadow that stretched as far as she could see, ringed with pine and with white-trunked aspen shivering their leaves. Wild iris, its flowers long withered, bore seed pods fat as clubs. Grass grew taller than her waist, bending in airs from the southwest, heavy with seed.

The narrow track led south. As she walked she stripped the shiny black grass seed with her fists and chewed it, spitting out the hairy husks. It tasted like raw wheat. The season's last grasshoppers, fat and slow, sprang away and crashed among the grass stems. She caught them, pinched them behind the head as Nine had taught, tied up the tail of her shirt to make a bag, and carried them to roast later.

She did not think about anything. She walked, the sun on her face.

There were fields of wild dewberries, but past harvest; she found scarcely a dozen of the tiny fruit, withering and soft. There were banks of some berry she did not know, purple-black, with a bloom on it like a plum's. She was afraid to taste it until she saw, away down the slope, a young bear stripping the bushes with her mouth; then like the bear she ate right off the branch. They ignored each other, both with purple tongues. Frost had opened the cones of the scrub pines; at each breath of wind the nuts pattered down, the squirrels and jays quarreled for them. She gathered her share and cracked them with her teeth as she walked. They tasted of pine sap and rain.

The meadow went on and on. In her mind vast non-thoughts built themselves, altered and dissolved, like clouds in air.

The mountain met the meadow as a steep gray cliff, and the little path ran at its foot. She laid her cheek on the sunny stone and heard Raím inside it, walking.

That was not sane. She pulled her ear away. But how was it crazier than seeing a raven on a man's arm before she drew it? Raím was in the mountain, walking through stone. Comfort drenched through her like a drink of milk. She whispered, "Raím!"

No answer. Only the feeling that he was there, scowling, too proud to answer.

"Raím! I'm here."

Nothing.

She said, "You are so irritating." It was true. Raím was irritating the way water is wet.

She felt stupid and stubborn at the same time, in the middle of nowhere hugging some rock, her cheek all crinkled from it. And yet. She was part of the world and so was he, even dead. How should she know how the world worked? All she had was her own experience. She said aloud, "Should I trust what the elders taught me about the world? Or should I trust the world?"

She kissed the stone. *I will trust the world.* She walked on.

ↄ

Come night, she trudged down into another little valley with its stream, not as stony as the first and full of scrub oaks instead of pines. Again she made her fire where she could sleep against stone, in a pile of new-fallen oak leaves. The air was colder. Her wounds ached and oozed. She roasted the grasshoppers in the coals; Nine was right, they were crisp and delicious as bacon. She parched handfuls of grass seed on a flat stone. She was still hungry. The high fear was over, and nothing was left but the fear that never stops, the one that asks and asks, *How shall I stay alive today?*

She waked in the night. Something moved in the woods beyond the firelight; she built up the flames and looked into the dark, but saw nothing. She thought, Something waits for me out there. I shall be food for it, as the grasshoppers were food for me.

She tried not to be frightened. She tried to think, This is just how life is, and fate. She dared not allow anything so real as the thought, *Please let it be quick.* Again and again fear woke her out of sleep, until sleep would not be put off longer and pulled her down. On the edge of it a different thought came, Suppose what waits to gather me into itself is not a beast?

She half woke. The flames shimmered, darkness beyond them. What could it be, if not a beast? *Trust the world.* What?

ↄ

In the morning she smothered the fire and walked south. The wind came up. To stay down out of it she walked among the trees, but in their shadows it was colder. The aspen were bright gold, quiver and hush.

There was less to eat. Bears had stripped the berry bushes, the grass was a different kind, with bitter seeds, and she did not know how to hunt anything bigger than a grasshopper. The squirrels watched her from the trees as they stuffed their cheeks with pine nuts; the ones they dropped were empty, each with a little hole where a beetle had eaten out the meat. She drank water, and walked.

Nights. As each dusk began she found a place where she could build a fire, roast what little she had found, and lie down between the fire and the stone. Sometimes she listened for Raím in the mountain. Sometimes she heard him, or pretended she did; she was getting crazier, or maybe only tired. She wondered what kind of story Ganu was telling Riinu and the rest so they would not do what she had done. When she thought about that she felt a strange freedom, as if she were the wind, without substance but going where she would.

What followed her stayed just out of sight in the woods and deep grasses. It was quiet. She was not sure what it waited for; it ought to have eaten her before she had walked so far with nothing but grubs for dinner. Her arms looked narrow, and even her hurt wrist looked thin. She thought, At my right hand Raím follows me in the mountain. He is a ghost; I am becoming a ghost. When I have walked to the end of the mountain he will be there, and I shall lie down against his shoulder, and stop walking, and be safe.

Sometimes she thought that. Other times, especially as she got hungrier and her thoughts went strange, she thought that what followed her at her left hand was a god: a lion-being, red gold, sometimes a lion and sometimes a man.

Little by little the sky went gray. She did not know how many days she had been traveling; she only knew how to walk and eat bugs. High fingers of cloud made a film across the sky. The sun went hazy and cool and set as if into dust. The highest peak was white and shining; one morning a glittering veil of new snow smoked off it on an invisible wind.

She walked south, stumbling a little. She found acorns, but they were bitter. And wild potatoes; Nine had shown her the strange way to eat them, first a bite of potato, then a bite of raw clay to ease their sharpness. They did not seem like real food. In the sunflower heads there were still a few seeds the jays had not taken. She left the last of the meadows and came among shelving sandstone cliffs. She heard the singing of wild dogs.

Late in the day the north wind rose, and a spark of snow touched her cheek. She stopped and looked up. All those days of walking south, clambering down canyonside and back up, and there was the mountain still—like a sleeper who changes position yet is always the same person.

She knew, then, that she would never get anywhere. There was only wilderness and she would die in it, of hunger and cold. Winter had come. She was not a bear, to find a den and sleep in her fat, nor a wolf, to hunt rabbits in the snow. She was a skinny girl in worn-out shoes, with an ounce of sunflower seeds gathered in her shirt. There was no way out.

Aloud she said, "Perhaps this path leads on even into the dark." She meant *into the grave*, but it frightened her to say that. Nor would there be a grave, just scattered bones left by the lion, or whatever it was that followed her.

Well, if the path led into death, to death she would go. Maybe Raím would be there, warm and impatient like Jip, and he would take her hand and teach her to walk in the dark.

She wiped her eyes in the crook of her elbow. She must find a slab of rock against the snowy wind, and gather wood, and build her fire knowing it might not be enough. She kept on along the foot of cliffs where the pines were so big they were like cliffs themselves. The day dimmed. She should have stopped but there was nowhere to stop, only cliffs and the brushy slope below. It began to snow. She thought, A little farther and I'll stop anyhow and build my fire against the foot of the cliff. Maybe the stone will open with a bang, and Raím will come walking out of the mountain.

A flicker of movement in the gray. Not where it always almost-was, just beyond the tail of her eye, but nearer, in the brush. In the day that had lost its color, a blink of reddish gold.

She stopped. Her heart stopped. When it began again it drubbed so quick she could not breathe. A flick above the bushes: the back of a leaping animal.

She put her hands to her throat and stepped back against the cliff. Two dogs as big as wolves, one black, one gold, leapt out of the brush and stood stiff-legged, smoke pouring from their mouths. Their eyes fixed her, glaring. Then as one they turned and sprang away into the blowing snow.

Her breath smoked like the dogs', the cliff was ice at her back. The sunflower seeds lay scattered where she had dropped them. And nothing happened. Snow fell. The dusk went blue. Her back warmed a patch of that cold mountain.

She said, "They had collars on."

She stepped away from the stone. She was afraid to go forward; there was no way to go back. She turned her face to the bushes, the valley whitening with snow, and when she looked ahead again the dogs were there, panting their steamy breath. Between them stood a cloaked being, a hand on either collar.

He crept down the iron pins. Under his feet and fingers, fat flakes of rust scaled off, whispering as they spun down and away.

He made himself think he was just climbing a ladder—at the apple harvest, or on his aunt's roof after cleaning the chimney with a rock tied to a string. Terror gripped him. The vacuous depth wanted a weight dropped down it. Numb, electric, his fingers loosened.

This passed. He climbed on down into the pit.

He tried to think of the shaft as solid dark, as if he sat at Ta Ba's loom weaving a vertical stripe of darkest black. The shaft grew warmer, a little, as he climbed down into it.

At intervals there was a different kind of pin: a bracket with both ends in the rock. He could put his arm through and rest a moment. "Thank you," he said into the dark. Then on down.

The rasp and chink of his footsteps changed. Instead of pins there were two brackets together; he swung to his left, into the mouth of a tunnel. No draft issued from it. He followed it. A rockfall had closed it. The fallen stones were huge; he could not move them.

He returned to the shaft. There will be more tunnels below, he thought. I can climb back up if I have to.

He went down. The air was distinctly warmer. He came level with the source of the sounding drip, perhaps a spring, somewhere out of reach on the shaft's far wall. Then many drips. All around him water tinkled and rang, like faintest rain. The chunks of rust that flaked from the pins were larger.

He had a companion, however: now and then his hand, if he swung it outward, knocked against the rope. The shaft must be a little crooked, and the rope did not hang dead center. The first time he hit it, it startled him so that he nearly fell, thinking there was something hairy out there. After that he felt for it now and then, something from the upper world.

Three more tunnels. At each he stepped off the ladder and felt his way about. In one a rusty hook had been driven into the wall, perhaps to anchor the basket; otherwise each was like the others, empty and still. Each must lead somewhere, but there was no way to know where: out, or further in, or nowhere in particular.

He stood in the mouth of the fourth tunnel, bleak. The bold madness in which he had taken refuge was wearing thin. He knew he would die. Not just death, but a bad death.

Since his blinding he had driven people away. He had refused his family and the Hold and Ta Ba, refused the Roadsouls; of everyone but Duuni he had demanded loneliness. Now, it seemed, some wandering god had heard his prayer and had given him what he wanted. He let that thought sink in. *But maybe with Duuni...*

He was not so foolish as to think that one *yes* could buy off years of *no*. "Then that's how it will be," he said aloud. His body

270

gave a little squirm of grief. "I'm sorry." He groped back to the rungs and went down.

The shaft got wetter, water rushing and falling on its sides. A pin, too rusty, bent under his foot. The next one held, but the one below it broke away at the rock.

He climbed back up to the last tunnel. Thought. Why should he go lower? There might be more tunnels, probably just like the others. He should try this one; if it led nowhere and he still had strength he could try the next one up, then the next, until he was too weak to climb and lay where he had fallen.

But the ladder led down. He thought, If I held onto the rope I could take half my weight off the rusted pins. I could get a little farther down, and be sure there's no other way.

He tried to catch the rope. Here it hung out of reach, he could not tell how far. He made a makeshift bolo of his breeks by holding one cuff and knotting into the other a rock from the tunnel floor. The bolo wound around the rope and fell off. In the end it was luck: As he shifted his footing for another try he stepped on a rusty mattock abandoned on the tunnel floor. By fishing in the air, he caught the rope and drew it close enough to hitch over the rusty wall hook.

He put the breeks back on, unhooked the rope, gripped it under one arm and went down. More and more he had to trust it, for the pins bent or crumbled. It wanted to hang straight, and as he felt for a pin with one foot it tried to pull him away from the wall.

"Better go back," he said under his breath.

To his left and below, a soft rush of water. He half dangled, not trusting the pins. Went down one more rung. Heard a change in the sound, crept down another precarious step and was sure of it: another tunnel. Water poured out of it.

He eased himself down. The pins would not hold him but the rope did, it swung him out into the shaft, swung back, he went down like a steeplejack and with a kick and a scramble stood to his ankles in a stream, hearing its waterfall spill down into the shaft. With the rope in the crook of his elbow he knelt, cupped the water and drank.

It tasted metallic and clean, faintly warm. He drank again, then stood, thinking, This is where I will go.

If he let go of the rope it would swing out into the middle of the shaft where he could never retrieve it. He felt around for a wall hook. There was none. Maybe he could drag a section up and weight it somehow? Then, if he had to, he could climb back up.

With both hands and all his strength he dragged a little arch of slack into the tunnel mouth.

The rope bent in his hands, as if it pushed him. From above in the shaft came a sound like bats or snakes, a whispering racket. He stood puzzled, holding the now-limp bight. At the last instant he had the presence of mind to let go as the whole length of the rope came coiling and slithering down the shaft with terrible weight, snapping the shattered basket after it into the pit.

Then only the rushing of water. He stood with his hands open.

He rubbed his face on his shoulder. "This is where I will go," he said again. His voice shook, but the noise of the water drowned it. Turning, he found the wall with his left hand and began to wade upstream, into the mountain.

20

Red heart that for an hour
or two can keep the darkness
there, not here.
We see our startled faces
made real by light,
while round us to infinity
lies endless night.

       Shrine poem, "The Campfire."
       Welling-in-the-Mountains.

The one who held the dogs loosed their collars. They came at Duuni open-mouthed, bounding through the snow, snuffing and nudging with their big muzzles.

"Blaze. Moon." A woman's voice. The dogs were at Duuni's thighs. The woman came forward, snow on her black cloak.

It was the prayer merchant.

In the falling light she looked at Duuni with her brows drawn together. Then her black eyes widened and smiled, though her mouth was grave; they closed, and with her hand she made a gesture of reverence. In Alikyaani she said, "So you are here."

Duuni gazed dumbly. The black dog licked her wrist.

"Come, then." She held out her left hand for Duuni's right.

As if this were a being she had dreamed, Duuni put her hand in the merchant's. She stumbled as the woman led her down the fading trail, around a wide shin of the cliff to sunset blazing in the stone: a fire, built well back under a ledge so deep it made a cave. A hobbled donkey chewed a handful of hay; the packs it had carried lay on the ground by the fire.

A striped blanket was spread there. To this the merchant led her. Duuni sat, or fell. The dogs shook snow from their coats and flopped on the warm dirt.

The fire was all blessing. A dented copper kettle spouted steam, a smoky pot simmered: meat and onions seasoned with *frenc*. Duuni began to weep, silently, with homecoming and fear.

The woman rummaged for a second blanket, Ganu shaking out a woven length. How could Duuni have come so far, yet be back in Alikyaan? The merchant pulled the blanket around Duuni's shoulders, poured a tin cup full of balmweed tea too hot to drink. Said, "Have you walked through the wilderness all the way from High Moles fair?" As if that were a common thing to do.

Duuni did not know how to speak in Alikyaani. She looked down and aside; then she raised her eyes. "Paidmen," she said in Plain, a whisper. "And Doctor Amu. But only the first day."

The merchant's face went sharp. She took Duuni's arm, where the scabs still itched and crackled, and turned it gently.

Duuni said, "I fell."

The woman took Duuni's chin in her hand and held it so she could not look away. "Did they rape you?"

This was not Ganu. "No. I kicked him. Amu. In his you-know-where."

Laughter made the woman's face radiant with wrinkles. The dogs beat their tails on the ground. "Kicked Amu in his privates? Oh, justice! And you ran?"

Duuni nodded. "Then I walked."

"How many days, brave one?"

"I don't know."

"As many as it took. Drink that up."

Duuni drank the tea she had not tasted since the Maidens' Balcony. The prayer merchant's face was broad and canny like Ganu's, but younger, and her wrinkles had not come from frowning. She wore uncut cloth; the outer robe was dusty from the road, but at her throat her day robes flashed green and crimson.

She ladled a wooden bowl full of rabbit meat and gave it to Duuni. Duuni wondered if she had painted a prayer to the god of rabbits so they would jump into her pot. From the saddlebags came a second bowl and a battered round of bread. Duuni felt like a poor relative who has nothing to bring to the feast, for she had dropped her sunflower seeds. She thought she would faint from hunger, yet it would be rude to eat before her hostess did.

"Blaze and Moon are coursers, they catch our dinner," said the merchant, as if Duuni had asked. The dogs drooled and flapped their chops. "You've had your share, dears," she told them. "They eat the guts and scraps, and hunt for themselves as we travel. We know ways through the mountains. I came away early from the fair; I was not sure of the reason, but here she sits. What are you waiting for? Eat!"

Still Duuni hesitated. "Alikyaani!" said the merchant, laughing, and dipped her bread. Then Duuni could eat too. Oh, it was good! The best of home, all comfort, and nothing frightening or evil. She said in Plain, like Raím, "Thank you." The words made tears start from her eyes.

The merchant gave her a warm look. "You're welcome."

To walk through the wilderness and be served, in the middle of nowhere, rabbit with *frenc*. Duuni remembered what she had vowed: that she would trust, not what she had been taught, but what the world taught her by being itself.

It would be rude to ask the woman's name, so Duuni gave her own. "I am Duuni Esremachaan. Please, how did you know I was from Alikyaan?"

"A guess. Just now, of course, you wouldn't eat until I did; that pretty courtesy is Alikyaani. My name is Aash, I use no surname. Your tongue is my own, for a long time ago I ran away from Muukra."

"Muukra!"

"Where it rains as it rains in Alikyaan," she said, for *Aash* meant rain; the best kind, not a downpour, but the quiet rain that hushes and gentles all night.

"You ran away?" Ganu's stories of disobedient girls who came to bad ends—had they been true? As surely now the grandmothers of Muukra were saying grimly to their guarded maidens, *There was once a wicked girl in Alikyaan...*

Duuni said, "I broke my batten. I set it at Mma's altar and broke it."

"Ah!" Aash bowed her head. Not in submission. "Why?"

Because they would have me marry a man so vicious that he raped children.

But it was not just that, nor that people could call such a man religious and look away. It was because the batten had belonged to a loom that wove only selvage to selvage.

She did not know how to name this. It was deeper than either good or evil, the way a river that flows underground is neither good nor evil but just river, flowing on.

"I had to," she said. Then, lest Aash think she had been forced, she said, "*I* broke it. I chose. Then I lifted up my hands and said yes. And then it got crazy."

Aash laughed, rocking backward. The dogs whined and squirmed. "That's what it does—especially at first! But maybe always."

"Did you say yes?"

"Not at first."

"But then you did."

"When I could not say no any longer I gave up and said yes."

"To them? To the Roadsouls?"

"In the end."

Yes to the Souls. Who had killed Raím for money. That feeling of falling; Duuni swayed where she sat. "But they—"

Aash took the bowl from her. "Sometimes the traveler's task is to rest."

"But—"

"Do you think you have come to your journey's end?"

"No."

"Then rest, and take up the thread in the morning." The thread! Duuni stared. Aash said, "I too was raised a weaver." She laid blankets on the soft sand of the cave floor and motioned Duuni to lie down, the dogs on either side of her. They were warm, they stank of safety. From beneath her lashes Duuni watched Aash where she sat tending the fire. Then she slept.

Right away she dreamed she was falling into darkness, down and down. She woke with a cry; the dogs leapt to their feet.

"Shh," said Aash, and they settled again. She began to sing in the tongue of Alikyaan.

> In a boat of sand I travel
> To the farthest shore;
> With a rope of sand I bind me
> To stray no more.

Listening, Duuni slept. She woke once in the night. The black dog had moved to make room for Aash, under the blanket next to Duuni. Her big body gave off heat like a stove.

☙

Morning.

Beyond the arc of stone, a changing gray sky and a dust of snow, the light unsteady. Aash of Muukra broke bread into water.

Shivering, Duuni sat up. Aash said, "Can you walk?"

Duuni nodded. She knew she could walk; she did not know how to get anywhere. "Where are you going?"

"To the Gatehouse at Welling-in-the-Mountains," said Aash. A quick glance. "If you come with me you shall see friends again, for the caravan you traveled with spends winters there."

But Duuni had known. The Souls were on their way to Welling. Like an ant to the ant lion's trap, a duckling to the muskrat's jaws, she must go back to Farki. The only way out of it was the way Raím had taken: death. As she sat by the fire she could feel him in the mountain at her right hand, the lion in the forest at her left. But she thought, I'm not an ant, a duckling. If my fate is with Farki I shall walk there choosing to go, not dragged.

This thought was a sharp wind. She rubbed her face in her elbow, pushed her hair back. She would go see what it was like, this Welling-in-the-Mountains. If the Gatehouse was bad she would run away from there, too.

"How far is it still?"

"Not as far as you've come."

"Do you live in the Gatehouse?"

"Yes, when I'm not traveling."

"Then…you know Nine?"

"Nine," Aash laughed, rocking backward. "Ah—Nine!"

They ate the hot mush, packed, and headed south.

ᔕ

The donkey was called Nim. When Aash had loaded him, he gave one shake, clattering kettle and pans, and set out on quick feet like a goat. They walked the faint path between orange granite and boulders of black stone shiny as glass. The sun rose. The snow melted, leaving its fresh cold on grasses still green.

Aash walked to Nim's right, where the mountain rose up. In her loose robes she moved like water flowing. Duuni walked to the left, where the hillside fell away to wilderness. The dogs did not bark, but sometimes they stopped and looked that way.

Duuni did not want to say, "A lion has been following me all the way from Alikyaan." But it would be evil not to warn Aash.

278

When again Blaze and Moon turned their heads to stare into the brush, she said, "If a lion were following us, would the dogs bark?"

Aash had been whistling to herself. She looked into the underbrush, then at Duuni. "It would depend what kind of lion it was," she said, and walked on.

Duuni followed. After some time she said, "I saw you at the fair."

"And I saw you. I saw your work."

Duuni shrugged. "Drawing on babies."

From Aash a bright, quiet look.

"In Muukra, do they paint the courtyard walls?"

"Of the Maidens' Balcony? Of course. We painted the Unclothed Gods, and the solar obeisance, and the worshiping universe—all. I was always the one chosen to paint."

"So was I."

"And you needed more than that. No wonder you went to find it."

Duuni frowned. She thought she had run *away*—from Tumiin, from selvage-to-selvage. Who can blame the victim who runs from oppression? But to choose to run *toward* a spaciousness as yet unknown—that is easy to call folly. Madness, even.

"I didn't want to," she said. But that was not true either. In her mind's eye she saw herself drawing the very line she followed: weeping and denying, yet walking forward. "I'm a coward," she said.

Aash's hand lay on Nim's pack, on the bundle that held her paints and brushes. The clouds had blown off, and the sky was bare and pale. "I was born in Muukra, as you know," she said. "To the Grooved Stick clan, born to the loom. A fat little girl, poor with the shuttle, good with the brush, a light dancer. In Muukra urda is used only by the grandmothers, or I would have learned that too. I would have liked it."

As she spoke she looked at the mountain. Duuni thought how Aash, like herself, must have looked at it from behind the lattice of the Maidens' Balcony.

"That was my life. I was stubborn, often beaten, but happy enough; my mother was a second wife, but she loved the first like a sister, and my father was a just man. I was my mother's eldest, very bossy and sure. At sixteen I was to be married to a man of thirty; I would be a second wife like my mother, in a household of good reputation. But I fell in love."

Duuni, walking, listened so hard she stumbled.

"A boy of the New Fire clan, dark as obsidian, seventeen. I saw him when I sat with my mother at the Sun ceremony. He saw me. He climbed the wall to the Maidens' Balcony." Duuni looked at her with big eyes. Aash shook her head. "He did not enter. He came close enough to whisper. In those days, of course, I could neither read nor write; whispers were all we had. Ever. Duuni of Alikyaan, I ran away with that boy, and never once spoke a word to him clear and loud."

"How could you get away? They watch the maidens—"

"I could have run away seven times over. Our warden was so sure of us she was half blind. And I was blind with love. We would go to the mountain, I thought, and live wild in the woods and feed our babies on acorns. Something like that." Aash smiled, her face a little sad. "At the dark of the moon he brought a rope; I was nimble; we climbed down from the balcony."

"Like the ballad of Jiin and Ekraaba!"

"Exactly. But easier. Away we went, my hand in his and luck with us, for we were not seen. It was low water, we waded the river, and as soon as we were well into the woods we lay down together and made sure the thing was done, so they could never take me back. It hurt, and I did not care that it hurt, and it was real—all of it. Whispering, embracing, we fell asleep." Her glance. "There the clansmen found us. Little fools, we'd left the rope dangling, our footprints in the sand like a pair of antelope.

They killed my lover in front of me. He was the fourth son of a third wife; there would have been no marriage for him anyway, he would have gone to the mines. His name was Ruus."

Duuni had put her hand on the pack next to Aash's, as if that might help her hear everything, everything.

"They sold me to the League. To the paidmen—but the League runs the business. They have the money, the paidmen do the work. I was raped immediately, that I might know I was now a prostitute." Her broad, calm face. "A dancing girl. I danced in the brothels of Rett, which serve the mills. Many a Leagueman have I seen put off his hat and his high black boots."

Duuni could say nothing. This woman had suffered everything she had so nearly suffered. Duuni was terrified of what might be, but Aash had weathered what was real.

"I did that work for four years," she said. "Three babies I killed in my womb because I would not carry them. I was like one stunned. I could not feel or think."

"Falling and falling."

"Yes. No earth. Only the dancing was right. When I danced I was, for a moment, whole. I was not a painter in those days; what does a sex slave paint besides her face? But when I danced I painted with my body. I wove without a loom." At Duuni's intake of breath she turned her head. "You, too?"

"Drawing. The line is the thread. There is no selvage."

"Therefore you will understand that I broke my batten."

"You had a batten?"

"None that was visible, yet a batten nonetheless: something in ourselves that we break on purpose so that we can never go back, we can only go on. What I broke was my laziness."

Duuni tried to imagine this woman lazy. Aash said, "Laziness of mind. I was not a thinker. I had been happy in my family; even when I ran away, when the elders killed Ruus, it did not occur to me to doubt the gods or wonder whether the world was as the elders said. I had transgressed; I was punished. That was all I thought. I was still Muukrai.

"But in the brothels of Rett, we were girls from all over, dancing the dances of every town and village, teaching one another. My body learned to move in ways that were not Muukrai.

"Perhaps my legs taught my brain, for I began to see and compare. The pious Leaguemen were like the pious elders of Muukra: different in language and clothing, but still men who placed themselves above women, who used their power to build worlds in which men were lords, with religion and its threats to enforce obedience."

Duuni nodded. It was what she had begun to see, dimly, for herself.

"I saw that by not thinking, not questioning, I had given my laziness of mind to the elders to be their tool. Your batten was not yours, Duuni. It was Alikyaan's, a tool to keep on making Alikyaan."

"Elder Tumiin...when he beat me he said 'You have broken Alikyaan.'"

"So you had, brave heart."

"I broke a stick. It made no difference."

"A woman walks beside me. What her life will be, who knows? But the daughters she bears will never weave their wedding shrouds."

Duuni wiped her eyes on her wrist, and Moon lapped at it. "I will never have children," she said. Not in this vicious world.

Aash made no comment. She walked awhile, then took up her story again. "Once I began to wonder and to think, how quickly the world I lived in became too small! The walls of the brothel and the dance hall, the arms of Leaguemen and strangers—I saw I was dancing one dance only, with many gestures: the dance that says *I want sex*, even when that is not true.

"I tried to talk with the other girls. They were too frightened or too sad. I rebelled. I talked back to the madam, to clients, even to Leaguemen. I was beaten. What I had begun to know was too big for those walls, but all disordered; there was no one to help me tame it.

"I fought, and was beaten more. My new knowledge grew so big it was like a child pushing its way out, all my unborn children at once. I could not bear it, and I could not get away even for a moment, for I was so wild they kept a watch on me. It was no use.

"I stole the long razor from a Leagueman's kit. To slit my wrists would be too slow; I would slit my throat, and be done. There was nowhere I could go to be alone, only the privy. I went there with the razor and stood over the hole. I thought of my blood pouring down among the filth.

"In that moment I remembered something. Like a vision, but it was a memory from before I entered the Maidens' Balcony.

"I saw the little otter who lives on the riverbank, quick and bright. Her fur jacket ripples when she runs, she moves like dancing, she plays and plays. She's funny! I knew in my heart I was like her: that quick, that clean. I thought, What have these people made me?

"I dropped the razor down the hole and went back to my cubicle. When I thought of the otter's bright face I felt a stillness, as if in that vision there was room for the bigness in me.

"I went back to my life. I danced. I lay with Leaguemen and drunks. I was so quiet that the madam changed toward me, and as the months passed she began to trust me with this or that.

"One day, at winter's end, she gave me a handful of copper and sent me down the street to buy bread. At the corner there were mountebanks and jugglers, and a crowd. I leaned against a cart. Only for an instant; it began to move, and above my head a woman's voice said, 'Are you coming with us?' I said, 'Yes!'

"I lifted up my hands, and in a moment we were gone." Aash smiled. "I traveled with them all summer. I was crazy with freedom, and just...crazy. It takes a long time to find out how to live without walls. By the time snow fell I was ready to go to Welling with the Souls—but only just."

Duuni said, "*What are they?*"

"The Roadsouls? What do you think they are?"

"Murderers!"

That grave, calm glance. "Tell me that story."

She could not. It was all choked with tears and confusion and things she had not said, not done; with the touch of his big hand, trembling with carefulness. But she would not be less brave than Aash. In stumbling half-sentences she told what she could of the man on the cart, proud and ashamed and glorious; of the mountain's mouth open, then shut.

"They sold him. They'll die for it," she said, wild. "A curse will come on them! They sold him like bread, the gods will wither them! The universe is just. It has to be!"

"Is a river just?" said Aash. "Does snow seek revenge?"

Duuni had been shouting. At Aash's words she stood still, gasping. Nim the donkey stopped, too, and the dogs. "Is that all there is?" she said. "Just rivers and dirt and snow, and no gods?"

"I don't know," said Aash. "How does it seem to you?"

Duuni cursed, using the words she had learned from Raím and Nine.

Aash touched Nim's shoulder; the donkey minced forward, nodding his head, the dogs wagged and walked on. Duuni could follow or be left. She followed, sobbing. Aash began to sing.

> Wind is the prairie tide. We are the wind.
> There is no wall the wind cannot unbind.
> Rain is the prairie tide. We are the rain.
> Rain turns citadel to sand again.
>
> Build proud, build high—air will unmake it.
> Build for eternity—water will take it.
> Even the gods in their high town
> Are by wind and rain and the Souls brought down.

Duuni felt the lion following. She hoped it would eat her. That would be easier than believing that retribution was not built into the windy world and administered by gods, or that *Justice* was an idea made up by humans.

She caught up to Aash and snatched at her sleeve. "Do the Souls destroy things on purpose?"

"Does the wind have an intent? Does time dismantle us on purpose?"

"But those are the universe, not the Roadsouls!"

Aash smiled. "You asked me what they are."

"I don't know what to believe!"

"That is a wise place to be. On that loom you can set your selvages very wide."

❦

At nightfall they unpacked in another cave shelter. The shelving stone of the cliffs was full of such alcoves, blackened by travelers' fires. The faint track had grown wider, but they saw no other human beings.

Duuni was heavy and bleak. She felt Raím's ghost in the stone; he had died for nothing but chance and the wind. What she had felt for him must be meaningless, too—only lust. They could have fucked. It meant nothing; his restraint had meant nothing.

Aash built a fire. Blaze and Moon went off and came back proud of themselves, each with a rabbit. Duuni fondled the dogs' ears and wished she were a dog too, that need only eat and sleep, and not think. Aash gutted the rabbits and threw them in the pot with wild onion, wild garlic. The night was cold and clear.

When they had eaten and the dogs had crunched the bones, Duuni meant to lie down with her heaviness and sleep. She could not think of another way to escape it. But as she stared at the fire, breaking a twig in one hand, Aash opened her pack and brought out the ink and brushes and coarse papers of her trade. She went to the little seep that made a muddy pool beside the shelter and dipped up water in the mug.

There was no morality in the universe; what difference did it make if Duuni was surly? She said, "Why do you paint fake gods for yokels?" Knowing she was a yokel herself.

Aash laid the paper on the board, wet the brush, wet the ink block.

Duuni said, "I suppose it's good money."

Aash smiled to herself. "Not very!"

"Why do you do it, then?"

She knew how rude she was being. She did not want answers, she wanted to be rude because it did not matter. Aash gave her a calm look. "Hush," she said.

Duuni shrank in shame and anger, jabbing the twig into the sand. Aash smoothed the paper with her palm and sat looking at it.

Duuni looked, too. She could see many things on it: not quite visible, shifting and clambering like kits in a litter, each wanting to be on top. She did not want to see them, could not look away.

Aash raised the brush, laid it at the left edge of the paper, and drew the thin, upturned arc of the crescent moon.

As she painted, some of the tumbling, not-yet-fixed possibilities fled. Some clustered at the brush. Some leapt out, calling the ink to themselves and settling down to be seen. Under the brush a woman rose, riding the boat of the moon.

It was Mma; it was not Mma.

In Alikyaan Mma stood still, hands folded. But this woman's foot was poised as if in dance; her balancing hands were spread. Mma's glance was always downcast; this woman's eyes were wide open, like the eyes Duuni had painted in Greencliff on the old woman's hand. Night-creep eyes. Around the dancing body Aash painted a glory, like rays of moonlight shining.

It was like watching a baby being born, a perfect child. Duuni whispered, "What goddess is that?"

"I don't know." Aash waited for the paint to dry. Then she laid the paper on the fire.

The sheet caught instantly and blazed up, it lit the cave's black ceiling and sent flakes of ash sailing into the night. Aash looked at Duuni's gawking face and laughed.

Duuni said, "Why did you burn it?"

"Why not?"

She could think of plenty of reasons why not. Because it was beautiful. Because she had wanted to look at it. Because Aash might have sold it, and grown famous and rich. It was as if she had burned a master tunic.

Aash rinsed the brush in the mug, laid it down, and sat with her hands round her knees.

"Did you burn it because nothing matters?" Duuni said.

"Or because everything matters?" Aash rocked back and forth, smiling. "They're prayers," she said.

But had the woman not as good as said there was no divine retribution, only rain and wind? "Then there *are* gods to pray to?"

"I don't pray *to*," said Aash. "I just pray."

They sat silent. Nim the donkey whuffed down his nose. Aash said, "Everything is as it is. It does not need me to bow down to it, as if I were its servant. Nor is it my business to try to push it around, as if I were its master; not that my pushing would have any effect anyway! So I just pray."

"By painting."

"Yes. For me, prayer is paying attention. When I draw and paint, that's what I do. How *you* pray is of course your own business."

Duuni thought of how she had felt when she drew in urda on a child's arm, or painted on canvas: perfect in that instant, right there and nowhere else.

Aash took another sheet of paper from her pack, laid it on the board and smoothed it. She handed the board to Duuni. Uncapped the ink pot, shook the water from the brush and put it in Duuni's fingers.

"Will you?" she said.

"Me? Paint?"

"Pray."

Duuni held the brush as if it were a venomous snake. "No."

Aash smiled, and took it from her hand.

☙

Each morning they rose in the chill mountain air and walked south. When she could find them, Duuni gathered grass seeds and nuts. She taught Aash to roast grasshoppers, which Aash thought disgusting until she tasted them. "Hot peppers and garlic," she said, "that's all they lack." Duuni felt proud, like Blaze and Moon with their rabbits.

The lion kept pace at her left hand. Maybe there were no gods of the sort Tumiin had worshiped, but there was *something*; she knew it was there the way the dogs knew, when they turned their heads and stared but did not bark. If she walked into Welling, would it follow her? Would it kill people? Where would it hide?

Thus she walked, paying attention, eating grasshoppers, trailed by a lion and a ghost.

21

A traveler, long time walking from the west,
and meeting friends at last, to them confessed:
"There at its source the River is so thin
and white a little freshet that no least
difference could I find between the twin
divided boundaries, west bank and east.
The water rises shining in the sun,
and from that source the stream goes down as one."

Shrine poem. Welling-in-the-Mountains.

The mountain's south face stood over them, snow-dusted granite sheer as an upheld hand. The cliffs at its feet were a jumble of different-colored rock, slabs and wrinkles and folds like blankets hurled aside by one who wakes.

"There's Welling," said Aash, pointing along the mountain flank. "We'll be there by night." Duuni saw only wilderness and stone. "Look farther," said Aash. What Duuni had taken for red rocks were red roofs, and mist was hearth smoke. "The town lies in a valley, but the outskirts nudge up to the mountain like kits to the mother cat. Come along, the day is passing."

Nim bobbed quickly, the dogs trotted, as though they knew home and wanted to get there. Duuni grew more anxious with every step. Yet had Aash been anything but kind? Why should she fear?

In the afternoon, still far from town, the dogs cocked their ears and bristled. Aash turned the donkey's head off the road, and like ghosts they fled into the brush. A minute or two, and with jangle and trot, four paidmen, three riding and one driving a light cart, came rattling downhill.

They did not so much as look in Duuni's direction, yet she sweated and shook. When they were past she said, "Were they going where we are going?"

"To Welling, yes," said Aash, watching her. "Welling is a town. But I don't imagine they're going to the Gatehouse."

"What if they are!"

Aash smoothed the donkey's white nose with one hand. "Woman," she said.

That made Duuni look at her.

"No place on earth is safe," said Aash. "Not with the perfect safety our souls want. Not even the baby in its mother's womb; it too takes its chances in this chancy world. But for you, Duuni of Alikyaan, I should guess that right now the Gatehouse in Welling-in-the-Mountains is the safest place on earth you could be." She smiled. "And the food is good."

Duuni followed her out of the brush and back onto the road. The paidmen had left behind them a smoke of fear like the dust behind a caravan. She walked on.

The afternoon grew late. They came among apple orchards, the fruit long harvested, a few windfalls making the air cidery and sweet. There began to be small brown houses set far back from the road, farmers who hailed them from the fields. Two children came shouting, "Aash! Aash!" When they saw Duuni they turned tail like calves and ran away.

"Shy," said Aash. She sounded weary. The sun set. Duuni grew more uneasy still, for Aash had always been careful to make shelter by dusk. Yet she followed her, past stone walls and the rustling skeletons of cornstalks, low outbuildings with cattle standing in the stony fields.

True dark came. The stars shone. They trudged over a last hill, and there in the darkness shone the lemon lights of a town, filling the valley and stair-stepping up the mountain now invisible with night.

Aash led them down the hillside. Duuni followed, slower and slower. At the valley bottom a brawly creek rushed out of the darkness, crossed by a wooden bridge. Aash did not cross the bridge but turned uphill, toward the town; when Duuni did not follow she looked back.

Duuni said, "Will they be there already? The Souls."

"Perhaps."

Duuni did not move.

Aash pointed across the bridge. "This road goes west along the creek to other villages, and at last to Rett and the sea. There's an inn that way. I know the innkeeper; she would put you up on my word."

Duuni petted Moon's ears so hard he yelped. Said without looking up, "I'll come with you."

Aash said, "Let's go home."

So they came out of the night, up the cobbled street of Welling-in-the-Mountains, into the light from open doors.

❧

The bars of light from the doors looked like the rungs of a ladder. Nim's hooves clicked on the cobbles. On either side, the walls of houses built shoulder to shoulder were broken by narrow alleys and wide doorways, some closed with wooden shutters, but most standing open to the night.

A carpenter's shop, a cobbler's, a saddler's. At each the worker, seeing Aash, nodded and waved. She waved back, but did not stop. Everyone stared at Duuni.

A weaver's workshop.

Duuni had been walking between Blaze and Moon, making a bulwark of their bodies. But when they came to the weaver's, with its scent of dyes and thread dust, she fell back and stared. In the dusk beyond the doorway wide planes of cloth stretched floor to ceiling like walls, lengthwise like beds, at angles like the gestures of hands. Dozens of looms, gathered in one room like the different peoples crowding at High Moles fair. From among them dodged a shaggy dark boy of eight or so.

"Aash!" He scrambled into the street and leapt on her, then the dogs.

"Willek! Where are your manners? We haven't been to the well!" But she laughed and looked him over.

He stared at Duuni. "Who are you? Are you new?" He fell in beside them, lurching on a crutch. He had a clubfoot.

Duuni said, "I am Duuni of Alikyaan."

"Where's that? Are there snakes? I caught a snake, they should be denned up now but it bit me." He offered his finger. It did not look bitten. "How come you're with Aash? Have you been with the Souls? Was Nine there?"

"Yes," said Duuni, amazed.

"I know where the snake is. It'll bite her and we'll be snake brothers, but she'll say, How come not snake sisters? When will she get here?"

"I don't know."

Aash said, "Run ahead, laddie, and tell the house we're coming."

"I can't *run*."

"Hobble quick, then."

He bobbed ahead like a lame goat. The street opened to a cobbled square crisscrossed by light from eateries and taverns with copper pots and arguments, the glow of a blacksmith's shop where the dark body of the smith, seeming larger than human, moved before the fire.

To the right of the smithy a rank of wooden columns front-ed a building whose upper stories made a jumbled step pattern against the sky. In the middle of this portico, light streamed from an archway. As the little dipping figure of Willek made for that light a swarm of children, shadows against the shine, poured from the arch and came running.

"*Aash!*" They were of every size—some too small, Duuni thought, to be tumbling about in the dark. Girls with pigtails half undone, jostling boys, and every color of hair and skin. One was missing her left ear, one his right eye; some had harelips, horrid scars. Some were untouched and beautiful—or perhaps they had scars that did not show. They fell upon Aash, they grabbed the donkey's halter, crying, "Nimmy!" They hugged the dogs, pointed at Duuni. "Is she a new one?"

"Yes. Her name is Duuni."

"Be welcome, Duuni," the boldest said, to show how polite she was. Then everybody had to say, "Be welcome," nudging and giggling.

Aash said, "These are the Gatehouse Mice. Most of them were brought by the Roadsouls."

"Not me," said a dark-eyed girl with a scarred mouth. "Song-sparrow brought me."

"I used to live under a rock," said a little boy. The others jeered. "I *did*."

"Tomorrow you shall tell her about it. Take Nim to the stables while we go in. Listen, Mice," said Aash. "Duuni is an artist. If you make her welcome perhaps she will draw on you with urda, whatever you like." She narrowed her eyes. "*If* your arms are scrubbed."

They put their dirty arms behind their backs. "Tomorrow? In the morning?"

"Tomorrow in the morning," said Aash. "If she will."

The dark-eyed girl said, "Will she be your novice?"

"If she will. But right now we need a bath."

They pelted off toward the alley and Nim trotted after, pack clashing. Aash strode on toward the lighted portico.

Duuni followed with the dogs, through the colonnade of posts big around as the pines they once had been, through an archway to an inner court full of a garden, tangled and wild—cosmos still blooming, and forlorn seedheads of healroot and bright-eye left standing for the birds. Through this thicket ran paths both wandering and straight. Here and there was a bench to sit on, or grass.

Not a soul was about.

"To the well," said Aash. "Always the well first. Once we have drunk from it the rest can greet us; but the Mice never remember that."

The path was of flagstones worn hollow in their middles. It led to the center of the court and a round parapet, waist height, built of river cobbles. There was no well hoist or tackle, just a thin cord, neatly coiled, tied to a small wooden bucket.

Duuni leaned over the parapet. A breath of water rose around her. Deep down, the shadow of her head and shoulders was framed with trembling stars.

Aash nicked a wooden bar across the mouth of the well and gave Duuni the bucket. "You cast it."

The rope uncoiled quick as a snake, the bucket struck the shining water mirror and splintered the stars. Duuni waggled the rope until the bucket sank, then drew it up heavy, hand over hand. Aash took a clay mug from a rack. "You first."

Duuni had never drunk such water. It tasted of stillness, or the dark; it soaked into her as rain enters earth. She drank again.

Aash, smiling, said, "Good water."

"Where..." Does it come from, she almost said, but that was foolish; it came from the well.

"Home," said Aash. She too drank. As she put up the cup, a man came down the path, still in a carpenter's apron, sawdust in his gray curls. As they greeted each other, she kept her face hidden, giving the dogs water in her palm.

"This is Duuni of Alikyaan, an artist," said Aash. "Where is everyone?"

"Gone up the mountain to the shrine, for the Late Light. Then to dance after."

"The Late Light! I'd lost track of days. All for the best, not to overwhelm this lass with numbers. Duuni, let's to our quarters, and bathe, and eat. Tomorrow can take care of itself."

The carpenter, smiling, said, "Be welcome, Duuni of Alikyaan." The stars were a circle of silver; the looming mountain made a dark notch in them, like her shadow on the water of the well.

☙

Aash's quarters were on the east side of the courtyard. "Two rooms. This one is my workshop. Those windows open on the alley, high enough for the sun to reach. As for the rhythm of the smithy, I like it." The brass lock yielded to her key, and she pushed the door open with the flat of her hand.

The gloom of long tables, a clutter of chairs, indistinct and forbidding like strangers not yet met. The bench-front fireplace, massive as an oven, gave off warmth like the flank of a beast. A row of steps went up the side of it, and in a loft under the black ceiling beams was a bed.

With the dogs at her thighs Aash lifted an iron cover from the hearth. Red coals glowed. She tossed in kindling, and the flames blazed up.

All around—hung on the walls, propped on easels, leaning against the big tables—were paintings.

A bull. Black, horned, male, with a tiny eye; he filled the page, swelled out of it. A woman with a body half fish, swimming in water that poured past her in a flood. A dog: Duuni's dog, her Jip, running under the moon in a landscape of stone. A raven all beak, a girl with a bunch of flowers but no eyes, a snake whose wide body was full of mice and lizards and birds. More. Everything. The world with its open doors, and all beings who enter them.

No lion.

Aash sat on the bench, her back against the warm fireplace. "This is where I work," she said. "It's my hope that you will join me."

Duuni said, "What is this place?" She waved her hand to mean not just the room but the Gatehouse, Welling-in-the-Mountains. "Is it...for catechism?" She had no other word that meant *a place to learn things*.

"Not that. Nor yet is it a school, though everyone here is learning. You might call a Gatehouse 'a place where one can ask any kind of question, among good company.'"

Duuni had been brought up not to ask questions at all, and when she had asked questions of the Roadsouls, she had been given answers she did not understand. Her dismay must have shown on her face, for Aash said, "Most questions are neither asked nor answered in words."

◎

Aash retired to her bedroom. Duuni lay in the high hearth loft, watching the fire's glow touch the living paintings. She had bathed with hot water in a steamy room. In borrowed clothing she had eaten soup at a big table in a room next to a kitchen, while Aash and the carpenter talked quietly. She had fallen asleep there, her cheek on her hand.

But now that she lay in a borrowed nightgown in the high bed, she could not sleep. The dogs were in the other room with Aash, and the door to the courtyard stood a little open. Footsteps sounded there, and new voices, mostly young: whispers, smothered laughter, a fragment of song. Four shimmering notes rang from some instrument she did not know.

Then all was quiet. But each time her eyes closed they flew open again. The painted creatures out there in the dark were alive as if they would leap off the paper.

She looked down into the room. Something moved in the shadows.

"Mma," she whispered.

It was the first time she had spoken that name since Alikyaan.

"*Mma*," said the shadow, and came streaking to her up the steps of the hearth: a narrow little cat, sleek as gray velvet. He turned around twice, treading, then plumped down and began to lick his breast.

She stroked him. He butted her hand with his head, and that was the last she knew until morning.

22

Hot-faced man,
bright one, brother.
In sleep the dark waters
of grief and silence
slowly rise to cover your heart.

Shrine poem. Welling-in-the-Mountains.

Into the mountain blind and hungry, following his left hand.

A little panicky voice behind his heart kept crying, *No way back! No way back!* But there had never been a way back. Again he said, "This is where I will go." He stalked up the narrow stream, his head bent to keep from banging it on the roof of the tunnel, trailing his hand on the wall.

The stone was grooved by miners' picks. He walked a long way. No sound but water.

The wall changed. The crimped ridges left by picks became planes and curves of stone. He thought, This is not a way men made.

The stream flowed toward him, sometimes quick and thin, sometimes spread across the tunnel floor. It made quiet, plishing sounds. He slopped along in his sopping boots. Drops fell from the low roof. The walls were slimy; where there was slime there might be little animals to eat, he thought. Snails, or fish.

If there were fish, there might be things that ate fish. Big things.

The thought slowed his feet. At home in Creek, the mountain was the Mother, one did not wonder what might be down in the middle of Her. But this was some foreign mountain. What might be here? Darkness. Well, what was darkness to him?

But what if there was nothing? What if at its root was the abyss, darkness forever?

He clung to a stony ridge with both hands. *I must go back.*

He went on.

He was splashing through ankle-deep pools, trailing his hand, when his sharpened hearing knew the tunnel had opened away from him, the roof had risen. The murmur of the stream echoed in a big space. Drops fell, cooler, from a ceiling far away.

He stood, his legs jerking with weariness and uncertainty. The wall where his hand lay was smooth, convoluted, wet.

He crept forward. The wall bellied and veered, swelling toward him, curving away. He followed it, creeping over slippery ridges, nubbly rubble, afraid to release himself into the cavern's space. A mouse that hugs the wainscoting, he followed his hand to the left. Stubbed his knees. Felt, with both hands, an enormous tooth.

He froze like a squirrel.

Nothing happened.

He felt it again. Felt about; found another tooth, and another. Whatever had owned them was dead and turned to stone, a dragon's skeleton. He stood inside its lower jaw. Some of the teeth were longer than his thigh.

He found the wall again. Heart drubbing, he took a step in the watery darkness.

Something cracked him on the skull. He crouched, his arms up to protect his face.

Nothing. Water music.

He stood up, banged his head a second time, felt for what was there and found a tooth hanging in air, the upper jaw.

It's dead, he told himself. Whatever it was.

Perhaps the dragon had been a creature like himself that had wandered in and died? Perhaps it had been buried here, or had crept up from somewhere deeper. He felt about for the rest of its body.

Teeth, teeth everywhere, up and down, no shape of jaw or skull. It could not be a dragon.

He returned to the left wall, thinking, How can I understand anything?

He wanted eyes and a torch. Had half a thought, What if there are things that even eyes can't—

Stopped himself. Felt his way forward, his right arm crooked over his head to protect it from the teeth that were not teeth.

Under his left hand were pearls and flutes, lilies and leaves, plums, wheat, the wings of butterflies. All stone. He crept slower and slower, touching them; he cringed from them, had to touch them. They were wet and smooth, not alive. He touched the wet cheek of a woman, her smooth lips, but where her eyes should have been was nothing, a pearly sweep. He touched a baby's fat hand.

I must have light! he thought. I *must* see!

But what if there was light already? What if he was creeping like a mouse at the edge of a great illuminated hall, a blazing gallery, touching green leaves and yellow wheat and purple plums and a baby's hand all rose and coral? What if something watched as he, a little blot of darkness in that glory, groped his way with his ignorant left hand?

He went on. The echoing vast space was left behind, and the tunnel closed in, narrower now, so that water and floor were one.

The stream grew warmer. He thought his non-light grew darker, though it could not grow darker. He walked stooped, the water to his knees, trailing one hand, then the other, his arm raised against blows.

The water was loud. But there was something else: a rap, the stream pushing at a rock, then dropping it—a resonant, aqueous ding.

He listened. Too regular. *Ding*, and *ding*, and *ding*.

Miners!

Miners hammering at the rock.

Panting, he groped on. The sound grew louder. *Ding* and *ding*, the clean clang rang through the rock, as though whoever it was hammered the very wall his hand lay on.

Almost running, he stumbled round a corner to get there, to be where the noise came from.

It faded.

He turned. Splashed back. There it was, crisp, distant. He searched left and right, up and down, looking for a crack, a broken place through which to crawl toward those clean blows.

Nothing. The wall was unbroken. He laid his cheek on the stone where the strokes were clearest, and wept.

After a while he thought to shout. Hammered with a rock. No good; unpausing, indifferent, the blows rang through the solid stone. He splashed on down the tunnel until the only sound was water.

His wet clothes bound every movement. He found a niche in the wall, big enough to creep into, where a stone made a sort of bench. He pulled up his feet and laid his cheek on his knees. Warm water trickled down his face. When it reached his lips he blew it off, or licked it off. Huddled, spitting water, he fell asleep.

It was a summer night. He lay across his great-grandmother's lap, her hand stroked his bare, dirty body, patted his bottom. His cheek was wet where he had drooled on her thigh. Old voice quavering, she sang.

Moonlight lies on wolf and doe,
On hunter and on lover,
As here upon my heart you lie
Until the night is over.

He opened his eyes to light: dawny, directionless. The night was over.

He waked, fell forward into the water. Struggled, coughing, to hands and knees. It was still night. He was still where he was.

He dragged himself up, wiped his face on the sodden tunic. Sat still, no heart left in his body. Maybe I never had one, he thought. Maybe I left it with that girl whose name I can't remember, who smelled of rosemary.

But he went on. After a while he went on all fours, for there was no headroom. The water rose to his chin. "Until the night is over, until the night is over," was the only lamp he had. The water rose to his lips.

The roof lifted. He raised his face from the water, spitting softly. Listened.

He could feel it was not a big space, the size of a hearth room, maybe. The water was quiet, a pool, not a stream. There was a slight current.

For the first time he moved away from the left-hand wall. Wading on his knees, he followed the subtle current. The bottom was sandy. Now the water came only to his waist. At breast height he stubbed his hands on a smooth ledge down which water slipped, slipped, without a sound.

It was the edge of a basin the size of his encircled arms. In it the water was flat and still. He placed the palm of his left hand on the surface of it, carefully, as if it were the mirror of water in a rain barrel. Felt a gentle welling up.

He sank his hand to the bottom. It was smooth as mother of pearl. Gently he pushed against the current's push and found his fingers quiet in a smooth gap like the mouth of a conch shell. From that place the water welled.

That was as far as his hand fit. The mouth was smooth. There was more beyond his reach, wherever that water came from, quietly rising. He knelt, touching back as far as he could, feeling beyond his hand some heart, the world itself.

He drew his hand out. Sat back on his knees.

Unbidden, his body gave a sigh, like a child's after weeping. He remembered bathing in the copper tub by the hearth, when he had been small enough to admire the pruniness of his fingers and toes.

He licked his fingers. They were pruny. Turning, he followed the current back to the wall, found the gap he had come in by, and felt about. There was a second gap. Through it, too, the water was leaving, going somewhere. It was big enough for his shoulders.

He turned to the welling basin, pressed the palm of his left hand to his mouth. After a moment he dropped it. "Thank you," he said, his man's voice strange in that place.

He squeezed through the second opening and crawled, slowly, down the new stream. The roof rose enough for him to crouch in the water, then to stand and walk.

No way to know how long he walked.

Days.

He walked through caverns so crusted with crystal that his hands bled. Through vaults of sandstone, grainy and soft. Through long cracks, slimed and slick, that smelled alive, tubes and tunnels full of the whisper of small beings skittering, running away.

He waded through pools thick with quiet fish. Fearless, they nuzzled his knees. He caught them with his hands and ate them raw, saying *Thank you* aloud in the dark.

Maybe he walked for years.

Sometimes he slept. Things that felt like spiders walked across his face and woke him, but they did not sting him, so he said *Thank you* and slept again. He did not know how many times he slept. He did not remember his dreams. The roof got higher. His boots were sodden but the rest of his clothes dried to damp, a good thing because the air went cool. He smelled the rose-petal odor of fallen leaves.

He walked as in a dream, where you cannot hurry. Following the stream, he turned his shoulders sideways and squeezed out into the world's air.

By the echoes he was in a cave, medium-sized. Shallow, for a low sun shone straight in. It touched his hands, his face. A little wind blew. The water was loud, spilling outward, downward, on its way to the sea.

He smelled dinner.

I've gone mad, he thought—calm, transported. He groped about. Found little rock piles, platforms, niches filled with clay dolls, toy carts, ribbons and papers and beads. Laid out among them were plates of roast partridge and apple cake, cornbread, sweet potatoes, little mugs of rum.

He thought, This cave is an altar to that place where the water rises.

"Thank you," he said.

He followed the cave wall until he was sure he had found the left-hand side of the shrine. Then, working his way around to the right, he ate all the offerings.

23

Where is life alight?
At the baker's spoon,
the singer's mouth,
the artist's and the writer's pen.
At each small wick, the candle flame
gleams in its hour;
behind these trillion points of light,
the great Fire.

Festival tune. Welling-in-the-Mountains.

 Sun.

He sat at the mouth of the cave, in the lee of a rock. Warmth lay on his arms, his eyelids. Because the sun moved, he knew the cave faced south, and that it was late afternoon.

He did not know how long he had been in the mountain. He knew that in this moment his face was warm and his belly full, and that he was happy.

I have had sun and food these five years, he thought, and I have been miserable. Why should I be happy now?

A rock squirrel piped. Such stillness. Reluctantly he thought, Soon the sun will go, the wind will grow bitter. Better keep moving, get down off the mountain and find out where I am.

He stood. It felt strange, as if someone else were standing. Or as if eyes were watching him; yet he was sure there was no one under the wide, stone-smelling arch of the cave but himself and the sunlight. He had always hated the feeling, even in imagination, of being seen when he could not see.

His old resentments showed up, a coat ready to hand; he struggled into them. They did not quite fit, as though they had shrunk in the water, but they were his.

I am to find Farki and kill him, he told himself.

Sunlight lay on his face like a blessing.

Where Farki was, Duuni must be; that was easier to think about. He turned to the cleft where the water of that nameless place leapt out of the mountain, and felt his way to the notch where it became a stream that misted the air.

Its clatter was easy to follow, but its path was not. It dropped down and down among boulders, bursting and re-forming at every fall; he had to clamber, grope, and slide down the water-worn jumble of rocks. He could not imagine what the land about him might look like. But he thought, Someone left those offerings where the spring leaps out. They must live on this stream. I'll follow it, and if I find them perhaps there will be more roast partridge.

He crept down beside the rattling water. The going was all but impossible. He broke through still-leafy bushes, stumbled among rough-barked larch and alder whose saplings sliced his knees. He forced his way through tall grass, hoping it was too cold for snakes. When the water plunged through a rocky draw he had to wade, slipping and splashing in the narrow stream.

Now and then he stopped, sure he heard footsteps, the little slide of gravel under an animal's weight; but it was only the water flinging itself against the rocks.

The air went cold. For years his overcoat of rage had kept him warm, but its new ill fit let the wind bite. He cursed viciously and felt more like himself. Farki, you fucker. Sell me, eh? Feel my grip! Feel my knee on your back, in the instant before I snap your spine.

But a stillness had come out of the mountain with him. It walked beside him, made his mind stray to the water sounds, to the wind in the leaves, to nothing at all.

The sun had gone. He found a path. Lost it. Shook himself, turned back toward the water's knock.

A creaking voice said, "*Ey.*"

He nearly jumped into the creek.

"Ey. You."

When he was sure it was not the voice of water, he touched his chest: *Me?* Had there been a thousand people there all along, watching him bash through the bushes?

"You that was cursing." Whoever it was kept his distance on the streamside slope and said in croaking Plain, "Why're you down there thrashing through t'brush?"

"I'm blind." It was the simplest answer.

"I seen that. Even so, seems a fool way to get there."

"Get where?"

"T'madhouse," said the voice. "Come up t'bank, I'll take you there."

"I'm *blind*," said Raím. "Not mad."

A hoarse old laugh. "T'maddies all say that."

Dragons that were not dragons, stone flowers, water that welled beyond his grasp. "*I am not mad!*" he said.

"Take you to t'sanctuary, then. Next door to t'madhouse. It's all the same."

Waist deep in brush somewhere in the universe, Raím felt his shoulders drop. He would go with the one who spoke. If they tried to chain him he would break a couple of heads. He tried to muster a determination to break heads. "Where have I come to? What place is this?"

"Ushumbre. Where else?" A branch poked at Raím's chest. "Take hold of t'stick."

Wherever the hell Ushumbre was. "You'll take me to the sanctuary? Not the madhouse. Do you understand?"

"You're blind, but I ain't deaf."

Raím grasped the branch. Once again kept at the far end of a stick like a beetle or a snake, he was towed up the bank to a path, smooth enough, that slanted downward in hairpin turns. When they had walked some distance in the sharp air, the dry voice said, "Come far?"

"Yes."

"Where from?"

To say "High Moles" would confirm him as a madman, though it would not be as strange as the truth. "If I had eyes I'd know where I've been."

"What's your trade?"

"Beggar."

"You're never a beggar," said the old man. "Not in them clothes, fine and ruined. All that comes to Ushumbre has trades. What's yours?"

"I'm the son of the Lord of the Ground." That sounded mad, too. "A wrestler. Bright Blood the Blind Magician." A madman's name. "That's for show, not my real name."

"What would that be?"

"Raím," he said. "What does that mean in the tongue of this place? Butterfly balls?"

He knew how rude he was being—and to a rescuer. Nothing in him had changed. He hated himself, must change, refused to change. Gods! He cast his end of the branch away. "Leave me!"

"I ain't leaving you. I'm Tarkark t'Keeper, and I know where you belong. Don't cross me." The branch whacked him, kept whacking until he took his end of it. They walked in silence until Tarkark said, "Raím."

"Yes, sir."

"Nay. T'word. Heard it in a song, but I had to think. In t'foothills, them Dras folk, that's how they pray. *Raím! Raím!* It means, like, 'Thanks.'"

Raím laughed—truly laughed, remembering a time when laughter had not hurt. "That's my other trade," he said.

"Could have fooled me," said Tarkark.

A little farther and Raím smelled hearth smoke, heard the screech of a windlass, the shouts of children in a last game of tag. He hunched his shoulders, ready for taunts and flung stones.

They did not come. What did spring up around their small parade was a murmur of voices low as prayer, the sound of feet that followed and then ran off, giving place to other feet.

Old, smooth stone underfoot, a canyon of stone houses. Sounds fell from the sky: the houses must be tall. Some stringed instrument played heartbreak, a girl's voice sang in a foreign tongue.

"Let go t'branch, now," said Tarkark. "Take my hand, don't you tumble down them steps."

His hand was dry and calloused as a goat's hoof. It led Raím down three steps into a small, low-ceilinged, earth-floored space. Flutter of candle flames, shuffle of slow feet. Tarkark said, "Mother, here's one of yours."

At what altar was he being offered? A little hand gripped his wrist, bony and thin-skinned as a frog's, and a skreeking voice said, "I can see what he is."

Tarkark poked Raím with one finger. "Lad, this old witch is Lenini. Give you a bite to eat and a bed by t'fire, if she don't suck your blood first."

"You old hide rack, it's you should suck blood, you're dry as a stick. Where'd you find this one?"

"Stayed after t'rest. I ain't young, I got my own prayers. Set down my tot of rum, and when I turn around he leaps out of t'mountain with t'water."

"Ah!" Lenini let go of Raím's hand.

"Like a kid out of a nanny," said Tarkark. "In that tunic, all chalked with clay like a ghost. Thought I'd die in my shoes. But he turns around and says 'Thank you.' Then he pisses on a bush.

Never seen a ghost do that. Then he sets to and eats every crumb
of what they left. Drinks my rum."

Raím blushed all over his body.

"So I think, it's a new maddie, that's who it is. But then I
think, Maybe he'll go back where he come from? But he sets off
down t'water. I follow him, and when I seen for sure he's a maddie, I bring him on in."

There was a silence, as though both of them looked him over.
Raím, who had discovered—not for the first time—that when he
thought himself most private there had been someone watching,
tucked his hands in his armpits. Had to ask, "Do people go in
there? Where the water comes from?"

Lenini said, "Nay. It's the most holy."

So he had desecrated. Perhaps he would be hanged in the
morning.

"I'm away to my grandson, tell him I found a new one," said
Tarkark. Raím heard his feet on the steps, then lost them in the
busy street. The door shut. Quiet flowed up from the earthen floor.

Lenini got a grip on the hem of the tunic and began to tug at
him. He stood still, a horse resisting a mouse, and said, "Mother,
what is the god of this place?"

"Any god you like."

She pulled him to a stool by the fire and gave him pea soup
with onions and barley bread, so plain and good he said "Thank
you" twice. He wondered when they would come and take him
to his fate.

Sleep came for him first, gentle as deep water. Sometime in
the long hours of the night he waked in the holy silence to find
that the bushes he had been thrashing through were poisonvine.

☙

"Look at you. *Look* at you," said Lenini. "All over your hands,
and your neck and your mouth. Holy Mother. If it's on your
hands it's on your privates—"

"Get away from me!"

310

She led him out to a kitchen garden, ordered him to strip in the chill morning air, and took away his clothes. Even the master tunic; too late, he realized it would never be returned. Duuni's lion must have faded from his body, for Lenini tutted only about the snake. Two girls, hysterical with giggles—acolytes of the sanctuary, he supposed—filled a tub with cold water, gave him soap, and left, or said they did.

He scrubbed viciously. Lenini inspected him, decreed a second icy tubful. When he stood shuddering she brought him a thin old towel and clothes that were so big, even on him, that he wondered from what giant she had borrowed them. She herded him into her tiny kitchen, sat him on a stool, and salved what he would allow her to; he took the salve away and did the rest himself. She wrapped his hands in rags.

The ointment was rank and cool, the fire was warm. "Thank you," he said.

"Blisterwort. It won't live in a garden. This is from the patch by Threadneedle Falls. I planted it myself the summer I married, and many a lad's paws have I salved with it." She sniffed. "Don't grow old, boy, you won't like it."

He thought, I have not much liked being young. "You have sons?"

"I do, and blessings they are, one living and three dead."

"The dead are blessings?"

"They were alive, and my sons."

He set his bound hands on his knees. "Mother, what can I do for you? Any work?"

"You've no eyes and no hands."

"A doorstop?"

"You bonnie silly lad." The cold little frog paw cuffed his ear. "What's the matter with your family, that they've made you wander?"

"They didn't make me. I chose."

"If you were son of mine—"

311

"—I'd be a blessing, even dead. So find me work, Mother."

"There's always work at the madhouse. So many mouths. Come along, then." She tugged at his sash. He did not move. "Up!" she said.

A sense of fate was on him, a dreadful rightness, what the coursed hare must feel when it surrenders to the dogs. "Will they try to chain me?"

"Hmph. There's some I'd chain. Smacking a scrum-ball off the garden gate in the small hours. Come."

She tugged him across garden flagstones, through a back gate and down an echoing narrow alley, through a second gate on a stone path. Had she stolen his garment of rage along with the tunic? He could have knocked her down and fled.

Running feet. Children's hands. Children in a madhouse? "Are you a new maddie?" they said.

"No."

"Yes!"

"*No.*"

"Yes, yes, yes!"

From the tumultuous kitchen a man's voice shouted, "There you are. Sissity, lead him, he's blind."

Lenini had evaporated. Raím's rag-wrapped hand was taken by someone small and placed on a shoulder, which moved. He followed it, thinking, in spite of his unease, This kid knows how to lead blind people.

"You're easy," said Sissity. "The Bat Man yanks me all over."

"Bat Man—"

"He works all night. He hangs from the ceiling."

Up two broad steps and through a doorway into warm air savory with onions. The man's voice came from here and there, as if he were running about. "Madness! Been expecting you. Carka, take out the pits, we don't want stone soup. Sissity, over here, please. Name's Raím? Funny, where I come from *raím* is a hole in something, like a doughnut. Slinker, chop *fine*. Gods, look at you—poisonvine this time of year, you must have had to work at that. Mott, drain the stock and throw the rest to the pigs. Raím—here's a chair, there won't be a cage free for you till after dinner." The voice was constant, calm. "Can't peel potatoes with your hands wrapped, can't sort beans with no eyes, let me think. Sissity, hands out of that. Ellu, what have we got for the new one?"

"Nuts."

"Right. Can you use your fingertips, Holey One? By life, the soup! Tita! Nutcracker. What's-your-name, Raím, can you work a nutcracker bandaged up like that?"

The nutcracker was the kind with a wooden screw. A sack of hazelnuts was dragged to Raím's elbow, a basket wedged between his knees.

It hurt to use the nutcracker. He would not admit it. After dinner they would put him in a cage? He'd like to see them try. He cracked a hazelnut, picked out the round meat and dropped it in the basket, dropped the shells on the floor. That was all he had to do so he did it. Walking onward, the next thing. A *cage*?

Now and then a hand clapped his shoulder. Talk was loud, broken, in Plain with weird accents. It was a madhouse, all right. Like Roadsoul madness, that made no sense and did not explain itself.

"It's opening. I thought it never would."

"Mine, too! A line of stitches down the middle. I pulled them out and my heart opened right up."

"Like a mountain in the air."

"You know what *he'd* say to that. 'Why do *you* think it's a mountain in the air?'"

"I pulled the eye closer to the nose but it wouldn't stay, I had to tweak out a yard of weft. Gods! I'm an oriole unbuilding its nest, I'm a snake shedding!"

The voices were male and female, mostly young, ordinary as carters talking about harness.

"I made the horns of the moon a little longer."

"Like a boat, you mean? Where are you headed in it?"

"Downriver, always. Downriver to the sea."

Raím twisted the nutcracker. He thought, I'm back in the newie cart, no one will explain, if I ask I'll be baited. Flea Butt.

Suddenly there it was: his lost rage in its fullness like a homecoming, rich, exquisite. For an instant he saw how much of it was terror. Pushed that aside and thought, These fucking clowns can't cage me!

The maddie who had reshaped the moon came close and said, in a twanging accent, "Crazy enough?"

Raím kept his head down. Twang asked someone, "He speak Plain?"

"Why not? Blind, though."

"Oh. And I'm brainless. Name?"

"Raím," someone shouted from across the kitchen.

"So, Raím," said Twang. The head maddie yelled at him to get back to the beets. "How'd you get here?"

"I'm not here," said Raím.

"No? Where are you?"

"In Ushumbre. I'm cracking nuts here, that's all."

"Cracking nuts in Ushumbre." Twang set it to music. "In Ushumbre—"

A girl's laughing voice said, "Raím, don't mind us. We're all crazy."

He drew in his head like a turtle. Twang said, "Yesterday the keepers let us loose. We trekked up to the cave to leave offerings, and nobody's really back yet. Where are you from?"

"Nowhere," said Raím in a panic. He had eaten their offerings.

"*Ohey!* What's nowhere like?"

Raím would not answer. Twang said, "Would nowhere be where everything is before it's somewhere? That's good. Before I take a step, where's the step? Nowhere. Before I touch the strings, where's the music? Nowhere, yet. Then I touch them, and the music's here."

Several voices said, "Ah!"

"Nowhere's the richest place in the cosmos. If that's where you're from, you're worth knowing."

Another voice said, "Don't bewilder him. He's new."

"He can't jump into the river without jumping into the river."

"We'll push *you* into the river. Raím, when *he* was new he tried to smash our faces in. What's your trade?"

Raím said, "I am not new. I am not mad. I don't live here, I don't have a trade, I'm a blind beggar, and I'm doing this for Lenini." He twisted the nutcracker; the hazelnut burst to shards. "Tarkark brought me."

"Tarkie! He was at the shrine. Is that where he found you?"

"He brought me down the creek, that's all. To the sanctuary, that's all. If you think you can keep me here, get out of my way!" He rose up like a bear. "I won't be put in a cage, and I have fists!"

The nutcracker went flying, the basket tipped, hazelnuts rattled across the flagstones like marbles. The crowd in the kitchen scattered away from him, knocking over chairs. Bad Blood the Blind Maniac, he crossed his arms, swung his head from side to side.

From high up, perhaps the safety of a cupboard, a girl said, "He thinks this really *is* a madhouse."

"Isn't it?" said Twang.

Raím ploughed forward like a grizzly, hands out to grab and wring. Ran into a table so heavy that when he tried to overturn it nothing happened. He swept his arm across it. Cups flew, a heavy bowl spun ponderously to the edge, fell, smashed. He slipped and went down on one knee in a welter of mashed potato.

"*Hist!*" said Twang. "*Drake!*"

Unseen beings dropped clanging spoons or ladles, scrabbled away like hens.

The noise stopped. The room rearranged itself. Bodies scrambled down from high places, up from low. Raím heard his own breath, and caught it in a gasp.

Silence.

315

Twang said, "Sir." Pause. Then, full of shame, "Sir, I baited him. It's my fault."

"No, it isn't," said Laughing Girl. "We were being wild. We all let it go on."

The kitchen shuffled its feet. A man's quiet voice said, "Raím."

"Get away!"

"Raím."

He struggled up. "I don't know who you are and I don't care, you can shove your madhouse up your asshole, sir, and I am leaving." But he had lost the door.

Silence, like the silence inside the mountain.

He said, *"Why can't I know where I am?"* To his horror, tears pricked his eyes. He covered his ears with his hands, as if to keep out that asking silence. "Shut up! Get away from me!" Felt all the wide, seeing eyes in the room fixed on him. "I'm a blind beggar," he said.

The quiet voice said, "You are a blessing."

"I am not!"

"You are a whole, good man."

The distant children's voices said, "You're it! You're it!" and in front of a houseful of strangers Raím wept, huddling his face in his sleeve.

He had thought shame was like the shaft in the mountain, down which he must fall forever. Yet the bottom of his shame turned out to be an ordinary place: not the best, certainly, but tolerable. There were a lot of people down there with him, shuffling their feet.

He raised his face. A blob of mashed potato fell off Lenini's clean tunic, *plop*. He said, "People give me things and I ruin them."

Footsteps. A hand took Raím's bound one and put it on a shoulder, tall this time. "Come," said the man. Raím followed him. Behind them a buzz of talk rose once more, and the clanging of pans.

୭

Through an echoing courtyard, up a stone staircase to a second story, down a shadowed balcony to an interior room that was warm and smelled of burning cedar. There was another odor, too, so familiar that Raím scarcely noticed it. His companion stopped. Said, "There's a chair to your right. Please sit down."

It was a broad wooden chair, smooth with sitting. Perhaps the room was paneled with tapestries, for sounds did not echo.

Neither of them said anything for a long time.

At last Raím said, "Who are you?"

"My name is Seu Drake. You came out of the mountain shrine."

"So hang me."

"The river springs from that place. Shall I hang the river?"

"I didn't steal anything." The offerings.

"It's not uncommon for a novice to find his way to his teachers in an unusual manner. But you're the first, to my knowledge, to come walking out of the mountain."

"Novice what?"

"What is your trade?"

Again that question! "I was a hunter once. And a weaver. Then a wrestler. And a beggar…no. I never begged. People gave me things."

"Were they things you wanted?"

"No." But that was not true. "Sometimes."

"What if you could have what you want most?" said Seu Drake.

"Oh, right!"

"What if what you want most—" a shift in the voice, perhaps toward humor "—is what you have?"

"What if I put your eyes out?"

"I'm sure you could."

A long silence. Raím said, "I wouldn't."

"You are young and blind. I am sighted and old. Who is better off?"

"Do you hate being old?"

"No."

"Then you're better off."

"I agree."

Raím ground his teeth. "You're happy."

"And you aren't?"

"No."

"Are you always unhappy?"

"Yes." But…that morning in the sunshine. "Almost always."

"When you aren't unhappy, what is happening?"

It was the strangest conversation he had ever had. "Sleep. Food. Fucking," he said, to shock the old man. He thought of Duuni laughing, kissing him through sugar. He turned his face aside. "Or…a moment."

"Sleep, food, fucking. None of those requires sight."

"But there are other things. Thousands. I want them."

Seu Drake said, "I have always wanted to fly."

"That was how—" said Raím, and stopped.

"How you lost your sight? Tell me."

"No. You'll take my words and twist them, you'll make it seem—"

"That you chose?"

"Oh, I chose! You'll make it seem that it was good."

"Was it?"

"Until I struck the rocks it might have been good, I suppose," Raím said bitterly. "If I'd been paying attention."

"Ah!" Silence. "You might have enjoyed it."

Raím rose from the chair, fists clenched.

"You can enjoy nothing else," said Seu Drake. "Not the sight you do not have. Not the woman who does not choose to enjoy herself in those long arms of yours. Not—" that hint of laughter "—not the arthritis in my hands; that's mine to enjoy. So let us arrange some things to match the life you have chosen, and perhaps one day you'll enjoy your arthritis."

"You took what I said and tangled it!"

"I took your thread and wove a different cloth."

Then Raím knew what he had been smelling: linen and cotton and lanolin, the dust of fabric-making. He was back in the Hold, where sunlight slanted through the roof in a spear of smoke and floating lint.

Seu Drake rose, took his bound hand, and led him to a loom.

It was a Great Loom, like those that divided Sunside from Starside. He stood again at the center of the universe. Seu Drake said, "There are two weaving masters here, and a separate workshop. But this loom suits me, so I keep it here to think with."

"'To think with,'" said Raím. "Gods. What is this place?"

"What does it seem?"

"I don't know!"

"Do you think *I* know?"

Of course you know, you fucking Roadsoul!

Then it was, suddenly, as when the last bead of sun slips under the western edge of the world: the blaze is gone, and all is mild and still.

Raím thought, He *doesn't* know.

He remembered how he had been in the mountain: groping, guessing, concocting theories, throwing them away. Seu Drake, it seemed, was saying this was normal: what everybody did. So Raím was short one sense out of five; did that make him so different from every other human?

"We go along asking one another questions," said Seu Drake. "Asking and listening at all the gates of being. That is all we can do. Hence this place, which is called a Gatehouse."

Ta Ba! She had been novice at a Gatehouse—not in Ushumbre but in Welling-in-the-Mountains.

"All of us here are makers," said Seu Drake. "It's in our art that we ask the questions, and if there are answers—" that laugh "—it's in our art they live. I don't use the word 'answer' much, myself."

"Makers," said Raím. "Weaving."

"And wrestling. And painting, and poetry, and woodwork, and smithing, and dance. All the making trades."

"Then those crazies in the kitchen—"

"Novices in one trade or another."

Gods. Raím passed his hand across his forehead. "There's a girl. I have to find her, I have to bring her here. It's hers." Then, "Does it take eyes?" Answered himself: "Inside the mountain, I was the same as anybody." Found he was gripping Seu Drake's shoulder. "You're saying…I am to stay here? And weave? And wrestle?"

"If you choose."

Raím blundered back outside until he bumped into the balcony and threw up over it.

Somebody below said, "*Hey!*"

Seu Drake followed him. He said, "It seems your life lately has had a lot to do with food. Perhaps we can find you another medium."

ᕼ

Seu Drake summoned the one who stood below. As it happened, it was Twang. When Drake had gone, it was he who steered Raím along the balcony. "You missed me," he said. "Though not by much. Does that mean the gods are merciful?"

"Where are you taking me?" said Raím, who between one breath and the next had conceived the worst headache of his life.

"To your room. It has an east window, when the wind sets right you'll get the bakeshop. Here's the door. Duck your…sorry. Sit on the bed. I suppose you smack your head often?"

"Yes," said Raím, holding it.

The narrow bed had a woolen blanket, coarse sheets, a pillow of common, quilly down. Since he had left his mother's house at eight years old, Raím had had no pillow but a rolled cloak. He had never had a room, only his place in the Men's Hold or his drafty hut. "What's all this for?" he said.

"The room? To sleep in. Where do you usually sleep? Horses sleep standing up. Fish don't sleep. Do they?"

320

"This isn't mine."

"No. Nor is your body, come to that. You use it for a while, then the worms get it, then the marigolds. Damn! I was supposed to spade the compost. For the moment this is your bed, though. You're to wash the sheets every couple of weeks, the steward won't stand for fleas."

In the Men's Hold everybody had fleas, dogs and men. "I don't know how to wash sheets."

"I'll teach you. Over there, the stove's lit and hot, don't touch it."

"You said there's a window?"

"Of course," said Twang. "This is a *town*."

When he had gone Raím felt his way across the worn floorboards, found the hot little stove, a table and chair, a stand with an empty bowl and ewer—tin, fortunately, since he knocked it over—and a tin chamber pot that rolled under the bed. At the casement he fumbled at the catch and swung the window open.

Cold air, sun slanting toward noon, aromatic smoke. Crows cawing in wide space. The sounds of the town rose past him: hammer on anvil, sawing, shouts. Clatter of carts. A snatch of whistling far away.

He listened. No thoughts; it was too big for thought. He itched, his head ached, a knot was growing on his forehead. Each itch and pain cried, *You are here!* He smelled the bakeshop.

From Ushumbre, where was Welling-in-the-Mountains? Was it far? He would find out, he would fetch Duuni somehow and bring her here. Duuni was with Farki. *What might Farki be doing to Duuni?* What if he had sold her? What if he—

"Brookie," said Raím. For a cat was toppling against his ankles, rubbing, toppling again. He was afraid to bend down lest it run away. "Nit, robber, pest," he whispered. He scratched at the window frame, hoping it might investigate. It leapt to the sill with a thump, and rubbed his bandaged hands.

321

He gathered the cat against his face, little, weightless, warm. There were footsteps at the doorway. But he was here, he had arrived somewhere, and he did not give a damn if anybody saw.

In the wilderness, walking, walking, around her only dark. She had to feel her way with her hands. Sometimes there was nothing to feel.

Duuni woke holding tight to the coverlets, and thought, I dreamed I was Raím.

Sun poured through the east windows—full day. The cat was gone. From the beam above her face swung a cobweb, the kind found only in houses.

She sat up. Beyond the courtyard door, footsteps and passing voices. Within the big room, quiet. From bench, table, wall, the eyes of the paintings gazed at her.

She looked away.

Then she said, "Gya!" She crept down the hearth stairs, shrugged into borrowed clothes, put on her broken boots, and went to look at the paintings. Not at all of them; there were too many. Anyway she did not need to look at all of them, only to know she could look.

She did not like them. They were too strange. Then she began to want their strangeness, though they frightened her.

Of the fat bull bursting his frame she thought, That's Tumiin. No. It's what Tumiin might be if he were not evil.

The painting of the girl who was half fish was easier to look at, but it made her sad—as if the girl were trying to be all girl, but with her legs bound together and nothing to breathe but water.

The courtyard door opened and Aash came in. Duuni jumped away from the paintings, in case she was not to be near them. Then she was angry with herself for lying, and said, "Good morning. I was looking at the prayers."

"There are some good ones."

"Are they what I am to paint?"

"Would you like to?"

"No."

A tap at the door. A girl a little older than Duuni entered, tall, in tunic and black tights like a mountebank. Her name was Liss. Aash introduced them, then called them to the table where an untidy pile of papers lay, saying, "Liss and her brother are novices of mine. This is her work."

The big, thin sheets were covered in faintest tracings, straight lines and measures. Drawn over them was a riot of vines full of creatures that were not strange at all: rabbits and grasshoppers and birds. Without meaning to, Duuni smiled.

"Yes, aren't they?" said Aash. The women spoke quietly. Duuni understood the words but not the meanings, things like, "If you'd let a little more wind into this," or "Think fire!" or "Try opening your elbow, it may flow better."

They spoke like Roadsouls.

Aash tapped a grasshopper with her finger. "These are delicious. Duuni, have you had breakfast?"

"No," said Duuni, hoping it would not be grasshoppers.

"Of course you haven't. I'm distracted. Go into town with Liss and her brother; take these drawings to Emerk the Blade and get something to eat. Liss and Thorn can show you a bit of Welling."

Liss rolled the drawings, picked a burned twig from the hearth, and wrote on the edge of one of the papers. She saw Duuni staring, and said, "We all learn to read and write. I teach the beginners. You can join us tomorrow, if you like."

Aash, laying out new paper, looked up and smiled. "You'll be able to write down the ballad of Jiin and Ekraaba."

When the girls were nearly out the door, Duuni turned and said, "Last night there was a cat."

"We call him Halfcat because he's so small," said Aash. "But he hunts like a lion."

❀

In the courtyard were banks of rosemary and bloodroot, and other plants that on the Maidens' Balcony she had seen only in pots. There was the well. Small figures moved under the portico; Liss's brother came hurrying, crying, "The hounds are upon us!" as, with a chorus of shrieks, Willek and the Mice surrounded them, holding out their newly-washed arms.

"This is why we don't do urda," said Liss.

Her brother drove the Mice away, saying, "She'll paint murals on you later. Maps of the known universe." They escaped to the street. "Time moves slowly when you're a kid," he said. "It's because we tell them *Later* all the time."

His name was Thorn. He and Liss were twins. They spoke with a strange, nasal accent, but where she was serene, his mind bounced like a six-week puppy. Duuni was afraid he would bait her for her borrowed clothing, but half the people in the town square were as motley as she. "You look like a novice," he said with a shrug. "That's to say, like a Roadsoul."

They walked down the street she and Aash had trudged up the night before. Duuni clung to Liss as she had clung to Tam Chivi and the rest on the midway, for the main street of Welling was like a fair that never stopped.

What she had taken for alleys were cross streets, made narrow by food vendors' carts and goods hung out for sale. Some had washing strung across. At the smell of new bread, Liss turned into a bakeshop, said, "Breakfast," and laid coppers on the counter.

Duuni said, "I have no money."

"My treat. You can buy next. A novice gets paid just about enough to buy buns."

She was to be *paid?* And learn to read and write into the bargain? They sat at a greasy table eating bread and drinking milky tea. She was afraid to say anything, for Thorn played with her words like a juggler with clubs. She began to see he was not teasing her but juggling with his imagination, like Nine playing cats-cradle, and she began to like it. When they walked on down the street, the sunshine on a bundle of besoms was spun gold.

They passed a tavern. At the door a man in a stained hauberk grinned and made a dirty gesture. From the dark interior, a hand reached out, grabbed his shoulder, and pulled him in.

Duuni went hot and cold and blank. Liss walked faster. "Plenty of novices can tell stories of paidmen," she said.

"And Leaguemen. And stepfathers, slave owners, bad priests, pimps," said Thorn, making a chant of it. "Pirates."

"Pirates! You believe Sharky?"

"Why not? You know how Batty says he got here."

"But up the river? On a *sea serpent*?"

Duuni looked back. The tavern doorway was empty.

They went first to a shop that smelled the way the air does after a hailstorm, of new-cut wood. Among leaning planks was the carpenter who had met them at the well, sawdust in the creases of his grin. Emerk the Blade.

"Ah!" he said. "The corbels." He set down a bright gouge and spread the roll of papers on the beam he was carving. From behind a rack of lumber, a thin brown girl joined them. She motioned for Duuni to look, too.

Duuni took a breath and said, "Please, what is a corbel?"

"Sticks out from a wall or a beam and holds things up," said Emerk. "Liss drew the designs on the plans here. Niki, my novice—" he nodded at the brown girl "—she'll carve it. These are for a house downriver in Oxbow."

They left the drawings with him. "Now we'll show you Welling," said Liss, which caused Thorn to make a chant of the names for Welling, in all the tongues of all the novices from all the villages—as patched and crazy, he said, as their clothes. He capered and clapped. Liss said to Duuni, "Imagine being trapped in the womb with him for nine months."

They went next to the glassblower's, where a man with wrinkled cheeks set glass jewels in lead strips to make a picture, a winged boy flying over a meadow of flowers. Liss pointed to a hare that stood on its hind legs, watching the boy fly. "I drew that."

The glassmaker said, "Why aren't ye youth working?" He scowled at Duuni. "Newie," he said, as if that were a weary thing.

On down the street, up this alley and that, the twins showed Duuni how the painter's work is used, where the drawn line can go. Everywhere there were novices. In the goldsmith's workshop a girl carved flourishes on bracelets. At the potter's a lad pulled a bowl out of a bit of spinning clay. In the stonemason's yard a young man with muscles that strained his shirtsleeves carved hearthstones and tombs; he shook Duuni's hand and said, with a grin and a thick accent, "Don't look's you need an epitaph yit."

At the cobbler's the proprietress took one look at Duuni's broken boots, scolded her in, measured her feet, then scolded her out again. "You novices ruin your feet. *Ruin* them. Do you want to be a cripple? Your shoes will be ready at the end of the week. You'll pay me soon enough; I'll harry you till you do." Behind her back her novice mimed her every gesture, until Duuni did not know where to look.

"She'll hardly charge you anything," said Liss when they had won free, "but you have to listen to her. We forgot to show you the designs she tools onto saddlebags, Thorn draws those."

They went to a shop where paper and brushes were made, then to one hung with stringed instruments of a kind Duuni had never seen, their bodies round like the bellies of puppies or people. The dark-eyed novice lifted one down and played a run of notes. "A *dindarion*," he said. It was the music she had heard last night, like water and voices. "Ah, but nobody can play like Songsparrow," he said, and hung it up again.

Duuni asked Liss, "Do they live in the Gatehouse? All the novices?"

"No. Some room with masters or tradespeople. But we gather at the Gatehouse. It's for all of us—" she smiled and shrugged "—who work at what we can't name."

"We try to name it, though," said Thorn. "By all gods, we try!"

Duuni was drowned in newness, and it was still only morning. "One last stop, then we'll go back and help with dinner," said Liss. "Thorn and I are in the kitchen this week." They turned off the bright street into the soft light of the weavers' workshop.

All the old smells and sounds: silk and raw cotton, swish of the batten, scratch of the comb. And new ones: heavy oil, the creak and cradle-rock of bizarre looms of which whole sections moved. Thousands of threads, a dozen weavers following them, each in a different pattern the way a dozen dreamers weave their thoughts a thousand different ways, weave their lives.

In spite of Raím, Duuni had not swallowed the idea that a man could weave; she had never *seen* a man weave. The weaving master was a straight-backed, dark-skinned old man, his hair so white and long that her first thought was that he might weave it into his work. He sat at a big window, weaving at a loom she could barely imagine.

It was part sash loom, for he was bound into it. Part moving loom, for its struts swung and creaked. Part she knew not what: wooden needles and curved hoops, delicate rows of brass eyes, underfolded wings, notches she could only half see. Over and through this his fingers moved, setting and knitting, shifting and strumming, delicate as a spider's feet on its silk orb. On it was half a white tunic, seamless. It shimmered.

"Sir," said Thorn, with more gravity than he had used with anyone.

The weaver turned his face. His eyes were the color of the cloth he wove: white. He was blind.

Duuni stumbled out of the shop, into the street. Liss followed her. "Are you all right?"

Duuni hugged her arms. *He would have come to this master! But Farki sold him.* "Novices cry in the street all the time. Nobody minds." Indeed, after a curious glance or two, the street went on with its business.

"I'm not crying." She felt too much for tears. "Have you heard of a man named Farki?"

"Of course. Farki of the Souls. He'll be here soon, with his troupe."

Was she to talk of murder in the street? She said nothing.

Liss watched her. At last she said, "You're trying to understand the Roadsouls. Everybody does, at first. But you can't understand them. They're too big for any loom. They plague and bless the masters the same as the rest of us. If they didn't, the Gatehouses would grow proud and stale."

Duuni thought of Nine's dirty face. Her heart unbound itself a little. "Did *you* ride with the Souls? You and Thorn."

"No, we're from a village downriver. Our parents didn't want us to be artists, but in the end they had to let us go."

"Did you say yes?"

"In the womb, I think."

Duuni thought perhaps she too had said yes in the womb, but without knowing it. "Are there other Gatehouses?"

"Oh, yes. I know of seven. The Souls travel one to another, bringing new novices and Mice. Upsetting everybody, making us curse and laugh, telling lies that are truth. You know how they are. If you're proud or timid, look out!" She laughed. "Farki's band will get here any day. He's the master wrestler. This is the Gatehouse where young wrestlers come, when they're called to that art."

Then Duuni did cry. Liss did not ask why, but pulled her back into the weavers' shop and gave her a handkerchief. The weavers kept weaving. Thorn touched the blind master's hand, then came to join the other two. All he said to Duuni was, "Something bite you? Let's go home."

⚭

At the Gatehouse the Mice waylaid them, their arms no longer quite so clean. Aash had mixed urda paste and found a press. While Liss and Thorn went off to the kitchen Duuni sat in a sunny corner of the courtyard in the familiar odor of rosemary oil, drawing ducks and snakes and bears as if she were still at the fair, still on the Maidens' Balcony. As if her life were a spiral that coiled back on itself. On Willek's arm she drew a kingfisher with its bright bold eye.

When the Mice had been drawn on and rag-wrapped they ran off to drive somebody else crazy until dinner. Duuni wondered where they slept, who took care of them. She went back to the room where she was to sleep and work.

Aash was not there. The lion was. She felt it.

From the bed above the hearth came a small complaint.

"Halfcat." She climbed up and found him among the tumbled blankets, tucked into the shape of a bread loaf. He had laid the rear half of a vole on her pillow. "Thank you," she said.

He stretched, bumped her with his head, and ran down the steps. She followed, carrying the vole by the tail, and tossed it in a lavender bush. Halfcat streaked up the stairs to the balcony. She stood in the sunshine, listening to novices hurry here and there and shout across the open space: her new companions, nobody she knew, a flood of names and faces among the thousands, perhaps millions in the world.

Suddenly she could not bear to be among strangers. She climbed the stairs and walked along the balcony, calling "Halfcat!" under her breath, glancing sideways through open doors into a room where a face looked up, then a room with nothing in it. In the last room, standing by the window with Halfcat under his chin, was Raím.

24

Begin with flowering flax.

Ripple it, cure it, ret it until the boon has rotted.

Break it, scutch it, hackle it until the fiber win free.

Spin it this way, that way.

Lay the two lines close as lovers. Spin them tight.

This makes strong thread, good to weave.

If the lion walks in the flax field,

the cloth is blessed.

> *"To make linen by hand."*
>
> A countrywoman outside Rett.

Stillness.

Inside the iron stove, crackle and hush. Outside the door, chatter and call; beyond the window, the smithy's clang. Right there, only quiet.

He spoke into her hair. "I can't kiss you. Poisonvine."

"I don't care."

"I do."

She touched her lips to his, light as a cat's paw. He groaned, put his big hand on the back of her head and mashed her face against his shirt. "I don't know where this is. I never do."

"Welling-in-the-Mountains."

"No. Ushumbre, they said."

"It has many names."

He started. Let her go a little. "Then they're all here. The Souls."

"No. I came by another way." She did not know how to tell him where she had been. "They say the rest will be here soon."

His face went secretive. "No matter. Oh heart! I don't know how to tell you where I've been."

They began to speak to each other, but haltingly, as if each were afraid to be thought mad. Her arm around his neck, his around her waist, they leaned together and spoke in whispers.

"Maybe we've been to the same place," said Duuni. "And we've come to the same place."

Something in him had changed. Yet something had not changed; she could feel it. He would not let anybody near it.

She wondered. Then she pushed that wondering aside, for he said, "Duuni. What should we do?"

This was the man she had seen chase a woman out of a mill-pond, stark naked and ready as a bull. They were alone together, there was a door to close, his arms were around her. Yet there it was, Jip's proud restraint.

She said, "We should hope your rash clears up quick."

He laughed, held her close. Willek appeared at the door of the room with his rag-wrapped arm, stared, and said, "Is that new blind man your lover?"

"Yes," she said.

"Huh. Can I take the rags off yet?"

"I told you, not until tomorrow. If you hurry, you'll spoil it."

❦

There are days in late autumn when the sun moves, but time does not. The leaves on the river poplars are at the same time green and gold, and the light pours through them as if they were colored glass. Soon they will fall; but in that moment they are

331

still part of the tree, flashing and trembling, and each moment you look at them is longer than your life.

These days are like that, Duuni thought. Raím, changed and unchanged; and the Gatehouse.

In two days Raím could find his own way to town. She watched him talk with Seu Drake, mingle hands with Meets, the blind weaver—trying to stay suspicious, but with the smile that he could not contain, like a trout's leap. She learned names: Carca and Finny and Slinker, Mott and Ellu, a gardener's novice called Holy Rot. There was another blind novice, the Bat Man, a jeweler, but he was visiting another Gatehouse. A blind jeweler! She was faint with happiness, and silent. It was beyond speech.

To wake each day to Halfcat kneading and purring, to shiver into her clothes and eat breakfast at Raím's shoulder; among quiet talk to prepare paint and paper with Aash and Liss and Thorn; with pencil or charcoal to sit at a wide table and draw—simple things at first, animals and birds and flowers—in silence. Only the whisper of the fire, the moving light from windows or lamps.

Later, to look at one another's work, to remark, to change a line. To *see*. To carry work to Emerk the Blade, and be praised with a look. To be paid for it! To lace her new shoes and put money into the hand of the master cobbler, whose name was She Sings.

No sooner had the Mice taken off the rags and squealed over the drawings than they wanted more. About every third morning they followed her, begging, and had to be told, *Not until those fade. That will be weeks. I mean it.*

No trace remained of the lion she had drawn on Raím's body. The blisters of poisonvine were gone, too. He shut his door, caught her round the waist, sat back on his bed and said, "Draw something new on me."

"Bunnies."

"You draw goddamn bunnies on me, I'll wring your neck."

"*Baby* bunnies."

He pulled her down against him. "Learn to wrestle, then. Better learn fast. I'll teach you." They pretended to wrestle. Kisses. Heat. The brink of mystery.

"Stop," she said, panting. "Stop."

"Duuni. Ah, Duuni. Let me in!"

There were pairs among the novices. She heard them making love in their rooms, but quietly. The days passed; yet she would not make love with Raím.

She knew herbs to keep from getting pregnant. She had been raised among women who had little other power. But she could not leave her fear. Sometimes she had to hold his left hand in both hers, just hold it, so as not to be afraid.

She confessed how she had gone with Doctor Amu, and what had come of it. He went white, then red. He said, "That's two."

"Two what?"

He turned his face aside. It was odd how the habit of avoiding someone's eyes was still with him. He said, "You were stupid."

"I know."

"But bold. That sack of slime! I would—"

His face was scoured by hate. She wondered what would happen if Doctor Amu and his paidmen came to Welling. To distract him with a second pain, as one eases arthritis by laying on nettles, she said, "Soon the Souls will be here."

It worked, but not the way she thought. The rich hatred on his face went subtle, private. Somewhere down deep, the door between them shut.

With whispers and touches it opened again, but never completely. He would not let her in. That was just; she would not let him in either. Each time—clothes rucked, their bodies hot and pressed together, Raím whispering, "Duuni, please..."—it was not just the old fear that kept her from saying yes. It was fear of being touched so deep, and changed, changed yet again. The only way she knew to approach it, and him, was the way Halfcat did: sidling, poised, ready to run.

He let her do that. *He let her do that.* They lay next to each other on his bed half-clothed, gasping, crazy with each other; yet when she said, "Stop," he stopped.

It humbled her. She told him that. She said, "I'm hurting you."

"Ah, it won't kill me. Just feels like it."

"Why are you so kind?"

"I am not kind!" He groaned, rolled away. Shrugged in that shamefaced way men do. "I didn't use to think how it must be for women. For my sister."

He told her how Thoyes had sold her hens that he might have money to run away. Duuni laid her hand on his neck where the blood jumped. "She has a good brother."

"Show you a better place than that to put your hand."

"No."

"Oh?" And they were at it again, panting. She learned something that is true in drawing, too: lines that almost touch are more powerful than lines that touch.

☙

She did not think much about the lion—or the lion-being god, whatever it was. It was a flicker among the shadows of Aash's workshop, a shine at the edge of a painting on the wall. She drew birds and flowers, no more. She was afraid to draw more. Sometimes she saw a reflection of the lion in Halfcat's round eyes—but Halfcat she could pick up and kiss.

There was no way to put this into words, not even the Roadsoul-speech that Duuni called "speaking in pictures" and that at first drove her crazy. Thorn might say, "Our blonde's out of bed" for *Sun's up!* Holy Rot might say, "root sleep" for *winter.*

Raím would take her aside and ask, "What blonde? What sleep?" She thought, Are we all blind in ways we do not realize?

Raím led her to the shrine where he had tumbled out of the mountain. Tarkark had taught him the way. When the world was not in constant change, as it had been among the Roadsouls, Raím needed to be led up a road only once.

They stood together at the mouth of the cave. It was like the shelters where Duuni and Aash had slept, an arch of stone with a broad, sandy floor lit to gold by the winter sun. The spring that would become the river burst forth at the back, where stones made rough altars. By then Duuni knew the novices had been born to many religions, and was not surprised to see offerings of toys and feathers and snake skins, papers written over with poetry in many hands. On the sandy floor were the footprints of deer and foxes and even a bear, as though all beings came to drink from the spring.

The moving air carried the mist of the newborn stream. Raím put his arms around her. The water broke out in bright spray; from the darkness behind it her mind drew back.

"Duuni," he said, low. "Do you pray?"

She had a feeling he had not meant to ask. "I don't know," she said. "No."

"Me neither."

As they walked back down the path to Welling, Raím's hand on her elbow, she thought it had been almost a prayer to go to that cave and stand by the water. But she did not know to what god.

Aash had an altar in the room, a niche built in the stone wall. Liss laid herbs on it sometimes. Duuni began to think she might make a little drawing of the lion-being god and put it there, the way Aash had drawn those prayers and put them in the fire. An altar, she thought, is a kind of fire.

But she could not draw it.

Sometimes she began. It should have been easy, like drawing on the Mice. But she could not see it clearly; it seemed always just at the edge of her vision.

There was a master papermaker in Welling, and the best her workshop made was a thick, felted sheet that was fine as Alikyaani cloth. Aash had set out a stack of it and told the novices they might use it, "if the painting wants it." Duuni asked how much each sheet cost, and was shocked; no painting but Aash's could justify that. But sometimes she picked up a sheet and rubbed it between her fingers.

She thought she might practice on a cheaper sheet. But each time—secretly, alone—she touched the tip of her brush to even the coarsest paper, the line stopped. Or it did stupid things: made a clumsy, dead drawing of a cat, or a cartoon with no dignity. She would crumple it angrily and throw the sheet in the stove, then feel guilty that she had wasted it.

So she stopped trying, and drew mice and roses and fish. She let the lion live in the corner of her eye and Raím in the middle of it, with his face that tried to look tough and sullen, but that with every glint gave away the secret that he too was happy.

⟲

She said nothing about Farki. She knew Raím brooded. She did, too. How could she think about someone who, for cash, sold a man to his death? The Gatehouse was paradise; how could she live in paradise with the devil? When novices and masters spoke of Farki it was with awe and praise. If angels praise the devil, are they angels?

Round and round she went, and could not make it fit. It was like being back in the newie cart, knowing nothing but the ruined patterns of Alikyaan and trying to wrench the Souls to fit them. That Raím did the same she was sure. She could tell when he held the question before him, dark, gnawing it like a bone. Any day the Souls would be in Welling.

"Nine," she said aloud.

Raím groaned.

"What will she say when she sees us?"

"*Gya!*"

⟲

Lenini pressed a coin into Raím's hand. "If there's no cardamom, bring me nutmeg."

Duuni liked her for not making him blind. She liked that he could come to town with her like a sighted man. With his big hand on her elbow, she was not so afraid of the paidmen who lounged in front of the taverns.

At the spice stall they bought cardamom in a twist of paper, then strolled on. Privately Duuni counted the coins she should have given to the cobbler. She said to Raím, "When's your birthday?"

He looked sly. "Don't have one."

They stood before the hardware stall. There were knives there, new and shiny from the smith whose hammer strokes they could hear from Raím's bedroom window. She wanted to thank him for letting her find her way to him, sidling like Halfcat. She chose a short knife in a sheath and paid the shopman, careful not to let the coins chime. "No birthday?"

"Raised in the forest by badgers."

"How did the badgers get you?"

"Bears didn't want me."

"Well, you got here." She put the knife into his hand. "So, happy."

He blinked fast. Put his arms around her. "Duuni—"

"*Aaa!* Flea Butt! You *got* here!"

A flash of silk, a blurred charge like a goat's: Nine barreled out of the crowd and butted Raím in the midriff. He staggered. A pyramid of saucepans dissolved in a brass crash. "Gya! *Pillbug!*"

The hardwareman roared round the counter, snatched Nine by britches and blouse and held her dangling. "You little...ah, it's *you.*"

"Put me down, Clangs," she said, giggling. "They're my *friends,* I ain't seen them since forever."

He dumped her on her feet. "You remember what I told you last spring, you little monkey?"

"I ain't taken nothing!"

He growled and began to stack saucepans. Nine leapt for Raím's sash and hopped about. "We thought you were dead and buried in there! Ate up by the mountain! Farki goes to fetch you out—"

"What?" said Raím.

"—he pays off the priest, he opens the door and you ain't there. Gone. Nobody but those poor buggers lying about."

Duuni caught her skinny arm. "*Farki went back for him?*"

"'Course he did. He *said* he would. Flea Butt's worth a bundle, Farki's not going to *waste* him. He calls about. No answer. Calls and calls, he takes his glim down the tunnels. Nothing. It's coming up dawn and he's got to get the key back, he locks the door again and that's that, we're leaving. Too bad! He said maybe you fell down some hole in there, or the mountain ate you." She teetered and leaned. "Farki got some fine shirts off those dead men. How'd you get out?"

Raím made a slight gesture with one hand. He looked as if he had been hit on the back of the head.

"And then *Pillbug* runs off. Farki says, 'They've both said yes. Either they'll find a Gatehouse or they won't. So it is.' Rags and Tiggy, they cried for you."

As Raím looked, so Duuni felt. The answer was too simple. "Where are they?" she said. "The babies and Auntie and the wagons?"

"In the fields back of the Gatehouse. I smelled the baker's. You got any money? Because if you don't I'll have to steal something. That would be bad."

Halfway to the bakery Raím stopped. Shook his head. In an iron voice he said, "Nine. Does Farki still own me?"

"Huh? You're *here*."

"He paid gold for me."

"Right. Too bad you weren't Bright Blood a little longer, Farki'd got his money back and some ugly townies'd got a thumping."

"If he tries to—"

"You got here your own self. You don't owe him nothing any more."

"'Any more'? When the hell did *I* owe *Farki?*"

"You get to the Gatehouse it's allee outs in free. Farki won't hold it against you. He ain't that kind." Nine ran ahead to the bakery, ducked under the baker's arm and snatched up a cinnamon roll. Raím paid for it. Nine said, "Where *were* you, Flea Butt?"

He seemed to gaze, inwardly, on some stone distance.

She kicked his ankle. "Pillbug, where were *you?*"

"With Aash."

"For sure! That's right."

Indeed, everything did seem right. Aash, the Gatehouse, Rags and Tiggy and the babies, Nine. *Allee outs in free.* Everything except, perhaps, Raím.

He stood in shadow. He thought he was alone; but he often thought himself alone and found later he had not been.

The sun had nearly gone. He was in the Gatehouse courtyard, his back against a stone that was taller than himself and half overgrown by a quince tree. The fruit had been harvested, but a few windfalls gave a cold perfume that mixed with the odor of fallen leaves and made him think of winter and snow.

He was considering how to kill Farki.

A few hours earlier he had stood within a few feet of the man, surrounded by the babble of welcome, the squeals of the babies borne off to be the newest Mice. He heard Farki's voice, brief and low, speaking to someone else. Raím did not speak.

It was not that he wanted to kill Farki outright. With his new knife, for example. Raím wanted, in fair fight, to cripple him so finally that he would cease to be Farki: who slid away like water, who violated sense and logic, who could buy Raím or rent him out or set him free. To kill Farki was to restore the universe to order, and Raím to his place in it.

This was what he contemplated, standing under the cold quince in the dark, rubbing a fallen fruit against his thigh and biting it, lightly, to taste the sour juice.

Duuni. Of course he thought of her. Sometimes he felt he was never not thinking of her, her warm body, the subtle approach that soon would bring her to say, *Yes, Raím, yes.* In the part of his soul where Duuni lived an awe had settled, like the awe of that secret place in the mountain; it held his hands open, waiting, never grasping. When she came to him of her own will she would truly come.

But in the part of his soul that had to kill Farki, nothing of Duuni existed. There, the only task in his life was to make Farki stop. For good.

He would kill Doctor Amu, too, but that was common revenge, and could wait.

He dropped the quince, took up the stick he had made, and set off across the courtyard to a meeting with Seu Drake. At the bottom of the balcony stairway Duuni came running lightly, smoky dusk in her hair.

As she pulled back from his kiss she said, "Everyone's here, Auntie and Dicey and all the babies. Maidy grabbed my knees and called me 'Peeba.' And I forgot to tell you: the woman you told me about, Ta Ba? She knows Aash! They were novices together. Her name is Bayami, she visits, you'll be able to meet her again. Raím! Everything's drawing together, coming home."

Raím said, "Farki."

"I'm so glad he—"

"—regrets what happened," said Raím. "Rents men for sacrifice every day."

She drew back a little. "He smiled at me. It wasn't impudent. Just a smile, like when you say, *Oh, there you are.*" She laughed softly. "And we are."

He ground his teeth. Women—they knew nothing of that deepest morality, how men must fight for it. "You think Farki... ah, to hell with it." He kissed her again, hard, so that anyone watching could see the blind man had a girl. *This* girl.

He went on up the stairs, knocked on the door of Seu Drake's chambers as he had been bidden, and entered at his voice.

Farki was there.

He did not need to be told. Farki made a perceptible gap in the universe, a not-precisely-thereness that was like wind: You could say, "There's a breeze," you could feel it, but you could not describe its whereabouts exactly.

Seu Drake was speaking. Raím swam out of the roar in his own ears, and heard.

"—Farki's mastery lives chiefly in wrestling. I propose that you plan your days to spend a portion of each with him."

"If that's what you want me to do," said Raím. He could not remember greeting or being greeted, assumed all that had occurred during the roar in his ears. What if he jumped Farki now, without warning? No. Not in Seu Drake's chambers.

"The choice is yours," said Seu Drake.

"If Farki wants to work with me, let him say so."

Farki's soft chuckle.

Raím folded his arms. There was an increasingly mortified silence. It continued. At last Raím turned to the vivid space that was Seu Drake and said stiffly, "If you think it necessary. Sir."

A second chuckle, Seu Drake's.

Raím sorted through ways he might save face. True, the last time he had tried a fall with Farki he had not been able to ground him; but he had not yet walked through a mountain, he had not touched—almost touched—that nameless place. He unfolded his arms, planted his stick, leaned on it. "All right," he said. "When do we start?"

"Now," said Farki.

⑤

Cold in his clout, Raím stood on the patch of sand behind the kitchen garden. He knew who was watching. Seu Drake, of course. Duuni, though he had made light of it and said it was not a contest. Lenini, and Liss and Thorn and Holy Rot and half the Gatehouse novices, a master or two. Nine, with a shrill contingent of Mice.

He set his hands on Farki's waist, his shoulder in the starting pose.

Indeed, something had changed.

There was even time to ask what had changed—as if a room had opened inside time itself. What is different? he thought. Answered himself: I am waiting.

As he waited for Duuni, he waited for Farki.

It made a spaciousness around him, so startling that when Farki moved at last, Raím lost his grip and they had to start over. The space was still there. When Farki made his move Raím melted under him like water. His old fear, that to let the other take him somehow unmanned him, was gone. Waiting for Duuni, letting her choose and move, had cured him of it. Inside this new space he opened himself, calm as a pond. Let Farki come into him. Come… Ah… Ah…

At the last half instant he turned, he thrust at Farki with an inner shout. *Got you!*

Farki was not there.

Raím flew through the air, landed heavily and rolled. Blind, he saw stars. Murmurs from the crowd, Nine's laugh. "Farki's still throwing old Flea Butt on his head!"

Farki's grunt. "Better," he said.

Better? Raím staggered to his feet. Was thrown again. And again. Miserable, furious, bruised, he began to chop and snatch, was thrown harder still.

Farki won every fall. Afterward he said, "You are learning."

Raím brushed the sand from his arms and crept away, praised for his failure, absolutely wretched.

๑

"Let me massage your back."

"No." He lay on his bed, face down.

"It might feel good."

"*No.*"

She laid her hand on his waist. He brushed it away. He would get at least part of what he wanted, prove he was a man. *Wait* for her? What shit—

He slammed around to face her, grabbed her arms.

"Raím—"

He kissed her as if she were Ellie, every goddamn woman who had never wanted him. Pulled her down, lay over her with all his weight. "No," she said. "*No!* Stop—"

The cliff's edge. The rock. Knowing what would happen if he jumped. Gathering himself.

Jump!

Don't jump—

With all his strength he wrenched himself off her, threw himself face down, fists under chest. "Get out," he said. "Get the fuck out!"

A scrabble. She tore away. Sobbing breath, her voice shook, terror or rage. "I love you," she said. As if terror, hatred were part of it.

The door clicked open, clicked shut. Outside the window, the late hammer blows of the smith.

He lay on his fists, saying "*Fuck, fuck,*" into the pillow. He did not want to be loved for being a ruin, cursed by all the gods.

☙

He got up and made his way, tapping and knocking, out through the Gatehouse garden. Thorn hailed him, laughing. He kept walking, over the uneven flagstones and out the round-echoed stone entryway to the street. He would go to the workshop full of looms and weave all night.

In the square he cracked his knee on a hitching post. A man took his elbow and said, "Need a hand?"

"No, thank you." His tone made it *Screw you.* He rapped with his stick. Workshops set their wares on steps or hung them from rafters, a labyrinth never two days the same. At the ironmongers he fell over a stack of pokers; a passerby said "Hup!" and set him back on his feet like a four-year-old. The cobbles were slimy with flung water. A tavern, smelling of piss and stale beer. A second tavern, raucous already, from which somebody yelled, "Blind man! Here's looking at you!"

His companions laughed. Raím groped on, grim as winter. Another voice from the tavern, not laughing, said, "Boys—that's Bright Blood the Blind Magician!"

A babble of comment. Raím stopped rapping the pavement.

Men came out of the tavern and surrounded him. The tavern keeper shouted, thinking they were running off with the tankards. These were not Gatehouse novices. "Bright Blood!" said one—yelling, because the blind are also deaf. "Hi! Seen you wrestling in High Moles!"

Raím leaned on his staff. Tried to look as if he ate human flesh.

"He near killed a man there, a big ugly wight," said the speaker to his fellows in a normal voice. Then, yelling, "Seen you near kill that big ugly wight!"

"Which one?" said Raím.

"Which one! Hark at him! 'Which one,' he says, like the Giant Killer. The one—"

"Don't go jabbing him, Renk, he'll rip your hand off," said another voice. It was a joke, but Renk stopped poking and said, "Come you, Bright Blood. Stand you a drink, won't we, lads? Tell us how you near killed that wight."

Raím shifted his weight off the staff and onto both feet. Jerked his head back to mean yes.

With roars of joy they gathered him, steered him to the tavern and up the steps into its fetid, comradely depths. They put a tankard in his hand. They pressed him to sit down, but he could tell he was taller than the crowd and preferred to loom, his back to the bar, feeling a warmth that did not come from liquor.

He did not smile. It would not have done.

They were already drunk. He guessed they were paidmen, which meant he was taller than savages, wilder than wicked men. The beer was spiked with strong spirit. He remembered the cure in Monsa's shed, and though his companions filled his tankard to the brim, he only sipped. A part of his mind thought, with a kind of sadness, Gods, I have grown old and wise.

The one called Renk, more sober than the rest, described in detail how Bright Blood the Blind Magician had turned the big ugly wight inside out. Raím listened, fascinated, to how it had seemed to eyes.

It all felt right: not to be slammed onto his head, not to be paraded in ribbons like a pig, but praised among men, even vicious men who stank and sloshed ale on him. They asked him how he had done it. Soon enough they were roaring at the tavernmaster to give them room to wrestle, Bright Blood would try a fall with them. The tavernmaster told them to get the hell out of his bar, they could go out back beyond the midden and kill each other there. They trooped out, banging Raím on the shoulders and singing.

He was cold sober and proud of himself. Smell of night, of midden, then sand. "Here," they said, and after some argument chose a man to face him. Not Farki but an ordinary man, drunk and happy. As Raím took the starting pose he thought, This is what it feels like to be Farki.

That was the last he thought for some time.

When he began to be aware again, he had a worse headache than he had had in Monsa's shed, all in his right temple. He tried to put up his hands to feel it, and found they were bound.

Above his head a hoarse whisky voice said, "There you are! Though in a commoner tunic than formerly—worse luck for me, eh?" Squeak of a cork twisted from a bottle neck, thump of it slapped back in. "The lads wanted to sell me a wrestler. But I'm no mountebank, and I must pay off a little debt to a mill warden, as the consequence of my not doing so would be quite unpleasant.

You're blind, but you're strong, and in the mills it won't matter that you are, shall we say, gullible in the extreme." The cart jounced onward. Doctor Amu belched, farted, and sighed. "Wisdom," he said to the world at large. "A hard road."

☙

Falling.

Not through air, though the air did get heavier, he could feel it, and warmer. But falling down the mountainside, slowly, on a rutted road, with halloos and the jingle of harness. By the laughter and talk, he knew some of the paidmen had come along with Amu. They shared his fire, nights. The cart creaked onto a barge, its wheels were lashed to the deck. It tilted in the current. Dogs barked from shores that drew away on either side.

Raím, of course, did not sit among the paidmen. He traveled in Doctor Amu's cart with the pungent remedies, bound hand and foot, and, after he tried to shout, gagged.

He had worn out his rage. Even his listlessness, his grief. There was left only some iron part of himself that would not bend; and despair. What glimpses he allowed himself of despair's face—the full knowledge of what he had lost—frightened him so badly that instead he chose to feel nothing. He lay in trance, as an animal does when it will die.

Sometimes he slept. Between sleeping and waking there was not much difference. He was given only water, and little of it. Was cargo, like a rolled rug. At last barge and cart bumped and shuddered, the watery sway became the customary jolts. Clatter and roar. A stink of coal smoke crept through the odors of medicine, rotten canvas and foul straw.

"Eh, lad. Here we are."

He could not stand. Did not want to. He was prodded, rolled this way and that.

"If he dies, Amu, you're still in my debt." A voice used to obedience.

"Dies? The lad's robust as a bull. Had I not trussed him he would have torn apart the cart. Ab Tate—in all my years of service, have I ever given you cause to mistrust me?"

Silence.

"All right," said Amu. "If he dies. But he won't die."

Nor did Raím die. His bonds were removed; shackles were locked to his wrists and ankles. He was hauled up, dashed face first into a horse trough and held under until everything in him that still wanted to live woke at once, gasping and thrashing.

"There, you see," said Amu.

He was set on his feet, clipped between two chains, and led, staggering, up stairs and down ramps, through narrow corridors and wide rooms. All of them were mad with noise.

Clash, crash, thud; hum and whine; scream and skirl of a thousand ungreased axles, a thousand pigs with knives in their necks. The part of his mind that constantly made maps reeled from the din, could not interpret it. Around him a breeze of motion, men's shouts, children's shouts. *Children's.*

"He's a weaver, sir. Will you take him straight to the frame?" said Amu.

"What you've left me of him," said Ab Tate.

"Now, now, sir."

Clatter and roar. A wall of gasping heat with an understench that curled the lip, an inferno of gnashing. Raím reeled, was snatched back. "Ha! Can't have you caught in the hackle on your first day," said Amu.

Ab Tate said with mild amusement, "That would be throwing money away, Doctor. Yours."

"Indeed." Amu kept his fist closed on Raím's sash until they had arrived somewhere in the completely inexplicable universe. The chain at Raím's ankle was clipped to something. He sat down on the floor, for his legs would not hold him.

"Hmh," said Ab Tate.

"A little food and water and he'll thrive," said Amu. "Never overfeed stock in transport. Hi! Lassie! Bring the dipper."

A quick scuffle like a rat's. A tin dipper rattled on Raím's teeth; he drank. "More," he said, gasping. Was given more, and still more.

"There," said Amu. "The will to live. And who wouldn't have the will, near such a pretty girlie as this? Eh? Does your mammy know you're such a—"

"That will do, Amu."

"Well and all, she'll be prettier when she's bigger. Though the hand, that's unfortunate. Oh…step back, sir, he's feeling better."

Raím had stood up. Not with the authority of Bright Blood the Blind Magician; but he was tall.

"Rogge," said Ab Tate. "You'll give this man the rules."

"Right." That was another voice, deep, from someone as tall as Raím. "You there. Blind, right? The rules is, you work. You don't work, I beat the shit out of you. Same if you damage the machines." The tip of a whip laid on Raím's shoulder a stripe six inches long. "Got it?"

"Yes," said Raím.

"Simple. Effective," said Amu. "Admirable."

"Rogge, take this man to the capstan. Amu, this is an experiment, to see whether a blind man can work. If he can't, you're still in my debt."

"Well. Come to that, there's a woman down Tillwood way has promised me a girl; but you'll see, the lad will serve." Amu struck his hands together softly, as one satisfied. "We'll save the girl for a rainy day."

☙

He was indentured. This he learned his first night in the men's dormitory, a foul closet of racks furnished with straw mattresses so filthy and bug-ridden that he hove his to the floor and slept on the planks.

He did not know what indentured meant. "Means you're working off your debt," said one of the men. They were mostly older, and weary. Such curiosity as they had was stirred by his blindness; at the thin supper of potato soup, one of them gave him a hunk of bread with onion pickle, brought from outside.

Raím could not think. If he thought, things jumped out of it and stabbed him with knives. Could the ghost of a girl's soft body kill? "I have no debt," he said.

"Why, then, you're working off the debt of him that brought you. What do you owe him?"

"Nothing."

Another said, "It was Amu."

A bitter laugh went round. The first said, "Aye, you owe him. Nor your four years here won't be enough. Better pay him back personal."

"Four years?"

"That's the term." They seemed to find savage pleasure in forcing him to hear it. Then shame, and a kind of camaraderie. "Or seven. Depends on the contract. When it's done you're free, and the mill will hire you for pay. That is, if they ain't got enough indentured they will."

"I was already free," said Raím.

"Then you're unlucky. Got family with money?"

He stopped asking. Listening, he understood that most of the millworkers were indentured, working off debt. Some had quarters outside, were married, even, with wives and children who worked at the mill too, the quicker to earn freedom. The unmarried ones lived in this dormitory; there was another for women, with ways into it if you knew them, and one for children, the mill rats. All workers were locked in at night.

He could not imagine what work children might do in a hell like this. As days went on—days spent chained at the capstan, walking in circles, a mule—he began to understand how, in the lint-filled air, they ran up and down the narrow alleys between the clashing looms, dodging whips and kicks and worse, replacing empty bobbins, mending broken warps, bringing water to the weavers who each oversaw a row of frames that wove as though driven by invisible gods.

He heard them crying at night. Once he came clean awake with the shout, "*Nine!*"

From his world of double darkness came the mutter, "Shut up or I'll give you ten!"

He slept, dreaming of the capstan. And, sometimes, of Farki.

෯

"Those wires, they pull the heddles," said the weaver. "And that under your hand…no, there…that's the feed. Don't move it, would you kill us both? Caught in the drive and carried into the cogs, that's the end of many a mill rat. Costs money." He stabbed Raím with his forefinger. "Don't you touch nothing without you know what it's connected to."

They lay on their backs in the crawl space under the loom. Raím had been in the mill for weeks, he thought. Longer. He was not counting days. The beater of this loom had jammed, and the weaver, a small man, had fetched Raím from the capstan for the length and strength of his arm.

He let Raím feel his way among the rods. When Raím set his mind to it wholly, he could parse how this maze of threads, wires, staves, and beams was Ta Ba's loom made vast, moved by some unseen agency: a waterfall, they said, in the great river that came from the mountains and by which he had been brought.

He had learned to keep his mind occupied completely with safe thoughts. Even so, in the least unguarded moment despair, like a dagger, struck. He would pause an instant and pant; gather himself; jerk out the blade; return to the capstan or to this fierce study of heddles.

"Up in there," said the weaver, guiding his hand. "Aye. It's got crosswise."

"I have it." It *was* Ta Ba's loom, though it wove wider than he could spread his arms. Before, behind, next to it was another loom the same, and another, and another. He was not clear how many looms were driven by the gears whose rattle and shriek made the room a hell of noise.

And of heat. It was a linen mill. That stiff fiber must be woven moist and warm, so there was some system of pipes and boilers that dripped and hissed and spat and sometimes sent out clouds of steam, scalding and scattering the mill rats. Out in the world it was winter. Now and then a draft knifed through a cracked wall, but inside the mill it was summer's thickest, muggiest heat, even at night. Sometimes, when he lay sleepless in the weight and stench of it, a kind of madness came over him and he thought, It is Farki. The universe is Farki; he has pinned me to the ground.

Not that he was allowed to lie down on the job. So far he had trudged at a capstan, hauled bolts of finished canvas up and down a gangway, pushed bales, put his shoulder wherever someone needed a blind mule. He was chained by the shackle, though if Rogge or another gang boss was there he might be loosed. When the weaver had fetched him to unbind the beater he had gone willingly. It was a loom, even if a monstrous and unholy one. Now he lay on his back, eyes closed in the linty drift. Delicately, at the extreme reach of his hand, he worked the beater free, then followed the rod that drove it as far as the cogs.

"Too much tension here," he said. "It's pulled the frame askew." He groped for the bolt and loosened it. "Try that."

"Eh," said the weaver.

The next day he took Raím off the capstan to find what was making a shuttle snag at the selvage. Then to fix a sprung heddle. After that Raím was mending as much as hauling. "Fetch the blind lad!" was the call. He would lie on his back in the crawl space under the maze of gears, groping, while weavers argued and Rogge, lest anyone forget him, slapped his thigh with the bundled whip. Raím, both arms raised into the motionless machine, tried not to think what would happen if someone, careless or malevolent, should push the lever that turned it on.

❧

It happened often enough. It had happened his first day at the capstan. A scream, a horrid shuddering grind, then other, different screams. A woman's braid had caught in the gears, they said, and dragged her into them. She was dead—her own fault, for workers were to crop their hair or tie it up. It meant time lost, costly repair. One of the weavers limped on a crushed foot. The little girl who had brought Raím water had lost half a hand somewhere.

He discovered this when he took the ladle from her. He had crawled out from under a loom and sat up in the windrows of lint, spitting dust and calling for water. She came pattering, barefoot in the steamy room. When his hand closed on the ladle it closed on hers too, a little claw made of thumb and one finger.

He did not say anything. He would not be like those who remarked on his blindness. But moments later, as he felt his way along a drive shaft, her little croaky voice whispered urgently, "Mister Blind! Don't touch it!"

He withdrew his hands. Nothing happened. For a moment he was angry, then whispered back, "Why?"

"Get out! Troopy ain't watching!"

He was out from under before she finished speaking, and a good thing, too: Troopy had thrown the lever that engaged the gears, and the loom lurched into motion with a squeal. Both Raím's hands would have been caught.

Troopy, who should not have touched the lever in the first place, was berated. Raím was inspected, found to be undamaged, and sent back under the loom. But the next time the girl brought water he said to her, low, "Thank you. Is that what happened to your hand?"

"In t'hackle."

He knew now what a hackle was, in fact had worked on those long belts, dense with meshing spikes, that raked the rotted flax stem clear of the fiber. He shuddered.

"You shouldn't have no hairs longer than that," she said.

"Than what? I can't see."

Timidly she laid her little claw on his palm, thumb and finger barely separated. "Nor that way the cooties can't hide, neither."

"What's your name?"

"Ratling."

"I mean your real name."

"Ratling."

"Oh. My name's Raim. How old are you?"

"Don't know."

"Gods," he said.

Someone called, "Water!" Ratling and her ladle went scuttering off.

That night he borrowed a dull razor from one of his dorm mates and shaved his head and face. Asked the one who loaned it where the kids in the dormitory came from.

"Sold," the man said with a South Road lilt. "Those that beget them have nothing. They sell their children. Amu buys them and brings them here—Amu, and others."

"And when they have worked their four years—"

"Seven. For children, seven."

"—do they go free?"

"Yes. But most of them die. And where would they go? They stay, and work at the mill."

After that he listened for Ratling's soft, hoarse voice among those of the doffers and the lint sweepers. Sometime he heard it at night, from the dormitory where children gabbled haphazard prayers to gods he had never heard of, or who even—after twelve hours at work—played tag, or hurled a tattered leather ball against a partition, chanting.

Yell, baby, yell!
Squall, baby, squall!
Grab it by the ankle,
Whack it on the wall!

They skipped rope, banging the drafty floorboards until someone shouted at them to shut up. Catcalls, slaps, silence; then some small voice, defiant, would sing a skipping rhyme one last time. That voice was never Ratling's. Raím wondered what she looked like. What Nine had looked like. The thought of Nine brought others with it. He lay on his blanket on the stained boards, his face in his hands, trying to think only of machinery.

☾

He dreamed his hands were caught in the loom, it dragged him in, and the more it gnawed the more he knew the loom was Farki. It had no selvages, no end. He screamed. His whole body, skin and flesh, was stripped away.

☾

He shared his bread with Ratling. It had to be casual, as if he did not want it. Even so the foul Rogge said loudly, "And what d'you hope she'll give you for that, eh, Darkie?"

Raím saw whiteness, fire instead of dark. Did nothing. It was no use.

A weaver whose loom he had repaired said, "No harm in him giving the lassie his bit."

"I'll give her my bit," said Rogge with his coarse laugh.

Later Raím said to Ratling, "Keep away from Rogge."

"I run under the looms. He don't fit."

"Good." But then he was eaten with anxiety that she would be caught in the gears. He could not imagine what she looked like, except the claw. "What color is your hair?"

"Don't got none. Like I said."

"But if it grew long, what color would it be?"

"It wasn't never long."

"What color are your eyes, then?"

A tiny chuckle, the first he had heard from her. "Nobody can't see their own *eyes*! No more like you can lick your elbow. Can you lick your elbow?"

He tried it. "No."

"Huh!" she said, like Nine. "Nor you can't see nothing out of *your* eyes, so there. Show you something," she said, and skittered off.

He was on his back, howking out the wadded lint that had bound the gears and hoping, as always, that Troopy was not on the lever, when he felt a damp pat on the back of his knee. Ratling whispered, "Put out your hands. Guess what this is."

He righted himself, sat on the floor close to the loom where Rogge would not see, and put out his cupped hands. Ratling's—one a claw, one a child's—were wet, they stank. What she put in his hands stank, too. It was small and slimy and it moved, he nearly dropped it.

"So, what is it?" she said.

Gingerly he felt it. "A turtle! Where did you get a turtle in winter?"

"How d'you know that's what it is? You can't *see* it!"

"Feels like a turtle. Here's its snout, pulled up in its shell."

"But how d'you *know*? Might be a rock shaped like a turtle. Might be a jewel box. Might be *magic*," she said. As if he were unworthy, she snatched up whatever it was and ran away.

He had fallen into the habit, when he ate his meager lunch, of leaving a half slice of bread behind a joist. Sometimes the rats got it, sometimes Ratling. When next he heard her there he whispered, "Where did you get the tur...the magic thing? The one you brought me."

"Retting hole," she said through the bread.

"Where's that?"

"Underneath." But she was gone. That night he asked Hakkai, the South Road man, what a retting hole was.

"Stink," said Hakkai.

"But what is it?" He had learned what *to ret* meant: to soak the flax plant until the pith of it rotted and left only the fibers to be raked free by the hackle, carded, and spun into linen.

"Under the mill. Half under, where they dump the water from the boilers. Takes warm water to ret flax, so most ret only in summer, in the sun, but not these lads. Hurry, hurry," said Hakkai. "They ret all winter in the boiler waste. Bundles of flax rotting. Stink. Why d'you want to know?"

"Kids had a turtle." It had certainly seemed like a turtle.

"Eh. All summer it's frogs. Kids not supposed to go down there, poor little buggers. Retting hole's where the trash water goes, from the pipes and privies. Across the pond's the city dump. Bad land. Tramps and drunks and Roadsouls."

"Roadsouls!"

"They camp there. Town won't have them. But there's worse than them in that place. Fouler than brothels. Best the little buggers play in the retting hole, worst can happen is they drown, and maybe—" the rustle of a shrug "—for them, maybe drowning's not so bad."

ᔦ

"So, what is it?" said Ratling.

It had become a game. She would bring him something from the retting hole in her wet, clasped hands, and he must name it. He lived in terror that Rogge would see, but Ratling was sharp as an alley cat, seemingly with eyes for two.

The rules were that he must then say, "I can't see it."

She was to answer, "So, what's it *feel* like? What's it *smell* like? How's it *taste?*"

A soft, dank knob with a gilly chin. A cool, flipping tongue that under the retting stink smelled like worms in rain time. A bristly, cold flake on the lip. Raím must name them: "A mushroom. A fish. A mint leaf."

Of each Ratling then whispered fiercely, "You *think* so, but you can't *prove* it! Might be the snout of the Holy Piglet! Might be a ghost's tongue! Might be a ice leaf, you ain't never heard of that because I just made it up!"

Each time Raím had to concede that indeed, it might be what she claimed, until he gave up altogether and made better explanations right off. Sand was the Stone God's flour; grass was snake ears; thorns were mouse daggers and certainly poison.

These seemed to satisfy her. Sometimes she leaned her cheek against his arm, and he dared not breathe, as if she were his old cat Brook come again from the owl. But she ran off. Later there was a fight, and he heard her crying. There was nothing he could do.

He asked about the retting hole. But he was an adult, and she clammed up.

He said, "Do you know about the Roadsouls?"

"Don't go over there," she said sullenly, like a catechism. "There's bad men."

"No. Ratling. Listen." He would teach her about the Roadsouls. She would creep out by night and swim the retting hole, then the pond; she would creep along the shore and across the dump to the scattered wagons, lift up her hands and be raised, like magic, into chaos and terror and a new life.

He himself could not go. That coin was spent. But she could. "Ratling. When the Roadsouls come in their carts, lift up your hands—"

"There's bad men there! They does things to kids."

He saw the reality of what would happen if he sent her to the dump to walk the gauntlet of tramps and pimps and procurers. How old was she? Seven, maybe? He cursed himself. There would be no Roadsouls for her.

Instead he said of a pebble, "It's squirrel bread." Of a tendrilly root, "It's the thread that binds the world together." He listened for her chuckle. Once he put his hand on her shaved head, plush as a peach. *Don't think.* Don't think about little girls walking the world of beings much bigger than they are, the dust of granaries. He took his hand away. Said gravely of half an eggshell, "It's a broken heart."

It was no good, loving a stray kitten in a world of dogs.

25

The river that always flows
knows the way from Cloudy Mountain
to the bottom of the sea.

      Song. Welling-in-the-Mountains.

Snow fell.

It fell into the courtyard of the Gatehouse as into the well, straight down. It winked out on the damp of the dark garden, then whitened and blanketed lilac and rosemary, deep.

Sometimes Duuni stood on the balcony and watched it fall, watched Nine and Willek and the rest roll in it with poppy cheeks. It was not like the snow she had walked through on the mountain, for now she had shelter.

Raím had been gone for weeks.

She went to his room. Not that there was anything in it; his borrowed possessions had gone back to those who owned them. The master tunic lay on the bare mattress, clean and folded, the rent over the heart still unmended. She went to the window. Snow fell into the alley, muffling the hammer blows of the smith.

Nine blew in, scrubbing icy dribble from her upper lip. "Willek and them are pigs. Button me, huh? Willek won't." Duuni rebuttoned her coat of bald rabbit skins, worn backward so she could slide on the front of it. Nine kicked snow from her shoes. "Think a wolf ate him?"

"No."

"He ran off again, that's all. Farki says, '*So it is.*'" She clattered to the door, clattered back and kissed Duuni on the face, slimy. "You should like Tam Chivi instead," she said. "He's a Soul and nothing else." She ran back out into the snow. Duuni wiped her face.

Not a wolf. She had felt the lion there. Almost seen it. As Tumiin, so Raím? She had been angry enough. But there would have been blood.

Later she stood by Aash's elbow, watching her draw the arched feathers of a crane. Liss and Thorn were not there, only the two dogs and the wintry dusk that was like a being itself. The candle flames trembled. Duuni said, "It was my fault."

Aash glanced up. Wiped the pen, laid it down. "That's what you believe?"

If I had said yes he would have felt like a man, in spite of Farki.
But I didn't say yes.
But he could have forced me. He didn't.
But another girl would have said yes.
But not me.
No.

If you pull on a knotted thread, the knot gets tighter. Duuni said, "I don't know."

Aash glanced at the stack of costly paper that lay ready.

Duuni said, "What good would that do?"

"None for him."

"You said a prayer isn't for asking."

Blaze and Moon groaned in their sleep. Duuni pulled on her hand-me-down cloak and went out through the courtyard to the big room, backed by the kitchen ovens, where the Mice played and slept. The pregnant townswoman who sometimes watched them was there in the big rocker, sewing. The babies were asleep in a rank heap against the warm oven wall. Duuni crossed to the outer door and picked through the kitchen gardens to the alleyway, then to the field where the Souls had their winter camp.

The mud was deep, the wagons half sunk in it. Paths made of stones and boards had been laid down, and sodden wads of straw. Here and there a fire burned; Auntie in a long gray shawl hunched like a condor over a black kettle. On the canvas of the newie wagon the tumbling cubs had already dimmed a little.

On the wagon's far side was the wrestling ground. There, year after year of strewn sand had built a drier place. The lads were grappling and tumbling: Shank and Ducktail, Barkem and Wheeze, Deu, others she did not know. What watched them from the canvas was just a painted lion. Farki was not there.

Tam Chivi was— Naked in his wrestler's clout, a flame. He grinned, tossed his head back.

She looked down and away. She went back to Aash's workshop, to her table in the corner. She pulled up a screen so no one would speak to her and began to trace out a pattern of leaves for the goldsmith to cut into the rim of a bowl: tiny, intricate, precise.

The year turned toward dark.

⟲

At solstice the novices went together to the shrine. Duuni would not go. She had work to do, she said. She had been at the task for some time. It was not interesting, copying the borders for a book, but she knew how to do it. She need only keep her head down, keep working.

Aash began to look at her. Duuni dropped her eyes, thinking, How I work is my own business. Her wrist cramped and something in her shoulder had started to click, but it was important not to stop, not to be thought lazy or lacking, and anyway once she started, bent over her desk, unmoving as an iron hook, it was hard to stop.

"Duuni."

She jumped.

"Get out."

Raím's words. It was Aash who spoke them. "Go to the shrine with the rest," she said.

"I don't—"

Duuni saw her face. Not angry, but absolute as time. Duuni laid down the pen and rubbed her third finger. It had grown a callous. Stiffly she rose, fetched her cloak and slunk out to join the others in the kitchen garden, where the snow was muddied from the steward's harvesting of kale.

Her neck hurt. As she walked it felt better. There were several dozen walkers, novices and Souls, laden with offerings and in a merry mood. The sky was glassy blue. They climbed the trail along the creek, higher and higher, looking out over the valley patched with snow, then west to where the river ran away and, somewhere, to the sea.

Tam Chivi walked beside her. He and Shank were soon to leave; in winter young Souls rode off to gatherings at other Gate-houses, in other towns. Sleepy and Shine had left already.

Duuni had not said much to anyone about Raím. Nor had anyone said much to her; certainly not Tam Chivi, who never spoke when a cocked eyebrow would do. He strode beside her. She thought, I have known him longer than Aash.

She had not been to the shrine since she had gone with Raím. It was winter now; the crevice where warm water sprang into cold air was dim with steam, shrouded in icicles. The novices laid their food and trinkets on the altar stones. Nothing came out of the dark cleft in the mountain but water.

It was too cold to linger. The rest packed up their baskets and headed down the icy trail, until there was nothing in the cave but their tangled footprints, and Duuni.

Tam Chivi left with the novices, but he came back. Made a little gesture with his head: *Better come along.*

She nodded. Did not move. The wind blew into the cave; the faded ribbons on the altars fluttered. He came in as though to fetch her. They stood together on the sandy floor, watching the pale water leap from the cleft in the mountain, endlessly, in gouts and rushes like blood.

He gave a short breath like a sigh. Put two fingers under her chin, and stooped, and kissed her.

She stared up at him.

He smiled, shrugged up the collar of his cloak. "I'll be back come spring," he said.

With the nod that meant *Come*, he turned to leave. She followed. They did not speak. Next morning he left, the iron shoes of his mare and Shank's gelding striking sparks from the cobblestones. They did not say where they were going.

She bent again to her work.

 It's praying, he thought as he lay on his back under the machines, stripped to his clout. To weave is to pray, even in the mill.

The hackle with its gnashing teeth, which yet made linen; the stench of the retting pond, without which there would be no linen for babies. Everything together— everything, bigger than the Farki of his dream.

If I could be part of everything there is, he thought as he lay on his back under the scutching machine, I could bring everything to bear upon Farki. I could kill him. No man could stand up to the universe.

He let his hands fall to his breast. Raised them, wiped his eyes, went on working.

A slight rustling beside him, a little poking hand. "Guess what this is."

"Can't play while I work." He did not like her to be under the machines, but there was nothing he could do.

Silence. Then, "*He's* here."

"Who?"

"Him."

Doctor Amu. When Amu was about, Ratling clung, whispered, whined. Raím did not like to think what happened in the dark beyond his hands. There was nothing he could do. "Stay away from him."

No answer. She pushed her forehead against Raím's ribs, lay flat and still. "Sometimes he has candy," she said.

He gritted his teeth. "Do you take it?"

Silence. In her smallest voice: "I don't like him."

"Me neither. Go, now. I have to work on the hackle."

"Don't!"

"I must." That was prayer, to see the evil parts of the machine in the pattern with the good. "Later I'll guess what you have."

"Some old dandelion," she said drearily. "That's all it is."

He felt bad that he had not made her some fine explanation: a mouse's cushion, a fur penny. "In winter?"

"By the retting pond there's lots." She slid away. He let her go to the world. There was nothing he could do.

Away down the line, he heard Ab Tate's precise voice, Amu's fruity one. He squirmed down the work trough and into the aisle, hoping to slide under the hackle before he was noticed. But Amu cried "Ah! There he is! Stop there, Raím, my man!"

Raím paused halfway under, leaning on one elbow, head bent. No reason to raise his face and pretend to see.

Ab Tate's boot heels, Amu's shuffle. "Ab Tate," said Amu, "They say the lad's your mechanic. What did I tell you?" He had been drinking, his words were genial and slurred.

No answer from Tate. Amu prodded Raím's shoulder with a cane. "A long way from the bumpkin I gave a lift to so long ago, eh? Mechanic to the finest linen mill in the region. A famous mill, with a canny manager."

Raím said nothing. Nor did Ab Tate, the canny manager; the measured click of his heels went on down the line. Raím slid under the hackle. But Amu prodded him again and said, in a lower tone, "A thought I ought to have had sooner. How did you get out of that mine, my lad? I wonder you came to me the second time without an armful of master tunics. They were there for the taking."

Raím said nothing. Amu bent down, a whiff of rum and sweat. "An offer. If you got out of that mine, you can get back in. Tell me how to get those tunics. I can free you from the mill. I have means; no one will see us. We'll go halves. You'll be a rich man. There was a pretty lass who went looking for you, a dark one. You could make her your wife."

In the night of Raím's sight, a sheet of fire. His whole body burned. Yet he did not move. The part of him that had spent so many hours under the machines calculated it: Amu is out of reach, by the time I scramble out he will have run. Do nothing.

He thought, Am I no longer a man? But it did not matter.

Amu grunted. "Opportunity knocks, my boy. Opportunity, that lovely wench—the man to whom she bares herself must take her, or she'll offer her favors to the next." His footsteps moved away. "Hi, you little scuttler, I see you. Come here."

Silence.

"Come here."

Rogge's growl: "Get along, give him water."

Raím gripped the hackle frame.

Reluctant soft footsteps, clank of the ladle in the pail. "Come, come, I shan't eat you. A little water for me, eh, pretty face? Just a sip." Sound of the bucket being pushed, perhaps with a foot. "Nay, now, you must dip it up. That's your job, isn't it? Dip me a little water. I'll give you a kiss for it."

Ratling's voice, barely audible. "No."

"Ah now, is that nice? With such an ugly hand there's not many boys will like you, you must take kisses where you can. Here. A peppermint, too."

"No."

"That's rude, won't you kiss your uncle?" A scuffle, a cry. "There now, a nice hug. That's good, isn't it? A nice—*Ai!* You little shit! Bite me?"

A resounding slap, a wail. Raím on his back under the hackle, moving as fast as he could, not fast enough. Another slap. The pail went over with a clang and a rush of water. Ratling fighting, scrabbling wildly to get under the hackle. Raím groped, grabbed her foot, yanked her free and under.

Amu fumbled among the gears. "Bitch! Little tart—"

It was as it had been when he wrestled. As if he had eyes. He knew exactly where Amu was, even his groping plump hand. Raím dragged Ratling into the service gutter, swept his arm over her to be sure she was not reaching up. Found the lever with his foot, slid it up the length, hooked with his heel and yanked the lever down.

Snarl of gears, shudder and lurch. Amu's shriek as his hand— Raím could see this—was pierced, dragged into the belts. His screams; the spiked belts shuddering, grinding as they closed upon his hand, then his wrist, his arm. They dragged him upward, toward the roof. Dangling, out of reach.

Other screams. Thunder of feet on the boards.

His shoulder. His torso, a thick load. Screaming. His face.

Below the noise, tiny-voiced as a junco, Ratling whispering, "He's killed, they'll kill us, you got to come." He wanted to lie there and listen to Amu being eaten. "Come on." She plucked at him, scrabbling like the rat she was named for. He would be hanged, and it would be over at last.

But Ratling.

"Come! Come!"

He followed her tugging hand, was in motion before he thought, She'll be all right, the same as always.

Her dreadful always.

She whispered, "Show you where," as on his back he shoved himself after her along the gutter. "Here," a rotten gap in the gutter's sidewall. She was through it; his head and one shoulder fit, he forced the other shoulder through, raking the skin. "This way. This way."

Joists, damp boards. He cracked his forehead on a beam. Above them, Amu's screams cut off in a horrid soft crunch, like a child biting candy. Shouts; the master rod and axles still grinding, someone vomiting. Rogge's voice, "Gods! How'd he pull the—"

Crawling. The space opened out. The beams were soggy, the gilly mushrooms she had brought him grew there, his hands slipped on them. He got to his knees. It was cooler than the mill.

"This way." A still cooler draft rose, and the stench. Rotten wood. The rusty pins in the mine shaft, the rotten rope; he tested each step. They held. They broke; he smashed down through three struts, head-under into tepid foul wet.

Not deep. He thought he had fallen on her, groped in the water. "Ratling. Rat."

"Come on," a yard away. "Come on."

Wading, he followed her voice, vile mist on his face, he followed the splash of her going. Rotting sheaves of flax. He shoved through and over them, half swimming, half dragging like a seal. The air colder, not the sharp cold of winter but a dank fug of sewage. The water deepened.

"They can't see," she whispered from heaped sheaves. "Because of t'water smoke. Not 'less the wind blows, then they come get you wif horses."

"Where are we going?"

"There."

"Where?"

"T'other side."

"Of what? The pond? Where the dump is? To—"

"Take me wif you," she said.

"Ratling."

"Take me wif you."

"I'm—" a blind beggar, what can I do? And you're seven years old, how old do you have to be to decide your fate?

A splash: she had flung herself into the foul water, gasping and paddling. He lunged, snatched her up. She clung like a monkey.

"Let go. I've got you, let go."

"*No.*" Strangling him.

"I'm blind, you have to tell me where to go." No answer. "I won't leave you," he said. "Heart's promise."

She did not let go, but she turned her face against his neck. "That way."

He waded on, nearly falling because now he had only one arm for balance. She weighed nothing. He floundered, sank, heard her cough and spit. Swimming with one arm—all the lakes and mill ponds he had ever swum in, clean water, hot sun!

His foot struck something rotten. He kicked twice, found bottom. Air cold, water shallowing, the retting stink fading to the rank smoke of burning garbage. Broken crockery underfoot. He must not drop her. The air knife-sharp. He walked on into nothing, into the world.

How was he to keep her? Soaking wet and shivering, little liberated rat; himself in a clout, trying to keep her from the wind that rose, that even now must be blowing away the water smoke, showing them to those with eyes.

If he ran he would fall. He walked, out of the water and into the ice air, just walking forward. Sand, the sloping shore. Hoarse shouts, a stench of ghastly smoke. Wild laughter; creak and jangle of a cart, the looming sense of something coming on.

"Let go," he said to her. "Let me go." She clung tighter. He wrenched her off his neck.

"*No!*"

"Say yes." He held her high, thrashing. "Say yes!"

She clung to his wrists. He felt her grow still, turn to look at what came. Her slight body went alert. "You say it, too?"

"I already did. Lift up your hands!"

His own were raised, for she was in them, held high as the cart swung by like the side of a living beast. The laughing voices said, "You coming with us?"

She let go of his wrists. He felt her reach up. "Yes," she said, and his hands were empty, held out to the dark.

Rumble of the departing cart. Ratling's scream of betrayal: "*Raim!*"

Heart's promise.

He let his arms fall and turned away. He had known his own chance was long spent. Let her see his back, it was easier. If he ever—

Hoofbeats on the soaked sand. Yells: the overseers, coming to get him. Death, or a dry shirt and slavery—he lifted his hands to it, crying, "*Yes!*" and then, "*Ai!*" as he was snatched up like a cock at a chicken pull, borne kicking between two whooping horsemen, and flung across a saddlebow with a grunt.

"Stinks," said Tam Chivi.

They drew even with the noisy cart and Ratling's wail. "By life," said Shank, the other rider. "Let Farki wash him."

Duuni set borders with a ruler, traced petals onto thin paper, copied scroll after scroll of twining leaves. The nights were all just winter nights.

Halfcat slept with her; Aash and the dogs were close. But in the dark, when from her high bed she looked down into the workshop, firelight made the paintings on the walls ripple and shift. She lay back and looked at the ceiling. Kept her hand on Halfcat until she fell asleep.

She fell asleep easily. But she had begun to wake, in that dead hour that is the night's heart, and lie listening to soft sounds that might be Halfcat hunting mice in the room below, or might be something else. So that whatever it was would not notice her she lay still as a painted leaf and in the morning woke stiff, one hand pressed to her mouth.

She did not speak of it. Just worked.

❦

Cold crackled in the eaves. She had been awake, unmoving, for more than an hour.

Halfcat was long gone. The slight noises in the room had grown, not louder, but more frequent. Something tried the steps to the hearth loft. Fell back with a slither.

She sat up.

She had stoked the fire well; light still played on the ceiling. She looked over the edge of the loft.

Nothing. But the air was thick with something living, invisible, like water thick with invisible fish.

She thought, I should pray.

To whom could she pray? She had desecrated Mma's altar. Yet it was of Mma she thought, patron of women and girls. She thought, I am a girl trying to be a woman, in this world I do not understand.

She whispered, "Mma."

The coals ticked in the grate. The invisible bodies of all the beings in the room rubbed against one other.

She gathered her robe around her. Crept down the stairs of the loft one by one, slipping through the thick air. She went to her table, tucked up her feet, opened the inkwell and took a sheet of the best paper from the stack.

She did not look at anything but the paper. She was afraid to.

She drew the bottom curve of the crescent moon. It was the drawing she had made a thousand times on the Maidens' Balcony, in ink and sand and urda paste. She knew how to draw Mma: robed, hands clasped in prayer, eyes downcast.

But she is not like that.

For a moment her brush hung at the tip of the crescent moon. Then it moved, and drew: Mma with strong feet, arms outspread, breasts bare. Naked, like an Unclothed God. Her eyes, big as Duuni's and wide open, looked straight into Duuni's own.

The rustling in the room had stopped. Duuni washed the brush and looked at what she had drawn. In Alikyaan she would have been beaten for it, or killed as a witch.

Carefully she tore the paper down the middle, then across. She took the pieces to the stove, opened the door and thrust them among the winking coals. Their flames lit the whole room, they made the shadows jig. She climbed again to her bed and lay looking at the ceiling. Halfcat came back with cold in his fur and curled in the crook of her elbow. She slept.

෧

"Aash. How do you know a prayer is real?"

Aash paused in her painting and looked up. "Real?"

Duuni stirred the ash with the poker. At dawn nothing remained of the painting, not even the shape of the paper. "A true prayer."

"For you, what would make a prayer real?"

Duuni looked down and away. "Maybe if you're real when you pray it."

Aash let the words sit in the air of the workshop for a moment. Then she said, "I wish I could say, 'Don't grieve.' But that would be saying, 'Don't paint the darkness.' Unwise instruction."

"It was all dark for him."

"No. His lights and darks were different, that's all."

"He was arrogant." But he had not been arrogant with her. Vain and ignorant and coarse, but not arrogant. Yet she had not been able to imagine the lion of him unchained, let loose inside herself, plunging over the ruled lines. No. Yes. No.

She said, "Do you always burn your prayers?"

"Oh no. But I think I must always give them up."

"How do you give them up?"

Aash had been painting a green snake in blue grass. She laid down her brush, turned up her open hands and said, "How do I hold on?"

❥

Still Duuni held on. To the pen, to Halfcat, to the routine of the Gatehouse. She kindled the fire, cleaned, drew water from the well. Kitchen work, she could do that, settled by the steward's fire to peel potatoes one after the other, precisely, beautifully, forever.

Nine would not peel potatoes. That is, she would agree to, but in two minutes she jumped up and ran about waving the potato, waving the knife, sticking the potato onto the knife and waving that, shouting, "Hammer of god!" Thus it was that, one afternoon, the steward took knife and potato away from her and made her run errands instead.

The day had grown late. Duuni was holding on by paying tight attention to everything: the glint of the blade, the starchy milk of the potato, how its brown skin fell away. Nine and the Mice thundered in and out, letting in cold air and the music and laughter that rose from the Souls' camp beyond the kitchen garden. Then—far away, yet right through the heavy door—Duuni heard, "Pillbug! *Pillbug!*"

"Hammer of god," said the steward. "Better go see who it fell on."

Duuni set aside the knife, wiped her hands on her apron, and went out into the garden. Low sun, boots crackling on old snow, breath in plumes. Nine's shrieks drew nearer. Duuni hugged her arms and hurried down the path, stepped into the back alley.

Nine, yelling. And Tam Chivi, and Shank, and half the Roadsoul camp.

And Raím.

Nine towed him by his sash. Was it he? His head had been shaved; in the low sun the haze of new hair was a fiery halo.

372

Clinging at his neck was a child so tiny and knob-kneed that for an instant Duuni thought, It's my Riinu!

In a breath she knew it was not Riinu, and that it was Raím indeed, in clothes so ragged they barely covered him. There was a bruise on his forehead; but then, there usually was.

"He never ran!" said Nine, leaping. "He got *snatched* by that stinking Amu, he's dead, he killed him, he's been in the *mills*, Tam Chivi saved him, him and Shank! He's fetched that little ratling!"

Duuni could not sort *he* from *he*. Could scarcely breathe. Yet there stood Raím, one hand gripping the child, the other reaching into the dark.

She spoke his name.

He drew back and held the child with both hands. Put out his hand again, a little, like a supplicant.

To touch it she had to step close. The child screamed and hit at her. Raím pinned her fists, saying, "Ratling. This is a good person. This is my friend." The girl buried her face in his neck and peered from under his chin like a rabbit from the grass. Her mangled hand, her desperate eyes. She was not blind.

༄

Ratling would not leave him for an instant. As the novices crowded around him where he sat on the hearth bench in the common room, she stood between his knees, her face pressed into his ragged tunic. He spoke almost absently, turning his head as if he listened for someone. Not for Duuni; she already sat next to him. He had not embraced her. Sometimes he slid his hand over to touch the edge of her hand.

He told of his folly with the paidmen. He did not spare himself.

"Tam Chivi says you didn't half stink of the retting pond," said Nine.

Ratling glared, tugged Raím's head down, and whispered. He said, "Ratling says it might not have been a retting pond. Maybe it was the black sewer of the world, and we swam through it, and

now we're here." He lifted her and set her on his thigh. Again
that listening look. He said, "Where's Farki?"

◎

No one knew where Farki was.

They went in to supper. Duuni sat next to Raím. They had
not said ten words. Nine sprawled on the bench at his other elbow, Ratling stood between his knees. Below table level the two
girls ate bread and butter and nattered in cant half Plain, half
Mill. When Ratling began to yawn and nod Nine said, "Come
on, you little ratso."

Ratling clambered over Raím's ankle, gave Nine her claw,
and the two of them went off like sisters. Raím patted his thighs
as if she had gone up in smoke. "Where did she go?"

"With Nine," said Duuni. "To sleep with the Mice."

"She's hardly let go of me since the mill." He looked offended. Duuni thought of how she felt when Halfcat left her to hunt
voles. "Well, good. *Good.* Duuni, I—" very low "—I can't talk
here. They said that room's still mine. My room, gods! Will you
meet me? I—"

Seu Drake came. Duuni rose and gave him her seat, saying to
Raím, "I'll wait for you there."

She put on her cloak, went into the frosty courtyard and
leaned over the well curb. That water never froze. A faint ghost
of mist rose from it, blurring the silver disk below.

She climbed the stairs to Raím's room. She had not set foot in
it for weeks. It was stone cold and felt like a storeroom, nothing
in it but the stripped bed and the master tunic. She built a fire
in the stove. The flames munched and snapped. She went to the
window and looked out over the cold rooftops to the stars.

She heard him coming. He had gotten a stick somewhere;
she heard its rap, his step. He opened the door without knocking,
came in, drew it closed behind him.

"Duuni."

"I'm here."

"I know." He stood where he was. Bent his head. Raised it. "I'm ashamed."

"I know."

The hand that held the stick clenched and unclenched. "Maybe that's all, then."

She said nothing.

His eyes were on her as if he could see, but there was still the telltale waver that was not of the sighted. "Is it?"

"I don't know."

"Maybe?"

"I don't know," she said.

But his face changed, softened by hope. "I'm a fool."

"Maybe everybody is."

"Maybe me most of all." That bitter pride: If a fool, be the greatest fool there is.

She did not know what she felt. She had kept her bounds so carefully, guarded against what wanted to come in; was it he who wanted to come in? Was it the lion? Was he the lion?

"I don't know," she said again.

"Don't know if I'm a fool? Then you're one. Duuni—" He held out his hand.

She lifted her own. Touched his fingertips. But he gathered her whole hand into his, enclosed it, drew her gently to him.

She could have pulled free. She was falling, sustained by that hand. His other arm came round her. The stick clattered to the floor. "Duuni. Duuni—"

"*Flea Butt!*"

Furious hammering. They jumped away from each other. The door flew open, Nine stuck her head in. "I banged, because I figured you'd be kissing," she said. "Flea Butt, you asked where Farki is. He's up the mountain at the shrine."

"The shrine," said Raím. He had dropped Duuni's hand.

"He told Shank, he said, 'The blind beggar's back? I'm to the shrine, then, and pray for my soul, for he'll want a fall with me.'"

"Did he say that." Raím gave a laugh Duuni had never heard from him. Short, hot. "Did he now."

"He said it like it's a joke and he's going to break your neck. Then he put on his cloak and away, that's what Shank said." Nine held the door open to the night; behind her rose a child's wail. "And that kid, she's screaming for you. She was right as rain, then she woke up and you weren't there. She can't half screech."

"*Raím!*" Thin, terrified.

"Go to her." He was groping the floor for his stick.

"Me? She bit me." Nine showed the neat red crescent on her arm. "It's you she wants."

"Tell her I'll come later."

"You think she'll listen?"

"She'll have to."

"I better tie her to a bedpost," said Nine, and left.

He found the stick. The wailing was terrible, a torn heart. Duuni said, "You...you won't go to her?" She meant, *You won't stay with me?*

"Nobody's hurting her." He was in another country, the one where men go and women cannot follow. He found the edge of the door.

"*Raím!*" Was it Ratling's voice? Her own?

He half turned back, his face intent. "It will be all right," he said. He went out into the night, drawing the door shut.

"*Raím! Raím!*"

☙

She might have gone to that screaming child. Nine had gone; no doubt Aash was there already, and those novices who were like aunts and uncles. She could have joined them. She could have tried to show Ratling, somehow, that when the boat sinks the river flows on.

She did not go. She stood in Raím's room, listening.

Yet it was not listening; after a moment she hardly heard the screams. Maybe she was looking, though not with eyes.

There was a darkness, but clear, as though the air were well water that went down and down, beyond the sinking of any stone. She was a cup brim-full of it, perfect, as water trembles above the brim like living glass.

She was afraid to move, yet not afraid.

She knew.

Carefully, as if she carried that cup, she bent to make sure the fire was safe. She let herself out the door, onto the balcony. The night was calm and still. Ratling screamed. Duuni went down the stairs. Met no one. Hastened along the colonnade to the workshop, let herself in.

It was dark. She put three billets on the fire, and lit a lamp.

Shadows. Through that clear darkness she carried the lamp to her table. Pulled the screen across. Opened the fresh water pot, set out brushes, ink, and paint. Took a sheet of the best paper, heavy in her hands, and set it on the slanted board.

Looked at it awhile. The lamplight flickered. She swiveled on the stool and looked into the shadows behind her. Saw nothing, not with her eyes; but it was there. Turned back. Took up the brush.

What she had never said to Raím, she said. Not in words.

Yes. Come in.

There was a shift—subtle, as though she had drunk well water, and was now, herself, that clear darkness.

All this absolutely quiet, perfect, like dawn.

She began to draw with the brush, beginning with the infinitely sharp point of the crescent moon, then swinging down. Yet it was not Mma she drew. She knew it was not. As the body made itself, standing not on the moon but in front of it, she knew it was male. She painted the big shoulders, hard loins, firm feet, the upstanding sex. The moon behind him was female, strong as he was, sharp as pain.

Then the frowning slanted eyes with their oval pupils, the triangular nose, the mouth half open like Halfcat's when he snuffed something new. Round ears, muscular neck. Lower down, the tail curving away. Hands big as paws, half raised, in blessing or before the leap.

Behind him and the moon, light blazed. She washed the brush and pulled over the paint box. The workshop still, except for firelight, the lamp's flickering flame.

Each color chose itself: this one, then the next. She liked it. A living peace not peaceful, a river. Thoughts came and went. The red-gold hide, blue moon, green grass, stars.

Blood. Here, blood was right—the god standing in his peaceful rage, blood radiant in the flaming nimbus around him. Blood for pain, for death and birth, broken battens and broken hearts.

She thought, Siibi was right. We must have blood the way we must have tears.

When she knew that, she knew she was nearly done. With her lion...not *her* lion, *the* lion. She sat back and looked at him. Touched paint a little, here, then there. Then, lest she do too much, she rinsed the brush, closed the paint box, and drew a rag over it. She propped the painting against the screen where she could look at it: the lion-being god, prayed whole.

It was right.

She did not think about this. Just looked at it and liked it, her heart quiet. The shadows still moved; they were just shadows, the lion was not in them any more. Maybe it would be again. For now, here he was—or she, in spite of the hard sex, because the moon that held him was the woman. The prayer was man and woman both, and all lion.

After a while she rose. She took the painting to the front of the workshop and propped it on the big table next to the lamp, where Aash would see it when she came in. She was not boasting; it was not her lion any more. It was itself, walking in the world.

Ratling's screams had ceased. Duuni put on her cloak and went out, stepping softly, to drink from the well.

Someone was there before her, a darkness sitting on the well curb in the starlight: Farki, drinking from a cup.

She stopped and stood. "I thought you were at the cave shrine."

"Tonight? Not I."

"He went there to find you," she said. "Raím."

"Did he now." Farki's teeth gleamed white in the dark. "At this hour? He must need something to wrestle."

"Yes."

"Perhaps he will find it." Farki dipped the cup full from the bucket and held it out to her.

"I hope he finds it," she said, and drank. She thanked him and went back to the workshop. For a moment she stood looking at the lion, where he shimmered in the light of the lamp. Then she went to bed. Halfcat leapt up the stairs and made himself a bundle against her side.

When she was near sleep Aash came in with the dogs. Duuni heard her footsteps enter, then pause. A little sound, a breath; then silence.

Duuni did not say anything, or even feel pride. She knew.

Aash turned down the wick, went to her chamber, and shut the door. The room was left to firelight and shadow. Duuni slept.

26

When the fight was done—
the rolling in the cloud, when I did not know
my face from my breast, nor any
pressure but that wrestler's thigh
over my knee, nor word
more than a beast knows—
when that was done,
in the falling dust a face
stood, steady as a flame;
it looked at me through the settling cloud
and ceased to shout my name.

Wrestler's Chant. Welling-in-the-Mountains.

Bright morning.

Halfcat was gone. Duuni lay looking up, so close to the ceiling that she could see, between the beams, the handprints of the plasterers. She crept to the edge of the bed and looked over.

There he stood, lion and god. He was still right. His curled tongue, his shining body. Awed, she thought, Did I paint that?

She knew she had. And yet it had not been she who painted him. She had gotten herself out of the way of something, and it was that something that had painted him.

She climbed down for a closer look. As she did, Aash's door opened and she came out, voluminous in her robes, her gray hair rumpled with sleep. Smiling. She leaned her head toward the painting. "Eh?"

Duuni said, "I know."

They stood together, looking at it. The more Duuni looked the more she could look, as though her heart rested in it.

"What will you do with it?" said Aash.

"I don't know yet." It was enough to look. As she looked she remembered Raím, and thought, How strange—while I was painting I did not think of him once. She said, "I don't need to burn it. But I'll go up to the shrine."

"Good. I don't hold with asking, but it's important to thank."

Duuni leaned the painting against the wall under Aash's, next to the altar. It felt right there, equal to the others, just itself.

She went to breakfast. Ratling was there, weeping and hitting, but gobbling oatmeal and stabbing Nine with her spoon. Raím was not. No one knew where he was.

Duuni had gone beyond trouble. Raím was who he was; he would be wherever he was. To grieve it was to long for swallows in winter. When she thought of his pride and folly and kindness, she did not know whether to laugh or weep.

"Nine," she said, "I'm walking up to the shrine. Do you want to come?"

"Nah, me and Tam Chivi's going up there in a bit, old Tarkark's got lambs for sale. But it's us to do dishes first," said Nine, for whom doing dishes meant dropping them. "If you see old Flea Butt, tell him come get this kid of his."

"*Aaa!*" Ratling clipped Nine with her good fist. Tam Chivi caught it and held it, kept on eating with his other hand.

"I'll see you up there, then."

Tam Chivi smiled. Duuni smiled back. How handsome he was! As if all of him were in his eyes, no mysteries.

Once away from the house she was glad to be alone. The day was windless and new, the sun brittle on the shining ice. She walked quickly, waving to the goatherds on the far bank of the stream. She had grown to be a fast walker, as if that were what she was born to do.

At the highest switchback, the mist from the spring floated on the freezing air like smoke. Something moved in it, leaving; she thought of beasts, but could see only the steam distilling into its private snowstorm. She slowed a little. What if Raím was still at the shrine? It would be like him, stubborn as death, to wait for Farki in the cold until the sun rose. If he was there, what could she say to him?

Then she thought, I'll know when I see him. The way I know, the instant the brush touches the paper, which way it must move.

So she strode on up the path and topped the rise into the cave, where the baby river spilled out of the body of the mountain.

He lay in the sand of the wrestling ground. Naked, face down, his arm outstretched as if to slap the ground in defeat. Still as stone.

She took one breath, and gave him to his death.

Then she was stumbling forward, afraid to touch him, his head wrenched sideways and crushed into the sand, leg twisted. Raím. Eyes shut. Mouth open.

His ribs moved.

She touched him. He was warm, he was musky with sweat and something else, rank, a beast smell. Who had done this? "*Raím—*"

In a whisper he said, "God."

Sound of water wrestling free, falling away.

"Duuni?"

"Yes."

"Don't move me." His lips drawn back. "Back broken."

Brittle chatter of ice on the frozen bushes. She laid her hands on him, that he might know she was there.

He was laughing.

Short, wincing breaths that made clouds in the bitter air, his face wrenched with pain. "Knew you'd come," he said. "I'm done."

"Who did this?"

Only that panting laugh. She took his hand in hers. He moved his fingers, his feet. She felt along his back. He cried out. She brushed away the sand and filth and found where the long muscle was torn from the spine, the flesh black, clenched hard as iron. "Not broken. But bad. *Who was it?*"

He panted. Grinned.

Then she knew.

The sand of the cave was cold; yet around him it was still warm. Pressed into it, all about him, were the footprints of a lion.

She bowed her head and laid her face against his musky shoulder. "Raím."

"Yes. And lay over me all night. I'd have frozen, else."

"You couldn't see him." As she, though she had summoned him, would never see him. Only the painting that had come through her hand. And Raím would never see that, either.

Again his laugh, like freedom. "Hurts," he said.

She laid her cloak over him and covered him with her body as well as she could, being much smaller than a god. The sun crept over them. Still it was cold. She got under the cloak too and lay against him, waiting for Tam Chivi and Nine, listening to the water leap into the light.

 With Tarkark and the shepherds they made a stretcher and carried him down the mountain. The steward set a bed by the kitchen fire. He could not stand, could not sit. He lay on his belly while Duuni worked on his back the way a weaver goes over torn cloth, hooking out the broken warps. She was not gentle. He held on to the bed frame and tried to stifle his grunts.

They did not say much.

No one asked about his night at the shrine. Sometimes the novices dropped their voices in his presence, the way the lads had back in the Hold. It did not sound like scorn. He would not have minded if it had.

Lenini came with scolding and liniments. He could not turn over without help. Because he was always there and in a warm spot, babies were put down with him for naps; he remembered bits of lullabies from Creek and sang them, patting, though he could not carry a tune. The Mice were warned against bouncing on him. Nine stopped calling him old Flea Butt and called him old Piss-in-a-Bottle.

When he could sit up a little, the steward brought him infinite piles of potatoes to peel, warm boiled beets to shuck out of their skins. Seu Drake brought him a sash loom, but the blind master brought a tiny neck loom of a strange northern type that wove in three dimensions. He spent hours with it. He designed a way to finish the pattern called Ravens' Flight Over Pines in which the harried hawk almost, though never quite, burst from the selvage.

Farki came. He sat on the edge of the bed where Raím lay propped on a pile of borrowed pillows. Said, "Tried a fall, did you?"

Raím said, "Mmh."

They played at pushing hands. As if to himself, Farki said, "Something waits for us out there. To meet it—for that we are born. So it is." He slapped Raím's palm and rose. "When you're afoot," he said, and left. Raím lay back, his arms at his sides because he could not lift them over his head. His thoughts were huge and slow as summer, without shape, without name.

He tried not to think about Duuni. He heard her laughing with Tam Chivi. She had moved out of Aash's workshop into a room of her own, next to his but one; he wondered if they went there together.

At last he could stand and shuffle as if he were ninety years old. He still slept in the kitchen, for he could not climb the stairs.

The weather changed. The eaves dripped, the gardeners tramped in and out, the steward shouted about muddy feet. Ratling brought him a beheaded crocus and said, "So, what is it?" She was plumping up, and her hair was growing out in furious curls.

He stroked her hair, then the cool petals, pollen silky on his finger. "It's an eye that looks up always."

"Gya, there's a million million of them," she said, and ran off after Nine, whom she imitated in all things. The Souls were gathering their gear for the road, talking of wind and wide spaces, clanking and jingling through the kitchen with harness and chain. Going, going, while he lay there, barely moving.

Duuni brought a letter. She was formal with him now. "There's a part in here for you," she said. "I'll read it."

Who would write him a letter? "You can read?" he said, amazed.

"Yes. And write. I'm learning. The letter's to Aash, from that man they call Songsparrow. He's a master of chants, I think. Listen to this part."

She read, stumbling over the longer words.

"Expect me in early summer. I would come sooner, but I have been delayed by a war and a birth. I bring you songs, of course, and a new Mouse for the nest. He is just turned four, newly blind, and so angry with it he is as if possessed: he shrieks, bites, hurts himself. We are at our wits' end, but knowing your wits have no end I shall bring him with me to Welling. Surely there is a lion tamer among you!"

Raím got up on his elbow—slowly, the way he did everything now. "Give him to me," he said. "Give him to me!"

"That was my thought." She folded the letter. "The boy's name is Arem, from some little seaside town. If you'll turn over now, I'll work on your back, so you'll be whole when the master brings him."

"I am whole," said Raím. He turned over, slow as time, and lay down again. "Broken and whole are the same."

She ran her hand the length of his back and let it lie, warm, on the tattooed snake. "Raím. Sometime, I want—"

She was silent. He said, "What?"

A pause. "Too noisy and crazy here to talk."

He said no more, because she put her knuckle in his kidney and he had to clench his teeth. When she had left him for dead, he lay a long time listening to the sounds of the Gatehouse: Thorn baiting the steward, Holy Rot singing as she spaded the squash bed, the Mice playing hopscotch beyond the open door. Maybe Duuni would write a letter for him, to tell Thoyes and Set and his mother where he was. And one to Ta Ba.

He shrugged. Regretted the motion. Nine came pelting to his bedside. "What you scrunching up your face for?"

"Heard you coming, couldn't run."

She flapped him with her jump rope. "You going to be some old cripple forever?"

"You'd better hope so. The minute I can run faster than you, you're dead."

She flapped him again. "I'm hiding from that Ratling. She's a hellcat. She ain't got but the one hand, but she *scratches*."

"Were you teasing her?"

"Me?"

He gave that up. "Why don't you ask Duuni to draw on her hand?"

"It wouldn't show."

"What do you mean?"

"What do you mean, what do I mean? She's blacker than a roast chestnut. Blacker than Duuni. Have to paint her with icing, like a ginger cake."

"Oh," said Raím, to whom this was news. "Why did she scratch you?"

"I said I'm going to marry you."

"Ah."

"She says no, *she* is, and she flies at me like a tiger."

He felt helpless. "You didn't hit her, did you?"

"Nah. She's too scrawny yet."

"You don't think I'm too old for you?"

"Well, right, you're old. But you're *available*. Duuni said she'd never marry you."

"Did she." Oh gods. The cliff. Falling into the dark. Always by surprise; he would never learn.

"Everybody knows she's going to be a master. Masters, they marry their art. So Duuni, she's married already."

The falling stopped, replaced by recognition, grief. It was true: Duuni was already married. He rubbed his mouth and thought, So am I.

"She loves you, though," said Nine.

"What?"

"You deaf? She says to Aash, 'I don't want to marry him, I'm just beginning. But I'd be his lover in an instant, if he had the sense the gods gave a hole in the ground.' So I guess it'll have to be me."

"Thanks," said Raim. "I'll think it over." Ratling shrieked in the back garden, and Nine was gone.

He levered himself to sitting. Swung his legs over the edge of the bed. Bent. Groped for his staff. Found it. Rose.

Slowly. Impetuous was out of the question. Across the garden, down the stone path. Past the well fragrant with new water.

Stairs. Up them, one, then one, wincing, clinging to the railing. He wondered whether he could make love. Didn't think so.

But maybe he could be made love *to*.

He began to laugh. It hurt.

Shuffling, down the balcony to her door. It was shut. He leaned his forehead on it. Scrape of a chair pushed back from a table, tiny clatter of a brush laid down. She said, "Who is it?"

"Flea Butt."

Latch click, hinge screech. Laughing: "Raím, you madman—what are you doing up here?"

"Duuni. May I come in?"

Silence. Then, "Lift up your hands," she said.

He could not lift them up. Only toward her, as toward light.

🌀 🌀 🌀

What were we before we were one?
I was the moon and you were the sun.
But moon and sun must dwell apart.
O child of night and day!
Not in the heart.

🌀 🌀 🌀

Author's Note

About the Roadsouls

Every society, it seems, needs to believe there can be humans who exist outside culture. Historically it is the Romani people—"Gypsies"—who have been unjustly described as glamorous, itinerant thieves who steal children, have special powers, and are unconstrained by the rules that limit the rest of us.

This need to believe—an archetype—must fulfill itself somewhere. Since it doesn't fit the Romani, I offer instead the Roadsouls: Roadsouls really *are* like that.

Biography

Betsy James is the award-winning author and illustrator of sixteen books and many short stories for both children and adults. She writes, paints, teaches, and hikes the desert backcountry around her home in Albuquerque, New Mexico.

Young Adult Books by Betsy James

Listening at the Gate
A Tiptree Award Honor Book

Dark Heart

Long Night Dance

Aqueduct Press 2016 Releases

The Merril Theory of Lit'ry Criticism
selected nonfiction by Judith Merril, edited by Ritch Calvin

Will Do Magic for Small Change
a novel of what might have been by Andrea Hairston

Hwarhath Stories: Transgressive Tales by Aliens
fiction by Eleanor Arnason

The Two Travelers
fiction by Sarah Tolmie

Time's Oldest Daughter
a novel by Susan W. Lyons

The Waterdancer's World
a novel by L. Timmel Duchamp

Conversation Pieces

Marginalia to Stone Bird
poems by Rose Lemberg

Unprounceable
a novella by Susan diRende

Sleeping Under the Tree of Life
poetry and short fiction by Sheree Renée Thomas